Mia Sheridan is a *New York Times*, *USA Today*, and *Wall Street Journal* bestselling author. Her passion is weaving true love stories about people destined to be together. Mia lives in Cincinnati, Ohio, with her husband. They have four children here on earth and one in heaven.

Mia can be found online at:
MiaSheridan.com
Twitter: @MSheridanAuthor
Instagram: @MiaSheridanAuthor
Facebook.com/MiaSheridanAuthor

Also by Mia Sheridan

BECOMING CALDER

CALDER

MIA SHERIDAN

PIATKUS

PIATKUS

Originally self-published in 2014 by Mia Sheridan
This updated version published in the US in 2023 by Bloom Books,
An imprint of Sourcebooks
Published in Great Britain in 2024 by Piatkus

1 3 5 7 9 10 8 6 4 2

Copyright © 2014, 2023 by Mia Sheridan
Excerpt from *Finding Eden* copyright © 2014, 2023 by Mia Sheridan

The moral right of the author has been asserted.

*All characters and events in this publication, other than those
clearly in the public domain, are fictitious and any resemblance
to real persons, living or dead, is purely coincidental.*

All rights reserved.
No part of this publication may be reproduced, stored in a
retrieval system, or transmitted in any form or by any means, without
the prior permission in writing of the publisher, nor be otherwise circulated
in any form of binding or cover other than that in which it is published
and without a similar condition including this condition being
imposed on the subsequent purchaser.

A CIP catalogue record for this book
is available from the British Library.

ISBN 978-0-349-44123-8

Printed and bound in Great Britain by Clays Ltd, Elcograf S.p.A.

Papers used by Piatkus are from well-managed forests
and other responsible sources.

Piatkus
An imprint of
Little, Brown Book Group
Carmelite House
50 Victoria Embankment
London EC4Y 0DZ

An Hachette UK Company
www.hachette.co.uk

www.littlebrown.co.uk

This book is dedicated to Maegan, my prima favorita and the most incredible mother I know.

THE AQUARIUS LEGEND

Greek legend tells of Ganymede, an exceptionally beautiful, young boy of Troy. He was spotted by Zeus, who immediately decided he would make a perfect cupbearer. Zeus, disguised as an eagle, swept up the youth and carried him to the home of the gods to serve as his slave.

Eventually, Ganymede had enough, and in an act of defiance, he poured out all of the wine, ambrosia, and water of the gods, refusing to stay Zeus's cupbearer any longer. The water all fell to Earth, causing inundating rains for days upon days, which created a massive flood that put the entire world underwater.

In time, Ganymede was glorified as Aquarius, God of Rain, and placed among the stars.

PROLOGUE

"I have taken away the mist from your eyes, that before now was there, so that you may well recognize the god and the mortal."

—Homer, *The Iliad*

I was assaulted by the smell of exhaust and rancid garbage as I stepped off the bus. My stomach rolled, and I moved left to avoid having to walk too closely to the overflowing waste cans a couple feet in front of me.

The half-eaten hamburger sitting on top of the pile caught my eye, and my instincts almost made me grab it and shove it in my mouth, but I clenched my fists and kept walking. I was so hungry, painfully hungry, but I wasn't at the point where I would eat garbage—at least not just yet.

I opened the doors to the station and looked around the dim interior at the signs for the ticket window. I'd need directions to get where I was headed.

At least everything's labeled in the outside world. As I

recalled those words, I felt a strong rush of grief that threatened to bring me to my knees. I straightened my spine and moved inside.

The ticket counter was situated in front of the back wall, and I started making my way through the people milling around, waiting for the next bus. I briefly made eye contact with a young man in sagging pants and an overly large sweatshirt. His eyes widened and he jogged over and began walking beside me. "Hey, baby, you look lost. Can I help?"

I shook my head, taking in the strange smell wafting off him—something slightly bitter and herbal. I glanced at his face quickly and noticed that, up close, his eyes were red-rimmed and heavy-lidded. From my peripheral vision, I noticed him move his head up and down, taking in my form.

I increased my pace. I knew I looked desperate. I *was* desperate. Scared, lost, grief-stricken, unspeakable anguish sitting just beneath the surface of my skin. I *did* need help. I wasn't worldly—this I knew clearly. But I wasn't naive enough to believe the man walking next to me was the helpful sort.

"You ain't got no luggage, baby? What's up with that? You got a place to stay?" He reached over and moved my hair out of my face, and I flinched back from his touch. I continued walking, even faster now. Fear raced through my veins, my empty stomach rolling with nausea.

"Damn, hair like spun gold. Face like an angel. You look like a fairy-tale princess. Anyone ever tell you that?"

All my life. A small half laugh, half sob bubbled up my throat, and I wheezed in a harsh breath to keep it from escaping. My heartbeat ratcheted up a notch as the man steered himself into me so I was forced to move left in order not to collide with him. I glanced to the side and saw he was attempting to steer me into a dim corridor that looked like it led to a maintenance closet of some sort. I looked around wildly for someone who might help, somewhere I could run, when the man's hand clamped down on my arm. I looked up into his narrowed eyes, his jaw now hard and set. He leaned in and whispered to me, "Listen up, princess. A girl like you has a whole lot to offer. And I'm a businessman. You wanna hear about my business, princess?"

I shook my head vigorously again, weighing my options for escape. I could scream. Surely there was at least one decent person in the vicinity who would help me. I could try to fight him, but as weak and tired as I was, he would overpower me quickly. That's when I felt the sting of something sharp press into me through my light jacket and the thin cotton of my T-shirt. *Oh God, there's a knife to my side.* I looked down at his hand holding the small silver blade against my body and then back up into his eyes, now shining with something that looked like determination mixed with excitement.

"You come with me, princess, and you won't get hurt. You'll like my offer, I promise. It involves all kinds of money for you. You like money, princess? Who doesn't like money, right?"

"Take your hands off her, Eli," said a deep voice behind us. I swiveled my head at the same time Eli did and took in the sight of a huge man standing casually, hands hanging at his sides, a seemingly bored expression on his face. My eyes widened as I took in all the designs and colors swirling up the left side of his neck, stopping just under his jaw, and his muscular arms, covered with the same intricate art.

"This ain't your business, Paul," Eli spat out.

3

"The hell it isn't. When I see a cockroach, I crush it under my boot. Cockroaches offend me. You're a cockroach, Eli. Let her go, or I'll crush you right here in the bus station for all the other cockroaches to see." Paul kept his eyes trained on us, but Eli's head moved to the right and I followed his gaze to a group of men dressed similarly to Eli, who were sitting casually on a bench at the front of the station, looking our way and snickering.

Eli turned back to Paul, and I felt his hold on me loosen slightly. He let out a disgusted sound and pushed me roughly toward Paul. "Got too many bitches on the payroll as it is. Take her." Then he turned and headed in the direction we'd come from.

Paul's hand clamped down on my wrist, and I let out a startled noise as he turned and pulled me behind him, tugging me back toward the entrance. I pulled against him, but he was built like a bear and my attempts didn't even slow him down. "Please," I said, "please, let me go." There was hysteria in my voice.

We exited through the door and the once-again bright outside world caused me to squint and flinch away. Paul let go of my wrist and turned toward me. "You a runaway?"

I backed up until I felt the wall of the bus station against my heels. "A runaway?" I repeated.

Paul studied me for a minute. "Yeah, you on the run? Someone looking for you?"

I shook my head slowly, his question causing some of the barely contained anguish to seep through my pores. "No. No one's looking for me." *They're all dead.* "Please, I just want to get out of here."

"What's your name?" he asked, a gentle quality in his voice now.

I blinked up at him. "Eden," I whispered.

"Where are you from, Eden?"

I stared, the word *Acadia* floating behind my lips. I'd heard it described as a cult, but I still wasn't sure what that meant.

"Where you headed, Eden?" Paul asked when I remained silent.

I took him in, seeing that despite his gruff exterior, there was concern in his eyes. I let out a ragged breath. "Grant and Rothford Company."

"Grant and Rothford Company? The jewelry store?"

"Yes. Can you tell me how to get there?"

"That's only about ten blocks from here. I'll tell you how to get there, but then, you don't come back here, you hear me? This is not the place for a young girl who's alone. I think you get that, right?"

I bit my lip and nodded. "I won't come back here." If all went as planned, I'd be sleeping in a hotel room tonight. I'd have food in my belly, and it would finally be safe to cry.

Paul pointed his finger down the block. "Walk in that direction until you get to Main Street, make a right, and go about six blocks down. You'll see it on your right."

I let out a breath. "Thank you, Paul. Thank you so much. And thank you for saving me from the cockroach." I mustered up a very small smile and then turned and began to walk in the direction he'd pointed me.

As I started to turn the corner, Paul called my name and I stopped and turned, looking at him questioningly. "There are more boot stompers than cockroaches in this world."

I considered what he'd said for a minute. "The problem," I said softly, meeting his eyes, "is that cockroaches can survive the end of the world."

Paul gave me a small confused smile right before I turned and walked away.

When I looked up the street and spotted the sign I'd been looking for, my cold hand automatically reached into my jeans pocket and wrapped around the heavy gold locket within—the one that had the name of Grant and Rothford Company on the back—the only thing of value I had to my name. I completed the rest of the block sluggishly, hunger, cold, and fatigue overwhelming me.

The comforting warmth of the heated store greeted me as I pushed open the door. For a second I just stood there and breathed, relieved at both having found my destination and the warmth seeping into my chilled skin. After a moment, I headed toward the sales counter. But as I passed a display shelf to my right, I caught sight of a glass jewelry box with pressed flowers between the panes creating the illusion they were floating over the velvet interior. I halted, looking more closely, my eyes widening and tears immediately blurring my vision, as I instinctively reached toward it. They were morning glories. I should know; I had fifty-two of them, carefully pressed and preserved in a plastic bag in the inside pocket of my jacket. The locket, the flowers, and a small round pebble were the only things I had grabbed before escaping. They were the only reminders I had of him. I'd left everything else I had ever known behind. A lump formed in my throat and anguish swept through me, so intense, I thought it might knock me over. I reached out to touch the glass, one finger tracing the deep blue petals of the flower I was so well acquainted with. But my body was worn down, tired, hungry, and my hand jerked ungracefully and knocked into a crystal vase sitting on the shelf next to the jewelry box. As if in slow motion, it wobbled and fell despite my unsuccessful attempt to grab it. It crashed to the floor and shattered at my feet. I sucked in a loud gasp and jerked my head up as a woman came rushing toward me, saying, "Oh no! Not the Waterford!" She brought her hands to her cheeks and pursed her lips as she stopped in front of the pile of shattered glass.

"I'm so sorry," I gasped. "It was just an accident."

The woman huffed out a breath. She was well-manicured beauty: stylish in a dark gray suit, hair swept up gracefully, and her face stunning, with perfectly applied makeup. I shrunk before her. I knew what I looked like. I was wearing clothes stolen off a clothesline from someone who was obviously quite a bit larger than me. I hadn't bathed for three days and my hair hung loose and lank around my face and down my back to just above my backside—far too long to be stylish.

The woman looked me up and down. "Well, accident or not, this will need to be paid for."

My shoulders sagged. "I don't have any money," I whispered, glancing around as my cheeks heated and the few customers roaming the shop looked away uncomfortably. I was almost surprised to find I still had a little pride left.

I brought the gold locket out of my pocket. "I was hoping to sell this—and maybe get some information about it too," I said, imploring the woman to help me. *Please help me. I'm so scared. I'm in so much pain. I've been broken in so many ways.*

She put her hands on her hips and looked from the locket to my face and back at the locket again. She took it from my cupped hand and held it up to the light. Then she looked back at me. "Well, lucky for you, this is gold. It will probably take care of the cost of the vase." She kept looking at the locket, turning it over in her manicured hands. "There's no way to give you any information about it though—no engraving or personalization." She looked over her shoulder at a man who had just finished dealing with a customer and was stepping from behind the counter. She pointed to the crystal on the floor and said, "Phillip, will you have this cleaned up while I take care of this…girl?"

"Of course," Phillip said, eyeing me curiously.

I followed the woman to the counter. "Wait here while I weigh this. You don't have the chain that goes with it?"

I shook my head. "No, just the locket."

I stood at the counter, my hands resting on the glass in front of me. When I noticed they were shaking visibly, I pulled them back and rubbed them together, attempting to still my body as best as I could. My heart thumped hollowly in my chest. Fear and hopelessness rose up my throat, making it difficult to swallow.

I looked behind me, where the woman had entered a door to the back of the shop, and saw her talking to an older man through the glass. He furrowed his brow as he looked up at me and nodded, his eyes lingering for a moment before he looked down at what he held in his hand. The woman turned and walked back through the door and behind the counter to where I stood. "We can give you twelve hundred dollars for the locket, which is a little bit under what the vase cost, but we're willing to give a discount on that so the matter is resolved."

Vomit rose up my throat. "Please, I need that money," I said, raising my voice. "It's all I have."

"I'm really very sorry, but there's nothing I can do. The vase has to be paid for. We can't just eat that cost. We run a business here."

"Please!" I said again, louder this time, bringing my hands down on the counter with a loud slap. The woman startled and thinned her lips, leaning in toward me so that I shrunk back.

"Do I need to call the police, miss?" she asked in a harsh whisper, barely moving her mouth.

Dread raced through my veins and I swayed slightly before pulling myself upright. I shook my head vigorously. "No," I squeaked out. I took a deep breath, "Please, I just…I don't have any money and that locket…" I sucked in another breath, refusing to cry in front of this woman, in front of all the customers who were pretending to mill around but were really listening to the exchange between us. "That locket is all I have. I need the money for it to find somewhere to sleep tonight. Please," I ended pathetically.

Something I thought might be sympathy flashed in the woman's eyes, but she leaned back, crossed her arms over her chest, and said, "I'm sorry, there isn't anything I can do. There's a homeless shelter over on Elm Street. The fourteen hundred block. I've passed by it several times. Now I'm going to have to ask you to leave our store."

I hung my head, too sick, tired, and heartbroken to put up a fight. How had I managed to squander my one chance for money and possible safety? Now I very literally had nothing of value to my name. Nothing at all, in fact, except the stolen clothes on my back and the pressed flowers and small pebble in my pocket. I turned and walked out of the store as if in a daze, thoroughly depleted of every ounce of hope.

I wandered the city streets for a while, hours maybe, I wasn't even sure how long. I grew weaker; my steps grew slower. I saw a bench up ahead and stopped and sunk down onto it, pulling my arms around myself. The night was settling in around me now, and the air was even chillier, my jacket too lightweight to keep me warm.

Where do you find your strength, Morning Glory? he'd asked me.

From you, I'd said, smiling and pulling him close.

But he wasn't here. Where would I find my strength now?

A heavy exhale ghosted from my lips as I noticed the street sign to my right. *Elm Street*. Did I have it in me to go just a little bit farther? Yes, I thought I might—for a warm bed and a meal—even if it was in a homeless shelter. I'd make it through tonight and then I'd come up with some sort of plan. Maybe someone at the shelter could tell me where to find a job...*something*.

My teeth chattered as I walked and I pulled my arms around myself again, tucking my head down against the wind.

A line was formed up ahead, and I craned my neck to see if it was the shelter, standing on my tiptoes to look around all the people.

"You here for a place to sleep?" an older man at the end of the line in a long dirty jacket with a head of wild white hair, asked.

I nodded, my teeth chattering harder.

"This place is only for men," he said. "But a pretty girl like you could probably make some good cash in the alleyway back there." He inclined his head backward and then leered at me and cackled.

So there it was again—sex. Evidently I did have something of value. I'd like to say I didn't consider it for a brief few seconds. I was so hungry, desperately hungry, and so cold. The list of things I wouldn't do to stop the pain of my empty stomach and the cold that had seemingly seeped into my bones was growing shorter and shorter.

I mustered the very last shred of my pride and turned away.

He's waiting for me, by a spring, under the warm sunshine. The thought made me want to give up, to invite death, to travel to that beautiful place in my mind's eye where he waited for me.

But then his words came back to me, shouted through smoke and heartbreak. *I'll wait for you. But I hope I'm waiting a long time.* He didn't want to me to give up. He'd want me to fight and live. But...I missed him so much. So much. It was a sharp ache in my soul.

I only walked about a block before the tears began slipping down my cheeks. Panic surged. *Oh no, oh no. You can't cry. If you cry, you'll lose control.* That thought brought the terror of my situation front and center. I needed someone. *Anyone.* There were plenty of people walking by, but I didn't belong to any of them and none of them belonged to me. They didn't see me. They didn't care. With neediness came overwhelming grief. I collapsed on a nearby set of steps, put my head on my knees, and cried.

"Miss?" I jerked my head up and looked through tear-blurred vision at an older man in a suit. He looked familiar. I sucked back my sobs, swiped wetness from my eyes, and attempted a deep, shaky breath, trying my best to compose myself.

"I own Grant and Rothford Company," he said quietly, his posture rigid as if with discomfort.

Then it clicked. He had been the man behind the glass door whom the saleswoman had spoken with. *The owner.* Oh no, had he decided I owed more money for the vase? Would he call the police now? I couldn't go to the police. I couldn't.

I stood up quickly, managing only two steps before the world tilted and fell away.

BOOK ONE
Acadia

"Everything is more beautiful because we're doomed.
You will never be lovelier than you are now.
We will never be here again."

—Homer, *The Iliad*

CHAPTER ONE
Calder

Ten Years Old

It was a Tuesday, the day the princess showed up. I remember because we were watering the bean crops, and the bean crops only got watered the third day of every week. I heard the white Jeep before I saw it, and when I looked up, it was coming around the bend in the road, kicking up dust as it drove toward where we were in the fields. I strained my eyes, putting my hand up like a visor as I squinted into the bright Arizona sun, and could see Hector Bias in the driver's seat and a blond head in the passenger seat next to him, but the glare and the distance was too great to make out much. "Hector's back!" I called out.

"Shh, Calder," my mom scolded. "Hector will be happy to see you working hard." But a smile crossed her face as she watched the Jeep getting closer and then turned back to her work. I rolled my eyes and stuck my tongue out at her back but bent down next to her again and continued giving those beans the inch of water they liked in order to grow big and tall and strong enough to feed all one hundred and twenty of us who lived in the community of Acadia.

I didn't see the blond woman after that. She lived up at the main lodge with Hector. She was his blessed one—the bride who would stand by his side when we, his people, were welcomed by the gods to the Fields of Elysium, the most glorious paradise within the heavens.

We were all curious about her though, the woman who it had been foretold, along with Hector, would one day lead us to the hereafter when those great floods came and the end of the world was upon us. I figured she was kind of like our ticket in.

The news that he had found her on one of his pilgrimages had come back to us through Mother Miriam, his first mistress. But Hector himself had lived away from us for a long time, almost two years, only returning to visit twice a month, as he directed his bride's education and made sure she was ready for her position within our family. She had a mighty big job ahead of her.

And so the day we would finally be introduced to Hector's intended was a pretty big deal. We all quickly shed our dirty linen work clothes, drawstring pants for the boys and men, and long dresses for the girls and women. After I was dressed in a clean outfit, I ran out the front door of our small two-room wood cabin as my mom yelled behind me, "Be on time, Calder!"

"I will!" I yelled back, clearing my throat as I made my way between the other cabins. I knew my voice had a hoarse, scratchy quality to it and sometimes yelling hurt my throat. My mom had told me that, when I was about three years old, I had cried and cried for a long time, and it

16

had injured my throat or something like that. She said she couldn't remember what had set off the marathon crying fit, but one day, it was like I just decided I wasn't going to be unhappy anymore and that was that. She said it wasn't in my nature to carry sadness. I guessed it was true because I sure didn't feel sad anymore.

I knocked on Xander's back door and his sixteen-year-old sister, Sasha, opened it, her long brown hair flowing loosely down her back. I swept my eyes over her and then looked up into her pretty face. "Hey, Sash," I said, raising my brows and standing as tall as I could to try to bring myself to her height.

Sasha rolled her eyes and looked over her shoulder. "Xander," she called. "Your little friend is here."

"Little?" I demanded, insulted. "I'll have you know, I grew three inches this summer. My dad marked it on the wall."

"Good for you." Sasha bit her lip, looking as if she was trying not to laugh. That's when Xander breezed by her, grabbing my arm so I was forced to take off running behind him.

"What the heck?" I huffed as we raced through the dirt paths, narrowly missing old Mother Willa with her herbs piled high in the wagon she pulled behind her. She yelled something at us, but she was always a little hard to understand on account of the fact she was missing so many teeth. Too bad for her there wasn't an herb for that.

Xander came to a stop, and when I caught up to him, I punched him in the shoulder. He laughed, dodging my next punch. "Whoa, you're gonna want to stay on my good side." He looked around, then leaned in close and whispered, "Look what I swiped." He opened his hand to show me four perfect sugar cubes.

"ranger station?" I asked, looking around too and then reaching out as Xander set two in my palm. I tossed them both back and crunched them in my teeth, closing my eyes and moaning as the sweetness filled my mouth and burst across my tongue.

Xander pulled me off the walking path and glared at me. I eyed him questioningly, my mouth too full of sugar to talk. "What?" I managed, shrugging my shoulders.

"Geez, Calder. What's wrong with you anyway? Don't you know how to *savor* something? When's the next time you're gonna get sugar, and you just devour them both so they're gone in an instant? Dimwit." Then he shoved me so I stumbled back, trying not to laugh and lose any of the sugar in my mouth.

Xander took one cube between his thumb and pointer finger and licked it delicately, and then he moved it away from his mouth so he could talk. "See, Calder, when you have something good, you have to make it last," he instructed, drawing out the final word. And then before he could bring it to his mouth again, two of the wild dogs that ran around our land raced past him, bumping him forward so he stumbled and dropped the sugar in his hand onto the dirt. The dogs ran over them both, grinding them into the earth as they dashed away barking.

For a second I just stared at the crushed sugar ground into the dirt at our feet and then up at his shocked face, his mouth hanging open. I burst out laughing so hard I had to double over so I didn't fall down. When I finally got hold of myself and looked up at Xander, the expression of shock was replaced by a small tilt to one side of his lips. Then he started laughing too, both of us howling away under the bright, late-afternoon sun.

That was one thing about my friend Xander—he knew how to laugh at himself, a trait I had already figured out most adults still needed to work on.

"Aw, come on, sugar breath," Xander said, taking off toward the main lodge where we had planned to sit to get a good look at the new bride everyone wanted to see so badly.

"I hear she has the face of an angel and the body of a goddess," Xander said reverently.

I nodded, sucking at the inside of my cheeks to get every small grain of sugar. "That's what the foretelling said."

"I bet she looks like one of those ladies from the Academic Awards," Xander guessed, squinting upward as if picturing the *People* magazine he'd swiped a couple months ago, the one we'd looked through together, hiding behind his cabin, the one with all the pictures of the painted ladies in long bright-colored dresses holding little, person-shaped gold statues.

I shrugged my shoulders. "Nah, Hector wouldn't marry one of them," I said. "They're too…" I paused, trying to think about what they were too much of for our family who lived far away from the outside world. "Colorful," I decided. Although they must be plenty smart to have won such a big academic prize.

Xander rolled his eyes. "Yeah, I know that. I meant, you know, take one of them with their pretty faces, and dress her in something like what Mother Miriam wears."

We were both silent for a minute. I was picturing drab old Mother Miriam with the frown on her face and the loose gray dress. When I looked at Xander, he'd squinched his face up, and I imagined he'd been picturing her too and found her lacking in comparison.

"Anyway," he said, losing the frown, "we'll know in a minute."

The sun beat down on our heads as we squatted in the dust against the log siding of the main lodge where the council lived. We figured we'd have the best view of them as they left the building to make their way to our temple, where Hector's blessed one was going to be introduced.

Xander picked up a stick and started digging in the dust at our sandaled feet. After a minute he glanced at me and whispered, "Bet I could sneak in there and swipe some butterscotch candies. I've looked in the window. They keep dishes of them around like it's nothing."

I gave him my best disapproving look and said, "It'd be a sin to steal from the council...from Hector. He provides for us."

Xander looked down at the ground where he was still using the stick to draw shapes in the dust. "I just wonder... why do *they* get sugar whenever they want it, but we have to...borrow it from the ranger's station?"

I picked up a stick nearby and started drawing in the dust too. I didn't really have an answer for Xander's question so I stayed quiet. I also chose not to remind him it wasn't borrowing when you never intended to return it.

Xander was part of the group of workers who kept our family safe, and whenever he could, he snuck off to the ranger's station that led into the state park a couple miles down the road. He found all sorts of good things there, from sugar cubes to magazines, once some Coca-Cola. I still thought about and longed for another can of the sweet, fizzy drink we had taken turns gulping down behind some trees near our crops. I was lucky he shared everything he found with me. I knew it wasn't right. But I didn't think it was enough of a sin that we'd have to stay behind when the gods came down to escort Hector's people to Elysium. I made sure to work just a little bit harder than I had to in order to offset the minor stealing.

"When I get chosen to be a member of the council and go into the big community and work, I'm going to keep a whole *barrel* of butterscotch candies in my office," I said with a laugh. "I'll bring some back for you."

Xander chuckled. "That'll be the day. If anyone is smart enough to get chosen for the council, it'll be me."

I snorted. "If that's the plan, we better both hope we get to Elysium soon and that the gods have butterscotch."

Xander's face got dreamy, and he leaned back against the wood behind us. "I bet Elysium's *made* of butterscotch."

I thought about it for a minute and didn't think that sounded so good. It might be good at first, but after a while, you'd probably get sick of butterscotch this and butterscotch that…everything sticky, and then you'd be stuck in a place made of butterscotch for eternity and—

Xander's voice, which had been droning on, interrupted my thoughts as I continued to use the stick to sketch in the dirt. "…butterscotch clouds, and butterscotch flowers, and butterscotch houses, and butterscotch furniture…"

Suddenly we heard what sounded like a soft, childish giggle and swiveled our heads back and upward, and caught sight of a blond head leaning quickly away from the window, likely a council member's kid. I looked back at Xander, who had a confused look on his face, and suddenly we heard a woman's voice calling, "Who's out there?" and the window above came slamming down.

Xander and I stared at each other for a second with wide eyes and then we jumped up and ran.

The large wooden temple was already crowded just like we had known it would be. As workers at Acadia, Xander and I had to sit in the back, and we grumbled about the bad luck of getting caught outside the lodge. Now we wouldn't have the close-up view of the princess before we made our way to the overstuffed building. In order to see the platform at the front where the council sat and Hector preached from, we'd have to crane our necks.

For the most part, the worker groups stood together in Temple: the crop and water keepers, the animal tenders, and the watchers (those who looked after our security) on the left side, and the teachers, weavers, sewers, and builders on the right side. Between our groups, we kept our four-hundred-acre community fed, safe, outfitted, educated, and sheltered.

And free of the sinful influence of the big community.

Hector had named it Acadia, which meant "Place of Plenty." And it was true, because we had everything we needed—well, other than Coca-Cola. But I supposed that wasn't technically a *need*, and it wasn't like I could talk about that anyway.

My mom smiled and waved me over when I entered the temple and Xander went to join his family, who stood to the right of mine. My dad pulled me in front of him and put his arms around my shoulders so his hands were clasped in front of my chest and we took up as little room as possible. I inhaled the smell of soap coming from my dad's skin and leaned back into him, feeling safe. Next to us, my mom stood with my sister, Maya, in the same position. Maya had been born with a leg that didn't work quite right, and so even though she was a member of our family and would naturally help with the duties surrounding the watering of the land and making

22

sure our people always had a supply of clean drinking water, because of her birth defect, she couldn't do physical labor. Instead, she helped the women who sewed the clothing and the bedding and, well, I wasn't quite sure what else needed to be sewed. I guessed if I looked around, there were plenty of things, but I didn't give all that a whole lot of thought. Maya was a year older than me, but she was a whole lot smaller and mentally younger because of something called Down syndrome. My parents told me it meant Maya had been born with an extra chromosome. I looked at her and she grinned up at me, wrinkling her nose. My smile grew as I grabbed her hand and squeezed it three times, and she squeezed my hand back three times too. It was our secret code for *I love you,* which I had come up with so she wasn't constantly yelling it to me in front of my friends. We were too old for that now.

The thing about Maya was it was like that extra chromosome was filled to bursting with love. So filled up, it was constantly leaking out of her in some shouty way, and she just couldn't keep it inside her. But I figured when you love someone, you put up with all their faults, even the especially loud ones.

A hush fell over the crowd as the doors right behind us swung open, and Hector Bias started walking purposefully down the center aisle with the council behind him. Hector was a tall, strong-looking man who held himself like the leader he was. He had a head of golden hair that he wore long and sometimes put in a ponytail at the back of his neck. His eyes were a bright, crystal blue that seemed to be able to see straight through you. The few times he had spoken directly to me, I had had to force myself to hold eye contact with him. Something about those eyes made you feel unworthy—like you weren't good enough to look too long at something so beautiful.

The doors behind him swung shut and I frowned in disappointment. Would we not meet his new wife today?

I looked forward as Hector took his place behind the podium at the front as the council, all four of them, took their seats behind him. He looked around at us with an expression on his face that made me stand up taller in pride. I felt my dad behind me do the same. One day, I was going to sit up on that podium behind Hector and take the place of one of the council members. I felt purpose flowing through me.

Hector raised his arms as if in slow motion, and his voice boomed, "Behold the blessed one. My bride and your mother. Eden!"

Two of the council members stood and walked back up the long center aisle and each opened one of the large wooden doors, stepping to the side as they held them wide-open. The crowd hushed as we turned in unison, and a feeling I couldn't explain swept through me—something that felt like a mixture of fear and happiness.

Everything was utterly still.

Suddenly, a breeze blew in, bringing with it swirling dried leaves that danced down the aisle and came to rest on the floor. At the same time, the wind chimes that hung in front of the temple started tinkling as if, until that very moment, the entire world had been holding its breath. I craned my neck to see what everyone was looking at and that's when I saw her—a little girl, even smaller than Maya, walking slowly down the aisle, a look of terror on her face. My eyes widened as I took her in. She was wearing a white lace dress—like a tiny bride—and her pale blond hair fell over her shoulders and down her back. And her face... I felt my heart lurch in my chest at the beauty of that small face. Her lips were full and pink, and I could see they were quivering slightly as her eyes darted around. Suddenly, they fell on me and my breath hitched as our gazes met and held. I couldn't see the color of her eyes from where I was standing, but something in them held me frozen in place. And then she looked away and the spell was broken. I let out a big exhale of breath as she moved farther down the aisle, and I could only see her small back.

Some strange instinct told me to run after her and take her hand. I suddenly realized I was still holding Maya's and my grip had tightened so much she was staring questioningly at me. I loosened it and smiled apologetically and then looked back at the girl who now stood next to Hector at the podium.

"My beloveds," Hector said, beaming at us and raising his arms again. "Today is a magnificent day. Today is a day filled with the glory of the gods." He looked around at each of us again. "Today is the day you all meet Eden." He put his hands on the small shoulders of the girl next to him and moved behind her. *She's just a little girl.*

I frowned in confusion and glanced at my parents' faces, and they both had matching looks of pure pleasantness. I mimicked their small accepting smiles and turned back around to where Hector and the child, the blessed one, *Eden*, stood. Evidently, I was the only one in my family thinking this was an interesting turn of events.

Hector continued, "I know you're probably surprised to see your mother is so small, so young. As was I when I first laid my eyes upon her and saw she had the mark." He turned Eden, who was looking around the temple with wide eyes, and directed her to a chair in the center of the council's seating arrangement. She sat down, her hands clasped in her lap—perhaps shaking slightly, although it was hard to see from where I was standing—her lace dress pooling on the floor. *Where are your parents?*

When Hector turned back to us and began speaking again, I tore my gaze from Eden with effort. Hector moved behind his podium, looking thoughtful. "The ways of the gods are not always clear to us—are not always predictable or easily understood. And yet, the gods always know best, do they not?"

"Yes, Father," we said in unison.

Hector nodded and leaned forward casually, resting his forearms on the podium and lacing his fingers together. "Yes, the gods always know best, and the gods always provide. And so the day I saw Eden and recognized the mark on her shoulder that foretold the identity of the blessed one—my perfect balance and harmony—I went and prayed to the gods. *How could this be?* How could the blessed one, my bride, my wife, the one to lead us into Elysium, how could she be nothing more than a *child*? My beloveds, I had the same questions I'm sure you have as well."

Hector raised his arms slightly and banged them back down on the podium, startling us. Raising his voice he continued, "That night I prayed to the gods: *Please guide me! Don't allow me to disappoint my people! My beloveds are the reason for my very existence!*"

He dropped his head slightly, looking weak with emotion. When he looked up again, his eyes were shining. "I cried and prayed all night long. And finally...*finally* in the early hours of dawn, the gods spoke to me in a whisper." Hector looked around the room and I held my breath, waiting to hear what the gods had said to him. It had to be good.

"'She is the one,' they said. 'Her name is Eden, and *she is the one.*'"

He paused and looked around again and then held out one arm to Eden, as if presenting her one more time before turning back to us.

"And so she has come to live with us, a child who before was an orphan, alone in the world. And when she reaches her eighteenth year, she will become my beloved, my one and only bride. And as the foretelling has said, we will live together as man and wife for two months and six days before the mighty flood comes and destroys the earth and all the people and animals, and we, the blessed people of the gods, will be escorted to the glorious Fields of Elysium where there is no more pain, no more struggles, and never, *never* any tears."

I felt a chill run through me, just as it always did when Hector spoke of the great flood and our journey to Elysium. Only now, we had a time frame, and *now*, we knew that the great flood was years and years away—because Eden couldn't be older than seven or eight.

"Eden will sit in her place of honor during every Temple meeting, and she will be looked upon with love and honor. Please welcome her with the adoration she deserves."

We all dropped down to our knees and bowed our heads, my mother taking Maya onto her lap, as Maya couldn't bend her leg. We kneeled like this for several minutes until Hector said, "Rise," and we did. I looked back up at Eden and she was gazing around, a more curious look on her face now as she took us all in.

I wondered what it had been like where she came from. I wondered if she had lived in a house or maybe an apartment. I wondered if she had eaten sugar cubes and drunk

Coca-Cola. I wished I could talk to her and ask her all sorts of questions. But, of course, that wasn't possible.

I realized Hector had started speaking again as my mind had drifted away to all my questions about the world. "As if Eden's presence isn't enough of a surprise, I have one more for you on this glorious day." He paused. "On my travels, I also came across Teresa. Teresa, beloved, will you join me, please?"

A skinny woman with brown hair and hollow cheeks stood up and started making her way to the front, where Hector stood, larger than life itself. Teresa joined him and looked around at the crowd embarrassed-like, finally bowing her head and staring at the floor.

"Before she came to Acadia, Teresa led a wicked life," Hector said, shaking his head with unbearable sadness. "I found her in an alleyway, offering to do depraved sexual acts for money." Teresa seemed to shrink in front of us even further as several people made disapproving sounds and others gasped and shook their heads. "She had been prostituting herself for drugs since she was sixteen years old. She's thirty-six now."

Hector towered over her as he grasped one of her bony shoulders in a fatherly way. Then he let go and walked past her to the side of the stage, where several vases of flowers stood on pedestals. He carefully plucked a perfect white lily out of a bouquet and walked back toward Teresa with it.

My eyes moved to Eden to see her following Hector's every move. Her hands still rested prettily in her lap and her shaking seemed to have stopped.

Hector stood in front of us all looking at the perfection of the lily before bringing it carefully to his nose and inhaling deeply. He closed his eyes and tilted his head back.

He simply stood this way for several moments before opening his eyes again and walking forward to Jeffrey Parker in the front row, where he handed the lily to him and nodded. Jeffrey nodded back and then passed the lily to another man right behind him.

We were all quiet as we watched the lily get passed around the temple, from one man to another and then finally back toward the front where Hector walked to Boris Friedman in the front row to retrieve it.

Hector gazed at the lily sadly. It was now bent and bruised, one of its petals hung down, ready to fall at any moment, a truly sad sight to behold. He brought it to his nose again and inhaled and then frowned as if the sweet scent was no longer there.

He looked pointedly at Teresa. "Who would want this lily now?" he asked, his voice lowering. "*Who* could love a used-up, passed-around flower such as this one?"

A single tear slipped down Teresa's cheek and she bit her lip, hanging her head again.

Now that I was ten, I understood what a metaphor was. I knew Teresa was that used-up lily, and I saw she knew it too. And no one on the gods' green earth *really* wants to be a used-up lily, despite their behavior to the contrary, or at least that's what my mom had explained to me when I first asked her about all that business.

"Who could want a flower like this one? Who could find anything beautiful about something *dirty* and *soiled* like this?" Hector boomed, spittle flying from his mouth as we all stared, spellbound by his intensity.

Teresa let out one small cry. But I had been witness to this same speech before, and so although I was as interested as I was each time I saw it, I just waited, as did the rest of us.

29

"Who?" Hector asked us more quietly. *"Who?"*

And that was our cue. "You can, Father! And we can, Father!" we all said joyfully.

Teresa's head came up and she seemed baffled as she looked around, her mouth fell open, and her eyes flew to Hector, as he walked toward her.

"That's right, my beloved. *I* can. *We* can. We can all love you, our flower, made new again with love, with *family*, with *purpose*, with *belonging*." And then he brought the lily from behind his back, and it was as perfect as it was when he first plucked it from the vase. New and fresh and so very beautiful.

I loved that part and it always made a chill run down my spine. It was like a plot twist that showed up in a story, and it made your heart jump and you wanted to tell someone about it right away. Only when Hector brought someone new up on the podium, the plot twist was part of their life and it was a good one, and they usually cried and carried on and on about it. Naturally.

Teresa gasped and I could see she felt the same way, and her tears began to flow even harder as she sobbed. Hector wrapped his arms around her, cradling her to his body, repeating, "I can, we can, I can, my love."

Hector looked out into the audience in my direction and I knew that was my cue to bring the water.

My dad stepped back, and I made my way to the marble font of water at the rear of the temple. I filled the small cup sitting next to it and walked down the center aisle toward Hector.

"My water bearer," Hector said, smiling. I smiled back proudly and handed him the cup and then stood to the side with my head bowed and my hands clasped.

As Hector gave Teresa a drink of the purifying water, I

30

kept my head bowed but moved my eyes to look at Eden to my right, trying to secretly get a closer look at her. My eyes met hers and she stared at me without blinking. I looked away, but I couldn't help the small smile that curved my lips, and when I dared to look at her again, she was smiling a very small shy smile as well.

I forced myself to bow my head again as Hector hugged Teresa to him and then handed the cup back to me. Then he presented her to all of us with a simple wave of his hand as she beamed out to the audience, wiping the tears off her cheeks.

And with that, Teresa was made new and would join our family, just as many had before her. And although Maya and I had been born into this community, my mother said that there was something extra special about those who chose it on their own.

She said the gods led Hector to them, but it was their choice whether or not to follow.

I rejoined my family, and we all filed out of the temple quietly, ready to begin preparing the evening meal. I glanced back as I walked behind my parents, and although other people moving behind me mostly blocked my view, I made eye contact with Eden several times, and I wondered if it was possible she was watching me leave.

CHAPTER TWO
Calder

Twelve Years Old

The dusty canyon trail was steep and narrow, but now that I'd almost made it to the valley floor, where the harsh rays of the sun couldn't reach, I sighed in relief at the feel of the cooler air. It was January, and the weather during the day was only in the seventies, but the shade still felt good while I was moving so quickly.

Even though it was a tough hike, I loved this biweekly ritual of collecting the purified water I brought and served at Temple. I made my way down the trail as quickly as possible, practically running in some spots, so I could spend extra time at the spring. Every so often, Hector would accompany me and say a blessing over the water himself, although it was actually the gods who provided the healing water for us so we would be pure and cleansed when the great flood came. It was this purification that would balance our systems and help ward off evil and temptation.

Whenever someone was injured or sick, I would fetch an extra dose of the water for them, as sickness was mostly a massive state of imbalance, or so Hector said. Hector also said that although the gods provided the water for us, and it would help with the situation, *ultimately* it was to be seen whether the gods' will was for healing or not. Sometimes they deemed healing to occur, and sometimes, Hector said, it was not their will, and we had to accept that and not question the reasons why. It was not for us to know—at least not yet.

That was the case with Maya. My parents had told me that when they saw the deformity of her leg and the fact that her features were different, they had dripped the healing waters into her small baby mouth, but apparently the gods had their reasons for keeping her the way she was, because that time, the water didn't work.

But just last summer, when I had served the water to Franklin Massey, who was doubled over in agonizing stomach pain, later that day, he suddenly straightened up and was healed, wouldn't you know.

Apparently it was true you never could know the reasons of the gods because from what I'd seen, Franklin Massey was a mean old crab who walked around with a puss on his face all the livelong day. And Maya, well, she was like a little ray of sunshine. It wasn't how *I'd* run things when I got some authority up in Elysium, that was for sure. Although that was a moot point anyway because there was no sickness in Elysium. Maya would run through the fields on two perfectly working legs and her mind would work just like everyone else's. I had to smile at the picture in my mind.

I knew for sure the water was magical though, because every time I drank it, a feeling of peace and happiness flowed through me, and I felt cleansed and strengthened.

I made a sharp turn and the spring came into view. The water was crystal blue and sparkling and it had green plants blooming around it. It always struck me as a small paradise and I stood simply admiring it for a few minutes.

I set down the canvas bag that held the water containers and dropped to the grass, lying back and lacing my fingers behind my head so I could gaze at the clear blue sky surrounded by the towering canyon walls. Everything around me was grand and beautiful and full of color and light. I wondered how Elysium could be any more beautiful than what the gods had already created right here on earth.

As I lay there, my eyes landed on some brush that seemed to have been pushed aside in a way I'd never noticed before. I frowned in curiosity and pulled myself up and walked over to the strange little opening. There was a break between the rocks I'd never seen because of the vegetation that had been in front of it.

I peeked inside a little nervously and then stepped in when I couldn't see anything much from where I stood. On the other side, it suddenly opened up and I stood upright and walked through the space, mostly consisting of dirt, rock, and a few sparse patches of desert grass. But as I walked farther, I heard running water and noticed more vegetation. Moving through another doorway-sized opening, I found another spring! I laughed out loud, looking around in wonder at the hidden pool of water. How was it I didn't know about this? I spent more time than anyone down at the healing spring. This one was even larger than the other one, just as clear and just as blue, with plants growing everywhere. There was even a very small waterfall, mostly a trickle really, that ran between two of the larger rocks.

Something caught my attention to my right, in between

two rocks. When I moved closer, I saw that someone had written in the dirt and there were several toys sitting neatly on a small blanket where both rocks met, creating a small alcove.

I tilted my head, taking it in. Two baby dolls, a plastic tea set, and a small pink horse. *Strange.*

My eyes moved down to the dirt in front of the toys and I saw "Eden" had been spelled out in small pieces of broken sticks.

I scrunched up my face in confusion. Was this where she played? The items looked older. Had she been playing here since she arrived? I stared down at the toys for a minute, curious and wanting to touch them, but I didn't. The council members' kids were given toys and the worker kids were not. Still, I kept my hands to myself. Something about those toys sitting there struck me as very, very sad and weakened my desire to pick them up and study them one by one. I thought about the many friends I had and how we played together every afternoon after our work was done—variations on games our parents taught us, like hide-and-seek, tag... From my experience, there was never a lack of someone to spend time with inside Acadia. As a matter of fact, you had to put some effort into finding some quiet if you got fed up with people chattering at you from sunup till sundown.

But Eden...didn't she play with the other kids who lived at the lodge with her? The council members' kids? Or was she forbidden for some reason? I had seen the way my friends looked at her as she walked to the front of the temple month after month—still with some interest—but clearly she was different than the rest of us. Separate...and looked upon with a certain suspicion, probably even jealousy.

Maybe it was the same with the council members' kids

too. She was separate from them as well—not just another ordinary kid, not yet a wife—sort of a strange mixture of both and not one of an "us."

I stood up slowly and chewed at my lip for several minutes, considering Eden, picturing her playing here in this place she'd found. All alone.

I was jolted out of my thoughts by the loud call of a hawk and made my way back to our spring to fill my water containers. My mom would be looking for me if I wasn't home soon.

I walked back through the brush between the two rocks and arranged it so it wasn't noticeable this time. Hopefully Eden would remember to do the same. For some reason, I didn't want anyone else finding out about that secret spring through the hidden passage.

I watched for Eden more closely after that day, more curious about her now, what she did, how she lived. She was so close and yet seemed so far away from the rest of us.

I looked up at the main lodge, brilliant with its electricity in the midst of the darkness of our small cabins, where we only had candlelight in the evenings.

I saw her now and again too, peeking through her window if we were playing in the large dirt area a little way from the main lodge, just beyond the first of the small worker homes.

One hot day at the end of that May, we were playing kick the can. Only in this case, our "can" was a small piece of driftwood I had retrieved from the river that ran behind our land. I tried to keep referring to the game in my head as "kick the driftwood" because thinking about a can made me think about Coca-Cola, and man, that would have tasted good right then and there, sweaty and thirsty as I was under a noontime sun.

All of a sudden, I noticed a blond head peeking out from behind a tree nearby. I pretended not to see her and just kept on playing, every now and again glancing over where I could now see Eden standing among the small grove of acacia trees, pretty much right out in the open.

Over the next fifteen minutes, she inched closer and closer to our game field, until she was standing right on the edge with some of the other players who had already gotten out.

As she got near, a small brunette girl named Hannah looked at her with wide eyes and blurted out nervously, "Should you *be* here?"

Eden pulled her shoulders back and glanced around, her eyes lingering on me as she whispered, "I was wondering if I could join your game."

Everyone backed away from her, looking around at each other with disbelief. None of the other council members' kids had ever asked to play with us, ever, not once.

Finally Aaron Swift declared, "No. Uh-uh. Go on back up to your palace, princess. You're not one of us." But then he softened his rejection by saying, "You're a flower. We're the weeds. You're either one or the other. You need to play with the other flowers." And he smiled a small, slightly nervous smile at her.

The rest of the kids standing around nodded as Eden's cheeks flamed. She looked down and breathed out shakily, resigned. I realized then she might have been working up the courage to ask us if she could play with us for weeks, maybe even months.

I thought of those toys hidden in the canyon by the spring and realized the council kids didn't play with her either. She was an outsider in both groups. I didn't know why exactly, because I didn't know what went on up in the main lodge. I just had this strong feeling that she was. Just as she started to turn away, and before I even thought too much about it, I blurted out, "That's not true."

Eden halted and turned back around toward me as several other kids came off the field to see what was going on and what the holdup was.

I walked over to Eden and made my way around her in a slow circle as she stood still, turning her head to watch me. "Do you know anything about morning glories?" I smiled as I looked into her deep blue eyes. She was just a kid, but I couldn't help notice she sure was pretty.

She furrowed her brow and bit her lip as she shook her head no.

I stood in front of her and crossed my arms. "A morning glory is a beautiful flower, delicate-like. Blue, just like your eyes." I paused and smiled again. "But the thing about a morning glory?" I leaned in closer and so did she, her eyes filled with curiosity. "The thing about a morning glory is if you let it, it will totally take over your crops because it's not *just* a flower. It's also a weed, totally invasive. Stronger than it looks." I looked around at my friends watching me. "The point is, you don't have to just be a flower or a weed. You can be both." I shrugged my shoulders. "I figure some people are both."

"Aw, geez, Calder, I swear sometimes you make things up out of the clear blue sky," Xander scoffed. "Fine, flower, weed, whatever, let's just play. Eden can be on *your* team."

Everyone ran to get in their positions. I looked back at

Eden as a slow grin spread over her face, and she laughed out loud as she looked at me. Her grin was contagious, because I realized I was grinning too as I ran to my own position.

What I had said, though, was true. Morning glories were flowers *and* weeds—at least here in Arizona. I should know. I'd helped to tug out whole batches of them trying to suck up all the water from our crops.

We played in that hot sun for at least an hour before Mother Miriam came stalking down from the main lodge looking annoyed. "Eden!" she shouted. Eden ran off the field past me, her long blond hair and long heavy skirt flying up behind her. She had played with more gusto than anyone else on the field, and within half an hour or so, everyone was treating her like one of the regular "weeds." I didn't think the smile left her face the whole time she was with us.

Eden, yeah…she was definitely a morning glory: as pretty as a flower, with the strength of a weed.

She looked back when she made it to Miriam, and although I could tell Miriam was already giving her a tongue lashing, Eden flashed me a smile as if to say it was worth it, completely worth it. I smiled back.

Suddenly, Eden broke free of Mother Miriam and came running back to me as Mother Miriam screeched her name. She stopped in front of me, breathing hard, and reached into a small pocket at the side of her skirt. She grabbed my hand hanging at my side, cupped her hand over my open palm, and then closed my fingers around something small and hard. We both looked up at the same time and our eyes met for several long seconds. Then she grinned at me and went running back to Miriam, who grabbed her arm and started walking even quicker than before, practically dragging Eden behind her.

I looked down at my hand and slowly opened my fingers. Inside sat a butterscotch candy.

I raised my head and laughed, staring after Eden. It *had* been her that day, listening to Xander and me as we talked about butterscotch candies beneath her open window. Eden and Mother Miriam reached the main lodge and disappeared inside. I unwrapped that butterscotch candy and popped it in my mouth, trying not to grin around the mouthful of sweet deliciousness.

CHAPTER THREE
Eden

Five Years Later

Through the years, it was our game, Calder's and mine. He would somehow sneak pressed morning glories places where I would find them. Mostly in the temple, around my seat, so any other person would think it was just a flower that had blown in from outside. Some months I found several, and other months none would show up.

After the second year, though, I started finding them in my room, and I would suck in a shocked breath and clamp my hand over my mouth not to laugh out loud. How he snuck them in there, I had no idea, and I wanted *so badly* to ask him. But after the day Mother Miriam had caught me playing with the worker kids, she kept a closer eye on me. I hadn't even been able to make it back to my secret spring I'd found when I first arrived. They had me practicing the piano all day long, and there was no way to sneak away from that as the silence would give me away. I loved the piano, though. It was my mind's one big escape. I'd sit there and think about Calder as the music floated around me, embracing me with its melodic comfort.

I watched him from my window on the second floor. I had a pretty good view of the path he took to carry the water from the river to the worker cabins. I watched the way he was always smiling and laughing and the way other people, whenever they were around him, seemed to smile too. It was like he just exuded joy and goodness. I knew from my own experience he was kind, but I also watched the way he rushed to help a woman whose cartful of vegetables had overturned when he could have turned away, and the way he carried his sister everywhere piggyback, turning up his head to laugh at something she said.

He was working on something too, but I didn't know what it was. He spent hours, after he'd finished his regular work, down by the river hollowing out logs and binding them together. I squinted, trying desperately to see what he was doing, but I didn't have any idea. All I knew was he must be smart and industrious.

Perhaps I'd built Calder Raynes up in my lovesick mind to be someone he wasn't. How could I really know? It'd been years since I'd actually spoken to him. But the looks we shared in Temple when I straightened from picking up one of his flowers made my stomach clench and my heart race. And finding one of them had me walking on air for days and days.

And he was beautiful. There was that.

He had grown tall and broad, and his skin was bronzed and smooth. He was constantly without a shirt in the summertime, keeping only a small piece of fabric hanging loosely around his neck so he could wipe his brow as he

42

worked. My eyes wandered unabashedly over his muscled arms and his flat, ridged stomach. To me, he looked like a god who had come straight down from Elysium.

It was sinful to watch his nakedness, I knew, but something in me was wicked and I couldn't stop myself.

His eyes were dark and thickly lashed and his brown hair was thick and shiny. And his smile...his smile lit up my world, even from afar.

He was perfect. And I loved him. I loved him desperately.

And I was destined to marry Hector. Or so I was told. Only destiny hadn't checked with me first. If she had, I would have told her that I was pretty sure Calder Raynes was my destiny—or at least I would have begged for it to be made so. Of course I couldn't tell him that I loved him.

Instead, I left him butterscotch candies.

It was hard at first. I was never allowed to leave the lodge for one thing, and for another, I didn't exactly *blend*.

But luckily, the workers in Acadia kept to a specific schedule and I always knew where they'd be and when. And so I would pretend I had to go to the bathroom while I knew Calder and his family were working, and I'd sneak out the back door and run as fast as I could to his small cabin and plant a butterscotch candy somewhere among his bedding or his things. I may have smelled his pillow once or twice, or okay, fine, every single time. I'd close my eyes and inhale the clean male scent, picturing him on his stomach, his skin a golden contrast to the white linens, his muscular arms wrapped around that pillow, his cheek pressed to it as he slept. And a flutter of butterflies would take up a thrilling flight beneath my ribs.

In any case, that's how I managed to leave those small sweets for him. I'd return from the "bathroom" slightly sweaty and just a little bit giddy, and I'm sure Mother Miriam, who was Hector's mistress and my piano instructor, wondered what exactly it was I did in there.

Everything changed for me one late afternoon when Hector called me into his office on the first floor.

"Eden, my love." Hector smiled as I took a seat on the small couch to the right of the fireplace.

"Father," I said, looking down and only glancing at him with my upturned eyes as I chewed on my lip nervously.

Hector sat down next to me and I felt the weight of his stare as I focused on my hands in my lap. I admired Hector, but he scared me a little bit too. Not only because I would one day be his wife, and this was confusing to me and not exactly in line with my personal wishes, but because he was a powerfully built man with an intense presence. He always seemed to tower over me, not just in person but in spirit somehow too. I imagined his large shadow following me everywhere, making sure I was acting in the manner befitting of both his wife and his blessed one. I understood why all the people of Acadia looked at him as if he were a god himself.

He sighed and moved some of my long hair back over one shoulder. I glanced nervously at his fingers next to my cheek.

"Eden, you grow more lovely by the day. The gods, in their infinite wisdom, have chosen an angel to lead us to the angels." He smiled again and pulled his hand back, and the breath I'd been holding came out in a sharp exhale. Hector didn't seem to notice.

He stood and walked the few steps to the fireplace and held his hands out to warm them, even though it was hardly chilly in his office. He straightened the fireplace tools, frowning down at them as if they displeased him. I remained quiet and simply watched him.

"I have to go away for a little while, my love." He turned to me fully. "Mother Miriam will be joining me on my quest this time. The gods have spoken and told me where I'm needed. I'll miss my little princess. But you'll be in good hands. Mother Hailey will be in charge of your care and will make sure you practice the piano and do your lessons as you should."

I nodded enthusiastically. I liked Mother Hailey much, much more than I liked sour Mother Miriam, and as it was now, I had very little interaction with Mother Hailey and her four boys. They lived in the opposite wing of the house with the other council members, and our paths didn't cross very often, except during meals.

When I realized I might look happy about Hector's impending trip, I lowered my head again and made sure my expression was properly depressed.

"How long will you be gone, Father?"

"I'm not sure just yet. The gods will tell me when my mission is complete."

I nodded. Hector had been on several missions since I'd come to live with him. He usually brought someone new back with him, twice a council member, more often a family or person to live among the workers.

He looked perplexed for just a second but then his expression cleared. "Our family is off-balance. I sense it, and so I must ensure it's put back in harmony. I'll know the person, a council member I think." He stared off into space for a second and then seemed to suddenly snap out of it. His sentence continued as if he'd never paused at all. "And when I find them, just as I found you once upon a time,

45

my princess—the girl to bring me peace and balance, to bring us *all* peace and balance—I'll bring them back here." He paused again. "The whole world is off-balance, Eden. Imbalance brings nothing but sin and greed...*pain*. I must protect Acadia from that."

I looked down at my feet, not really sure what he meant. "I'll miss you, of course, Father." And I thought I would, at least just a little. After all, he was the only father I had.

Hector was silent for a minute. Then he walked behind me and put both hands on my shoulders. He moved my hair off the back of my neck, and I froze as I felt his warm breath on my skin right before his lips pressed against me. I shivered, forcing myself to stay still on the couch.

I felt Hector lean away and he returned both hands to my shoulders. My heart thudded in my chest and everything within urged me to flee. But I didn't.

"It won't be long now that we'll be married and I'll take you as my wife. And the foretelling will truly come to pass."

Dread raced through my veins. Suddenly, a year and a few weeks seemed so very near. The foretelling had said I would be his only wife and that couldn't be made so until I was of legal age. Eighteen loomed like a death sentence, literally and figuratively.

A flash of Calder's face raced through my mind, and I wondered momentarily if I would have to watch him marry as well. Most likely. Despair made my chest ache. I'd have to bear that pain alone, as I did all my sadness. But I was used to that by now.

"Yes, Father," I whispered.

Hector and Mother Miriam left the following week, and so Mother Hailey and her four boys moved into our wing of the main lodge.

Mother Miriam had never been blessed with children, and so to now have the noise and laughter of kids around brought me happiness.

Mother Hailey had a kind, quiet demeanor and I loved simply being near her. Although I wasn't allowed to cook or clean like Hector's mistresses, Mother Hailey didn't seem to mind that I sat with her as she prepared meals and did laundry.

The first week they were there, I watched her play a game of jacks on the floor as her littlest boy laughed and chased after the small rubber ball whenever it bounced away from someone.

Standing off to the side, watching them from behind a large column, I felt deep sadness and a memory I chose not to explore skated around the edges of my mind.

Once, once, I was loved. I remembered how it felt.

The tears began to fall and so I picked up my long skirt and walked quietly up the stairs to my room, where I sat on my bed staring out my window at the city lights far, far beyond. I had come from lights just like those—another world entirely, a world almost as distant as the glow of the stars above.

Suddenly my door squeaked open and Mother Hailey stood there, smiling gently at me. She moved her long, light brown hair behind her shoulder.

I wiped the tears from my cheeks, and Mother Hailey came and sat on the bed next to me and took my hands in hers. "You're always sad. Why, Eden?" Her gentle blue eyes regarded me with concern.

I sniffled as another tear made its way down my cheek. "I watch you play with your boys and I..." I looked up into her kind, pretty face. "I guess I was just wondering, with so many boys, if maybe you...could use a girl?" My last word came out on a squeak and my cheeks heated. I knew I was far too old to be useful as somebody's child. I didn't even really know what I was asking her exactly. I felt the loneliness I'd lived with so long consume me.

But she squeezed my hands in hers and she seemed to understand what I was asking for, even if I didn't. "I've always wanted a girl. I love my boys, but, well, to have a girl would be just lovely." She stood up and clapped her hands together. "Well now, this is cause for celebration."

A breath shuddered from my mouth and then I grinned up at her as relief and happiness flowed through me.

She took my hand and we went downstairs and I watched her as she prepared and cooked dinner, and for the first time since I was a little girl, I felt the love of family around me. I soaked it up like an overly dry sponge suddenly plunged into a sink full of water. Hailey and Hector's four boys raced around the large kitchen, laughing and playing, and Hailey hummed as she worked, shooting me smiles every once in a while.

As she peeled the potatoes, I asked her, "Mother Hailey, do you like being with Hector?"

"Yes, Eden, he's a kind man if you're obedient."

"And if you're not obedient?" I asked, my warmth creeping up my neck as I studied Hailey, hoping she wouldn't be angry at my question. It's not that I planned on being disobedient; it was just that I had so many hopes and dreams, and I didn't know what I'd do with those once I was certain they could no longer come true. Could I simply pack them away in my mind, like old clothes meant to be handed down to someone else? Did Hailey have hopes and dreams that were her own too?

Hailey stopped peeling and met my eyes, a concerned look replacing the gentle one that had been there a moment before. "Eden, you must always be obedient. You of all of our people. You have an entire family depending on you. The foretelling is the key to our salvation and you are at the center of it. I know you understand that."

I nodded. Yes, I understood. It was the only thing I had been educated on since the day I left my home with Hector. That and my music. But in my room alone, I daydreamed. I allowed my mind to wander in ways that were far from obedient.

My days after that were filled with the first real happiness I'd known since I had arrived. I spent the mornings playing with Jason, Phineus, Simon, and baby Myles and the afternoons reading from the Holy Book—a compilation of the teachings and foretellings of the gods, as spoken to Hector. Then I would practice the piano in the early evening as I continued my real full-time job, which was daydreaming about Calder Raynes.

It was now easier for me to sneak out and leave butterscotch candies for him, and so I ramped up my efforts. Calder had a belly full of sugar those first few weeks.

But it was on my way back to the lodge, right next to the field where Calder had first called me "Morning Glory," that I saw him bending over a worker girl to help her with something on the wooden table where she was sitting.

She said something and glanced back at him, and he leaned his head back and laughed like it was the most hilarious thing anyone had ever said in the history of life on earth.

Red-hot jealousy spiked down my spine and I stopped in my tracks and simply stared as my heart clenched with pain and longing shot through my body, so powerful I actually jolted where I was standing. My face felt hot and I was slightly dizzy, but I couldn't look away.

The girl laughed too, glancing over her shoulder at him and shrugging innocently.

Calder straightened, and the girl turned around, and that's when they both caught sight of me, standing there like a big, dumb fish with my mouth in an *O*, my face filled with heat, gawking rudely at them.

Embarrassment overcame me as I turned and ran as fast as I could back to the main lodge.

When I got there, I slammed the door behind me and stood against it, trying to catch my breath and calm my racing, hurting heart. I'd never have him. He'd *never* be mine—*not even his laughter.*

Mother Hailey came into the room and saw me. "Eden, I've been looking for you. Did you leave the lodge?"

I just stared at her, unable to form words right at that moment. "Uh…"

Mother Hailey pursed her lips and then sighed. "Eden, you mustn't leave the main lodge. Hector forbids it. I'm to watch you and check on you often during the day." She paused. "Of course, I have to give the boys their lessons from noon to two every day, and it's easy to get distracted with those four, that's for sure." Her eyes hung on mine before she winked and left the room.

I stood there for a minute digesting her meaning—the veiled permission—and although anguish still clawed at my heart, I let out a surprised breath. It was the first hint at freedom I'd had in over five years.

CHAPTER FOUR
Calder

The small amount of water at the bottom of the jugs on my shoulders sloshed as I made my way down the steep slope. I usually carried smaller containers in a pack, but today I needed extra. Helen Whitney was in labor and the midwives required plenty of the holy water in the birthing tent to assist in a healthy delivery.

I walked as fast as possible, lost in my own thoughts. It was a peace I craved, to be away from the others for just a little while. These days, I constantly longed to be away from the incessant noise of Acadia, away from my parents who were always discussing Hector's sermons late into the night. And most of all, away from those tiny two rooms of our family cabin that I had outgrown, literally and figuratively, years before.

This was my seventeenth year. I'd be eighteen soon and it was almost time for my water purification ceremony. I didn't know if it would happen right on my birthday or not since Hector was gone on another pilgrimage. If he wasn't back by then, it would have to wait until he returned.

Being purified meant I'd be washed clean of all my childhood sins and officially be part of the temple. I would be responsible for my own choices, and I'd reap the consequences if I sinned.

As I walked, I considered what that was going to mean. First of all, it meant no more enjoying the benefits of Xander's trips to the ranger's station. This, in turn, meant no more Coca-Cola for me when and if he brought it back—which, for the salvation of his own soul, I hoped he wouldn't. He would be eighteen in a couple months too.

At the thought of forsaking Coca-Cola, I groaned in despair. That might be the very worst of it.

It could be argued I was employing a loophole by acting as if it was okay to sin at all when I *knew* it was a sin, "child" or not. Still, that *washed clean* part of the deal made it really tempting to get as much good stuff in while I still could. Yeah, I knew it wasn't supposed to work that way, but I was still only human after all.

My mom told me I had a wicked way of justifying things in my own favor, which I admitted was probably true. It was just that life seemed full of so many pleasures. I wondered why every single one of them had to be sins. I couldn't help but picture the gods in Elysium with pinched faces and constant displeased expressions, which didn't make it seem all that great if I was honest. But I supposed there was no way I'd be disappointed in Elysium. After all, it was paradise.

My dad said we just had to prove ourselves here, with all the temptations the gods put in front of us, and the rewards for our sacrifice would shower down on us in the afterlife. Although there probably wouldn't be Coca-Cola in Elysium, and that was a truly depressing thought.

So I needed to stop thinking about Coca-Cola. And I

really needed to stop thinking about sex. My body tightened at the thought of the word alone—which spoke for itself as far as how much I needed that purification. I didn't know if the ceremony alone would help redirect my thoughts somewhere more appropriate, somewhere more befitting of a council member, but I sure hoped so.

I had been working on my irrigation system for over two years now, and I was pretty sure it would work as I'd planned it to and using only the materials available to us from the land. I also hoped fervently it was what would convince Hector I deserved a place on the council, and I'd be able to go out into the big community and work like some of the other members did.

Hector said we should use only the tools and materials from the land the gods had bestowed upon us, rather than the wicked instruments of society, where laws and rules were all based on greed, sin, and selfishness. It pleased the gods that workers only used that which was provided by them. It made us a holier people.

I couldn't help but wonder, though, why so many of those tools and instruments seemed to be in use up at the main lodge. I watched my own mother scrub our clothes down at the river on a flat river rock, and from what Maya told me, there was a big machine that did the job up at the main lodge—just toss a whole bunch of clothes in there, push a button, and they all came out shiny and clean, she'd said. I figured Maya was exaggerating, but it couldn't be denied that life was a lot easier for Hector and the council members.

I tried not to think about it too much because a sinful feeling of anger, and way more questions than I wanted to consider, would bubble up inside of me, and I knew that was wrong.

I made it to the spring and set the water vessels on the grass. I noticed immediately that the plants and brush had been moved aside and the crack in the rock that led to the larger spring was visible.

I had been back there a few times over the years, but I knew Eden hadn't been. Her toys sat unmoved and the few times I went in, there was no sign of any human disturbance at all.

I made my way through the rocks and open areas until the spring was in view, and it was then I saw her. Her back was to me and she was facing the large rock sitting at the back edge of the spring. Her hands were fisted at her sides and a glorious spill of pale blond waves cascaded down her back, covering most of her. But her legs were bare, as were her shoulders and I blinked at her nakedness. With her back to me, I allowed my eyes to move slowly down her body— her delicate shoulders to her narrow waist, to her hips that rounded slightly, down her slim legs and back up again. My body stirred, tightened, and blood pounded in my ears. I swallowed heavily, unable to move, rooted to my spot as I watched her.

She, *Eden*, put her hands on her hips and made a strangled, angry sound. I leaned in farther to get a better view of what she was so angry about and I saw the small snake sunbathing on the rock, just like he owned the place. Apparently, Eden wanted him gone and hoped her sounds of anger would compel him to move along. I almost laughed but sucked it back before I made a sound and gave myself away.

Eden fisted her hands down by her sides again and then stood still for a good minute, seeming to be trying to decide what to do. I waited, enchanted by her; there was no other word for it. I gave a small surprised jolt as she suddenly darted out into the water and waded across the shallow pool, only up to her shoulders. It was the only way across, as large rocks sat on either side of the small spring. The only rock accessible was the one that snake was currently occupying. Eden emerged from the water and marched up the slip of shore. Then she climbed up on that rock as I watched, spellbound, grabbed that snake, and flung it into the foliage beyond. She then brushed her hands together and plunked herself down, having evicted said snake with a swiftness I sure didn't see coming.

I couldn't help it then. I started laughing out loud. I didn't think I'd ever seen a spectacle quite like that one before.

When I finally opened my eyes and got control of my laughter, I looked up and Eden was sitting there in nothing but her wet undergarments, staring at me with wide eyes and her lips parted in that same *O* shape they had been in when I'd looked up to see her watching me talking to Hannah Jacobson.

I went serious, now in control of the initial lust that had swept over me at the sight of her. As I stared, a strange feeling gripped me, almost like a sort of déjà vu, as if this moment was a memory—not one that was in my mind, but in my *blood*, in the very fiber of who I was. It felt like some sort of recollection or maybe a vision. Or perhaps a misty, long-forgotten dream coming true.

"Hi, Morning Glory," I finally managed.

She just stared at me for several beats before she sat up straighter and said, "Hi, Butterscotch."

I cleared my throat, as Eden seemed to remember she was half naked and covered herself with her arms. "Will you…will you"—she pointed to her clothes discarded on the grass next to the spring—"bring me those?"

I went over and gathered them up and waded through the spring, only up to my chest, and handed her clothes to her as I pulled myself up on the rock. She put them on quickly as I glanced away. When I looked back, she was doing the last of the buttons up the front of her blouse, and I saw her hands were shaking.

"Are you okay?" I asked.

Her eyes darted to mine and her cheeks turned a pretty shade of pink. "I...I hate snakes," she said, her lips quivering now. "Like, really, really hate them."

I stared at her for a couple seconds. "It sure didn't seem like it to me. I don't think it seemed like it to that snake either." I grinned at her.

She let out a gust of breath and then smiled timidly back at me.

I had been half-right. Her eyes were the color of a deep blue morning glory. Only, up close I saw gold flecks along the outer rim. They were the color of a blue morning glory bathed in sparkling early-morning sunlight.

She looked down at her lap and said quietly, "It's just I haven't been here in a while, and I was really looking forward to it. It's all I wanted. Just to swim across the spring and sit on this very rock, the only one in the sun. And then I saw that snake, and I...I never get what I want." Her eyes flew to mine again. "And I know that's selfish. I shouldn't just think of myself. I just... It made me so angry..." she trailed off.

"I understand," I said, taking her hand in mine. Something raced across the inside of my skin when our hands touched and I pulled away quickly.

Our eyes met again, and Eden blurted out, "I've kept every single morning glory. All forty-six of them."

I grinned. "I've eaten every single butterscotch candy. All...well, I lost count, but all of them."

Her eyes widened and she let out a small breathy laugh before turning toward me more fully. "How do you get them in my room?" she asked.

I laid back on the large rock and laced my fingers behind my head. I was soaking wet, but the sun was shining, and I'd be dry soon enough.

I squinted up at Eden above me, closing one eye against the sun. She had turned and was looking down at me, waiting for my answer.

"My sister delivers things. I send them with her when she has a delivery up at the main lodge."

Eden nodded her head vigorously. "Yes. The girl who..." She paused and I tensed, waiting for her to make note of the ways in which Maya was different. "Sews so beautifully."

I relaxed and smiled, nodding. "Yes, that's her."

Eden tilted her head. "Well, now I'm going to have to deliver two butterscotch candies. I didn't know you had an employee." She smiled at me and I chuckled. Gods, she was so pretty. She dazzled me with her pale blond hair and those big, dark blue eyes that seemed to have a whole world behind them—a world I suddenly wanted to know, to explore.

"How old are you, Eden?" I asked. "Hector never mentioned..."

"I'm sixteen."

I was surprised. She looked younger and I had always assumed she was. To me, her age was directly linked to the foretelling of those great floods. I nodded, doing the math and suddenly feeling more anxious than I had before. I moved that aside. "Can I see it?" I finally asked.

"It?" A look of confusion came over her face.

"The mark."

"Oh yes, the mark." She hesitated briefly but then turned around and moved her hair away from her left shoulder and brought her blouse down to bare it.

I moved closer and squinted my eyes to see what looked like a smallish birthmark near her shoulder blade that was supposed to be an eclipse.

"'And the moon shall move in front of the sun as the waters rise and cover the earth,'" I whispered, quoting from Hector's Holy Book.

I felt Eden shiver slightly as I traced the mark on her back. I supposed it did look like an eclipse, as much as any birthmark could.

Eden pulled her shirt back up and turned toward me again. She suddenly looked shy, and I wondered what she was thinking. I watched her, waiting to see if she'd tell me.

Her lashes fluttered and her lips curved gently. "In the church I went to before I came here, I think there was a story about the first man and woman in a place I imagine to look like this one." She waved her arm around at the towering rocks and the spring right in front of us, glistening in the sunlight. Her smile widened. "There was even a snake!" She laughed and I couldn't help smiling too.

"I remember it because my name was in it somehow…" She gazed off as if trying to remember.

I tilted my head, squinting again. "Tell me more."

Her smile disappeared. "Well, I wish I could remember more of the story. I don't think it ended very well for them." She paused, looking thoughtful. "Or maybe it was the rest of the people who didn't fare so well."

"No, I mean, tell me about the place you lived before

this. Tell me about your house, and your car, and the city you lived in."

Sadness altered her expression. "I don't remember much, feelings mostly. The pictures in my mind are so blurry. And it's like, when I try to remember them, my head starts hurting." She rubbed her palm over her forehead as if it was hurting now, and then stared off in the distance behind me.

I studied her for a minute, wanting to ask her more questions but also wanting that far-off look of sorrow to disappear from her eyes.

Suddenly her eyes met mine. "Will you tell me what you're building down by the river in your free time?"

I raised an eyebrow. "Have you been watching me, Morning Glory?" I smiled teasingly, but her eyes widened and she looked down, as if she'd just been caught. I laughed. "Eden, I'm kidding. Is it okay if I call you Eden?"

She laughed a small laugh too, but it quickly faded. "Yes, of course." She glanced away. "And I do watch you sometimes," she whispered. "I'm sorry. It's very rude...how much I...watch you."

My heart did something strange in my chest and I just stared at her for a minute. This beautiful, quiet girl—the blessed one—had been watching me? I felt momentarily baffled. I didn't know what to say to her, so I opted for simply explaining my project. "Uh, I'm building an irrigation system. All this carting water in jugs and containers seems really...time-consuming when there could be an easier way." I sat up. "I actually read about it in a fiction book I can't remember the name of now. I mean, you know, before Hector banned fiction books. But it's not like it came with directions or anything, so it's a matter of figuring it out. I think I've got it though. And if it works, it could water all the crops in about half the time. I'm hoping it will mean a spot on the council for me."

Eden looked surprised. "You want to be on the council?"

"Yeah. I want to go out into the community and work."

"What kind of work?"

"I don't know. From what I hear, the council members work in businesses all over—I'm sure Hector or one of them could find a place for me, you know, if I prove myself."

"So you'd live up at the main lodge?"

I nodded. "That's the plan."

Eden blinked and then she glanced down at my mouth, her gaze lingering there as if she was thinking about kissing me. My heart galloped but I looked away. Even I had more sense than that.

I stood up and Eden jolted slightly, my sudden movement obviously surprising her. "I better go. I'm expected back with some holy water."

"Oh, okay," she said, standing up too. "I'm here every day from noon to two." Her cheeks turned that pretty shade of pink again and she shifted uncomfortably. "You know, if you ever want to have lunch here instead of with your friends…or, I mean, not that you would, but…if you did, or…" She shook her head, giving a subtle grimace. "Why would you?"

That strange feeling came into my chest again, warm and weighty. "I'd love to," I said. "It would be an honor to have lunch with Hector's princess."

The smile that had begun spreading across her face faltered slightly. "Okay," she whispered.

I studied her for another moment. "Speaking of Hector though, he probably wouldn't approve of this, you know," I said. I waved my hand around, meaning her being at the spring alone...or with me. I assumed she'd managed to be there—to sneak away—because Hector was currently gone, but she had to know it was a risk.

"No, he wouldn't," she replied, and I couldn't read the expression on her face now.

I paused, knowing I should tell her I wasn't going to be back, but somehow not being able to. Being in her presence after all this time felt so good, and it seemed the idea of spending time with me brought her happiness too. "Goodbye for now, then." I gave her a smile and then turned and made my way back to the spring, where I gathered the water needed at the birthing tent.

I was too late. When I got back, Helen Whitney was holding a healthy baby boy.

CHAPTER FIVE
Eden

The next day, I settled in at the spring, my heart beating triple time, filled with hope that Calder would join me. He never did and as I hiked back to the main lodge, my mood was melancholy, lonely, and severely disappointed.

I had loved him for so long it seemed. But talking to him, getting to know him just a little bit, made that love seem silly and juvenile, made-up. He still made my heart beat out of my own chest and his beauty mesmerized me, but now the desire to know who he really was filled my thoughts.

I wanted to talk to him all day long, to hear that deep, throaty laughter that washed over my skin and made me shiver. His voice sounded like warm spring rain falling on a gravel road.

He didn't show the next day either, and so the third day when I sat down on my rock, sans snake, thank the gods, I didn't expect him to show. And so when he suddenly appeared at the rock entrance to the spring, I gasped out loud.

Calder smiled, and another boy with black hair appeared

behind him, pushing him through, so he stumbled and laughed.

The other boy bent over and put his hands on his knees and stood there for a minute obviously trying to catch his breath.

Calder nudged him and said, "Wimp," as he waded through the water and pulled himself easily up onto the large rock. I scooted over to make room for them.

"What's for lunch?" he asked with a grin.

"Lunch?" I put my hand over my mouth and then took it away. "Oh no! I told you to meet me for lunch and I didn't bring anything." I grimaced, embarrassed. "I'm so sorry. How rude."

Calder laughed. "I'm teasing you, Morning Glory. We already ate." He tilted his head toward the black-haired boy now wading through the water toward us. He wasn't as tall as Calder, but the water still didn't come close to his shoulders, like it did to my own.

The boy made it to the rock and pulled himself up on it with effort. Calder and I both moved over as he lay back, catching his breath again and massaging his side as if he had a stitch.

Calder chuckled. "Eden, this here sorry, out-of-shape person is Xander Garen."

"Out of shape? Who's out of shape? I walk miles every single day. I just don't jog straight downhill with heavy water containers on my shoulders. Ridiculous." Xander turned to me. "Lovely to make your personal acquaintance, Eden. I played kick the can with you once years ago. You probably remember me. I was the star of the game. Not that I particularly remember that game itself, but I was always the star, so it can safely be deduced I was that day as well."

I laughed. "I do remember that game, Xander, because

63

it's the only game I ever played, and yes, you played very well, and so did Calder." I blushed when I looked over at Calder because, well, he was so handsome and I wanted to stare at him, and the way he was looking at me made me feel like he could read my mind.

Xander narrowed his eyes slightly, looking between us. "Right. Well, thanks for allowing us to share your oasis today. I had no idea this was here. When Calder told me about the spring, I assumed it was just a little water hole with a few rocks around it. You've been holding out on me, Calder." He winked and I let out a short laugh before moving my gaze back to Calder to find him staring at me with a strange expression on his face. He seemed to come out of a trance and his face broke into a smile, too, as he nudged Xander.

"Nah, I'd never hold out on you. You just never seemed interested."

Xander huffed out a breath. "Well, you know I have so much excitement as it is, what with walking around the perimeter of Acadia a thousand times a day."

"It's an important job, just like every job here," Calder said, but there wasn't any emotion in his voice, as though he was simply repeating a line, Hector's most likely. We sat there for a minute silently until Calder cleared his throat and went on. "Anyway, I know I sleep better at night knowing a big, strong manly man such as yourself is in charge of my safety."

Xander chuckled. "Who doesn't, pretty boy?"

I giggled, taking delight in their banter. It had been so long since I laughed and felt the lightheartedness of friendship. I wondered if I'd ever experienced it…*before*.

"So, Eden, what is it that you do every day?"

I blushed and looked down. "I'm not allowed to do much, really. I practice my music and I study the Holy Book.

That's the extent of it." I let out a small uncomfortable laugh. "Makes walking around the perimeter of Acadia a thousand times a day sound more interesting, huh? You must think I'm the most pathetic person on earth."

There was silence for a minute and when I looked up, both Xander and Calder had matching surprised looks on their faces.

"You can't be," Calder finally said. "Xander already holds that title."

"So funny," Xander drawled as I giggled again. He elbowed Calder. "We'd never think that about you, Eden. You're the blessed one."

I felt my face heat slightly at the reminder I was different than them, and I cleared my throat, not knowing what to say.

"Seriously, you don't go to school?" Xander asked after an awkward moment.

"No. Hector says as the blessed one, the only thing expected of me is to be well-versed in his Holy Book."

"Well, I guess that's true," Xander said slowly, spacing his words as if several could have been inserted between them.

Calder looked down and began tracing something on the rock, almost as if he was unconsciously drawing, which made something occur to me. "Oh, Calder, I've wanted to ask you this forever," I said. "That day you and Xander were talking about the butterscotch candy beneath my window, what was it you were drawing in the dirt? It was only half-done. I looked down on it for days, trying to figure out if it was a girl or a horse or...I thought maybe it might be a river for a few days, but then I was sure it was a—"

I stopped talking when Calder burst out laughing.

"What?" I demanded, looking over at Xander, who was smiling too.

65

"Nothing. You," Calder said, smiling, but not in a way that felt mean. "You gave that dirt drawing a lot of thought."

I let out a small laugh on a breath. "I told you, my days are pretty boring."

"I was just teasing you," he said. "Uh, let's see… I'm sorry, I can't remember what I might have been sketching."

"Calder's constantly sketching," Xander inserted. "It's the bane of our teacher's existence. Anytime he's allowed near a writing instrument, it's like the gods possess him to sketch."

"And yet he's not allowed to?" I asked.

They both shook their heads. "Workers aren't allowed to partake in the arts. That's only for the council members and their families."

"Why?" I blurted out, thinking of all the instruments, paints, charcoal, and paper kept at the main lodge. Hector was *big* on the arts. He was constantly insisting we practice, practice, practice and that the arts pleased the gods. I wasn't aware of the many rules the workers lived by, as our lives had always been kept so separate. I had seen for myself the fact that they didn't have electricity like we did at the main lodge, but I thought, other than our living conditions and that they tended to the work in our community, that we participated in pretty much the same things. Of course, not counting the Holy Book, I wasn't educated in anything *other* than the arts, but that was only me. The council members' children were schooled in the usual subjects, just like the workers. It suddenly all seemed so confusing.

Calder shrugged. "We all have our jobs. My dad says each one is equally important." He was quiet for a beat and then continued. "They all balance the community."

I nodded and Xander looked toward the entrance to the spring. "We should get back," he said after a moment.

Calder nodded, his eyes lingering on me. His eyelashes were ridiculously thick, his eyes such a deep, rich brown. He tilted his head and pursed his lips as if he was considering something. "I have an idea."

"Oh no," Xander said. "No good can come from this."

Calder glanced at Xander. "You haven't heard my idea."

"I stand by my statement."

Calder rolled his eyes and focused on me again. "What would you say if I offered to teach you the subjects you're not being taught in exchange for some art paper and paints?"

"Oh, whoa, whoa, whoa," Xander said, putting his hands up as if to ward off Calder's very, *very* bad suggestion. "Even worse than I thought. That's just asking for trouble, Calder."

"Look who's talking," Calder inserted, not taking his eyes off me.

"Yes," I blurted out. I did want to learn. I was hungry for it. But the truth was, I wanted to spend time with Calder and I was willing to do anything I could do to make that happen. I had surprised myself with my impulsive acceptance though. I rarely interacted with people other than Hailey and her boys, and occasionally Hector, so why was it I could so readily agree to Calder's idea? Perhaps I felt a greater comfort level with him because I'd spent so long with him in my own mind, even if much of what I "knew" were assumptions.

Calder smiled. "Great," he said softly, not taking his eyes from mine.

Xander stood. "All right, well, you two have fun sitting in the cellar."

Calder finally looked up at him. "The cellar would be worth it to finally get to draw on a big clean piece of paper." He talked about paper like it was a delicious meal he couldn't wait to devour.

I chewed at my lip, not quite as sure now. The cellar was a very large, cavernous space under the main lodge where Hector would bring all two hundred or so of us at least once a year for a drill to prepare us for when the great floods came. I shivered just at the thought of standing in the cellar with all those bodies pressed together, feeling sick, scared, and claustrophobic.

There was also a small room down there with a heavy metal door used during the rare time someone did something that went against Hector or the gods. They would be jailed for the amount of time it took for them to repent and then brought back up and made to sit to the side of the podium where Hector gave his sermons. They had to kneel on a piece of metal with little bumps on it from the beginning of Temple until the end. It wouldn't pierce the skin, but the look on the faces of those who had been punished that way let me know it sure felt like it had after kneeling on it for two hours.

I never knew exactly what the transgressions were, but I watched those people—three since I'd come to live in Acadia—and I silently sent them strength as I sat behind Hector. I swore my own knees ached as I walked back up the aisle, away from them.

I came back to the present and Calder was staring at me as if he saw the newfound doubt in my expression and was waiting for me to reconfirm my acceptance. "Maybe Xander's right. The cellar seems…" My voice faded away as Calder's face fell. "But my answer is still yes," I inserted quickly and nodded, unwilling to disappoint him. "I agree. When?" I took a deep breath. "I mean, when should we meet?"

His face broke into a grin, his straight teeth flashing. His grin transformed his face, making it, impossibly, even more beautiful. My stomach muscles tightened. I'd seen him use his grin with others, but to be the recipient of it myself was thrilling. "Tomorrow?" he asked.

I nodded, smiling too, probably looking slightly giddy. "Okay, tomorrow." I wanted to see him tomorrow and every tomorrow after that.

He studied me for a minute and I wondered what he was thinking. "I'll see you then."

"Bye, Eden," Xander said and jumped from the rock into the water. Calder followed behind him. They waded across the water and then walked up the small bank. My eyes wandered down Calder's muscular backside, clearly defined in the wet linen pants clinging to him. I caught myself and looked away, but before I could muster up any shame, my gaze was sliding back again. Just before they ducked through the rock opening, Calder looked back at me and smiled once more. I was glad he couldn't see my blush from where I sat.

The next day when I showed up at the spring, Calder was already lying back on the grass with his hands behind his head. I couldn't help the joy I felt to see him waiting for me.

"Hi," I said as I approached him, and he sat up. I took the large canvas bag I had brought off my shoulder and set it down on the grass. He immediately pulled the large pad of paper out and glanced up at me with a look of sheer happiness. My heart started beating triple time at the look of delight on his handsome face. He continued to rummage through the bag, and as he pulled the items out, he placed them neatly on the grass in front of him. There were several paint containers, four brushes, and a set of charcoal pencils.

"It was all I could take without making it obvious," I explained when he kept staring down at the items.

He raised his head, his eyes meeting mine. "This is way more than I expected. Thank you, Eden." He looked as if he wanted to say more but was at a loss. He rubbed his hands on his thighs. "So what lesson should we start with today?"

"Why don't you draw something first?" I suggested.

He opened his mouth to say something but then closed it and started again. "Are you sure?" I noticed his fingers moving as if he was barely controlling himself from reaching for the items.

"Yes. I'm very sure."

Calder grinned. "Okay. Hey, how about we do both at once? I'll draw and give a lesson at the same time. I can multi-task like that. You feel free to ask any question you want."

"Okay, if you're sure that won't distract you."

He shook his head. "No. Remember, I'm used to drawing under my desk while listening to a lecture."

I laughed. "All right then."

He scooted until his back was against a rock and he was mostly in the shade, and leaned forward to grab the charcoal pencils and the pad. Then he brought his knees up and leaned the pad of paper against them.

"First tell me what you know."

I know I love you and you're the most beautiful boy I've ever seen.

That was *all* I really knew for sure. I looked down, ashamed that I had no real education. I cleared my throat. "I know how to read. And that's really all."

I looked up to find his pencil still and that he was studying me, a small frown on his lips. "No math? No science? None at all?"

I shook my head again, scooting back so I was leaning against a rock too.

Calder started sketching again. "Okay. So we'll start with the basics then."

And so we sat there as he sketched, and he taught me the basics of mathematics, addition and subtraction. I caught on quickly. Somewhere in my memory, I knew I had begun learning this before. It was hazy and unclear, like all of my memories before this place. If I closed my eyes, I remembered a smell—like cleaning products and chalk—and I remembered being happy in that place, a school probably. But that was all I could muster.

After an hour or so, Calder set his pad down. "You'll be up to speed in no time," he said.

"Why exactly are you doing this?" I gestured my hand toward the paper. "I mean, other than for the exchange? Hector wouldn't approve of it, and we could both be severely punished. Why are you taking this risk?"

Calder watched me for a few seconds and then looked out to the spring. He bit his full bottom lip and his brow creased. Finally, he said, "Xander talks to the clerks at the ranger station at the entrance to the state park a few miles from here."

I was surprised. We were strongly encouraged not to engage with other members of the "big society" where wickedness, evil, and imbalance prevailed. Except for the council members who worked and Hector who went on pilgrimages when the gods ordained it, no one else had any reason or desire to venture from Acadia. Aside from the main lodge, we were totally self-sufficient, reliant on no one other than ourselves. "He does?"

Calder nodded. "He's formed friendships with a few of

them. When we were kids, we used to steal from the station. Or rather, Xander did the stealing; I just did the partaking. Anyway, a couple years back, he got caught red-handed. Only, instead of turning him in, the woman who caught him asked what he liked best of all the things he was taking. He told her, and now sometimes she brings candy and other things just out of kindness." He rubbed his chin. "I don't think every single person out in the big society is wicked and evil, Eden. Maybe some are, maybe most. I don't know. But the point is, I don't think Hector's completely right about that." He shrugged. "And if he's not right about that, maybe he's not right about a few other things too—like the fact that you shouldn't have an education. I know the gods talk to him, but he's also human. Maybe he…misunderstands messages now and again."

We sat there looking at each other silently. The small waterfall next to us provided gentle splashing sounds, and somewhere far away, a dog barked.

He exhaled, breaking eye contact. "It's why I have to get a place on the council," he said quietly. "I have to see what's out there, Eden." He met my gaze again, his expression filled with tension. "No matter how much time we have before the floods, I just have to know."

My heart was beating fast, not just because of Calder's closeness, but because talk like this simply wasn't done, at least as far as I had ever known. Something stirred deep inside of me, as if just beginning to wake. "You trust me," I said, knowing he wouldn't have told me what he did if that wasn't the case. And his trust… it felt like a gift, like a wonderful gift.

He nodded once. "I started trusting you a long time ago."

A sudden and fierce feeling of pride filled my chest. Being trusted by Calder Raynes made me feel more special than I'd ever felt in my whole life. I had already admitted to myself that I had made many assumptions about Calder, but those assumptions weren't just based on my own fantasies. I knew he was kind—knew that I was right to feel proud of earning his trust—because I'd felt kindness before. "My parents were kind," I said. "I remember so little of them, but that's one thing I know. They were kind."

Calder's gaze moved over my face. "Will you tell me about them?" he asked very gently.

I sighed, struggling to remember. "They were both blond." I took a piece of my own hair between my fingers and then let it fall. "Surprising, right?" I smiled and so did Calder. "And, um, my mother, she smelled like flowers." I closed my eyes and inhaled as my mind conjured her sweet, delicate scent. When I opened my eyes a minute later, Calder's head was tilted as he watched me, and his eyes looked darker somehow. I swallowed.

"What else?" he whispered as though we were telling secrets. And I supposed we were.

"I think my dad did some kind of work with other people's money. And my mom, she didn't work, at least not that I recall. We lived in Cincinnati, I do know that. I know they were good friends with Hector. I remember him being in our home. I remember my mother telling me we were coming to live with him. Here I'm assuming. But then... they died, and it was only Hector and me in a different house for a long time, years maybe. That's it. I've tried so hard to remember more from the time before, but it simply won't come. Because I was young, I suppose."

"How did your parents die?"

"It was a car accident. That's all I was told."

Calder had his bottom lip between his teeth again in that way he had when he was thinking hard about something.

"What?" I asked.

He let his lip free, licking along it with his tongue before responding. "Nothing. I'm just sorry you lost your parents."

I had the feeling he had been about to say something else but didn't. I nodded anyway. "Thank you."

"So," he said, starting to get up. "Tomorrow? Same time? Same place?"

I stood too and nodded enthusiastically. "Yes. Um"—I nodded toward the pad in his hands—"can I see your sketch?"

He looked down at it as if just remembering it existed. "Oh. Yeah, sure." He turned it around and my breath caught.

He had sketched our—for suddenly that's what it was, *ours*—spring. He had only used charcoal pencil, but somehow it was lush and beautiful, the shadows and highlights hinting at the depth of color in the water, the rocks, the grass, and the sky. It was…breathtaking.

"Calder. You're… I've never seen anything that good. You've never had any lessons?"

He shook his head, watching me closely as if it mattered very much to him what I thought.

"You're just gifted, then. Very, very gifted." I felt awed by his talent and I was sure it must have shown in my expression.

He held it out to me. "It's for you."

I grinned, accepting it. "Thank you. Today, here with you, was a wonderful birthday gift." I began to carefully roll up the sketch so that I could carry it with me.

His expression took on surprise. "It's your birthday?"

"Tomorrow. I'll be seventeen. But this here"—I hugged the rolled paper to my chest delicately—"is the best gift I could have ever asked for."

"No. No way. If I had known it was your birthday, I would have sketched one of you. A portrait." He smiled. "Tomorrow. On your actual day."

My heart squeezed with happiness. "Okay." I held up the canvas bag with all the supplies in it. "Should we hide this somewhere?"

Calder looked around and then took the bag from me and walked it over to a group of rocks to his right, placing it between two sitting at an angle so it was like a mini-cave. He picked up a flat rock next to him and put it directly in front of the opening so it couldn't be seen.

We headed up the trail and when we got close to the top, he stopped and nodded at me to go before him so we wouldn't exit together.

When I returned to the main lodge, I walked quietly upstairs and unrolled the sketch of our spring, looking at it for several long minutes before rolling it back up again. I hid it in the far corner under my bed, and I stowed my time with Calder in a quiet, private corner of my heart.

I hadn't been completely certain Calder would return today, whether he would decide it was too risky or if he would decide he wasn't interested. And yet he had. His patience was unending as he taught me basic math. I hadn't felt stupid or ashamed as I started to grasp what must seem like such elemental things to him. It felt good to learn, to stretch my mind further than its normal boundaries. And as I went to bed that night, my heart felt full.

CHAPTER SIX
Calder

While I waited for the birthday girl, I looked around for the perfect portrait location, finally deciding on a large rock just to the left of the spring. It was lightly sun-dappled, mostly shaded by larger rocks. It would be perfect for her to lie back on while I sketched her.

I pictured Eden reclining there, her dress outlining her slim shape, her shirt molded to her small round breasts, and my blood heated.

Don't, Calder. Don't even think about it.

No, thoughts like that about Eden were a very bad idea. She was off-limits in the biggest way possible, and I needed to remember that. It would have been for the best if I had ended our exchange and never looked her way again. But the desire to be close to her was too hard to resist. I could be punished severely, but maybe it would be worth it. I struggled to think pure thoughts around her, but her beauty... *Stop, Calder. Don't think about sex when she's about to arrive.*

I picked up the small bouquet of flowers I had brought

for her and placed them on the rock, thinking of that day so long ago when she had bravely marched out onto our game field with hope in her eyes.

Morning glory. As pretty as a flower, as strong as a weed.

I had loved our game through the years. To me it was an adventure, a secret, and yes, a risk. I had even used some morning glory seeds to plant a small bush at the edge of the field where I worked. It had been true what I said about morning glories being stronger than they looked. That bush worked to take over, but I kept it small and contained, just big enough to easily provide me with the blue flowers I left for Eden as regularly as possible.

"Hi," I heard behind me and smiled before I had fully turned around.

"Happy birthday," I said, walking over to her and taking her hand as I led her toward the rock and gestured for her to lean back. "I think this is the perfect spot or your portrait," I told her.

"I'm a little nervous," she said. "One of Mother Hailey's boys drew me last week and I looked like a squash with eyes."

I laughed. "I'd like to think my skills surpass his."

"Oh, yours definitely do. What I'm more worried about is I actually *do* look like a squash and your skilled portrait will confirm it."

I laughed again as I placed both hands on her shoulders and turned her. "You? A squash?" She laid back against the rock so I was now over her. I walked closer and moved her hair the way I wanted it. Our eyes locked and suddenly we both went serious. *You're the most beautiful girl I've ever seen.* "Not even close," I whispered.

She remained still, her lips parting as her gaze moved to my mouth like she had done the other day.

Oh, Eden, don't do that. Don't let me know you want to be kissed.

I leaned back quickly and turned to my supplies. "Are you comfortable?" I asked, not turning around, clearing my throat. I took a deep breath and willed my body to settle down too.

"Yes, I'm fine."

I sat down on a rock a few feet away, put my drawing pad on my lap, and began to trace her outline. Primal thoughts and urges coursed through me as my eyes moved back and forth between her body and my pencil. *Get ahold of yourself.*

"So, what's our lesson today?" she asked quietly.

"Our lesson? Oh, lesson, right. Uh, more math?"

"No, I'll keep working on my addition and subtraction in my room in the evenings. How about some science today?"

My pencil kept moving. Once I got started, it was almost as if my hand took over. I barely had to think about what I was drawing.

I tried to remember back to what I had learned when I was eight, about the age Eden would have been when she came here. "Do you know the states of matter?"

"No."

"Okay, we'll talk about those today and whatever else I can remember from first-year science. I figure…well, I figure anything I can't remember probably isn't that important anyway. Or at least, it's not that applicable to life."

She sighed. "What *is* applicable to life, Calder? Maybe Hector's right. If we're all going to go to Elysium soon enough, why should I bother learning about this world and how it works?"

My hand kept moving as I considered that. "Remember what I told you about the morning glory that day?" I glanced up and she nodded. "I learned about them in an agriculture class field-workers had to take." My eyes moved over her parted lips as I traced their shape on the paper. My heartbeat quickened. I imagined it was my finger, not the pencil, tracing those ripe lips. It felt intimate and personal and made my skin feel flushed. I cleared my throat. "Anyway, what if I hadn't known that detail and therefore hadn't been able to convince the other kids to let you play? That specific knowledge resulted in years of butterscotch candy for me." I shot her a wink and she laughed softly.

I focused on the paper and drew quietly for a minute, shading her bottom lip. "My point is, you never know when a small piece of knowledge is going to come in handy or maybe...maybe even change your life. I think you should try to take in as much of it as possible, and anywhere you can get it. No one should ever stop you from gaining knowledge if that's what you seek."

She was quiet for a minute. "Thank you, Calder."

"For what? This is an even trade. I'm benefitting here too."

"You're *risking* here too."

I outlined the swoop of her delicate cheekbones. "Somehow...it feels worth the risk."

I stood up and went to her and arranged her hair again so that a portion of it was in the sunlight where it glistened like gold. There was something shimmery about her, a glow that seemed to come from the inside. *No wonder she's the chosen one to lead us through darkness*, I thought. *She shines.* As my hand moved through the heavy silk of her hair, our eyes met.

"Calder..." she started.

"Yes?" I asked, my voice even raspier than it normally was. Time seemed to still—she and I were the only ones moving, the world around us pausing. Her full, rose-colored lips parted and I almost groaned.

"I..." She looked down as a pink flush rose up her neck. Then her eyes bravely met my own. She leaned forward and planted her lips on mine. I startled slightly, my eyes remaining open, as her lips simply pressed against me, firm but soft, her eyes closed. I knew I should move—*I knew I should*—but I was rooted to the spot, immobile, incapable of rational thought. And then her tongue poked out tentatively and before I even realized it, mine had too. Her taste—it surrounded me—sweet and delicious as our tongues met and played gently, testing, experimenting. Eden sighed and her hands came up to grip my shoulders as she pulled me closer. She tilted her head and her wet tongue slid more deeply into my mouth.

The power of the need to mate, hard and vigorously, shocked me, clear pictures forming in my mind of us, sweaty and tangled. I wanted her. I hadn't known this pull before today, but I knew it then. I wanted her desperately, but I stepped away, turning and attempting to cool my raging blood.

When I finally felt in control enough to turn back around and face her, she blinked at me, her blush deepening. "I'm so sorry," she said quietly. "I just wanted...to kiss you. Just once. Even if you don't want to very much." She shook her head slightly, the expression on her face vulnerable but also full of a wary strength. From the very first time I had talked to her, when she asked to join our game, there was a determined force about her. She appeared gentle and subdued, even meek. Yet a depth of bravery was evident too. I wondered how often she pulled forth that courage.

She sat up straighter, squaring her shoulders. "If I have to live in Elysium for eternity with someone I don't love, I thought maybe a kiss from you, even just one, would make it bearable." Her eyes rose to mine and I stared at her.

I turned her words over in my mind. I felt shaken, not just from the kiss but from what she'd just said. I had lived my life with the knowledge that a great flood would come and our community, Hector's people, would go to the promised land. I had dreamed of what Elysium would look like, would smell like, would *feel* like. I had even secretly feared it, wondering if it could possibly be everything Hector said it was. After all, he'd never actually *been* there. But I had never considered Eden might dread it, have dreams of her own that would never be fulfilled because of her role in the foretelling. I had even figured she looked upon her role as a gift, like the rest of us had been taught to. But clearly, that wasn't the case.

And yet…the gods knew best. *Didn't they?*

"That can't happen again, Eden." I took a few steps back, not trusting myself to be too close to her just now, not to reach for her against my will. Eden's face fell and the blush seemed to deepen even more. She licked her lips, the lips I had just tasted, and I almost groaned but caught myself.

She gave her head a small shake. "That was so very, very wrong of me. I'm sorry for putting you in an unwanted position," she said.

I almost laughed. Unwanted? Hardly. That was the problem. I stepped back to her and placed my hand on her arm. Her skin was warm and soft and I removed my hand quickly. The temptation to touch more of her was too great. "No. I want to kiss you again, and I want to do it better. More than I'm willing to think too much about."

Eden's eyes widened with hurt. "Then…*why?* Why won't you?"

"Because you're going to be Hector's *wife*, Eden, and all of our fates are tied to that. I don't know what Elysium is going to be like. I don't know a lot of things." I put my hand in my hair and gripped a handful. "But what I do know is you're going to be his wife a year from today. You're going to *belong* to him. He'll never have it any other way." *You'll never belong to me and I can't let myself want that.*

She sat up. "Yes. I know. I count down the days. I count down the days of my freedom, which is a poor excuse for freedom, by the way. But it's better than what I'll have to endure against my will—*forever!*" She brought her shoulders back and straightened her spine. "It might be Elysium to all of *you*, but to me, it sounds like *hell*."

Shock ratcheted through me. "Eden…" I said, but didn't know where to go from there. There were so many conflicting emotions running through me, I wasn't sure how to untangle them. I ran my fingers through my hair again and stepped back as she pulled her dress straight and began gathering her things.

"Please don't go."

Her eyes cast downward. "I think I should. I'm sorry. I've humiliated myself and said things I shouldn't have said and—"

"You can always be honest with me."

She finally met my eyes. "I don't want to stop meeting you here. Or put an end to our…sessions. But for today, I need to go." She smiled a small trembling smile. "Tomorrow?"

No. Not tomorrow, not ever. This was a terrible idea. I can't trade flowers and candy or let my eyes linger on you in Temple. I can't think about kissing you or touching you. I can't meet you here again. "Yes, tomorrow," I said. She paused as if she'd heard the struggle in my voice. I knew we were playing with fire before this, but now…it was even clearer it would be better for everyone involved if we put an end to our *sessions* right here and right now.

But try as I might, I couldn't bring myself to say those words. In fact, suddenly my desire to see her, to be near her, was overwhelming. Her bravery stunned me. She had dared to dream beyond what Hector had ordained her destiny to be, beyond what even the *gods* had destined. And instead of that looking blasphemous or just plain stupid, something about it felt powerful, beautiful, brave.

Just like the bravery she had shown that day on the playing field.

As beautiful as a flower. As strong as a weed.

And something inside me felt like it had shifted too, because I had dreams as well. In that moment, right there and then, I admitted to myself that I longed for more for my life, even beyond Acadia, and maybe those dreams were beautiful too. Brave. I had always pushed that desire away, ashamed of it, thinking it sinful, selfish.

But maybe, just maybe, my own dreams weren't as sinful as I'd always thought them to be…*somehow.*

I watched her silently as she retreated. And somewhere deep down inside, somewhere where there were no rules and no limits, somewhere where only the beating of my own heart could be heard, a feeling I could only describe as love took root.

"Morning Glory," I called as she began to duck through the rocks. She turned. I walked over to her and handed her the rolled-up portrait. It wasn't completely finished but close enough. "Happy birthday." I smiled. And then against my own better judgment, I stepped forward and wrapped my arms around her, leaned in, and kissed her forehead. The sweet smell of fresh apples clouded my brain and I moved away, just a little bit dazed. Eden released a breath and then gave me a small smile. And then she was gone, and my arms were empty.

———

Later that evening, after I had delivered the next day's drinking water to the cabins, I saw Xander making a pass around the perimeter of our land and jogged out to where he was. When I slowed to a walk and came up next to him, he gave a small jump. "You scared me."

"I see you'd be pretty useful in an attack," I said, ribbing him.

He snorted. "Lost in my thoughts. But yeah, you're right. You're all pretty much sitting ducks with me out here."

I eyed him sideways. "What's on your mind?"

He sighed and stopped walking. "Do you really want to know?"

I stopped too, and frowned.

Xander squinted out to the darkening desert. "I have a lot of time to think out here walking around ceaselessly." He paused. "Probably too much time."

"Hey, spit it out, Xander." I glanced around to make sure no one was nearby.

He paused again. "This thing with Eden—"

"Don't try to talk me out of it, Xander. I know everything you're going to say and I—"

"You're wrong," he interrupted. "You don't know what I'm going to say. This does have to do with Eden in a round-about way, but not how you're thinking." He rubbed the back of his neck. "I've been considering this for a while, and I never said anything because, well, I've been trying to get past my own sinful thoughts…I guess. My head is all jumbled

84

most of the time. But I"—he looked around quickly like I'd just done—"*question* things, Calder. I question Hector."

My muscles were tensed and I relaxed my body slowly as I considered Xander. I was surprised but also relieved after I'd just been having similar thoughts.

"I go around and around it in my mind out here," Xander went on. "I work it like a puzzle, and it doesn't add up. So many things…"

I looked away, in the direction of our spring, Eden's and mine, and said softly, "No, I question things too."

Xander let out a breath that sounded as if he had been storing up air for hours, years, perhaps a lifetime. We'd never spoken of our doubts. Maybe our actions had done that for us, the stealing, the *sinning,* but we'd never said the words. "The irony is, I walk the *outside* perimeter of Acadia a hundred times a day, and I feel like a damn caged animal."

"Why haven't you said anything to me before now? We talk about everything."

He looked off somewhere behind me. "Yeah, I know. I was trying to make sense of it…or get over it…or something. I swear to you, Calder, I don't even know."

I remained quiet while he ran both hands through his hair, leaving it looking like he'd just traveled through a windstorm.

"I guess when I saw you with Eden, when I realized the risk you'd be willing to take to be friends with her, I thought maybe you might have some questions, or doubts, too."

I paused. "Have you talked to Sasha about this?"

Sasha was several years older than us and already married to another worker. But along with us, she was among those who had either been born here or had come to Acadia as a baby. We hadn't chosen this life. *It* had chosen us.

Xander shook his head. "No, Sash is happy. She likes her life. I think she truly loves Aaron. She's never seemed restless."

I nodded. "Listen, Xander, the best we can do is achieve a place on the council. We can go out into the big community that way. We're not stupid. We can learn things. We'll have more choices there…more opportunities to find answers."

"But we still won't have anything that's our own." Xander grimaced and looked off into the distance, muttering, "Even saying that feels wrong."

I frowned. We'd always been taught that wanting anything for yourself, rather than the group as a whole, was sinful and selfish. It wasn't an idea easy for me to shake either. And maybe that was a good thing. It was all so damned confusing.

"We don't have a lot of time, Xander. We need to get a place on that council—even just one of us—before the floods come."

Xander looked down at his feet and finally said quietly, "What if Hector's wrong about that too?"

Something that felt like a mixture of dread and hope surged through my blood. *What if.*

Xander's eyes met mine and were filled with what looked to be the same thing I was feeling. "Kristi at the ranger's station told me lots of *so-called* prophets have foretold the end of the world, and not one of them has come true… obviously."

"Hector would say Kristi's a blasphemous liar who's doing work for the devil."

Xander huffed out a breath. "Yeah. I know. I'm well versed in what Hector would say."

"I didn't realize you and Kristi talked that much."

"Yeah…she's…" He paused, looking as if he was trying to come up with just the right word for this mysterious

Kristi. "Kind. And she's about our age but she's completed two years at the community college. She's transferring to a university soon. She's…worldly."

Someone slammed a door to a cabin, and even though it wasn't very close to where we stood, we both startled. I lowered my voice when I said, "Let's not talk about this again unless we know we're somewhere where no one is around."

Xander nodded. "Is it really safe to discuss this kind of stuff around Eden?"

I thought about that for a second, certainty filling my chest. "Yes. Yes, I believe so."

He paused. "You have feelings for her, don't you?"

I thought about that for a second and simply settled on "I won't be that stupid."

Xander watched me silently for a moment. "The thing is, Calder, it's not always a choice who you develop feelings for. You're playing with fire in more ways than one. Any fool can see the way you two look at each other. And the more time you spend together—"

"We have a history, Xander. We're fond of each other."

"Fond of each other?" He snorted. "I'm *fond* of your mom and sunsets. You are not 'fond' of Eden, trust me."

I gave him a wry smile. "Okay, so it goes a little beyond 'fond.' I'm okay, I promise. You don't need to worry about me."

Xander studied my face and then nodded again. "Okay, brother." He started to back away. "Have a good night." And then he turned and walked off, leaving me to return home and my mind to go over and over and over what we had discussed. What if Xander was right and Hector was wrong? What if there wasn't going to be a great flood? *What if I had the choice to leave Acadia and travel out into a world that wasn't ending? At least not anytime soon.*

87

CHAPTER SEVEN
Eden

The next day, Calder didn't show at the spring and I felt both sad and humiliated as I shuffled back to the main lodge. I had ruined everything. I'd acted like a fool—a stupid, honest fool who'd declared my deep desire to kiss him, and the sinful nature of my secret thoughts. He'd looked both shell-shocked and torn after our kiss and all I'd wanted to do was to get away to lick my wounds and cower from my shame. And now, I had lost my only...friend. Or I'd thought he was my friend. I groaned in despair and put my hands over my face as I leaned back on the inside of my bedroom door. *Good job, Eden*, I thought bitterly.

I spent most of the day lost in my music—my only refuge, my only comfort.

Later that night after I'd helped bathe Hailey's boys and gotten them dressed for bed, I walked back through the main room toward the stairs. I saw Maya, Calder's sister, with a stack of folded clothing in her hands opening the front door to leave and I halted in my tracks. I gave her a smile, but she blushed, lowered her eyes, and ducked out the door before I could say anything to her. *Gods above!* Calder didn't tell her about yesterday, did he? *No, surely not.*

I was so weary of everyone looking at me like I was a breakable doll rather than a living, breathing girl. I clumped up the stairs slowly, my heart heavy.

When I stepped into my room, I immediately saw the dark clothing item lying at the end of my bed. I stopped, confused, and looked back over my shoulder nervously before closing the door and picking it up. My heart jolted, then soared, settling into a quickened pace. My smile grew as I stared at the hooded cloak the workers sometimes wore in the evenings.

Was I meant to wear it? The hood would certainly hide me, especially if it was dark. Could I wear this and dare walk out among the workers? I let out a soft sound of excitement. Maya had left this for me. Had Calder sent it with her? What else? This was a piece of worker clothing. Perhaps he *wasn't* angry or disappointed in me. I brought the cloak to my chest, holding it tightly as I let out a small joyful squeak.

The rest of the evening went by at a snail's pace as I waited for it to grow dark and for Hailey to go to bed.

Once the main lodge was mostly quiet and the night sky was deep and black, only the sliver of a new moon showing, I crept down the stairs and through the front door, closing it very quietly behind me. Once I had made it around the main lodge, I put the cloak on, tucking all of my hair inside and pulling the hood low over my face. Then I walked briskly toward the worker cabins, where several bonfires lit the night.

As I moved unnoticed for the first time since I'd come here, I took in all the sights and sounds of this very different life. People sat around three main bonfires in the large open area in the center of all the cabins. There was soft laughter and conversation and I heard small portions of stories people were telling as I walked past. I wished I had the nerve to sit right down with them and listen in, but I didn't want to risk anyone noticing me. Just walking around like I was—feeling *free* and anonymous—was thrilling.

At one of the bonfires, a man was singing softly, his voice deep and melodic as everyone around him sat quietly and listened. I stopped for just a second, lulled by the peaceful sound of his low voice, wishing I could play the piano while he sang. I felt the keys under my fingers, finding the notes that would accompany the melody he sang.

Suddenly, a hand grabbed me, and I almost let out a shriek as the person began walking and I was forced to move with him, stumbling slightly.

"Shh, it's me," I heard Calder's voice say. My heart soared. I'd know that voice anywhere. I'd know that voice in the midst of a thousand clanging symbols or in the deep darkness of a never-ending cave. It *moved* inside me, it scratched gently over the inside of my skin.

I grinned. "Where are we going?"

"You'll see." I could see his gentle yet mischievous smile in the dim glow of a nearby fire and my heart flipped. I wanted to groan and raise my face to the gods, calling out, *Why? Why did you make him so beautiful to me if I can never have him? Why? Why? Why?*

Calder picked up the pace and soon we were running, the breeze blowing in our faces as I laughed out loud, feeling wild joy in the moment. My lips had been on his, and it would probably never happen again. *But I had lived it*, even if only just once, and if that was all I ever had, I would hold it dearly, deep inside where no one else could ever take it from me.

We stopped, our breaths mingling as we stood in the darkness. I glanced around and saw we were right on the edge of the fruit orchard. "Why are we here?"

"Our lesson of the day. Come on." He took my hand in his again and we walked slowly through the fragrant, moonlit trees. The perfumes of the earth—the soil, the grass, and the sweetly scented air—surrounded us. Calder's hand held mine—gripped me tightly—spreading warmth through my body.

This. This is Elysium—not some far-off, fathomless place. This.

When we got to a small clearing in the trees, Calder sat down on the grass and I followed him. He lay back and pointed up. "Look."

I lay back too, and sucked in a breath when I saw the stars, clear and brilliant in the dark night sky, glittering above me. "They're so clear," I whispered.

I felt Calder nod next to me. "This is far enough away from the main lodge's electricity and our bonfires. Plus, it's a new moon…"

We lay in silence for a few minutes, looking up at the sky full of glowing stars. I cleared my throat. "You're going to teach me about the constellations?" I asked.

"Yeah. What I know anyway."

I turned my head toward him. The starlight provided just enough light that I could see Calder, mostly in shadows and highlights but enough to notice his expression.

"So…you're not feeling strange about yesterday?" I asked softly.

He paused and I held my breath. "You mean the kissing?" I heard the smile in his voice. "I've barely given it a thought."

"Well, gosh, that makes me feel so much better."

Calder laughed, turning his face toward me, his smile fading. "Can I be honest with you, Eden?"

I groaned. "This is going to get worse, isn't it?"

Calder chuckled. "No. In the course of a few days, life seems to have become complex. The simple part is this." His eyes moved to my lips and he seemed to catch himself as his gaze darted back to mine. He cleared his throat. "If I were just a boy, and you were just a girl, I wouldn't kiss you once like you asked." He paused and my heart dropped. *Oh.*

"Eden, there might not be enough air in my lungs to kiss you as long and as often as I wanted to."

Oh. *Oh.* I blinked and sat up. "That's supposed to make me feel better?"

Calder sat up too. "No. But we have to be honest about our situation and the risks we're willing to take. We're attracted to each other. I admire you, and I like to be with you. I want to be your friend. But, Eden, nothing more can ever happen between us. I'm sorry about that, but it's just the way it is."

I felt stung, angry, and bitter, the joy I'd been feeling just a few minutes earlier, fading. "My destiny," I bit out.

Calder paused, furrowing his brow and running one finger absentmindedly over his bottom lip. "I don't know about that. All I know is life as we know it would be over for us if we gave in."

"Right. Thank you for being honest with me. I admire you too, Calder. You're very…obedient." I felt angry. Angry with Calder? Angry with the gods for bringing me here and putting me within arm's length of this wonderful boy? *Why?*

Calder furrowed his brow and then looked away. I suddenly felt guilty. I had meant it as an insult and he had taken my statement in the vein it had been said. In truth, I was just hurt and filled with bitterness at the unfairness of my situation. And here Calder was, a boy, practically a man, who was trying his very best to be honorable, to be my friend, my only friend.

"I'm sorry," I said. "That was unfair."

"It's okay. I *am* obedient. I like to think I'm obedient to the gods, even if Hector is prone to the same mistakes or misinterpretations any human being could be. I like to think I'm obedient to this community, to the needs and happiness of others here. What would happen, not just to me, but to our people, if it was known I was cavorting with Hector's soon-to-be bride?"

"Cavorting? You make it sound so tawdry." Hector often used that word. He said sinful actions were like cavorting with the devil.

"It would be wrong. Just meeting like this…it's as far as it can go."

I was silent for a good minute, mulling it over in my mind. Like the day before when I'd kissed him, all I wanted to do was leave, run. Although his points were valid, doubt still assaulted me. *He knows how I feel about him. Is he just being nice here to avoid hurting my feelings?* Oh, what did it matter? Either way, he was rejecting me. And it wasn't as if what he was saying didn't make sense. It just hurt. "I suppose you're right," I said, feeling defeated.

Calder turned toward me. "My point in being honest about my attraction to you is I think it's better if it's acknowledged. We need to tread carefully here, Eden. It would be far too easy to cross a line. I want to be your friend. I want to teach you things. But not to the detriment of our entire community and not to the detriment of our own hearts… and our own dreams."

Truly, my heart was already his for the breaking, and breaking it was, but I nodded anyway. I knew he had dreams for his own life. And he was risking those just by meeting me like he was, most definitely by teaching me things. If anything, it made my admiration for him stronger. How could I ask him for more?

We were both silent for another moment. "The portrait was beautiful," I finally said. "It's nice to know I'm not squash-like at all in your eyes." I had unrolled the paper the night before and my breath had caught in my throat at the absolute beauty of the picture. Did I really look like that? Hector had told me since I was a child I was beautiful and angelic. But something about the way Calder had drawn me made me look powerful and strong, the look on my face sure, confident, but also serene as I gazed upward.

He let out a small chuff. "If only you were just a little more squash-like, this whole situation would be easier for me to bear."

I held back a grimace. If this was going to have any chance of working, he couldn't flirt with me.

He seemed to read my mind as his expression became serious and he cleared his throat and lay back down. "So, speaking of squash, our lesson today is going to be on the stars."

"What does squash have to do with the stars?"

"Oh, you've never heard of the constellation Squasharius?"

I laughed as I lay back too. "I swear, Calder Raynes, if you're teaching me all kinds of things I'm going to have to unlearn later, I won't be happy."

Calder grinned. "Okay, so maybe there's no Squasharius." He was quiet for a minute. "Did you know that when you're looking at stars, you're actually looking back in time?"

"How's that?"

"Because the light from a star takes millions of years to reach the earth. So, for instance"—he pointed upward again to one tiny blinking star—"that's actually what that one looked like millions of years ago."

Something about that seemed magical to me and I decided not to try to wrap my mind around the science of it, not that I really could anyway. "It's like I can imagine the gods up there, somewhere behind all those stars, looking down on us right now." I paused. "Can I tell you a secret though?"

"Anything."

"I only pray to one of them." I blushed, glad he couldn't tell in the near dark. Saying that out loud, despite the fact I read hours and hours of the Holy Book on all twelve deities every single day, felt blasphemous.

Calder turned toward me. "Which one?" he asked, surprise in his voice.

"The God of Mercy."

"Why him?"

I considered his question for a moment. "Because…I just figure there's not much that grace and mercy can't fix. And I guess I figure that he…he cares the most about what happens to us. Or maybe he's able to love us despite how much we mess up, how imperfect we are, and how much we want what we shouldn't want," I finished quietly.

"Then he has the hardest job," Calder finally said.

I breathed out a small laugh. "Yes. I always imagine that when I get to Elysium, I'm going to find him first."

We were both silent for a minute. "What would your own dreams be, Eden, I mean, if it wasn't your destiny to marry Hector?" Calder asked.

You. You're my dream.

"I don't know. To see the world, like you, I guess. To know what might be out there for me. If anything at all."

"Are you proud of being chosen?" he asked softly.

"There's no sense of satisfaction in something you didn't do anything to achieve," I answered.

"But obviously the gods see something in you perhaps you don't even see in yourself. You were chosen by them because you have a beautiful, brave heart."

I laughed softly. "No, it can't be that."

"Why not?"

"Because it's my heart that makes me want to *deny* my so-called destiny."

It's my heart that wants you *to be my destiny.*

Calder remained quiet, seeming to ponder my answer.

"What's that one right there?" I asked, pointing at a bright star all by itself on the edge of the sky.

Calder turned back over onto his back and looked to where I was pointing. "I don't know."

"Maybe you can ask someone tomorrow."

"I won't be able to see it tomorrow to point it out." I heard his mouth move into a smile.

"Hmmm, I guess the stars teach us things, even from a million years ago."

"What do the stars teach us?"

I paused for a second. "That some things are seen more clearly in light…and some things are seen more clearly in darkness."

Calder's head turned my way and I looked over at him. His expression seemed wistful. He didn't say anything, but after a moment, he grasped my hand in his, and we both turned back to look at the sky.

We talked about the stars, his beautiful, slightly gravelly voice moving over me like music.

As I lay close to him, the warmth of his body next to mine, I listened to him talk. I felt content, something I hadn't known before and I closed my eyes for just a second.

What seemed like a few moments later, someone shook me. "Hey." I heard Calder's voice and looked around, disoriented. The sweet smell of the fruit trees awakened my senses and my eyes slowly opened. "I have to get you back," Calder said. "We both fell asleep."

"No one even knows I left," I said sleepily.

"I'll be missed though," he said, standing and reaching for my hand.

He pulled me to my feet and I brushed myself off. I guess his family *would* know he hadn't come to bed since they only had two rooms.

We started walking and Calder grabbed my hand again, leading me through the darkness. We took the long way around the outer perimeter of the cabins, walking as quietly as possible, not speaking.

The bonfires were all just dying embers now, and most of the people had already gone inside.

I walked as slowly as possible, wishing I could stay out all night, just roaming, doing as I pleased. With Calder.

"Meet me at the spring tomorrow?" Calder asked.

I nodded. It was lighter now as the electricity from the main lodge reached the path we were walking.

"Thank you for this," I said, glancing at him, feeling shy. "It's hard to explain what this meant to me, but thank you." Freedom. He'd given me a few blessed hours of freedom.

Calder smiled. "Maybe we'll do it again."

Hopefulness filled me and I nodded, smiling and

removing the cloak that had provided me anonymity and then handing it back.

He left me at the place where the cabins ended, and the large courtyard between the workers' homes and the main lodge began. I looked back several times to see him standing where we'd parted as he watched me walk the rest of the way. His hands were in his pockets, and as my steps separated us, he became nothing more than a shadow. As our distance grew, so did the loneliness in my heart. I missed him already.

When I entered the lodge, someone grabbed my wrist and I cried out in surprise.

I looked up to see Clive Richter, my least favorite council member, a shifty-eyed man who used too much hair product. I thought it fit his personality—greasy all around. Why Hector considered him holy enough to be one of the leaders of his people, I didn't have a clue.

"You're not supposed to leave the lodge, are you? Especially at night."

My heart began racing and I swallowed. If Clive knew I was leaving the lodge for something Hector hadn't approved, it'd all be over. No more lessons. No more Calder. I cast my eyes down, trying to look as obedient as possible.

"I just wanted to see what the workers did at night," I lied. "I walked through their camp once. That's all. How can I lead people if I don't understand them? If they don't think I care about who they are or how they live?" My eyes remained lowered as I waited for him to respond.

"They're all a bunch of degenerates, you know. You're lucky you didn't get raped by a group of them."

"Degenerates?" I asked, my eyes rising to meet his.

"Yeah, degenerates. You hear their stories when they come to us," he said, referring to the information Hector gave us about their lives when they joined our family in Temple.

"Yes, but they're here because they want to be washed clean."

Clive snorted. "The point is, don't go walking around the camp again, Eden. I'll be checking every night to make sure you're here. Don't do it again or I'll have to mention this to Hector."

I nodded, lowering my gaze again. When I finally looked up, I found his eyes raking over my body, a dark glint to them. He focused on my breasts for so long I almost brought my arms up to cover them under his scrutiny, but I made myself stay still. *A perfect princess.*

"Hmm hmm," he said, finally raising his eyes to my face. He pushed a lock of hair behind my ear and I bit down on my tongue to keep myself from spitting at him.

"Such beauty," he hummed. "You're almost eighteen, aren't you, Eden?"

"No. I just turned seventeen."

"Hmm. I can only imagine Hector is impatient for the day you'll become his." He leaned closer so I could smell his stale breath. "You'll be a good wife, won't you, Eden? So lovely. So obedient."

"I'll hardly have time to be a good wife, will I? The floods will come and it will all be over."

Clive leaned back and smiled. "No, just beginning, my lovely. Just beginning." He laughed and caressed my cheek once more and then turned and walked away. I shuddered as I watched him retreat, not understanding what he had meant with his statement. I hurried to my room where I quickly undressed and got in bed.

My dreams were filled with Calder bathed in starlight.

CHAPTER EIGHT
Calder

It rained for the next couple days so I wasn't able to meet Eden at our spring. I actually wasn't able to get out at all. I supposed the gods had decided I needed a minivacation and were overseeing my work in the fields.

Instead, two long days after I'd lain with Eden under the stars, I stood in the doorway of our small dim cabin and looked up toward what I knew to be Eden's room on the second floor. It glowed with light and I wondered what she was doing up there while I was down here. Was she lonely? Bored? I believed I knew enough about her now to guess that she was. I imagined standing a ladder against that window, climbing up to her, and then taking her hand as we ran laughing through the warm rain, the smell of apples scenting the air, her dress clinging to her, revealing her pink skin beneath. A lightning spear of lust arrowed through my body and I let out a soft groan. This line of thought was not productive. I had told her we couldn't kiss, that we couldn't be more than friends. But half my mind and my body—certainly my body—didn't seem to agree with that plan at all. In fact, there seemed to be a full-out mutiny to that plan as my thoughts constantly turned to Eden, visions of her, of us together, setting my blood on fire. Several times I had given in to temptation, gone up into the hills and leaned back against a rock, and stroked myself until release flooded from my body, potent and intense. I knew it was sinful, but in the moments right before, it felt necessary, vital to my very survival. That water-cleansing ceremony had its work cut out for it where I was concerned.

"Quit pacing. You're like a caged animal," my mom nagged.

I snorted softly, recalling Xander using those same words a few days before when we'd spoken.

"This damn rain," I muttered, sticking my head out the door covered by a small wooden overhang.

"You want something to do; I have a hundred cans that need filled with tomatoes," my mom said, looking over her shoulder from where she stood at the table. Cans were lined up neatly in front of her as was a large pot of peeled, cooling tomatoes. She was helping stockpile food for the winter months. It didn't get very cold here in the desert, even in winter, but everything had a season, and tomatoes only flourished through November.

I sighed and reluctantly went to help with the canning. We worked in silence for a few minutes before I picked up a can, turning it one way and then the other. "Cans aren't provided by nature," I said.

"What?" My mom paused in her work, eyeing the can I was holding.

"Hector always says we should use the instruments and materials the gods have naturally provided for us, that

101

using the wicked tools of the big society only corrupts our purity."

My mom returned to her task, not acknowledging my statement for a few minutes. After a bit she said, "We use as *little* as we can from the big society. Some things simply can't be fashioned from rock, dirt, and tree branches."

"Oh, I see. So when it's *convenient*, we use what the gods have provided. I didn't get the updated version of the Holy Book. Maybe that's in the new edition," I said sarcastically.

My mom looked up, her gaze sharply disapproving. "You're being blasphemous, Calder." Her voice was a whisper, as if someone were listening in—the gods themselves perhaps—although you couldn't hide from the gods so why bother trying?

"We make many, many sacrifices as Hector's people." She waved her hand around the cabin. "No running water, no electricity."

"Yes, but clearly Hector doesn't make those same concessions. Why? Has anyone ever asked him? Perhaps the gods ordained it so? Is that it?"

"Calder," my mom hissed. I had never spoken to her this way and I was suddenly ashamed.

I set the can down with a sigh. "I'm sorry, Mom. I shouldn't have said any of that."

"It's the rain. It's gotten under your skin. This cabin is small for four. It will clear tomorrow, and this mood will lift. You'll see." She gave me a thin smile and patted my cheek. I did my best to smile back.

We were quiet in our work for a minute. "You'll be able to marry soon if you wish. As soon as you've had your water cleansing," she said. "Have any of the girls caught your eye?"

Yes, as a matter of fact. Funny story though…

102

"No."

"Oh, Calder, surely *one* has." She hesitated in her canning, looking upward as if thinking. "Let's see, there are four girls here about your age. Lucie Jennings, Hannah Jacobson, Leah Perez, Sadie Campbell."

"What does it matter anyway? The great floods draw closer every day," I said.

"Yes, and that's precisely why you want to take a wife. So you can bring her to Elysium with you."

I laughed a humorless laugh. "Maybe I should wait until I get there. What if the options are better?"

My mom narrowed her eyes and put down the ladle that was in her hand. "What's gotten into you?"

I let out a breath. "I just… Don't you ever question things, Mom? Don't you ever have questions you wish someone other than Hector would answer?"

Her eyes moved to the window for a minute before she met my gaze. "We'll never have all the answers to every question, Calder. But Hector is *good* and Hector has only our best interests at heart. That's all I need to know, and that's all you need to know. The devil is testing your faith and you must win against him." She picked up the ladle and began working again before continuing on. "You know, if not for Hector, you wouldn't even be here. He saved my life, Calder, and he saved your dad's life too. He gave us a family, a purpose."

"I know, Mom," I responded. She had told me the story many times, how she and my dad had grown up in loveless homes where harsh beatings were a daily occurrence. They had met Hector when they were both eighteen, when he was on one of his missions. My mom had been pregnant with Maya and they didn't have anywhere to go. Hector treated them with the first fatherly kindness they had ever received, and they were thrilled to know they were meant to be two of his people, and among the first to live in Acadia. It was the very first time they'd felt their lives had meaning.

My mom waved her hand around our small cabin. "This may not look like much, but there is peace here. There is *order* here. There is faith, and there is purpose. We're all very lucky. Blessed. I know sometimes the simplicity of life here seems difficult. But there is *peace* in simplicity. The big society is filled with chaos, uncertainty, and hurt. Believe me, I know." She looked at me out of the corner of her eye. "Have you had a good life, Calder?"

"Yes, Mom." *But I want more.*

She nodded as if she'd known what my answer would be. "Then you have Hector to thank for that."

"I have you to thank for that."

My mom looked like she was about to say something more when my dad and Maya came laughing into the room from the bedroom, where they had been doing their Holy Book reading, their matching red hair glinting in the sunshine coming through the kitchen window. My mom had red hair too. My mom said I had gotten my dark coloring from the "black Irish" in our genes.

My dad sat Maya down on the chair directly beside me and I put my arm around her small rounded shoulders, tickling her ribs with my other hand. Maya was nineteen now, but she still had the mind of a child—a sweet, angelic child.

She laughed but it turned into a coughing fit. She had had this same cough for days and days now and I was a little worried about her. When she finally cleared her throat, she said, "Calder. Take me out in the rain on a piggyback! I want to get wet!"

I laughed, thinking that she needed to stay right here in this cabin, probably under a warm blanket. "I can't. Know why?"

She shook her head, her eyes wide with curiosity.

I leaned over and whispered in her ear. "You know how I bring you sugar cubes sometimes?" I leaned back up and put my finger over my mouth to indicate it was our secret. I glanced at my dad and mom, and they were talking in hushed tones about what other canning needed to get done. Truly, it wasn't even our work, but in bad weather, we all needed to occupy ourselves, so each of us helped out with whatever inside work there was.

"Well, you're just as sweet as those sugar cubes. You get sweeter every day. And if I bring you out in the rain, you'll might melt away, just like sugar."

Her eyes widened, but then she laughed. "That's not true!"

I winked. "Well, the part about you being as sweet as sugar is. Come on though; if you bundle up, we can sit under the porch and I'll draw you something in the dirt."

She clapped. "Do I get to guess what it is?"

"Yup. I won't tell you. Let's see how quickly you can figure it out."

I helped her put on a sweater and a pair of warm socks, and then we sat under the overhang as I drew small pictures in the dirt and she guessed what they were.

When I looked up toward Eden's room, I saw her outline in the window. And I swore that despite the distance and the rain, for a brief second, our eyes met.

The next day was dry, not a raindrop in sight. I bounded down the trail even faster than I usually went, my calf muscles burning with the exertion. I had a strange feeling I couldn't even explain swirling through me from not seeing Eden these past few days. Was it protectiveness? Maybe. I wanted to know she was okay. I wanted to know she was being cared for, happy. Those feelings were friendly, right? Only, I had never felt anything remotely similar for Xander. I pushed that aside, unwilling to ponder every emotion and work myself into a headache.

When I squeezed through the rocks, at first I didn't think she was there. Disappointment, swift and strong, hit me. But then her head surfaced from the spring and she took in a big breath of air.

She caught sight of me and grinned.

"What are you doing?"

"Swimming," she answered, smiling happily.

I walked closer until I was just at the edge of the spring.

"Well, yes, I can see that. Why exactly?"

She squinted at me, sunlight hitting her face, making the water droplets on her skin sparkle and dance. Her hair, although wet, was still golden and it cast a halo around her beautiful face. She looked like an angel or a mermaid—a magical, mythical creature. I took a mental photo of her, meaning to draw her later just like that.

"Well, I've decided this"—she waved her hand around, indicating our spring and the surrounding rocks—"is my school. And I mean to learn every little thing I can while I'm here. I mean to soak up every piece of knowledge possible. And I didn't know how to swim. And now I do." She laughed. "Sort of."

I raised an eyebrow. "You taught yourself to swim in the last"—I looked up at the sky to see how far past noon it was, when I assumed she'd arrived—"fifteen minutes?"

She nodded, leaning down and taking some water in her mouth and then spitting it out. Something about that had my body stirring in ways that, again, didn't feel friendly.

"Do you know how to swim?" she asked.

I nodded, willing my body to cooperate. "Yeah. I bathe in the river. Us worker kids have been swimming since we were young."

"Come on in, then. The water's nice." It was almost winter, but the temperature was still in the seventies. I'd bet it *did* feel nice.

I hesitated though. This felt dangerous in ways that had nothing to do with drowning or stubbing my toe on a rock under the water. Nonetheless, I took off my shirt and waded into the water in my pants. I moved to the other side of the spring and regarded Eden. I noticed she was fully submerged, but she was still wearing her long modest dress. Although it would be less modest now that it would be sticking to her skin. Lust swirled dizzily through my system, leaving a fierce longing in its wake.

I moved away a little farther and Eden rolled her eyes. "You don't have to be afraid of me, Calder. Friends, remember? And actually, I've been up in my room thinking about it these past few rainy days and you're right. It's better this way. Not just for the community as a whole, but for me too. I've been too fixated on you these past few years. You didn't know that, but now you do, and I'm only telling you because it was silly, really. I mean, think of all the things I could have been teaching *myself* if I had had a different focus. There's knowledge everywhere! And instead, I've been wasting time staring at your face and your muscles." She laughed as if it was the most ridiculous use of her time imaginable.

I felt slightly elated at the knowledge that she'd been

"fixated" on me for years, and slightly offended by the fact that she'd deemed it silly. "Well, I wouldn't call it a complete waste of time," I muttered. Only...really, wasn't she right? Not only because she could have been putting her time to better use, but because I'd made it quite clear nothing could come from it.

Eden laughed again but it quickly dwindled. The swell of her breasts was just barely showing over the surface of the water and try as I might, I couldn't keep my gaze from moving there. "No, but really..." She swirled her arm across the water, causing it to ripple. I watched as the ripples moved away from her, reaching toward me as if she meant to span the distance between us using the water as an extension of her. When the first small wave hit my naked stomach, I almost groaned as if it were her hand stroking my skin. *Oh, for the love of the gods, what's wrong with me?* "When the rain hit my window, it fogged up. I remembered your lesson about the states of matter, and I was able to figure out the window fogged because of the different temperature of the glass on the inside and the outside." Her eyes lit up, like she had just solved the mystery of the universe. I couldn't help but smile at her enthusiasm.

"And music," she continued. "It's all numbers. I don't know why Hector never taught me math. I could have been an even better piano player than I am." Her eyes widened. "Last night I snuck down to the kitchen and read through some recipes. There's lots of math in those too... Some you still have to teach me." She took some water into her mouth again, puckered her lips, and then spit it out in an arc. My body responded to the image without my permission and I was thankful I had the cover of the water. "Anyway, my point is, you taught me a couple things, and I was able to apply them in other ways. And now I want more. I want to learn everything you have to teach me. And I want to teach myself as much as possible." She paused, looking thoughtful for a minute before her eyes met mine. "It's a sort of freedom for me, Calder. And maybe that's hard to understand. But... most of my life, I've had so many questions and no answers. And now...well, I might not have all the answers, but I have a few, and my life feels fuller. And I can carry all that knowledge inside me and no one else can ever take it. It's mine. It belongs to me. In a world where nothing else does, I have that, and you gave it to me. Thank you."

I stared at her, captivated in every way possible. She wasn't only beautiful. She was kind and brave and full of life. And gods help me, the seed of love that had taken root, the seed I had *vowed* not to nourish, started to flourish anyway. I swore I could feel the velvety tendrils stretching through me, twisting around the vital parts of who I was. I was helpless to stop it. She had invaded me. I was the field and she was the morning glory. I had been overtaken. Just like that. Or maybe not just like that. Maybe those tendrils of love had been growing for years as we enjoyed our private game, trading flowers and candy and glances and covert smiles. A secret kept between us in a world where secrets weren't allowed. Perhaps that in itself had told me things about Eden before I'd ever spent time with her and learned from her own lips what was in her mind and her heart. But in that moment, I could no longer deny what I felt.

She isn't yours, I told myself. But my heart rebelled against the internal words, as if the thought itself were a virus to my system.

Eden continued to swish the water with her arm, looking distracted but serene as a battle raged inside my mind and heat continued to flood my system, filling me with want. *Breath. Just breathe.* So, okay, I wanted her. But that didn't mean I had to act on my feelings, my attraction. I had sacrificed before in one way or another. I could certainly do it now. I stared at the rock to my right, attempting to find inner peace.

"Calder? Are you okay?" My gaze flew to Eden, who had ceased the movement of her arm, and she was now looking at me strangely. "Are you well?"

Not really. "Uhh…" I cleared my throat, still feeling overly hot and off-balance. "Yes, I'm fine. So, uh, speaking of all the knowledge you need to soak up, what should we get started on today?"

"Oh. A new lesson." She smiled. "Okay. But first, ask me my multiplication tables. I know them all."

"Oh, uh, seven times seve—"

"Forty-nine."

"Good, nine times eigh—"

"Seventy-two."

I laughed, and the laughter brought the calm I'd been seeking. "You pass."

"No, really, I know them all."

"I believe you."

"I just don't want you to think that your time's being wasted here. I'm a very committed student."

"I don't think you're wasting my time, Eden, not even close."

She smiled and we stared at each other across the water for a few weighty seconds. Finally, she looked away and said, "All right. Well, my basic math is coming along. How about we just practice some swimming today?"

I thought that might be a decent idea, considering it was

still not the most opportune moment for me to get out of the water.

Eden paused as she seemed to contemplate something.

"What is it?" I asked.

She dragged her teeth over her bottom lip. "Do you think…well, do you think when the great flood comes, there'll be any chance of survival?"

My skin prickled strangely but I shook my head slowly. "That's not what the foretelling says."

"I know. It's just…like you said, Hector is only human, and, well, maybe he misinterpreted something? Is it possible?"

I paused for several beats. My heart had begun beating more rapidly for reasons I didn't necessarily want to investigate right then. This line of conversation felt…dangerous on a few levels. "I don't know, Eden."

She let out a breath. "Well, just in case, I'd like to learn to float. I'd like to learn how not to drown."

I stared at her for a few moments. This girl was going to attempt to survive the end of the world? I had to admit I'd questioned whether the great flood would really happen. But I'd never gone over the ways in which I might try to live despite its arrival. "Where do you find your strength, Morning Glory?" I asked softly.

She grinned but shook her head as if I was crazy. "I'm the least strong person at Acadia. And by the way, Calder, you can come closer, you know. You really don't have to worry about me."

"I'm not worried about you. I'm worried about me," I blurted out.

She stilled and we stared at each other over the expanse of water between us, the only sound the quiet splashing of the small waterfall hitting the spring. Speaking of dangerous…

I broke eye contact as I cleared my throat. "You know, if you're with Hector, you don't have to worry about surviving. We'll all be led to Elysium. The point is sort of… not to survive."

She watched her own hand move back and forth in the water again. "Maybe I'd rather take my own chances. Maybe I'd rather not end up in Elysium with Hector."

"Eden…"

She didn't wait to hear what I was going to say, which was fine because, truthfully, I didn't know anyway. She leaned back and brought her body up in an attempt to float and promptly sunk. She came up sputtering. I moved quickly over to her. "Whoa, you okay? Here, I'll hold you up until you get a feel for it, and then I'll let you go."

I put my hands underneath her back, only touching her with my fingertips. She straightened her body out and leaned her head back and closed her eyes, a small peaceful smile on her face. I gazed at her, drinking in her features and her golden hair floating around her face. And then my mutinous eyes roamed down past her face to her body, her dress pressed and clinging to her delicate curves. I swallowed and my eyes paused when they got to her hardened nipples. Then they moved slowly downward over her flat stomach and down farther to that small mysterious, feminine mound. Again, my body surged to life, blood pulsing hotly. I'd never felt this way before, even those times when I'd touched myself out of sheer necessity. And right now, I was about to go up in flames and the only part of me touching her was my fingertips. This had disaster written all over it. Even if I could successfully control myself around Eden, it would be disastrous for *me*.

And yet. And yet, I couldn't stop myself. Looking down at her, I felt a rush of heat but also a rush of tenderness.

"I'm floating," she said, not opening her eyes, a smile still curving her lips.

"Not yet," I whispered and very slowly removed my fingertips from her upper and lower back. I took a small step back. "Now you're floating."

Her eyes opened slowly, but she remained still, gazing up at the sky.

"Can I teach you an even better way not to expend energy in the water?"

She gave a barely noticeable nod and so I stepped forward again and put my hands on both of her arms. "I'm going to flip you over. Take a big breath and then let yourself float so that the back of your head is just above the water. Just let the water support you. Then, when I touch your arms, let them float toward the surface with your elbows bent. Have you got it so far?"

Another small nod.

"Okay, good. Then when you're ready, press downward on the water with your hands until your mouth clears the water. Breathe out quickly and then inhale. And then go back under. You could hang out in the water all day doing that if you needed to. Even if the whole world were underwater."

Eden took in a big breath and then I turned her body over slowly until she was facedown in the water. I removed my hands and let her float there for a minute until I knew she had it, and then I touched her arms and she let them float upward until her elbows were bent and her hands were above her shoulders. She pushed downward gently and her mouth came up above the water and I heard her exhale and then inhale before she let herself float back down.

There you go. You already got it. I smiled and she brought her head up and set her feet on the bottom of the spring so she was upright. She let out a little triumphant laugh and threw her arms around my neck. I froze. Every part of her was pressed up against every part of me. I prayed she couldn't tell how hard I was. Maybe she didn't even know what that meant. She tilted her head back and gazed at me, that same triumphant smile on her face.

I let out my breath and smiled down at her. "Add floating to your list of accomplishments," I said.

She laughed. "I will." She let go of my neck and I felt the loss of her as she started walking through the water to the large, flat rock. She pulled herself up and then lay back. "We don't have much time to get dry," she called. "Better get up here in the sun."

I waited a minute, until my body had settled down, and then waded toward her and pulled myself up on the rock too. I lay back and we turned our heads, our faces mere inches apart. "Thank you for teaching me things, Calder," she said.

"You teach me things too, Eden." *About courage and triumph and the secrets of my own heart.*

She regarded me silently for a minute and then simply smiled in answer.

Then we both tilted our faces toward the sun.

CHAPTER NINE
Eden

Over the next few months, I met Calder mostly every day for my lessons. Some days we missed seeing each other when his chores got in the way or when there were too many council members at the main lodge. Those days were the hardest. But the days we did meet, Calder would recline lazily against a rock and draw something or another while he taught me math, science, and the rules I didn't know about the English language. Often, he'd have to stop and go over something in the notebook I filled with everything he talked about. But mostly I just took notes, and then the next day, he'd quiz me a little. I was an excellent student. Of course, I knew the value of knowledge, having been deprived of it for so long.

I didn't just learn the academics Calder taught me; I learned them from his specific point of view. Not just the information he remembered, but the way he saw the world. When we lay on the grass and looked up at the sky and talked about the color spectrum, he told me about a rainbow he'd seen once as he watered the tomato crops in the fields, after too short of a rainfall to do any good. It was as if each time a rainbow appeared, that rich smell of soil came back to him, and Elysium and earth were joined for just that moment, even if only in his own mind. We'd both gotten slightly sleepy, lying there together, and he'd been musing when he said it and he almost looked embarrassed when he realized he'd been speaking aloud. But I loved those moments—when just for a second, I was a part of Calder's innermost mind. It humbled me and warmed me, as if for a brief span of time, I'd stepped into a ray of sunlight.

He was goodness—raw, unguarded goodness. It glowed in him. I'd seen it before when he'd been the only one in a group of children to let me into their game, or when he smiled so lovingly at his sister, or laughed at his friend's joke, his whole spirit shaking with it. He exuded joy and kindness and a passion for life. And in a place that often seemed bleak and passionless, it was impossible not to want to drown in that type of beauty...to feel like I could happily wrap around his bones and suffocate in his skin.

It alarmed me—and comforted me.

As we lay by our spring day after day, Calder not only told me the things he remembered from each year of his schooling but he told me the things he'd learned from the others living in our community who had previously lived in the big society. He had learned about gambling from a man who had come to be a part of our family five years previous. He'd told Calder, as he worked alongside him, that he'd had a real problem with going to big casinos, places where adult games were played for money. If you won, you went home with more money than you'd arrived with, and if you lost, you went home with nothing. That man had lost far more than he'd won, and in the end, he lost everything: his wife, his children, his job, and his friends. No one wanted him. That's when Hector had come along. And Hector had wanted him.

There were many of those stories, and I listened intently to them all.

Physically, Calder kept his distance from me, flinching when I got too near, watching me like a hawk. I wasn't so naive I didn't understand he was having a difficult time with our closeness, and I had been telling the truth when I'd said I was going to pour all my focus into learning, but it still stung. And the unfairness of it made me angry. Because I realized that what I'd felt for Calder before had been nothing more than a childish infatuation. Yes, I'd observed his thoughtful nature. But I *knew* him now. I knew his genuine kindness and his protective nature. I knew his patient spirit and his sharp wit. Simply put, my love had blossomed from a bud to a flower. As if my love for Calder could ever be simple.

Meeting him at our spring for an hour and a half every afternoon, as my friend and my tutor, wasn't everything. But it would have to be enough.

We didn't meet again in the evening. Clive Richter was home at night, and he always seemed to be watching for me. It was safer to keep our lessons to the daytime hours. I wouldn't jeopardize those.

We talked about the names for groups of animals one day. "Gorillas come in a band, grasshoppers come in a cloud, pigs come in a team," he said as I wrote down the list. He named a few more and then couldn't remember any more. I sighed with disappointment, which wasn't exactly fair. It wasn't like I could expect him to be a textbook—his memory did have limits.

"Sorry," he said with a laugh. "I told you, I could only give you what I remember."

"The problem is," I said, tapping my pencil on my chin, "if you were prompted or given a choice of a few, you could probably remember a lot more than you think. It's *somewhere* in there." I bopped my pencil on his head.

"Ouch."

I rolled my eyes. "But me, all I have is what you give me. There's literally no more."

"Well then, good thing I'm smarter than the everyday person." He winked. "I figure, even having a quarter of what I ever learned, you're better off than the average numbskull."

"Ha-ha. Well, how comforting that I'm an *above average* numbskull."

Calder grinned. "Penguins come in a colony."

I scrawled it down.

He looked thoughtful like he did when he was trying to recall something specific he'd learned on a certain topic. "Penguins spend seventy-five percent of their lives in water. I wonder if they'll survive the flood. How could they *not*?"

We both quietly mulled that over.

"We had cockroaches in our cabin last year. My mom said in the big community, the joke is that cockroaches can survive anything."

"Even the end of the world?"

Calder shrugged. "Maybe. But that's probably a good thing. Who wants cockroaches in Elysium anyway?" He grinned. "Let 'em stay."

I let out a small laugh, picturing the great flood finally receding and the cockroaches climbing out of their holes in the earth.

Calder turned toward me and propped his head up on

his hand. "Anyway, back to penguins. There's a certain kind who proposes to his mate by giving her some thing or another."

I looked over at him with interest. "Really? What does he give her?"

"I don't remember. Maybe a feather or a stick or something."

"You don't remember? Why not? That's so romantic. You remember precisely what percentage of time a penguin spends of its life in the water and how cockroaches will survive us all, but you don't remember what gift a male penguin gives his mate to propose to her? That's ridiculous." I shook my head in exasperation.

Calder laughed. "Why should I care? I'm not a penguin. It's not exactly information that was going to come in handy when I pick my own mate."

I sucked in a breath and looked away from him, out at the spring water, glistening in the sunshine. "Do you plan on picking a mate?" I'd never asked him, but I wondered. Why shouldn't he? It's not like he could pick me, even if he wanted to. But surely he must want one. He was a man now, with a man's body. He must have...needs. I had seen other girls our age look at him with interest. With them, he wouldn't have to hide. He wouldn't have to lie and sneak. And sin. My heart sunk. When I looked back at him, he was staring at me thoughtfully. *What does he think when he looks at me that way?*

"No. I can't even think about that. The only thing I can think about right now is getting a spot on the council and going out into the world."

I blew out a silent breath. I nodded, my gaze moving over his handsome face. Calder had turned eighteen in January, and it seemed in the span of a year, he had grown even taller and broader in the shoulders. He was lean but hard everywhere, and I couldn't help but let my eyes roam over him while his eyes were focused on his sketch pad. Sometimes, he showed up with a shadow of dark stubble on his jaw. That was my favorite—it's how he would have looked if I had had the opportunity to wake up beside him. He looked extra tired those days too, but when I asked him what was wrong, he just told me he hadn't slept very well.

One day, as I sat waiting for Calder, my face tilted toward the sky, I was surprised when I looked up to the sound of him coming through the brush and saw Xander instead.

"Hi," I said, standing up as he approached me.

"Hey, Eden. Calder can't make it today. I wanted to come tell you so you didn't worry."

I hadn't seen Xander in several months and he looked bigger to me too. It seemed like both of those boys had shot up several inches in half a year.

"Oh, okay. Is he all right?"

"Yeah, he's fine. His sister isn't doing so well, though. She's had a pretty bad cough forever, it seems like, and she does get better, then worse, then better. She's worse right now."

I realized then I hadn't seen Maya in weeks. But I had just figured there wasn't much mending to do in the main lodge. Why hadn't Calder told me? Was that why he had looked so haggard recently? It hit me how separate our lives truly were. It made my heart ache. "Why didn't he tell me?" I asked Xander.

Xander sighed. "Knowing Calder, he just didn't want to burden you. And he was hopeful. He's always so damned hopeful." He stared off behind me for a second as if considering something. "You know he has feelings for you, right?"

His words surprised me. I opened my mouth to say something, decided I didn't know what, and then closed it again. *Did* I know Calder had feelings for me? He'd admitted he was attracted to me, that he'd kiss me if he could. But we'd set all that aside. As far as feelings? I thought about that for a moment. Yes, I knew that he cared for me or he wouldn't be putting himself at risk to spend time with me, to break Hector's rules. Calder obviously considered me a friend. But just knowing Xander could clearly see Calder had feelings for me had my heart soaring with hope.

It made everything better. But…it also made everything worse. I let out a sigh. "Whatever his feelings mean, he won't do anything about them." I didn't know if Xander was worried about this situation with me and Calder and was looking for reassurance, but I figured he probably was. His fate would be affected by our decisions too, after all.

"No, I don't guess he will." He didn't look exactly happy about that, which confused me. He rubbed his eye and let out a breath. "Want to sit for a minute?" he finally asked, indicating the small patch of grass with a large rock behind it where Calder usually sketched.

I nodded and walked the few steps to it and sat down on my knees. I felt awkward, and the unfamiliar feeling in this place made me realize how comfortable I'd grown with Calder. And how much I *missed* him, even though I'd just seen him yesterday.

Xander sat down next to me and brought his knees up and wrapped his arms around them loosely. "Any word on when Hector's coming back?"

"No, Mother Hailey receives letters from him, but he doesn't write to me. She told me he's living with some people who he believes the gods want to become part of our family."

Xander was silent for a second and then nodded his head once and said, "Has Calder talked to you about his plans to get on the council?"

"Yes." I shot him a worried look. "I don't know how likely that is."

Xander scooted back so he was leaning against the rock. "Yeah, I don't either. Tell me why you say that."

I let out a breath. "It's just…the other council members… they're different than Calder. I don't see Calder fitting in. He's too—"

"Good," Xander finished.

I nodded slowly and lowered my eyes. "Yes."

We both sat silently for a few minutes. "He's going to try as soon as Hector gets back, you know. And I don't see it working out well for him," Xander finally said.

"So what do we do?"

"I don't know there's much we can do. Calder's going to do what he thinks is right for him because he believes the council is where he can best serve." He picked absently at the grass for a minute. "Calder, he breaks the rules once in a while, but he'd never do anything he thought would hurt someone else. He's so damned honorable."

"Yeah, tell me about it," I muttered.

Xander chuckled. "I should get back. I'm going to take some holy water to Maya." He pulled himself up and so did I.

"What can I do?"

"Not much, Eden. Just pray for her."

"I will. Xander, if I leave some candy for her under the bush on the right side of the main lodge's porch, will you retrieve it and take it to Maya for me?"

Xander smiled. "Sure."

"Okay, thanks. And thanks for coming to let me know about Maya."

"You're welcome."

I thought he'd turn and leave, but he looked up at the clear blue sky for several beats before his eyes met mine. "There's a storm coming, Eden."

I nodded, not looking upward. "Yes," I said simply. I didn't know if Xander meant today or in general, but both might be true.

He frowned, and then he turned and left me standing there, alone.

Calder didn't show up at our spring for the next few days. I left the candy by the front porch diligently, though, and made sure to see if it was gone. It always was. Xander was doing the job I'd asked him to do.

I did see Calder at Temple, but Maya wasn't with his family, and even from far away, he looked so drawn and tired. I gave him a discreet smile, and he smiled back, but it looked like he did it with effort. I was screaming inside as I quietly and obediently went about my religious duties.

I wanted desperately to ask someone if Maya was okay, if she was getting better, but who could I go to? Hector wasn't here. What if I just walked myself right over to Calder's small cabin and knocked on the door?

I threw myself backward onto my bed and groaned. Someone, probably one of the council members, would drag me back in about seven seconds, that's what. And then they'd start watching me like a hawk again and I might not be able to meet Calder down at the spring. I couldn't risk it for either of us.

I lay there contemplating what I could do when I suddenly heard the distant sound of an engine on the road. That wasn't too unusual. All the council members had vehicles they used to travel to and from work in the big community. But for some reason, I sat up anyway and went to my window to look out. I strained my eyes to see what kind of car it was drawing closer. It was a black Jeep. I kept watching, disbelieving for a few minutes, but as it came nearer, it was unmistakable. Hector had returned. He had been gone for almost six months, and now he was back. The back of my neck prickled and I drew my shoulders up. My access to the spring, *to Calder*, would now be practically nonexistent. All these months, that fear had loomed, and now it was reality.

Mother Hailey rushed into my room, saying, "Hurry, Eden, make yourself presentable. Hector's returned. He'll want to see you right away."

I didn't reply but moved to put on my lace dress, the one he favored. It was slightly tight on me now, as I hadn't had it altered in six months since he'd been gone. There'd simply been no need. I despised that dress. It was a symbol of everything I hated about my life.

Still, I pulled it on and then Mother Hailey brushed my hair and put a ribbon around it. I looked like a child.

"Mother Hailey," I murmured as she ran her hands through my hair, "can I still call you Mother?"

She was quiet for a moment before she said gently, "No, Eden. You'll be *my* mother in a few months now. You must simply call me Hailey."

Tears gathered in my eyes and Hailey turned me toward

124

her and led me to the bed, where we both sat down and she grasped my hands in hers. "Eden, you don't need to be scared. Hector is a very kind husband. And if you're lucky, you'll be pregnant with Hector's child before the great floods come. And picture it now, the two of you leading us all into Elysium, a blessed child in your womb." She smiled warmly, squeezing my hands in hers.

"A child wasn't part of the prophecy," I murmured.

"No, but the gods can't send every detail, I don't imagine. That wouldn't be practical."

I didn't try to imagine how all that might work, but the thought of making a child with Hector filled me with dread. And it made the reality of what I'd be expected to do with him even more vivid. I wasn't sure what "that" was precisely, but I knew it involved things I had no desire whatsoever to do with Hector. He had raised me for all intents and purposes. I thought of him as my father. I tried to swallow down the bile that rose up in my throat when I pictured him kissing me the way I'd once seen him kissing Hailey in the corner of the kitchen when I'd passed by.

The way I'd kissed Calder.

"Hailey," I finally managed, keeping my eyes cast downward, "are you happy? Don't you ever want someone just for you?" I brought my eyes to hers.

She was quiet for a moment, but I swore I saw sorrow in her eyes. "Sacrifice is what makes us the blessed people of the gods," she answered. "It's human nature to be selfish, but we must fight against that sin. It's what sets us apart from the people of the big community."

I let out a soft huff of breath. She was simply paraphrasing from Hector's Holy Book. "What sacrifices does Hector make?" I asked boldly.

"Hector makes many sacrifices. His life is lived with all of us in mind. Everything he does is for us. None of it is for him. For over twenty years, he's built Acadia, built our family, kept us strong and balanced."

"What if...what if I loved someone other than Hector? What if I wished to marry someone else?"

Hailey let go of my hands and joined hers in her lap. "That's not what the foretelling says, Eden. You must obey the foretelling."

I looked away. "The gods can't send every detail, I don't imagine," I repeated, picturing Calder bursting into the temple to interrupt my marriage to Hector, scooping me up, and carrying me away. To where? That was the problem.

"Eden—" Hailey started, a warning tone in her voice.

"Don't worry, Hailey," I interrupted. "I'm always very obedient."

She narrowed her eyes. She knew better than that. "Where do you go while I'm schooling the boys? I know you leave the lodge."

I stood and went to study my hair in the mirror, pretending to smooth it into place. The truth was, I couldn't care less what my hair looked like. "Just up into the hills to lie in the sun." I turned to her. "All my life, I've felt like a china doll sitting up on a dusty shelf. The sunshine makes me feel half-alive."

Hailey studied me for a minute. "Eden, I moved to the main lodge with Hector when I was nineteen years old. He's the only man I've ever been with. He's given me four boys and a life of peace. I have a role here too. If a meaningful life is a measure of happiness, then yes, I'm happy," she said, answering my earlier question.

"But who judges whether your life has meaning?" I

asked boldly. "You or Hector?" I had never asked Hailey what her life had been like before she lived in Acadia and she had never offered that information.

A door slammed below, and Hailey stood up. "He's here. Come, put a smile on your face and come downstairs to greet him. All your doubts will melt away when you see the adoration on his face." Hailey smiled reassuringly and took my hand, and together we walked down the main staircase. If Hailey herself felt anything other than adoration, she didn't show it.

We turned into the large two-story foyer, and there he was. He turned toward us, and although he was still the same large, broad-shouldered man he'd always been, something about him appeared older, more haggard than when he'd left. And I noticed that he looked softer around the middle, his shirt stretched over a small paunch. His smile was radiant, though, when he saw us.

"Eden, Hailey, my loves," he greeted us, opening his arms wide and walking toward us.

"Hector—" Hailey said.

"Father—" I said at the same time.

We looked at each other and smiled and then we walked into Hector's embrace and he kissed the tops of our heads.

"My girls," he said. "Now I finally feel at home. Eden, please, play something for me. It will do my heart good."

I nodded and hurried to the piano. As I played, I pictured myself at the spring, lying on the grass with Calder, our hands grasped together, the noontime sun above us, warming our bodies. I let the melody surround the vision of us in my mind, the notes dancing over our skin.

When the last note was played and I came back to myself, the room was silent. I looked up to see Hector and Hailey staring at me.

"Eden, your playing is even more beautiful than it was before I left. You must have been practicing very diligently."

"Yes, Father."

Hector stood and came to sit down next to me on the piano bench. I scooted all the way to the edge to make room for him.

"Eden, you must call me Hector now," he said. He ran one finger down the side of my cheek as I kept staring ahead. "We'll be married very soon. I'll be your father no longer."

I didn't speak, couldn't speak. Hector continued to stare at my profile. Finally, after what seemed like hours, he let out a shaky breath and said softly, "So sweet. Just what I needed." And then he stood.

I glanced up to see Hailey still seated with her eyes downcast.

"Where are the boys?" Hector asked.

"They're with Monica," she said. Monica was one of the council members' wives who helped Hailey with the boys once in a while.

"Good," Hector said. "Come with me to my room. I'd like some time with you. Mother Miriam will be home later today and she can help me unpack."

"Yes, Hector," Hailey said.

They both turned and left me there. I wasn't sorry for the solitude. I returned to my room and retrieved the notebook from under my bed and filled my head with the algebra I'd been learning with Calder.

CHAPTER TEN
Calder

"Better?" I asked Maya, removing the glass of water from her lips and placing it on the table next to her. She nodded, her eyes sleepy. "Good."

I smoothed her hair back from her face and she smiled at me. "Are there any more butterscotch candies?" she asked.

I smiled. "No, you ate them all."

Her lips moved into a pout. "Maybe Eden will leave more for me today."

"Maybe. You remember that's our secret, right? Eden would get in trouble if anyone knew she was giving you candy."

She nodded very seriously. "I know. I can keep a secret."

"I know you can."

Maya closed her eyes for a minute and then opened them. "When I get to Elysium, Calder—"

"Maya, you're not going to Elysium anytime soon."

"I know, but when I do get there…well, will I be beautiful like Eden?"

My heart squeezed as I looked down at her beloved face. "You're already beautiful, Maya."

She shook her head and pursed her lips as if I was purposefully being difficult. "Will I be beautiful *like* Eden?"

I knew what she was asking me and it broke my damn heart.

I tucked the blanket around her more tightly. "I think in Elysium, we'll get to be whatever we want to be, anything our hearts desire."

Maya smiled at that. "Then I'm going to look just like Eden, and I'm going to be able to run as fast as a cheetah."

I couldn't help chuckling. Maya's heart was one of the sweetest and most wonderful things in my life. She'd been my source of joy since I was a small child. And if she wanted to be a cheetah...I could go with that. "Okay, then, I'm going to be as strong as a hundred oxen and I'm going to be able to *fly*," I told her.

Maya laughed softly, but then it turned into a cough. Sometimes it sounded like she couldn't catch her breath. I gave her another sip of water and she leaned back on her pillow, smiling. "I think Elysium is going to be wonderful."

"As long as we're there together, it will be."

Maya smiled again and then closed her eyes. "You get some sleep," I said quietly. "I'll be back in a couple hours."

She nodded but didn't open her eyes. I could hear her quiet snores as I ducked out of the healing tent, a large tented "room" close to the temple. Maya's cough was markedly improved this time after the holy water, and I said a silent prayer of thanks to the gods, most specifically the God of Mercy, who Eden loved so much.

My parents and I had been taking turns sitting with Maya night after night so she wouldn't be alone, but they were older than me and staying up all night took its toll on them, so most nights I volunteered. As a result, during the day I felt like the walking dead. I hated missing my time with Eden, but if I was going to be any good to Maya, I needed to sleep during my midday break. Maya didn't like the dark, and I'd never let her stay alone in that small unlit space in the evenings and through the night. She slept well with me there. But she was sleeping quite a bit during the day now too, so she must have needed extra rest.

I took a quick trip to the river, shed my shirt, and then used my hands to bring water over my head and chest before scrubbing at my face. I used my shirt to dry myself as well as I could and then draped it around my neck. Feeling a little bit more refreshed, I walked back toward my cabin to get some breakfast.

Glancing at the main lodge brought a sharp ache to my chest. I would have given anything to walk up there, stride right through the front door, and up to Eden's bedroom. I wanted to wrap her in my arms. I wanted her clean scent and her gentle voice to soothe me. I wanted *her*.

But Hector was back now and I couldn't risk it. I had walked up to the main lodge yesterday and made an appointment with Hector for later this morning. I needed to show him my irrigation system. Thankfully, Hector was always open to meetings and inquiries from the workers. I had to make sure to present my idea well, as a spot on the council was at risk. The rest of my life hung in the balance.

Xander jogged up alongside me and I looked over at him, surprised.

"Sorry, didn't mean to startle you. How's Maya?"

"Better this morning."

Xander nodded once. "I went down to the spring and

hung out with Eden for a little bit yesterday. It was nice to get her to myself for a little while. I'm really hoping that phrase we use, 'Whatever I have, you have half,' applies to her too."

I froze in my tracks. Rage, hot and wild, shot through me, turning the world red. The next thing I knew, I had Xander up against the side of a worker cabin. "You were alone with Eden? What the *hell* are you talking about?"

Xander put his hands up against the cabin, a huge grin spreading slowly over his face. "Whoa, it's even worse than I thought," he said.

"What's worse than you thought?" I asked, narrowing my eyes and pressing him harder against the wall.

"You. You're in love, killer. *Deep.*"

I released him immediately and stepped back as I stared at his still-grinning face. *You're in love. You're in love.* His words seemed to echo in my mind. I let out a harsh exhale. Gods, I'd just attacked my best friend because he'd said he had been alone with Eden. *You're in love.* I couldn't deny it. I'd *tried* to deny it. I *wanted* to deny it. I wanted to *ignore* it. I'd vowed to. But it was so obvious, Xander could see.

I laced my fingers behind my neck and looked up at the sky. Then I walked in a slow circle as I got control of my rapid breathing. Finally, I stopped and just stared at Xander. "What am I gonna do? What in the hell am I gonna do?"

Xander's smile dipped, then disappeared as he considered me. "I don't know, Calder. I wish I did."

"Why'd you do that?" I demanded, my chest still rising and falling as my heartbeat slowed. He'd tried purposely to get a rise out of me and it'd worked. I felt ashamed and overwhelmed by my reaction.

"Because it was time you admitted it to yourself."

I stared at him, trying to maintain some kind of anger, even some annoyance, but finally, my shoulders sagged in defeat. "I'd already admitted it to myself. I just didn't want to say it out loud. Anything but that." Because saying it out loud felt like it suddenly had weight, a *presence*, it was a living, breathing thing that would be impossible for me to pretend didn't exist.

Xander stepped forward and put a hand on my shoulder. "Aw, geez, Calder, I didn't mean to make this worse. I swear I didn't." He studied me for a minute. "Whatever happens… whatever this means…brothers," he said solemnly and put his fist out. I let out a breath and bumped his fist with my own.

"Brothers."

When I got back to our cabin, I went straight to the room where I slept and started pulling on a clean shirt. I willed myself to put what I'd admitted to Xander out of my head for now.

My parents were already out in the fields, but they weren't expecting me. They knew I was meeting with Hector. My parents didn't necessarily agree with my ambitions, but there wasn't anything they could do about it. My dad wasn't much of a talker anyway, and he seemed perfectly content with the life he led. His belief in Hector was unwavering. I'd never tell him that my ambitions stemmed from a desire for more of life in general, not just more of life in our small community. He wouldn't understand. To be perfectly honest, I didn't exactly understand it either. What was it about me that made me want more? What made me stand in our doorway night after night, staring out at the distant city

133

lights with fear, yes, but also with a strange longing in my gut? Maybe I could compare it to the way I felt when I looked at Eden—terrified and electrified all at once. This spot on the council could mean more than just a means of going outside Acadia…

You're in love, killer. Deep.

I saw what looked like the corner of a piece of paper sticking out from under my bedding and frowned. I picked up the lumpy pillow and there was a folded note with two butterscotch candies on top. My heart lurched and I couldn't help the smile that spread over my face. I unwrapped one quickly and popped it in my mouth, that familiar buttery sweetness bursting across my tongue.

I unfolded the note and read Eden's small concise printing:

Calder,

I hope Maya is having a better day today. I've been thinking about her nonstop and wish somehow I could visit her. I hope the candy has put a small smile on her face, even if only for a minute.

I could have given this letter to Xander along with the candy for you and Maya, but I kind of wanted to leave it for you myself—sort of for old time's sake, I guess.

The spring has been quiet without you there, although the days haven't been without a small measure of excitement. Yesterday, it came to my attention that the snake I threw off our rock months ago is actually the offspring of a twenty-foot (two hundred forty inches when converted—I pay sharp attention to my math tutor), two-headed serpent that has been stewing in a venomous rage (quite literally) since the mistreatment of her beloved son or daughter. (How do you tell one from another? I guess that's a lesson for another day.) When confronted, I was forced to wrangle the slippery beast. As it turns out, the reptile (cold-blooded vertebrate) is rendered weak by verbal algebraic word problems. Despite the shouted math (me) and subsequent weakening (snake), there was still much physical thrashing and hissing (on both parts), but in the end, I was victorious. The rock remains our domain (or is it domaine?). All in a day's work.

And you were right about knowledge. You never know when a little bit of it will come in handy at just the right time, and save your life (and your rock domain(e?) as the case may be).

I miss you. Maybe I shouldn't say that, but it's true. More honesty? My days have dragged by, and at least a thousand times an hour, I think of something I want to tell you or ask you. I've written them down because I don't want to forget and because it makes me feel closer to you.

Today, Hector has a meeting with the council at noon. I can meet you at our spring if you're able? From now on it's going to be harder for me to meet you, and so I hope you can come. I don't want to think our time there is ending, but at the very least, it won't be regular anymore. That thought brings me such immense sadness, I can't even tell you. I'll always consider it to be the place where my life truly began.

I'll be waiting.

Yours, Eden

Yours. Mine. I wished I could go to her, hold her, tell her I loved our times together too, and I missed her as well. But what would be the point? *Yours.* Mine. I moved those thoughts aside. But I still stood there grinning at the note like a damn idiot for longer than I had time to. I had business to attend to today and I needed my focus to be there.

You're in love, killer. Deep.

I folded her note up and put it under my pillow so I could read it again later.

An hour after that, I was walking up to the main lodge, clean-shaven and bathed more thoroughly. I felt purpose surging through my veins. This had to work.

When I stepped up on the large porch, I heard piano music playing and hesitated in knocking. Could that be Eden? She'd talked about her music often, but was she that good? The music floating out the open window next to the door made my heart clench in my chest at its beauty and mastery. I walked farther down the porch and turned to an open set of french doors. There she was, sitting at a large black piano, eyes closed as her fingers flew over the keys. My breath hitched. She was mesmerizing. Gracefully beautiful. Ethereal. *Mine. That's the girl I choose. Mine*, my mind insisted. And this time, I didn't correct myself. I leaned against the doorway and put my hands loosely in my pockets as I watched her. I was lost to everything except my beautiful Eden and the melody floating from her fingers. Nothing else existed. In my chest, I felt...*pride*. I was so damned proud of her. I watched until the last note was played and she opened her eyes. They met mine. Her mouth opened as if to say something, but we both knew our station. Even so, I felt the electricity singing in the air between us even after the music was gone. A small smile played on Eden's lips, and her cheeks flushed as her eyes held on me.

Suddenly, the small hairs on my arms stood up and a strange coldness moved down my spine. I pivoted, and Hector was standing there watching the silent exchange between Eden and me. *No.* I closed my eyes very briefly and took a deep breath.

"Father," I said, attempting to sound much more confident than I felt inside. "Your...Eden is a beautiful piano player. I didn't realize she was so gifted."

Hector's eyes, which were narrowed on me with suspicion, moved over my shoulder to where Eden was, his expression clearing. He gave himself a small shake as if casting off an idea he found distasteful. "Water Bearer."

I have a name. My name is Calder.

He walked toward me and clapped me lightly on my back. "Yes, Eden is very talented. The gods have blessed her with many gifts. To be the man who has been chosen to...bask in those gifts is humbling indeed." He glanced at me sideways, but I pushed my own emotions regarding that statement aside. *Focus.*

"You had a purpose to scheduling an appointment with me, I presume," Hector said as I fell in step beside him.

"Yes, Father. I'd like to show you something if you'll allow me."

Hector nodded. "I always have time for my water bearer," he said, his expression warming.

"Thank you."

We walked the distance between the main lodge and the bank of the river in silence. When we arrived at the riverbank, Hector followed my lead a short way along the pebbled shore until we got to the start of my irrigation system.

It was mostly a series of thick, hollowed-out branches tied together and elevated where necessary to keep the water running downhill to the edge of the crops, which were about three hundred feet from where we were standing. We'd already been using this one for the last three months or so, and it made our work much easier and quicker. We no longer had to make trips back and forth to the river for hours a day. We simply made one trip to undam the system and then spent about a fourth of the time we had before filling containers that were right there at the edge of the area we were watering.

"What's this?" Hector asked.

"It's an irrigation system, Father," I said. And then I explained the simplicity of how it worked. "With your approval, I'd like to build several more of these. I think we can cut down on the time it takes us to water the crops even further…maybe even plant a few more once we have the means to water them all."

Hector's gaze moved over the system for a minute and then looked at me, his eyes moving to my arms.

"You hollowed out those branches yourself?"

"Yes, Father. I did it on my own time, after my work was done."

Hector rubbed his chin thoughtfully for a moment. "What was your ultimate goal here?"

"My ultimate goal?" I cleared my throat. "Well, Father, I was hoping to be of use to the Acadia community at large of course but also that you'd possibly consider me for a position on the council. There's been an empty spot since Father Nagle passed away, and I'd work hard for you. I'd be diligent and—"

"Oh, Water Bearer," Hector interrupted, his lips tilting in a tight smile. "Son, are you sure this doesn't have to do more with wanting to live up at the main lodge?" He raised his brows. "You should always be honest about your motivations if you're hoping to please the gods."

I remained silent for a moment, feeling as if I was about to walk into some kind of trap no matter how I answered.

"In all honesty, Father, my motivation is to offer my services to our family in a bigger way. I feel called to serve as more than a water bearer, not just for myself but also for our community as a whole. I know it's not my place to determine who does what job; all I can tell you is—"

"In the grand scheme of things, each and every job here is important. You play a role in keeping our family nourished. Do you think the God of War feels loftier than the God of Grain? He may be a mighty soldier, but without the God of Grain, he would starve, as would all his men. No job here is insignificant. I am the prophet, and you are a worker. The gods have deemed it so and you must learn to accept and thrive in your role. If you're finding that difficult, I can assign you some readings, and I ask that you start going to Temple every day."

I took in a long pull of air, trying to steady my rising anger and frustration as I felt my hopes crumbling all around me. "And if I'm not able to accept what the gods have ordained, Father?"

"Try harder. There are paths much rockier than the one I'm offering you. I'd hate to see you choose the more difficult one." He looked at my irrigation system and then back at me, regarding me with such derision I wanted to look away in shame, but I held my ground, forcing myself to hold eye contact. Something about it felt disrespectful—almost challenging—but it was almost as if I responded by instinct alone, one man to another.

Finally, Hector was the one to look away, back to my

system. "It took a lot of strength to build this," he said, almost as if to himself. "But brute strength alone doesn't get you anywhere in the long run. In any great endeavor, mind power is your greatest tool. Planning, strategizing. For example, you can obviously lift stone and hollow out trees, but the problem is something like this isn't completely structurally sound, because no thought went into its construction."

I blinked, a current of anger buzzing steadily over my nerves, causing my vision to blur. "With all due respect, Father, it's extremely structurally sound. I strategized the whole thing in my mind long before I began construction. We've been using it for months, even through several storms. It's proven a big help to the laborers, not only for crops but for other water needs as well." I was talking, but I felt as if my jaw wasn't moving and my words came out clipped.

He shook his head as if what I said was nothing more than a bald-faced lie and then he took one foot and kicked the section in front of him violently.

I startled, unable to comprehend for a second exactly what he was doing.

"No," he said, shaking his head again. "Not structurally sound at all. Practically anything could bring it down." He kicked at it again and again, and several sections beyond the one that had taken the blow, came crashing to the ground. I was frozen, disbelieving. He was destroying everything I'd worked so hard for. *On purpose.*

"Father—" I started, stepping forward.

"See, son? When you build something from the ground up, you have to build it in such a way that no man can ruin it. It can't be flimsy and easy to destroy. Why, if that were the case, anyone could knock it over, take what was yours as if they had that right. When in fact, they should know that would be a disastrous thought and action on their part. Do you understand?" His eyes bored into mine, making his point very clear.

I felt hot, my skin prickled, and my hands automatically curled into fists.

"I'm sorry I have to cut this meeting short, but I'm expected by the council now. Remember what I said, Water Bearer," he said as he started to leave, kicking over other sections of the system as he walked away from me. "Don't ever try to be something other than what the gods have ordained."

I stood there, watching him retreat, the world shimmering around me as if filled with heat. What had just happened?

My feet started moving before my brain had a chance to stop them. There weren't any thoughts in my head, just a loud whooshing sound. I didn't even remember covering the ground from the river to the edge of the trail leading down to the spring, but suddenly I was there. I made my way downhill, my calves straining, dust clouding at my feet as I practically ran down the steep incline.

Anger coursed through me, but below that was deep hurt. I had *trusted* Hector. I had trusted his respect, in the very least—for me, for all of his people. All my *life*, I had trusted Hector. And in an instant, that was gone.

I moved the brush aside roughly, practically crashing through the small opening to our spring. When I stepped out onto the other side, there she was, just turning toward me from across the grass. *Calm in the wake of a storm. A smile that soothed my wounded heart.*

"Calder," she breathed, her smile growing. Her pale blond hair shone in the sun and her gentle eyes blinked and widened as she took me in. "I didn't know if you'd be able to make it."

I strode toward her, and as she took in my expression, her smile faltered. "Calder, what are you—" Her words died as I made it to her, still breathing hard from my fast descent down the trail. I took her beautiful face in my hands, glanced at her lips, and then back at her eyes. There was no reason she shouldn't be mine. No reason at all. Her eyes widened even farther and she breathed out, "Ohhh," understanding suddenly filling her expression. And then my mouth was on hers, and I plunged my tongue into the forbidden fruit. *Hard*. Demanding. Despite my harshness, her mouth opened under mine, and she let out a breathy sigh, her arms wrapping around my neck. I pushed my tongue deeper into her mouth with no finesse whatsoever, wondering if she'd pull away, but she didn't shrink back. She met my probing tongue with her own and sucked lightly on mine. A growl rose up my throat as if I was a savage. I was on fire everywhere, not only from anger now, but from *her*, from her taste, from the soft yet bold way she was responding to me. She took everything I had to give unflinchingly and gave more in return.

And just like that, the whole world was a place I no longer recognized. I didn't know my place, or my purpose. I didn't know who I was or what I could be. It was freedom and fear and excitement and floundering. And so I gripped her harder, holding on to the only thing that felt solid. *Eden. Eden... Mine.*

She hooked her leg around my own, pulling me closer, offering me what I desired as if she'd somehow read my mind, giving comfort when I needed it so desperately. My senses cleared and our kiss slowed. Suddenly, the only thing I was focusing on was her: the way her hands were gripping the hair at the nape of my neck, the way her skin smelled like apple blossoms, the way her mouth tasted like the very first springtime. It occurred to me that this was her first *real* kiss, and I had practically mauled her. I felt a moment of shame but I couldn't stop and she didn't seem to mind, her soft mewls spurring me on. I kissed her with all I had and everything I was worth, which unfortunately wasn't anything at all. But in her touch was promise, the promise that dreams mattered and the world was bigger than we'd been told. That there was *more* beyond what I'd been taught all my life because no one had ever mentioned that Elysium could also be right here on earth. I was experiencing it now. This was my first real kiss too and Eden's lips were the only ones my mouth had ever touched.

We kissed and tasted and sucked and nipped at each other's mouths, lips, and tongues until we were both so breathless I had to pull away. She let out a small moan and her head fell back as I dragged my lips down the satiny skin of her throat. She raised her leg to wrap around my hip and I put my hands under her bottom and lifted her up so we were at the same level. I took a few steps and pressed her against the flat rock behind her; both her legs circling around me. My erection, hot and pulsating, was pressed to her core now and we both moaned together. It felt so blessedly good, so *right*.

As I nipped at the skin of her neck, words came flowing out of my mouth unbidden. I barely knew what I was saying. It was as if a dam of emotion had opened and I was helpless to stop. "I've wanted you for so long. So long. Every waking minute, in my dreams too. I want to bury myself in you, *drown* in you, and never come up for air. I want you to be mine and *only* mine. I'm so sorry, Eden, so sorry—"

"Please don't be sorry," she breathed out, her head still

back. "Anything but that. Please don't be sorry. I'll never be sorry. If this is the last piece of heaven I get before I'm dragged down to hell, then I'll gladly take it."

I groaned, part misery, part overwhelming desire. "Don't say that, Eden." I put my lips to the pulse beating strong and sure at the base of her throat and used my tongue to trail around it. Eden pressed her body into mine, gasping softly. Was this evil and disgusting? Was this wrong? And if it was, then why did it feel like I would die without it? Why did Eden's touch suddenly feel necessary to my very existence?

And so I continued to kiss her, despite what I knew to be right and against all reason except for that which spoke to me through every heartbeat.

"We should stop," I said, totally unconvincingly since my mouth met hers and I slid my tongue inside to taste her again and again. Her tongue joined with mine and we kissed for long luxurious minutes, completely lost in each other. *Yes,* this was my Elysium. This beautiful girl in my arms. I'd longed to hold her close for so long. She was so soft, so beautiful.

She broke away, drawing in air and gazing into my eyes. Her lips were swollen and red, her face flushed, and her eyes heavy-lidded with desire. In that moment, I knew I'd never see anything as beautiful as Eden's face after she'd been kissed. Not the sunrise, not a rainbow, not anything I'd previously looked at with awe and gratitude.

"Make love to me," she whispered. "I want you so much I ache."

I froze, all except for the parts between my legs. Those parts surged forward with attention, apparently under the impression their services were needed. Now.

I used every shred of willpower I had to calm my raging

144

blood. I leaned forward so our foreheads were touching and I let her down gently onto the ground. We breathed together for a minute, our heart rates slowing. "I can't, Eden. Not here. Not like this."

She looked down, hurt.

"I want to. Believe me, I want to—more than I've ever wanted anything in my life." I grabbed her hands in mine and brought them to my heart. "But I have to know you're mine—"

"I am yours. I've always been yours. I'll be yours here on earth, in Elysium. I'll fight the gods if I have to. I'll stand before them and declare it."

Tenderness engulfed me and I smiled down at her. She would. I knew she would. "Where do you find your strength, Morning Glory?"

"From you," she whispered, her gaze direct and filled with trust. "What will we do, Calder?"

"I don't know. Something though. Something has to be done."

She nodded, her gaze searching my face. "Why did you kiss me today? What made you do it?"

I hesitated. "Hector rejected my plan. He kicked over my irrigation system." I paused as the humiliation washed over me again but I pushed that aside. I met Eden's eyes and took a deep breath. "That was the catalyst. But I swear to you, Eden, I swear to you on every part of me, it's because I've wanted to kiss you for so long that it was brewing inside me like an out-of-control storm. I'm sorry it started in anger. You deserved better than that."

Eden regarded me for a minute and then she smiled. "I'm not sorry. I don't care how it started, just that it did." She paused. "As long as it'll happen again."

I kissed her lips again softly, nipping the bottom one with my teeth until she smiled against my mouth. I leaned back and she brought a hand to my cheek, her expression filled with care and kindness. I nuzzled against her palm.

"I'm sorry Hector did that." She paused. "I heard him talking to Clive Richter. Something went wrong for him on the pilgrimage he was just on. I don't know what, but something…something's different about him. And also, he sees you as a threat, and rightly so. He saw us today."

I stepped back, took her hand, and led her to the smaller rock where we sat down together. "I know. It's part of the reason, and I see how he's different too, but…I also see clearly that I was never going to get a spot on the council. It was a pipe dream."

"I'm sorry," she whispered.

I stared out at the spring for a minute, realizing nothing in me felt overly surprised. I turned to her and let my gaze roam her beautiful face. My goddess of the spring, bathed in sunlight. For just a second, I wanted to fall to my knees and worship at her feet. But I rejected those thoughts. Eden had been "worshipped" all her life. She didn't want to be a goddess or a princess. She wanted to be a girl who was allowed to learn and dream and choose. And she'd chosen me. And though I felt a fierce surge of pride at the knowledge, I also felt a responsibility because her dreams were now mine. "This changes everything, Eden. We can't go back. We can't pretend this didn't happen. *I* can't pretend this didn't happen. I don't want to. Not anymore."

She nodded. "Yes, I know. Me either. I don't want to pretend anymore."

"I don't know exactly what to do, but I'm going to come up with something. You trust me, right?"

"With my life."

My chest tightened and I leaned forward and kissed her again. "We need to get back now. Hector's meeting will be ending. No more coming to my cabin, all right? If you need to contact me, you leave a note in the bushes for Xander. I'll have him check every day."

She took her lip between her teeth, drawing my eyes. I wanted to kiss her again, but there wasn't time. I wanted to kiss her again and again for the rest of forever and never stop. "Are we going to leave here?" she asked, her eyes pleading for some sort of confirmation.

I pulled her into my chest, holding her tightly against me. She laid her ear over my heart and we just sat like that for long minutes. *Could we? Could we leave here? My family? My friends? Our lives? Our destiny?* "Only because we have to," I finally said. It was the only way.

CHAPTER ELEVEN
Eden

I was walking on air. Life was going on around me, but it had a distant, dreamy quality. I was lost in my own head, at our spring, Calder's lips on mine, his tongue claiming my mouth, his hard body pressed against me. I shivered just recalling the feel of him—overwhelming, delicious, beautiful—everything I'd ever dreamed of and more.

A few days after Calder kissed me, I put a handful of butterscotch candies in the bush in front of the lodge for Xander to take to Maya and my hand touched a folded piece of paper. I grabbed it and stuffed it in the pocket of my skirt, looked around, and quickly returned to my room.

I recognized the thick paper. It was a piece from the pad we left at the spring, torn in half to make it smaller. I sat down on my bed and unfolded what I hoped was a note from Calder with shaking hands.

Eden,

A pebble. That's the answer to the question you asked a

while back about what the male penguin uses to propose to the female penguin. He sifts through all the pebbles until he finds the smoothest one he can to give to his chosen female. Then he presents it to her as a token of his love. If she takes the pebble and places it on her nest, that means she accepts him as her mate.

I asked a girl I took classes with and you were right. That was, of course, the part she remembered.

I feel your lips on me, Eden. When I close my eyes, when I'm awake, I taste you. You are my first breath and my last. I feel you, and I hope you still feel me too. I need to see you. Can you meet me at our spring? Leave a note for Xander and he'll bring it to me. It will seem like a thousand years until then.

Yours, Calder

Yours. I sat there holding Calder's note to my chest, a giddy smile on my face. I was somebody's. I was *Calder's.* I belonged to him. And he belonged to me. It seemed so simple, but of course for us, it was anything but.

I turned the note over and laughed out loud when I saw the entire back side of the paper was filled with a sketch of a penguin nosing a small shiny pebble along the snow-covered ground toward another penguin sitting on a nest, her head turned away from him. In that one quick sketch, he had managed to put an expression of pure hopefulness on the boy penguin's face and a haughty indifference on the girl penguin's face, as she waited to be impressed. I let out another small laugh.

I looked around my room for a piece of paper but realized I didn't have any in my room. There'd be some downstairs. I glanced at Hector's Holy Book on my bedside table and bit my lip. Then I picked it up and opened it slowly, hesitating. I quickly turned to the back and ripped a page out. My eyes widened in disbelief at my own small act of rebellion. But I sat down on my bed and used the cover as a hard surface to write my note.

I used the empty margins of the page, and I had to keep it short, as the white space was limited.

Calder,

Who could have guessed that penguins are so romantic? This world really is filled with love in the most surprising of places, isn't it?

I feel your lips on mine too. I taste you. I breathe you. I long for you like I've never longed for anything in my life.

Meet me at our spring on Sunday, after Temple? Hector has another council meeting and I'll tell Mother Miriam I'm ill so I don't have to attend the Sunday meal.

Always yours, Eden

I walked as quickly as I could in my sandals and skirt down the trail. My heart beat rapidly, not just from the exertion but from the excitement of knowing I'd see Calder in a matter of minutes.

I ducked through the opening and there he was, reclining on our rock, his arms behind his head, his wet clothes clinging to his skin. I stood there for a minute simply staring. He sat up and his wet shirt stuck to his stomach muscles bunching underneath the fabric. My mouth went dry. *Yours.* I met his grin with one of my own.

I waded through the water and Calder offered a hand and pulled me up on the rock. I lay back next to him. We lay there for a minute or two, our breathing and the splashing of the water the only sound around us. Then we both moved at once, turning toward each other, Calder taking my head in his hands and weaving his fingers through my hair. He paused for only a second as he gazed into my eyes, his own darkening and growing slightly lazy in a way I'd never seen before. A tingling began between my legs and I squeezed them together to relish the sensation. And then his mouth met mine and the taste of him was all I knew. I moaned, a wordless confession of my complete willingness.

He tilted his head and our kiss went deeper, our tongues dueling gently. The scrape of his rough jaw against my cheek was inflamed me and I moaned again, pressing my body closer to his, wanting to experience all the ways he was so different than me. Wanting to touch those mysterious bunched muscles of his stomach and the rough texture of his skin…and other things that made me blush just to imagine.

When Calder broke away gently to trail his lips down my throat, I sighed, tilting my head back to give him better access to my skin. I gazed up at the blue sky, clouds floating lazily by.

"The gods created this place for us," I whispered, smiling dreamily.

Calder paused, brushing his lips once more across my throat before responding. "Yes." I felt him smile against my skin. "Why do you think they did that?"

"So we'd have a secret place to fall in love."

Calder lifted his head, his gaze latched to mine. "You're

mine, Eden. You always have been, from the very first second I saw you."

"Yes," I whispered. It seemed like the simplest truth the world had ever known.

Our lips met again. Calder kissed me in a way that made me believe I had not only always been his but I would be his forever. In this life or any other. In his kiss was a claiming and a promise that wherever he and I existed, we would belong to each other.

After several minutes, Calder broke away, panting. His expression spoke of deep need, but I saw confliction there too.

"Please don't stop," I said, leaning up and kissing his lips again softly.

"I'm afraid if I don't now, I won't be able to later," he said, his voice even more gravelly than it normally was.

I wanted to tell him not to stop now, or later, but the words themselves felt brazen, too bold, even in my mind. My actions would have to speak for me.

I put my fingers on the top button of my shirt and started slowly unbuttoning each one after that, one by one. Calder's eyes jumped between my fingers and my face, his eyes seeming to darken as each button popped open. I watched his throat move as he swallowed heavily.

I opened my shirt to expose the simple white bra beneath and shrugged the wet garment off, letting it fall from my shoulders. Then I reached behind my back, unhooked my bra, and let it slide down my arms and drop to my lap. I felt the heat creeping up my neck, but I kept eye contact, refusing to feel shame in this beautiful place where I'd finally found escape from all those rules and judgments cast on me by others. A soft moan ghosted from Calder's parted lips, as his gaze lowered to my breasts. My nipples hardened under his stare, and though I refused to feel shame, this was the first time I'd ever been naked in front of anyone.

"Eden," Calder murmured, "you're so beautiful."

And then in one swift movement, he pulled off his own wet shirt and sat bare chested before me. My eyes roamed his bronzed skin and his sleek muscles before I reached out tentatively to touch him. Time seemed to slow down; the flowing water became a trickle; the clouds bobbed lazily above us. Our bodies came together and my hand made contact with the warm, smooth skin of his chest. A breath escaped from his mouth and my eyes darted to his. I had seen Calder shirtless before but never dreamed I would one day get to touch him, feel the strong muscles I had admired for so long, let my fingers roam the singular dips and swells of him. He felt so firm, so masculine, his skin smooth and warm. I could hardly believe this was real.

"Please don't stop," he said, repeating my words from a few minutes before.

I released a breath and let my fingers continue their exploration, over one pectoral and down to a nipple, where I used my pointer finger to trace around it gently.

"Eden," Calder choked. "You're killing me. I'm dying."

I smiled, my eyes still watching my fingers as they trailed even farther down his stomach. "No. You're living. *We're* living. Right here, together. It's been suggested dying would separate us forever, and I refuse to let you go." My eyes met his then and something seemed to spark between us right before he leaned forward and took my mouth once more, his tongue thrusting slowly and leisurely. I moved even closer so I could feel his bare skin against my own. *Bliss.*

I was being bold now, but this moment was ours, no

one else's. Never in my whole life had I been given what I wanted or even asked what that might be, so I was going to take it. Right here under the gods, at our spring, I was going to take what I wanted for myself. And I wanted Calder. And he wanted me. And that couldn't be wrong, could it?

I rubbed my achy nipples against his hard chest and moaned into his mouth at the delicious sensation. Nothing had ever felt so good and I wanted more. I wove my fingers through the short soft hair at the back of his neck and tangled my tongue with his, exalting at the taste of him, the smell of him: clean water and male skin.

We lay down together, our mouths never breaking contact. My heart beat furiously and there was an intense tingly feeling between my legs. I felt hot and frustrated. I didn't know what I needed, but I was desperate to get whatever it was. I broke away from his mouth. "Are you…? Do you…?" I asked breathlessly, not knowing how to verbalize what my body was asking for.

"Yes," he said, seeming to know. "Yes."

I let my eyes move boldly downward and took in the bulge at the front of his loose pants. Keeping my eyes trained there, I said, "I learn things here. Teach me, Calder." *Bold. So bold.* Who was this new version of me and why wasn't I more shocked by my lack of fear?

Calder groaned and fell backward on the rock, covering his face with his hands. "How am I going to survive you?" he asked.

I didn't know exactly what he meant, but I heard the teasing note in his voice, and I saw desire clearly in his eyes. I smiled, laying my body on top of his and kissing his throat. "I'm the least of your concerns."

He chuckled. "No, you're by far the biggest of my

concerns." But he looked at me with so much tenderness, that my smile grew.

I laid my cheek on his chest and, after a minute, allowed my hand to move down the muscles of his stomach, taking a moment to trace the indents and ridges. He sucked in a breath and my hand halted, but when he didn't object, I let it continue on to that mysterious fullness under the fabric. I got to the waistband of his linen pants where a small trail of hair disappeared and he seemed to freeze, the bulge right beneath my hand jumping. *Oh.*

I dipped my fingers below the loose waistband and moved my hand lower, through a thatch of coarse hair, seeking that part of him that was a mystery to me. Calder's chest rose and fell in pants that grew increasingly shallower and a tremor went through him. A heady feeling of power surged through my blood, emboldening me even further.

My hand reached what I was seeking. I wrapped my fingers around the silky length of him, surprised to find it hard. He moaned deeply, pressing toward my hand in a wordless plea to continue.

I let go for a second and a another groan escaped him, but I needed to get his waistband lower so that I could see what I was doing. He lifted his backside so I could accomplish my goal, and when I pulled his pants lower, he sprang free. *Oh.* It was standing straight up. I wrapped my hand around him again, my eyes widening as I took in the dusky organ, the head deep red, a shiny drop of fluid right at the tip. I knew what boys looked like—I'd helped Hailey bathe her children. But I'd never seen a *man* before. It was so… *large* and it jutted toward me so stiffly. For a minute, I simply stared at it.

I sat up and put my other hand on the rock next to me.

I looked back at Calder, but his arm was thrown up over his eyes and so I couldn't see his expression well, just that his lips were parted and his jaw tense.

"Eden, Eden…" he breathed, sounding so desperate I almost laughed but was too enthralled by his body, by this moment, to interrupt it.

I gazed at my hand encircling him and I used my thumb to rub the drop of fluid in a circle, fascinated by him, by how different his body was from my own. "Show me," I whispered.

He hesitated for a brief second but then took his own hand and put it on top of mine, using it to slide it up and down his length.

After a minute, he let go so I could do it on my own. I continued to stroke him as he'd shown me. His moans and breathing told me I was doing something right and so I continued, mesmerized by the way the skin moved beneath my fingers and the way he swelled even larger in my hand.

After a few minutes, his breathing grew even more ragged and he began thrusting his hips upward into my hand. As I listened to his moans and soft panting, the pressure between my legs intensified, and I felt moisture trickling down my inner thigh.

His body tensed and then froze as white liquid came bursting out of him. I sucked in a breath, my eyes widening as he moaned, gasped, and then relaxed, his body softening beneath my hand.

When I turned my head, I saw he had lowered his arm and was looking at me with an expression of sleepy bliss. *Wow.* I leaned down and kissed him, and he brought both hands up and cupped my jaw as he kissed me back deeply. We kissed for long minutes, already experts on each other's mouths. Calder rolled me over onto my back as his tongue continued to dance with mine.

"That was… I can't even put into words what that was," Calder said, gazing down at me.

I didn't know if what we were doing was wrong or right. I had been told all my life sexual impurity was a sin. But this felt the furthest from a sin any person could get. How could this be a sin when my heart was bursting with love for this strong, kind, incredible boy—the one who continued to teach me things patiently and lovingly? How could this be a sin when it was the most joyful moment of my whole life?

Could it be wrong to be so happy? I just couldn't bring myself to believe it was.

I whimpered into his mouth when his bare chest again rubbed over my hardened nipples. My body was suddenly enflamed again and my fingers dug into his biceps where I was rubbing up and down the hard muscles of his arms. I loved the feeling of his big hard body hovering over mine, his scent surrounding me, the knowledge he was as helpless to resist me as I was to resist him. It was power and surrender all in one and I'd never known those two things could exist simultaneously.

He pulled away from my mouth and bent his head and suddenly, his lips were at my breast and he was kissing my nipple. My eyes blinked open and a sound of surprised delight escaped my mouth. *Oh, that feels so blessedly good.* He nuzzled his face against my breasts and licked around the sensitive buds for several minutes until I was panting and dizzy with desire.

I pressed the aching part of me upward, into his manhood, and he groaned and lifted his head. Our eyes met and he gazed at me with that same tenderness, right before he leaned in and trailed his lips up my throat. Before I realized it, I felt his hand under my skirt, trailing up my inner thigh. I froze, only able to concentrate on that rough hand moving upward, toward my most secret, private part. I swallowed heavily and tilted my head back, opening my eyes to stare unashamedly up toward the gods and the heavens. *You were wrong*, I told them in my head. *This is my destiny.*

Calder's fingers feathered over my skin and then reached the waistband of my underwear. Just as he'd done for me, I lifted my backside to allow him room to pull my underwear down. His hand moved tentatively over the soft curls covering my sex and one of his fingers slipped through and touched a spot beneath that made me cry out in unexpected pleasure. His hand paused but then he continued to use one finger to touch me there, exploring. I moaned and pressed up into his hand, overcome with the bliss he was giving me. "Calder," I breathed, "please don't stop."

His finger continued to circle for a few minutes, as the pleasure rose higher and higher. He stopped momentarily and I made a sound of loss and pressed unabashedly up into his hand again. He moved his hand lower and dipped one finger into my opening and it felt so good I cried out again, begging him for more. He moaned too and pressed his finger deeper, filling me.

Calder kissed and sucked at my neck, sending goose bumps across my torso. *It feels so good.* His voice was thick as he said, "I want you so much."

"Yes, yes," I answered.

"My Morning Glory," he said.

And then his now-wet finger moved back to that

magical spot and all thoughts vanished as I submitted to the pleasure.

"Is this…show me if this isn't—" Calder said, sounding uncertain.

"No, that's perfect. That's… Ohhhh, Calder," I moaned.

He moved his finger back and forth slowly and then faster as I panted and moved my head from side to side, not knowing if I could handle the thing I felt swirling through me, ready to drag me under.

And then as suddenly as the thought came, overwhelmingly intense pleasure washed through me as I cried out, all the muscles in my body contracting so deliciously I thought I might die from it. It felt like the world gave a sudden jolt as time resumed, the sound of flowing water meeting my ears and the clouds moving swiftly overhead. I was dizzy and giddy and loose-limbed.

The pleasure slowly faded and I sighed, my lips tipping in dreamy satisfaction. Calder leaned down and kissed me tenderly. "That was beautiful," he said.

I nodded, awestruck by everything that had just happened and not able to form words. Calder smiled and then I followed his lead as we both stripped off our still-damp bottoms and washed ourselves in the spring.

We held our clothes over our heads as we crossed to the other side and then dressed on the bank.

We lay down on the grass in our underwear, leaving our clothes to dry fully on a rock.

"I don't want to go back," I said, my eyes suddenly filling with tears. *I don't ever want to go back.*

He didn't speak for a minute. "I know. I don't want to send you back. If there were any other way…"

"Please come up with something," I begged.

He tucked a piece of hair behind my ear and wiped a tear from my cheek. "We'll need to leave here. There's no other way we can be together. Are you ready for that?"

"Yes. It's what I want."

Calder's eyebrows moved together. "It will take some preparation though. We'll need money…and somewhere to stay. I'll need to figure out a few things about how the big community operates before I can know I'll be able to keep you safe, provide for you."

"I don't need much," I whispered. "Just you."

Calder smiled and then flopped back on his back. "You make it sound easy, Morning Glory, but it won't be easy. Hector's left us completely ignorant and unprepared. I don't know if that was purposeful or…" He looked over at me. "In any case, we need to make sure we have a shot."

"I trust you."

Calder studied me for a minute and then smiled, but his smile held more worry than joy. "I know you do," he said very seriously. Then he gathered me to him and held me against his chest as the warm sun dried our clothes.

When we were both dry and dressed, Calder leaned forward and kissed my lips softly. I suddenly felt irrationally shy, standing there after we'd just touched each other in such an intimate way. Would this change things in ways I wasn't prepared for? Did he think differently of me? I had no one to ask.

"Leave another note for me when you can meet me again," he said.

I nodded and then we walked hand in hand to the base of the trail, where he kissed me one more time before I left him to ascend alone. I felt alive. Invigorated. Hopeful. I never wanted to feel any differently again. Could we make our dreams come true? Could we really *leave*?

CHAPTER TWELVE
Calder

Calder,

My thoughts are only of you. There are six hundred seventy-seven steps between my home and yours. I'm sure of it. I've counted them. I walk them in my mind. I step out of my front door and I come to you in the night. I slip into your bed and your heat burns into me as we quietly touch. Your mouth finds mine in the darkness and the taste of you makes every part of me ache with want—my body, my skin, and my heart. I know you in the dark, just as I know you under the bright daytime sun. I'll know you in Elysium and in any other place the gods deem to send me for loving you. I'm not afraid. But I miss you, and I don't want there to be any steps between us. I want my bed to be your bed, and I want your nighttime heat to be within arm's reach. Every night before I fall asleep, I pray that day comes quickly.

Yours always and forever, Eden

P.S. I suppose my academic lessons have ended for now. I have to say I like the new curriculum very much, E.

I grinned down at the paper and then hid it under my mattress with the other note Eden had written me. I flopped down on my bed, which was really nothing more than a straw-stuffed mattress and a wool blanket, and lay there trying to cool my body. I'd probably be wise to go jump in the river quickly before I went back to the fields. Eden's note had the blood coursing through my body and images of us in bed together filled my mind. I groaned and put one arm over my eyes, trying in vain to empty my brain.

After a minute, I sat up and unfolded the blank piece of paper Eden had provided with her own note.

Eden,

My thoughts are only of you. When I bathe in the morning, the water running down my skin is your fingertips, touching me everywhere. When I work in the fields, the feel of the velvety plant leaves reminds me of your skin. As I stand in my doorway, looking toward the main lodge and you, the deep blue twilight sky is your eyes. I burn for you so intensely, I feel like I could light every worker cabin, all fifty of them, and we'd no longer need candlelight. I'm going to take you away from here, to a place where my bed is your bed and my home is your home. And in that place, I'll never be more than an arm's reach from you, my beautiful, brave Morning Glory.

The spring festival planning is underway for the workers and I've been assisting where needed. I won't be allowed to come near you during it, but I'll see you, and I'll know you see me too.

Yours always and forever, Calder

I turned the paper over and did a quick sketch of myself, standing in the doorway of our cabin, looking toward the main lodge. I drew light emanating off my skin and cast a glow over all the cabins surrounding my own and smiled as I folded it up.

I walked the half mile to the edge of the field where Xander was standing, leaning against some sort of light green box by the side of the dirt road.

Xander turned when he heard my footsteps and cocked an eyebrow. "Decided to come see where all the action is?"

"Is this what you do all day? No wonder you're mostly crazy."

He snorted. "I'd disagree with you, but…"

I smiled and leaned against the box next to him and then gave it a light pat. "What is this anyway?"

He glanced at it and then back toward the road. "It's an electrical box. It houses some wires or something that bring electricity to the main lodge."

I nodded slowly. "So aren't you supposed to be walking around or something?"

"What's the point, Calder?"

"Hector would say it's how safety is ensured."

Xander let out a humorless laugh. "More like how slaves are ensured."

I stared at him. "Slaves?"

"Isn't that what we are? Don't we work out here all day for no pay?"

I stared at the road for several moments not knowing exactly how to answer that.

Xander turned toward me. "Hector would say we work for our family, but, Calder, if the floods don't come, if Hector's wrong about that, then we're going to end up old men out here."

I looked around to make sure there wasn't a soul in sight. "I wanted to talk to you about that." I pulled in a deep breath. "I need to leave. It's not safe here for me anymore. I need to take Eden with me and leave."

Xander didn't look surprised, but he studied me for a few beats before responding. "Yeah, you do."

I gave a singular nod. "I need help."

Xander laughed softly, little amusement in the sound. "Yeah, you do."

"Will you come with us?"

"Yeah."

"Seriously?" I felt a sudden release of tension. He was in this with us. We had a three-person team. "So we're really going to do this?"

Xander squinted up at the sun. "We're gonna try. But listen, in all honesty? We have a lot going against us. Hector educated us only because the state would've cleared us out if he didn't. But we're gonna be like fish out of water out there." He waved his arm in the direction of the city miles beyond us, or maybe he meant the entire world. Both would have been accurate. "I mean, we're eighteen-year-old men, and we have no skills other than farming and walking around for hours a day, which isn't much of a talent."

I massaged the back of my neck for a second. "I've been wondering." I paused, gathering my thoughts. "That woman from the school system came out here every month to look at our lesson plans, right?"

"Yeah, I remember her," Xander said. "That's what I meant about Hector educating us because of the state laws."

"Right. So why didn't anyone ever check up on Eden? How did Hector get away with not educating her?"

Xander stared out at the road and then shrugged. "I have no idea. Maybe since he's her guardian, he can do as he pleases?"

I frowned. That didn't sound quite right but what did I know about state laws? Little to nothing. "Do you think Kristi would help us? I don't even know where to start."

"I think so. Let me talk to her and I'll let you know what she says."

I extended my hand and he gripped it. "Okay. Thank you."

"Whatever I have, you have half," he said.

"Same goes for you, brother," I said solemnly.

I looked back at the road stretching to places I couldn't even picture and I steeled myself for what might be to come.

A few days after I talked to Xander on the edge of Acadia, I was returning home after my work in the fields when, from a distance, I saw Eden entering the temple. I was far away, but she couldn't be mistaken for anyone else with that long fall of golden hair. Mother Miriam stopped at the front and sat down on the small stone bench to the side of the doors as Eden disappeared inside.

I turned hastily and made my way to the other side of the field, where I was able to walk straight to the back of the temple without being seen from the front or the sides of the building. I glanced around covertly, and when I didn't spot anyone nearby, I tried the back door, found it unlocked, and quickly ducked inside, latching it behind me. In Acadia, there was little reason to lock doors. Our security walked the perimeter, so we felt secure that the only people inside were family.

I stood listening for a minute and then I peeked around the open doorway that led directly to the platform at the front. I spotted Eden alone, kneeling in prayer before the twelve candles on the left wall, each one representing one of our gods. Her eyes were closed and her lips moved ever so slightly.

I advanced, my footfalls creating no noise at all, and stopped next to Hector's podium.

"I thought you only prayed to one," I said softly.

Eden startled, her eyes flying open as she brought a hand to her heart. She stared at me for a beat and then her face broke out in a stunning smile. "In my mind, I do. The other ones just happen to be represented here."

"Does he ever answer you?" I asked, raising my eyes heavenward.

Eden gave a small shrug. "If you mean does he talk to me like Hector says the gods talk to him, no." She stood and the candlelight behind her in the dim, windowless room outlined her shape beneath her white skirt and blouse. My body stirred. "But every once in a while I hear something… *something* between a feeling and a whisper." She began walking toward me, a serene smile on her lips, tendrils of hair falling around her cheeks. I watched her, awestruck by her beauty. Sometimes she seemed unreal to me—a vision. Had I really just touched her so intimately? *Me?* A lowly worker. How could that not have been a dream? "Do you ever hear them whisper?" she asked.

"No," I said, turning more fully toward her as she approached me.

"Maybe you're not listening closely enough." She raised a delicate brow. She was teasing me.

My lips lifted in a small smile, but I still felt slightly dizzy, standing there in my dirt-streaked clothes in front of this beautiful, pristine girl who I'd been taught was so far above me, and yet had let me kiss and touch her. I felt something close to *fear* looking at her—like no matter what I did, no matter what I tried, I'd never get enough of her. I'd never resist her pull. I'd felt it my entire life, but now... now it was a burning hunger and I had no desire to resist anymore. "Maybe."

Eden smiled a mischievous smile and reached her hands up and around my neck. "Perhaps they told me to come here today," she said softly. "Maybe the sense of claustrophobia that overcame me in my room and made me tell Mother Miriam I was feeling pious was really the gods whispering to me, letting me know my arrival would be perfectly timed to you leaving the fields for the day."

I let out a breath and chuckled softly. "Will she come inside?" I asked, nodding toward the front door where I knew Mother Miriam sat outside.

Eden shook her head. "How can I properly say the Twelve Petitions if I'm interrupted? Then they have to be started all over again..."

I gazed down at her and her lips parted. I groaned and leaned in and took her sweet mouth, my tongue pushing between her lips to gain access. I hardened and instinctively pressed into her, moaning again. She let out a little gasp and pulled me in closer. *Oh, Morning Glory.*

As her tongue wrapped around mine, she reached down

between our bodies and rubbed me through my pants. Oh holy hell. Pleasure pulsed through me and I squeezed my eyes shut tighter, reaching up with my hands to cup her cheeks as my tongue plundered deeper. I was dizzy with lust, with the taste of her in my mouth and her smell—apple blossoms and springtime—surrounding me.

I pressed toward her hand and felt her body bump something behind her. *Hector's podium.* Thank the gods it was attached to the floor and wouldn't tip right over.

Eden continued to rub me through my pants, leaning back slightly against the podium. I went down on my knees in front of her and looked up at her beautiful face, worshipping her, only not exactly the way I'd been taught. The thought brought a wicked smile to my lips and her eyes widened slightly as she ran a hand through my short hair.

Suddenly, I needed to taste her more than I needed to draw in another breath. I bunched her skirt up and put my face against her soft mound. Eden sucked in a breath and moaned softly, igniting me. Both her hands were in my hair now and she ran her fingers through it, her nails scoring over my scalp.

I brought her underwear down her hips and heard her suck in a breath. "Calder," she moaned but didn't say more.

I brought my face to the soft patch of blond curls and inhaled. Heat pulsated through my body, accompanied by half-formed thoughts and visions: instincts that told me to thrust into her, plant my seed inside her, protect her, lay a bounty of food at her feet. Gods above, how could one woman's scent convey all those commands and even more?

But when I opened my eyes and looked up into hers— filled with tenderness—it was my heart that swelled and clenched. She had every part of me. *I was hers.*

I turned my face back to her and licked down the crease of her sex with my tongue. "Oh!" she gasped, pressing herself into me. I couldn't help the moan that came up my throat either. My mouth found that little piece of flesh that made Eden moan and pant, and I circled it with my tongue. She tasted so good—sweet and musky, like a more intense version of her skin. *I love it. I love her.* Her hands gripped my hair and I growled softly against her. I circled that small spot until Eden was crying out and grinding herself into my face. I felt animalistic, needy, like I wanted to devour her, mark her, and claim her as my own in any and every way possible.

Eden tensed and shuddered and panted out her climax right against my mouth. It was the most intense thing I'd ever experienced in my entire life. I wouldn't have been able to get up now if I tried though. I was hard as stone. Pulsing with my own need for release.

After several still seconds of me breathing against her, I pulled her underwear back up and let her skirt down. I raised my gaze, my eyes widening first with confusion, then with horrified realization at what I saw. "Oh no. Eden, I…I'm so sorry. I didn't even consider that I…"

She blinked, obviously still a little dazed. "Sorry? For what?"

I brought my hands up, my palms still smeared with dirt from the fields. I had forgotten and apparently she hadn't noticed in the dim room.

She looked down at herself, her white skirt covered with dirty marks where my hands had been. It appeared as if a dirty dog had pawed her. Shame descended, the marks on her somehow conveying how unworthy I was of touching her. *Was she thinking the same thing?*

I cringed as she stared and then she suddenly burst out

laughing, clutching her stomach and leaning back against Hector's podium. I started laughing too, and it took several minutes before we finally got a hold of ourselves.

"Seriously, this isn't funny." But I let out another chuckle anyway. "How are you going to get out of here?"

Eden wiped at her eyes. She looked around, her gaze finally landing on the ashes next to the twelve candles. She pushed at me. "You need to go. They won't let me come here again after what I'm about to do, but it was worth it." She grinned. "I'll look for you at the festival."

"All right." I was worried though and didn't want to leave her. "Are you sure you'll be okay?"

"Yes, I promise." She leaned forward and kissed me once more on my lips and then pulled away, smiling.

I let my eyes roam over her beautiful face and down to her skirt, where there was an extra amount of dirt smears right between her legs. *Gods above.* "Bye, Morning Glory."

"Bye, Butterscotch."

I snuck back out the rear of the temple, standing against the building for a minute, until I was sure I didn't hear anyone walking nearby.

When I moved to the side of the temple, I heard Eden let out a shriek and then a minute later, the front doors banged open. Mother Miriam's voice came quickly, "What did you do?" she shouted.

"I'm sorry!" I heard Eden cry. "The ashes! It wasn't my fault. They tipped over and…"

"All over you?" Mother Miriam asked harshly. "You always were a clumsy thing. Come on. You need a bath. You're lucky I don't take this to Hector."

I leaned back on the wall of the temple, chuckling softly. I should have attempted to hold on to the momentary shame

I'd felt inside, but I didn't seem able to. "Morning Glory," I murmured. I started my walk to the river, where I took my time washing off every bit of the dirt on my body, sad at removing her essence from my tongue, a feeling of pride infusing me when I pictured Eden, my dirty handprints all over her. "Pride is a sin," I reminded myself softly. But as with the shame I probably should have felt, I didn't feel sinful either. I just felt happy.

In Acadia, the workers hosted a festival every April. It was a celebration of winter ending and that the spring crops were bursting with life again. No one worked that day, and everyone chipped in to cook for the different booths and to set up the games. Generally, we just celebrated the blessings the gods had bestowed upon us and the peace and success of our community.

I'd always enjoyed it in the past. It was a chance for a day of leisure and for my friends and I to compete at the different booths.

But the morning of the festival, I rolled out of bed at dawn, feeling antsy with pent-up frustration even though sleep was still clinging to me. I walked to the door of our cabin and stepped outside, my head turning automatically toward the main lodge. Eden's window was dark. She was still sleeping. I pictured her lying in her bed, her eyes closed, and that golden hair spilling over her pillow as her breasts rose and fell. I scrubbed a hand down my face and closed the door, none too quietly, and began my walk to the river.

"Wait up, Calder," I heard Maya call behind me.

I stopped and turned around, bending to pick her up when I reached her.

"No, don't carry me. I wanna walk," she said in her slightly slurred speech, right before she coughed.

"Maya…"

"It's morning. You don't need to be in a hurry yet," she teased.

I smiled. "No, I guess I don't. Come on." And I took her hand in mine.

After we'd visited the outhouse, we made our way to the river. I took my shirt off and waded in slowly, getting used to the cold water. Maya stayed closer to the shore as she splashed water over her face and hair, coughing more in the cool air.

I swore under my breath. Her cough had gotten better for a while, but now it was back. And it didn't sound good.

As I watched her, I suddenly felt filled with anger that my sister had to splash cold water on her head in the chilly morning as the people at the main lodge woke up to a warm shower and indoor plumbing.

I had been taught my entire life that our sacrifice was pleasing to the gods, and it made us holier to live with the amenities they alone provided. But suddenly, standing there, it enraged me that Maya should have to sacrifice and the council members' kids didn't.

I reined in my emotion and dove into the water, coming up a short distance away and shaking the water out of my hair. I heard Maya laugh behind me. "You're like a fish," she called.

I laughed and dove back under the water, coming up just the same. Maya laughed again and clapped her hands. She mimicked casting a fishing reel and I pretended to be caught, floundering in the water and attempting to make an escape. Maya laughed louder and began to "reel" me in. I pretended to fight and strain as Maya reeled me toward shore, where I finally flipped and flopped on the ground, creating a dramatic fish death. Maya kept giggling and finally, I opened one eye and grinned back.

I stood up and splashed some water in the places I'd gotten sand on me and then Maya handed me a piece of fabric, and I used it to blot the water off my chest and run it over my hair.

"Do you like it here, Maya?"

"Yes. It's my home. I like it anywhere you and Mom and Dad are."

I nodded, watching the water pool in the rocks at my feet. "You know if I ever left here, that I'd come back for you, right?"

Maya squinted at me. "Why would you ever leave here? If you did, you couldn't come to Elysium with us. You'd be lost in the great flood with the rest of the sinners. Please don't ever leave here, Calder."

I held back a flinch. "Okay, Maya. Anyway, today's not the day to talk about this. Today"—I scooped her up and she shrieked and then laughed—"is the spring festival and I'm going to win you whatever you want."

"I want a flower wreath for my hair."

"Then that's what you'll have."

Back at our cabin, Mom and Dad were awake, so we all started the day. Mom made breakfast as Dad loaded the small wagon outside our door with the baked goods my mom had been preparing all week.

For the festival, those baking were given a bag of sugar to use as an ingredient and Xander and I usually went from booth to booth, shoveling in treats, making ourselves sick by the end of the day. For some reason, the thought of sugar didn't fill me with my usual enthusiasm.

I stood in the doorway again, needing the air as all four of us clambered around the small space. It had always seemed crowded in our cabin, but now it felt tiny, claustrophobic, and I could hardly breathe. If I wasn't sleeping or working, these days I spent most of my time on the little porch.

"Make yourself useful, and help your dad," my mom said, a bossy tone in her voice.

I took a deep breath and went and grabbed a couple wrapped plates of desserts off the table.

By noon, the setup was done and I walked through the rows of booths slowly, checking out the various items: cakes, cookies, cupcakes, hair wreaths, bouquets of wildflowers, soaps that smelled like different herbs, scented candles made from beeswax, jars of clover honey. Although the workers had made or collected the items, everything that was out was a gift from Hector, and we were encouraged to take what we needed. Everyone seemed happy, full of excitement today, but the whole festival suddenly seemed to me like a small morsel Hector threw to us workers to keep us happy when *he* lived like this every day of the year, taking his fill of whatever treats and luxuries he desired.

I'd take Eden away from here, yes, because there was no other option, but would I miss any of it? It was all I'd ever known. And it would break my mom's and dad's hearts. And Maya…I'd come back for her. I'd have to. Once I got settled, I'd come back for her.

I massaged the back of my neck. Just thinking about it was overwhelming. And Xander was right—I was wholly unprepared for the world outside. I didn't fear it so much as Hector had taught us to. I wasn't even sure exactly why… Maybe it was the people Xander had met at the ranger station… maybe those happy-looking movie stars in the magazines we had swiped and hid under the floorboards of Xander's cabin. None of *them* looked evil or cruel. I hoped I was right to be optimistic about the way other people lived and acted outside Acadia, because I knew one thing for sure: we'd never be allowed to rejoin this community once we left.

I was interrupted in my thoughts by the sound of voices rising and some calling out, and I looked behind me to see the small, horse-drawn wagon, draped in bright fabrics, that Hector used to ride through the festival as people waved and clapped for him. Eden was sitting beside him, solemn in the white lace dress she always wore to Temple and special events. Hector leaned over and whispered something in her ear and a look of discomfort passed over her features before she smiled demurely and nodded at him. Anger and jealousy spiked through me as I leaned against a tree at the edge of the clearing where all the booths were set up. He had no right to her. If I could, I would have scooped her off that *stupid*, pompous wagon right then and there and walked off with her. But to where? And with what? So that she would be hungry by dinnertime and I'd have nothing to feed her? She couldn't know all my doubts. She was counting on me and I wouldn't fail her. But inside, I was nervous, frustrated, and filled with questions I had no way to answer.

I walked back around the small grove of trees and weaved through the booths until I was next to the wagon, about a hundred feet to the side of it. I moved along at the same pace, ducking behind booths here and there so I wouldn't be seen. Finally, Eden turned her head and caught sight of me, her eyes widening before she coughed into her hand. But I'd seen the smile before she'd hidden it.

I ducked behind another booth, and when I stepped out, Eden was looking around for me and, spotting me, started to "cough" into her hand again. I walked along with her like that for a few minutes, loving that I was making her smile. We'd played games like this for years, but I'd never been quite as daring.

When the wagon made it to the first of the game booths, Hector stepped down and then offered his hand to Eden, who took it and stepped down as well. I moved closer, blending in with the rest of the people now crowding around the booth.

The game booth was a series of three platforms, one close, one farther, and the third one all the way at the back wall. There were three heavy beanbags on each platform and the object was to throw a larger beanbag with enough force and just the right placement to knock all three off.

Hector leaned in to Eden again, pointing up at the variety of flower head wreaths. I moved closer and Eden caught my movement and looked over at me and then immediately down, obviously forgetting Hector had just asked her a question.

Hector raised his head to see what was distracting Eden, and his eyes locked on me, his expression cold. "Which one would you like, love?" Hector asked loudly. Eden startled and looked up at the booth, hesitating and then pointing to a wreath of pink and yellow wildflowers, long pink ribbons hanging from the back of it.

"Then that's the one that will be yours," he insisted.

He took the beanbag from the little girl working there and threw it at the first platform, easily knocking all three smaller bags off. The crowd cheered like he had just knocked a ten-ton boulder over with his bare hands. He turned toward Eden and took her hand and kissed it, brushing his lips across her knuckle. My gut clenched and I felt a clawing need to rip her away from him.

He turned back around and Eden looked toward me, biting her lip and then giving me a very small smile.

He threw the beanbag at the second platform and cleared those too, the crowd going wild.

Suddenly, Xander was beside me. He leaned in. "Relax. It's all a show. She wants to be next to you as much as you want to be next to her."

I relaxed my hands, which had balled into fists.

Hector took the beanbag in his hand again and hesitated as he aimed for the farthest platform. He made his throw and two of the three smaller beanbags slid easily off, but the third remained. Hector smiled, letting out an exaggerated sigh and raising both hands in an "oh well" gesture.

"I'll win one for the princess," I blurted out loudly.

I felt all eyes turn toward me, but my focus remained on Hector.

"You idiot," I heard Xander mutter, but my pride ruled the day and I stepped forward.

"Here, Calder," the little girl at the booth said, grinning and showing a gap where both her front teeth were missing. I took the beanbag from her and watched as she set up the three platforms again.

"Go ahead," she said. I threw the first one and cleared the platform easily. The crowd clapped, although not as exuberantly as they had for Hector. I threw the second one and cleared that one easily as well, and the crowd cheered a little bit louder.

I moved over to the third one and glanced back at Eden. Hector had moved behind her and had both hands on her shoulders. My clenched my jaw. Eden widened her eyes and opened her mouth as if she wanted to say something, but didn't.

I turned back around and aimed at the third platform, all the anger in my body seeming to collect in my hand as I threw that beanbag as hard as I could. Silence surrounded me as the bag made contact with the three smaller bags and they all flew off in different directions, the larger beanbag plowing through them and hitting the back wall. There was a second of silence before a loud groan came from the wood of the booth wall and it wobbled and then crashed backward, landing on the ground with a loud thud.

I stood frozen for several seconds, and then the little girl in front of me whose mouth was hanging open moved slowly to the wreath Eden had requested and silently took it down and held it out to me.

I took it from her and turned around. Eden was standing there with her hand over her mouth and her eyes shining with laughter and delight. And Hector stood behind her, his face a red mask of anger.

I handed the wreath to Eden slowly, and she took it from my hand, her skin brushing mine as she blinked up at me. I tore my eyes away from her and met Hector's irate gaze. "Father," I said, bowing my head and turning away. I moved past the booth, where two men were already reassembling the wall, and pushed through the crowd. Xander jogged to my side and walked with me silently until we got to my cabin, where I put my hands on my lower hips and paced in front of it.

"You impulsive *fool*," Xander said, glaring at me. "Calling attention to yourself and Eden when we're planning to leave? Are you *stupid*? Now you probably just made it that much harder. Did you see the look on his face? You threatened him."

"He had his hands on her," I gritted out.

Xander moved closer, his face right in front of mine.

"Yeah, he did. He plans to *marry* her. He plans to have his hands all over her…*forever*. And you have to stop acting like a prideful idiot and ruining any chance we might have to get out of here with any ease."

I scrubbed a hand down my face. "You're right. I know you're right. I'm a fool." I sat down on my front step, bowed my head, and laced my fingers behind my neck. A couple seconds later I felt Xander sit down next to me.

We were both quiet for a few minutes before Xander spoke again. "I talked to Kristi. She says we need money, enough to last us three months or so, just long enough to get a job. She estimated three thousand."

I raised my head and looked at him incredulously. "Three thousand dollars?" I laughed. "Where are we supposed to get three thousand dollars?"

Xander shrugged. "I suppose that might be where Eden comes in. Surely the council members keep some money on them. She could start taking just a little, so they don't notice when she does it."

"Stealing again."

Xander let out an annoyed breath. "Do you have a better idea?"

I shook my head and squinted up at the sky. "No."

Xander was quiet for a minute. "Does Eden know how to count money?"

"*I* barely know how to count money. I mean, I know in theory but obviously not in practice."

Xander ground his foot into the dirt. "I don't know if we can risk bringing anyone else in Acadia into this."

"No, we can't." I thought for a minute. "What about the Castle family? Think there'd be any way of contacting them?"

"Ah geez, I don't know," Xander said, running his hand through his hair.

Bob, Tina, and Melissa Castle were a family that had come to live with us several years ago and then one day, in the middle of the night, they'd taken their things and left, right after Bob Castle had been punished by Hector for insolence. I never knew what the "insolence" was exactly, but Hector talked about those who weren't righteous would never feel comfortable in Acadia and would be lured back out into the sinful society, as had happened with the Castle family. But I wondered if the Castle family would have another story to tell. Who knew if we could even trust them? My brain was all scrambled most of the time these days. The only people I knew for sure I could trust with my very life were Eden and Xander.

"They might not help anyway," I said. "I never knew them very well."

Xander sighed. "Let's see what Eden says about the money situation up at the main lodge. One step at a time, okay?"

"Yeah. Okay."

"And no more stupid, jealousy-fueled stunts with Hector. In fact, you might be wise to apologize to him."

I grimaced. "I'm not sorry."

"Fine. But at least pretend you are."

I tensed my jaw as I pictured him bringing Eden's knuckle up to his lips again. But Xander was right. If I wanted to get her away from him, I needed to be smarter.

As it turned out, I didn't have to go to Hector on my own to offer an apology. The next morning, he summoned me to the main lodge.

CHAPTER THIRTEEN
Eden

The morning after the festival, Hailey woke me early with the message that Hector wanted to see me after breakfast. I sat up in bed, rubbing the sleep from my eyes, feeling a nervous flutter in my belly. "Did he say why?"

Hailey shook her head, opened my closet, and pulled out my clothes. She laid my skirt at the end of my bed and then sat down. I propped my pillows behind me so I was sitting up too.

Hailey studied me for a few seconds and then looked down at her hands. "Your wedding is drawing near, Eden." She paused as if uncomfortable. "Hector would like me to educate you on the details of your wifely duties. He instructed me to do it as soon as possible."

I froze, her meaning immediately clear, and a feeling of dread raced down my spine. I took a deep breath. I would never be Hector's bride. Calder was going to take me away from here before that could happen.

But I could use the lesson, couldn't I? I wanted to know all the ways to please a man. I wanted to know all the ways to please *Calder* without him having to show me himself.

"Please do," I said softly.

Hailey glanced at me and her cheeks turned pink. Before she looked away, I thought I saw distress flash in her eyes.

"A woman doesn't *enjoy* these things, Eden, but a mistress or a wife performs them anyway. Do you understand?"

I shook my head. "No," I whispered. "Doesn't Hector bring you pleasure?" I felt my own face fill with heat and knew my cheeks were flushed too.

Hailey pursed her lips. She took one of my hands in hers and said, "It is not always unpleasant, and you shouldn't fear it. But only a loose, impure woman takes pleasure for herself. You should focus on your husband only."

I frowned. Was I loose and impure? I must be, for I had surely enjoyed pleasures of the flesh with Calder. In fact, *enjoy* might be an understatement. I *loved* pleasures of the flesh. My body was tingling just thinking about them.

Hailey took a deep breath. "Things happen to a man when he is aroused. You'll know he wants you in bed when he…hardens."

I lowered my gaze demurely. I already knew that. And the thought of it alone, of Calder…*hardened*, sent a bolt of electricity between my legs.

"He will then want you to touch him, with your hand and with your mouth." The last word came out as a squeak and my eyes widened.

"My *mouth*?" I whispered, incredulous. Calder had used his mouth on me, but I was expected to use my mouth on him too? "What do I do with it?" I asked.

Hailey let out a short, hysterical-sounding laugh, her blush deepening. "Well, uh, you put it in your mouth and you…uh"—she let out another small laugh—"*suck* on it."

"*Really?*" I whispered. I liked it when Calder used his

mouth on me, so would he like it if I used my mouth on him? I wanted to squirm with the increased tingles, but I held myself still.

"I know it sounds absolutely terrible and awful, but you'll get used to it."

"Oh yes, awful," I whispered again.

Hailey cleared her throat. "So, uh, then he'll put his hardened manhood between your legs and *enter* your body. The first time will hurt and you'll bleed, but after that, it will be okay. Do you understand?" Hailey looked like she wanted to flee.

I kept imagining Calder naked with me, his tight muscles and handsome face clear in my mind's eye. I swallowed again, flushed all over, and became wet between my legs. Yes, I understood. And I wanted it. I wanted it right that very second. I wanted Calder in my bed, putting his *manhood* between my legs. Surely I was loose and impure. And I didn't care.

Hailey stood up and took a deep, shaky breath, inching toward the door. "We'll discuss this more before your wedding night, of course. And if you have questions... well..."

"Thank you, Hailey," I said. "You've been very helpful."

I had asked Calder to make love to me, not knowing exactly what that was. But now I ached for it. I felt dizzy with wanting.

I stood under the warm spray of the shower, thinking about what Hailey had told me. When Calder made love to me, he would enter my body. Goose bumps erupted on my flesh at the thought alone. I washed myself slowly, cleaning between my legs, and as I did so, I slipped the very tip of my finger inside my opening as Calder had done. Heat bloomed over my skin and my nipples puckered. My finger felt snug and squeezed. How would Calder's manhood…*fit*?

I heard voices and footsteps outside the door to the bathroom, so I finished my shower quickly and then got dressed. I ate breakfast and walked to Hector's office as he had requested, and smiled meekly at him when he opened the door and ushered me in. My mind was too focused on Calder's *manhood* to be nervous about the reason Hector might want to see me, and so when I walked inside and saw Calder standing in front of the fireplace, I didn't catch my expression soon enough. Calder's eyes widened in warning and I startled, realizing that a goofy grin was plastered all over my face. I went serious, but not before Hector turned from the door and caught me staring joyfully at Calder. I bent my head and chewed on my lip but when I glanced up, a storm was passing over Hector's face and then he, too, schooled his expression as he walked over to his desk and stood behind it.

"Please," he motioned to Calder, "sit down. Eden, you may remain standing." Hector's voice was cold and a chill moved up my spine. I clasped my hands in front of me and stood still, waiting to see what was going to happen.

Calder moved cautiously toward the chair in front of Hector's desk and sat down.

Hector shook his head. "No, I meant sit down on the floor, not the chair."

Calder looked confused and glanced uncertainly at the chair in front of him. "I'm sorry, Father, I don't—"

"Kneel on the floor, Water Bearer. You'll understand when I explain it to you," Hector commanded.

Calder narrowed his eyes. His hands flexed and unflexed. But he glanced at me quickly and then paused before pushing the chair aside and kneeling on the floor in front of Hector's desk. My stomach clenched in fear, but I raised my chin and looked unflinchingly at Calder. Hector was meaning to humiliate him in front of me but I wouldn't be embarrassed. I understood this was about the festival. This was about Calder showing Hector up in front of his people.

Hector focused on the objects on his desk, seeming to suddenly notice something distressing about them. He rearranged them and then frowned, putting them back the way they'd been. Then he frowned again, straightened them all, using his arm to line them up perfectly.

Calder and I glanced between each other and then back to Hector. Hector suddenly furrowed his brows and took one of the objects, a glass statue of a woman, and threw it at the fireplace so it shattered loudly. I gasped and Calder's alarmed gaze shot to me.

Hector sat back, his lips tipped up in a small smile. He took a deep breath and looked at Calder, continuing as if nothing strange had just happened.

"I see you've noticed how very beautiful my blessed one is," Hector said slowly.

Calder simply regarded him for several beats. "Yes, Father, you're a lucky man."

Hector regarded him coldly. "Yes, I am a lucky man. I have the gods to thank for that. I have the gods to thank for Eden."

Calder waited, not seeming to move a muscle. I glanced between the two of them.

Finally, Hector continued, "It's understandable you would notice Eden's beauty. But things will be made difficult for you if you think to take it further than that. Am I clear?"

"Yes, of course, Father," Calder said.

Hector studied him, seeming to consider his sincerity

before he went on. "Good, that's good. Now, Water Bearer, I can tell you're an ambitious boy. Your"—he waved his hand around dismissively—"system thing, was not pleasing to the gods, but"—he sat down in his large black leather chair—"you have always served me well as my cupbearer." He looked at Calder thoughtfully. "I can see a promotion in that same capacity could serve us both well. And so from today on, you'll be my *personal* cup bearer, serving not just the temple but me as well."

Calder's expression didn't change. "Thank you, Father. What is it I'll be expected to do in this capacity?"

Hector leaned back in his chair, steepling his fingers. "You'll serve me when I require it. If I need something, you'll fetch it. And you'll kneel before me to do it."

Calder's eyes flashed at Hector and I flinched. For several long seconds, they stared at each other. Finally, Calder said slowly, not breaking eye contact, "Thank you for your faith in me, Father. It will be my pleasure to serve you."

Hector tapped his fingers together, regarding him. "Yes. The gods will be pleased with your sacrifice, as am I. It will serve to make you more holy, to further wash the sin from your soul. You may stand."

Calder stood, looking powerful as he straightened his lean but muscled body. I resisted the urge to drag my eyes up and down him. I thought it safer to bow my head.

"In order to best serve me, you'll need to move to the main lodge," Hector said, standing as well.

Calder looked shocked for a second before replying, "Of course, Father. Should I pack my things?"

"What things would those be?"

"I suppose…nothing much. A change of clothes."

Hector waved his hand. "If you want. There isn't

186

anywhere to store anything in the back room, but bring what you like."

My mouth fell open. The back room was where the laundry machines were and where the dogs slept. I snapped my lips together and looked down again so as not to reveal any emotion.

"There's no bed, either. I trust you can make do," Hector went on.

"I'm used to making do."

Hector regarded him. "Yes. The sacrifice of my workers is most pleasing."

Calder didn't answer.

Hector waved his hand toward the door as if shooing him. "You're dismissed. Gather your things and return here. You will follow me and attend to my requests beginning today."

"Yes, Father." Calder turned and headed toward the door but not before making momentary eye contact with me. I held it until he had passed and then looked back at Hector, who was straightening things on his desk again.

"Eden, do you know why I called you in here while I spoke to my new server?"

I shook my head. "No, Father."

"Because, Eden, it is my job to help that boy. I want you to understand the order the gods have ordained. There are workers, and there are leaders. I am a leader, as are you. We must trust in the gods in their ultimate wisdom and not try to change that which has been foretold. Satan attempts to alter our course by averting our attention from the ways of the gods. But we must not listen. Dire consequences will rain down if we are swayed. Do you understand?"

"Yes, Father."

"Good." Hector stood and came to me, cupped my face in his hands, and gazed down into my eyes. "My princess, I've waited so long for you. Nothing must get in the way. Satan will try his hardest now that our union is so very near. You must ignore all temptations."

"Yes, Father."

Hector let out a breath and then leaned forward and planted his lips on mine. I froze, pressing my lips together. After a minute, Hector leaned back up, disappointment in his expression. "Has Hailey spoken to you yet?"

"About what, Father?" I hedged.

"About the marriage bed."

I cleared my throat. "A little," I said, averting my eyes.

Hector nodded. "Good, that's good. Soon, so very soon. I feel as if I've waited a lifetime for you, my love. If only the foretelling…" He frowned, glancing away for a moment. "But we must follow the instructions of the gods, not our own selfish wants." He studied me for a moment longer and then released my face. "You may go, Eden. And I want you to increase your Holy Book reading, especially the section on temptation and sacrifice."

"Yes, Father," I repeated, backing away toward the door. When I was almost there, I turned and exited quickly, shutting the door behind me, releasing the breath I'd been holding for far too long.

Calder was moving into the main lodge. And all I could feel was dread. Xander's words came back to me. *There's a storm coming.*

The next day at Temple, I walked in with the other council members and sat down in my usual chair. Calder walked

188

behind Hector, Hector's appointed slave. He didn't use the word, but it was obvious that's what it was: a method to humiliate Calder. Anger and defiance battled the fear inside me at what Hector would do to make our lives more unbearable before we could leave. We needed to be careful, I knew that, and I was well practiced in that role. But seeing Calder degraded by Hector made me want to stand up and declare my love for Calder in Temple, right in front of everyone. My love for Calder would serve as a mighty sword against Hector. There was nothing he could do to fight that, nothing he could do to enslave that. It was true and untouchable and it was ours.

Hector signaled to Calder, and Calder kept his face blank as he kneeled on the floor to the left of the last council member. I bowed my head as Hector took his place at the podium and leaned forward, waiting as the people quieted. The council members bowed their heads and closed their eyes.

Something blue caught my eye, and I turned my head slightly to look just under my seat, where a lone morning glory sat. I bit my lip not to smile as I shifted my gaze over to Calder and saw he was turned slightly toward me and he saw the morning glory too. So why did he appear confused? I watched as he turned toward the audience to where Xander was standing. Xander winked at him quickly and then bowed his head and closed his eyes too.

My eyes met Calder's again, and he shot me a very small, covert smile before he, too, bowed his head.

"My people," Hector said, his deep baritone commanding attention. He moved from behind his podium and stood quietly in front of the congregation for a good minute before speaking again. "Today, I am going to talk about disobedience and then I'm going to perform the water purification of one of my beloved workers, the boy who has served as my cup bearer since he was old enough to follow instruction. Calder Raynes."

My eyes darted to Calder and his face showed a brief moment of surprise before he frowned. I looked back out to the people, all eyes now on Calder.

Hector turned and paced for a minute, his finger on his lips as if he was deep in thought. Finally he stopped and looked up. "The gods love us, just as I love you. But we must remember that although the gods bring us the gently flowing river, so do they bring us the violent thunderstorm that stirs up the waters of the sea." Hector paused, looking around. "The storm may be violent, the storm may cause wreckage, but ultimately..." Hector paused again, pivoting on his foot to turn and look at the other side of the room. "Ultimately, the point of the storm is to show you where you've gone wrong and to guide you once again to peaceful waters."

The doors to the temple opened and two younger worker boys carried a large white tub down the main aisle and set it gently on the floor. Calder had always been part of the ritual of filling the baptismal tub in the past. I didn't recognize the two boys who did it now, although they must have known Calder, as they eyed him with admiration. After several trips with large jugs, the tub was mostly filled.

Hector motioned to Calder to step forward, and Calder did, rising to his full height and walking over to Hector, where he stood next to him in front of the tub. Hector was a tall man, but Calder stood just an inch or so taller. Something inside me took satisfaction in that. Perhaps it was the knowledge Calder outmeasured Hector not only in inner qualities but quite literally as well.

"Kneel," Hector said coldly.

A shiver moved down my spine despite the warm temperature in the temple.

Calder went down on his knees in front of the tub and bowed his head over the water.

"Beloved gods!" Hector boomed, raising his hands. "Those who believe in your goodness and your never-ending power shall be saved and cleansed of their sins!" He took ahold of the hair at the back of Calder's head. "Calder Raynes, you have been educated in the ways and truths of the gods and instructed into obedience to them. Through your life, you will avoid evil, acknowledge your faith, and fulfill the promise to always serve the gods and *only* the gods. As you are purified by water, so your heart and soul are washed clean of whatever is displeasing to the gods."

Hector pushed roughly on Calder's head and plunged his face into the water and held him there.

"Calder Raynes, do you desire to obtain eternal life in Elysium, serving among the gods?"

I waited for Hector to bring Calder's head up from the water, but when he didn't, my heart picked up in speed and my gaze flew around the congregation. No one else seemed to be wondering what was going on. I looked back at Calder, anxiety settling in my chest.

"Calder Raynes, do you vow to love the gods with all your heart, mind, and soul?" He paused, again not bringing Calder's head up.

I stared at Calder's kneeling frame, my eyes wide, my hands clenching and unclenching in my lap.

"Calder Raynes, will you live in such a way that will daily be pleasing to the gods and always serve them before yourself? *Before yourself?*" he repeated loudly.

My nerves turned into flapping wings of fear as Hector still held Calder's head submerged in the water.

"Calder Raynes," he paused, looking around slowly, still gripping Calder's hair, "do you promise to cast off the powers of darkness, which often will seek to steer you from the truth and the wisdom of the gods?"

I scooted to the edge of my chair, a lump rising in my throat. How long could someone hold their breath underwater? Panic twisted between my ribs. If Calder struggled, would Hector let him up? *Why isn't he struggling?* Had he quietly drowned?

"Let us pray!" Hector boomed.

He bowed his head, as did everyone else. If they noticed Calder had been underwater for far too long, no one said a word.

"Gods, banish all sin, selfishness, and evil from this boy. Take the darkness from his heart and deliver grace and righteousness into his soul. Let the water purify him today and forever, so this boy may become a man." He kept his head bowed, eyes closed. My body trembled with the need to stand up and scream, every muscle primed to attack Hector before Calder drowned right in front of us.

But just as I started to move, Hector raised his hand, bringing Calder's head out of the water, droplets flying out in every direction. I could just see the side of Calder's face as he drew in a huge breath, kneeling back up, a beautiful smile spreading across his face.

I gaped.

Hector walked to Calder's side and seemed to falter slightly but regained his balance. His voice seemed just a note weaker than it had as he gazed down at Calder, a look that was a mix between anger and confusion.

"Do you forsake Satan?" he boomed.

"I do, Father," Calder said, his voice strong and clear.

"And all his evildoings? All his temptations?"

"I do, Father."

"Do you renounce the wicked lusts of the flesh and of the eyes?"

"I do renounce the wicked lusts of the flesh and of the eyes, Father."

"Do you promise to love the holy way of the gods?"

"I do, Father."

I watched as water dripped down Calder's hair and face, the droplets wetting his shirt and causing it to cling to his muscles. There was something fierce and happy on his face and I couldn't guess what he was thinking. It was as if water was his element and it had not only cleansed him but also empowered him. I sat confused, still fearful, but *proud*.

"Then I pronounce you purified, made new. You are strong and clean. Depart in peace. Go forth in holiness."

Calder stood slowly, smiling at the congregation as they peered at him. He walked back to the place next to the last council member, where he knelt again.

As the two young worker boys came to collect the tub and take it away, I couldn't help but notice that the one with black hair and light blue eyes looked at Calder as if he were a god himself.

That night, I lay in my bed picturing Calder downstairs, lying in that small room, sharing a bed with the house dogs. I tried to focus on my own anger at the injustice of the situation, but my mind kept going back to the picture of him, lying there, no shirt on, the moonlight shining on his golden skin. He was so very near to me.

I wanted to speak to him about the fact that he now lived here. I wanted to ask him about what had happened during his water purification, what he'd been thinking, if he'd been as scared as I had been. He was my best friend and I longed to talk to him.

I tossed and turned for a while longer. Hector's plan was to keep Calder close so he could monitor his every move. But would he expect me to be so bold as to seek him out in the night, especially after he had just been cleansed? I knew Hailey was in Hector's room tonight. Perhaps she was keeping him busy.

My feet touched the floor seemingly before my mind had even directed them to. Apparently, my body knew what it wanted, even if my brain wasn't certain it was such a wise idea.

I put the blanket at the end of my bed under my quilt and formed it into a semihuman shape and then tiptoed to my door and opened it very quietly. I peered down the hall, and when I saw no one was there, I snuck out and closed the door behind me. I had to walk past Hector's room to get to the large stairway, and when I got there, I paused and listened. I heard a masculine grunt and the very soft noise of what sounded like skin slapping against skin. I hurried past it to the top of the stairs.

Somewhere in the next wing, I heard soft voices. I moved quickly down the stairway and across the large expanse of the two-story living room. I darted through the empty kitchen and down the back hallway until I stood outside the laundry room, my heart thundering in my chest. Everything was utterly quiet now.

I turned the doorknob very slowly and it opened on a quiet squeak. I paused, and when no other sound came from anywhere in the house, I pulled the door wider and slipped inside. A hand went over my mouth and an arm came around my waist, Calder's narrowed gaze meeting mine. He let out a harsh exhale and removed his hand from my mouth.

"Are you crazy?" he demanded in a harsh whisper.

I threw my arms around his neck and buried my face at his throat and inhaled his delicious scent. I nodded yes to answer his question.

He let out a small grunt and brought his arms around me. I leaned back and whispered, "It's making me crazy that you're so close but so far away. I couldn't sleep. I—"

His mouth came down on mine and he kissed me passionately, as if to tell me he had been feeling the same way.

After a few minutes, he broke away from my lips and put his forehead to mine. "Eden, we can't risk this. Hector's... I don't know. Like we talked about, he's different. I don't know if it's just what he's seen between us, or something that happened on his pilgrimage, or something more. But if we're going to get out of here, we have to be so careful."

"I know. Calder, what happened today? I was so worried about you. I thought you would drown. I didn't know what to do."

He put a finger to my lips. "I was fine. I'll fight if I need to, I promise. But you have to trust I'll know when that's necessary and when it's not, all right?"

I nodded and he smiled again. "Good." He looked over my shoulder for a minute and then back at me. "Today, Eden, when my head was under that water and I could just make out Hector's words, I..." He paused for a minute, seeming to collect his thoughts. "I don't know, this feeling of peace filled me, like I was being told everything was going to be okay. It was as if the gods weren't cruel or judgmental like Hector wants us to believe. I felt this feeling of *acceptance*. I felt like they were offering me strength to get out of here, to make a life for us. It's hard to explain. Do I sound oxygen-deprived? Do *I* sound crazy?"

I smiled and shook my head. "No. What you're saying is the first rational-sounding thing I've ever heard. I think it was the God of Mercy whispering to you."

Calder chuckled. "It made it more clear to me that we need to get out of here as soon as possible. And that's why"—he kissed my lips softly—"you can't be down here."

"I know. I'll go in a minute. I just…I need you so much, Calder. I want you. I want all of you. And I want you to have all of me. I want you…inside of me." My eyes widened and so did his. "Maybe if you took me, and we told Hector… he'd *make* us leave. He'd throw us out."

"Shh, Eden," Calder said, smoothing my hair. "I'm not taking your virginity when it has anything to do with Hector at all. And if Hector made us leave today, we'd have to come begging back by morning." He gave his head a shake. "When we leave, it has to be for good."

I nodded and he took my hand and led me to a blanket and a flat pillow that was lying on the ground under the window. Two dogs, overly friendly mutts that did nothing more than raise their heads and moan softly, lay on dog beds in front of the large washing machine, beds far more plush than what Calder had been given.

We sat down on the blanket and Calder lay back, bring-ing me with him so I was lying against his bare chest. I turned my nose into his skin and inhaled.

"I've always slept on the floor. This is no hardship for me. In fact, see this," Calder said, pointing his finger out the window. "Now, I have a perfect view of the moon and the city lights. I've never slept next to a window before. I've never had cool air that came right out of vents in the floor," he said, gesturing over to the other side of the room. "Soon, we're going to be out in that city, under that same moon." He wrapped both arms around me and pulled me tightly against him. "And when you go back to your room tonight, I'll know I'm closer to you than I was yesterday, and my bed will have your sweet scent all over it." He smiled down at me and leaned forward and kissed my forehead.

"On the floor with dogs or in a bed fit for a king," I whispered back, "I'd choose you, Calder. I'd sleep on a bed of nails if it meant I was touching you."

"Don't give Hector any ideas."

I laughed softly. "I mean it. I would." I leaned up on one elbow so I could see his face better. "Do you think there's a life out there for us? One where we can be happy and...free?"

Calder paused for a few beats. "I'm going to *make* a life for us out there. A place for you and me. But until then, yes, I'm going to believe that there is."

I put my leg over his and snuggled into him again. "Someday we're going to sleep every night like this." I tilted my head, so I could gaze up at him.

"Yes," he agreed. The look on his face was so serious as he pushed a piece of hair off of my cheek. "I love you, Eden."

My heart soared. "I love you too," I whispered.

We lay there together, silent, the words *I love you* seeming to float in the air above me like silent music. *He loves me. Calder Raynes loves me.* I'd always been referred to as *the blessed one,* but for the first time in my life I truly felt like it was true. After a few minutes, I leaned up and sighed. "I better get back."

He nodded. "If anyone sees you, tell them you were in the kitchen. They probably won't believe you, but—"

I sat up on my knees. "I won't let anyone see me." I hesitated for a second. "I hate watching him treat you the way he is."

"It's okay. He's using me to prove a point to the rest of the people. As long as I know you're strong, I can play his game. I have to know you're not worrying about me, though, okay?"

"Okay."

Calder frowned. "I don't like sending you out of here not knowing you'll get back to your room safely." He sat up and we both stood together. Calder leaned in and kissed me softly on my lips. "When you get back to your room, look out your window up at the moon. I'll be looking at it from here." He smoothed a piece of hair away from my face. "As long as we're both under the same moon, we'll always find a way to each other. The God of Mercy wouldn't have it any other way."

I leaned in and kissed his lips one last time. "Good night."

"Good night, Morning Glory."

I opened the door quietly and slipped through it and then snuck quietly through the great room and up the stairs. When I got to the top, Hector's door suddenly started opening and I ducked quickly into the room across from his, an empty guest room. I plastered myself up against the wall, my heart beating triple time. If Hector went down the hall to my room, would he look in and see me gone?

I heard Hailey say something from inside Hector's room and his voice answering as he moved back inside. I peeked around the corner and saw that his door was still open. I tiptoed hurriedly past it and down the hall to my own room where I opened the door and closed it quickly and quietly behind me, releasing my breath on a loud exhale.

I threw back the covers and removed the quilt and got in. Not two seconds later, my door opened and light from the hallway flooded in. I opened one eye just enough to see Hector's outline standing in my doorway. I continued to pretend to sleep. After a long minute, my door closed and I heard his retreating footsteps. I rolled onto my back, attempting to get my wild heartbeat under control. A shiver moved down my spine. I'd taken a huge risk. Still, I couldn't help feeling thankful for the small amount of time I'd had with Calder. And thankful I hadn't been caught.

I turned over in bed and looked out my window, my heart slowing into a peaceful rhythm as I stared at that full moon I knew Calder was gazing at too.

CHAPTER FOURTEEN
Calder

The next morning, I woke when the rising sun hit my eyes through the uncovered window next to my bed. I groggily made my way outside, through the back door, where dew was still glistening on the ground. It'd burn off in the next hour or so, and no one who slept later than five thirty would ever know it had been there at all.

I went to the river, where Hector still insisted I bathe. I knelt on the bank and used my hand to bring the water over my head and behind my neck, and then shook my head like a dog, sending water droplets into the air to land back in the water in a mini rainstorm. I used my shirt to blot the remaining water from my face and neck and then started toward the outhouse all the way at the back of where the worker cabins sat, about a quarter of a mile away. But first, I took a moment to look back up at the main lodge behind me. No one would be up for at least an hour. Per Hector's rules, I had been trekking back and forth to the outhouse since I'd moved up to the main lodge, but who would know if I used the small bathroom all the way at the back of the house?

The main lodge was still and quiet as I made my way to the small bathroom I'd only glimpsed on my way to the laundry room. The door made a tiny click as I closed it behind me as softly as possible and then looked around. There was no shower in here, just a toilet and a sink. I had never used indoor plumbing before, but it was easy enough to figure out what was what. Plus, I'd heard often enough the things others who had come from the big community missed once they were living in the worker cabins. I could see why. I turned the handle on the sink and startled slightly when water came streaming out and then turned the handle up, watching the water flow more quickly. I let it run for a minute, just watching it and marveling at how much easier something like this would make life in general. As I watched the water run, I thought about that ridiculous irrigation system I had made to water our crops. As much as Hector talked about sacrifice and living off the land, he had probably been laughing inside at the simple stupidity of what I had come up with. Suddenly, that irrigation system seemed utterly ridiculous as I pictured myself down by the river hollowing out logs for months and months, my muscles burning and the sun beating down on my head. I started laughing, as silently as possible, leaning on the sink as I got ahold of my hilarity. I was laughing, but I had to. It was either that or cry in humiliation.

Once I'd reined in my laughter, I simply watched the water flow for another minute and then quietly shut it off.

The running water made me realize how much I needed to empty my bladder, so I used the toilet and then pushed down on the small silver handle. Water swirled and washed down the drain and then refilled as I stood there staring down at it like some neanderthal who was seeing the modern world for the first time. Which, in actuality, was probably pretty accurate. I flushed it again, marveling once more as the water swirled and drained.

As I stood there, it hit me what stepping out into the big community was going to be like for me. If I was rendered incredulous by the workings of a toilet and sink, what was it going to be like to take in the many new and overwhelming things all at one time? It wouldn't be the same for Eden—at the very least, she'd lived with running water and electricity her whole life. And it was going to be my job to take care of her, protect her. I was probably going to look like a bumbling fool. Heat flushed through my body when I realized how unprepared Hector had left us to make any choice for our lives other than to live here, in Acadia, for the rest of our days.

I leaned against the sink, picturing Eden's trusting eyes, which served to cool my anger, a sense of purpose returning. It'd be overwhelming, yes, but I wouldn't let Hector decide the course of my life anymore. If the great floods really did come, I'd be washed away, but at least I'd be washed away in possession of my own freedom, and Eden would be washed away with hers too. And wherever we ended up—in Elysium or in hell—*we'd end up together.*

I used the soap to wash my hands, rubbing the silky liquid between my palms and watching the bubbles form. The only soap I had ever used was a homemade concoction of herbs and oils, and it never lathered like this. I dried my hands slowly as I studied myself in the mirror. We didn't have mirrors in our home—vanity was sinful—so I had rarely seen my own reflection. I studied myself now, turning my face in different angles, touching the dark stubble on my jaw, and moving closer to examine my teeth. I took good care of my teeth, always cleaning them well with a rough cloth and salt, and chewing on mint leaves. I was lucky they were white and straight like Eden's. Not everyone here in Acadia was as lucky in the teeth department.

I opened the door quietly and then closed it behind me. As I was turning, a male voice said, "Breaking the rules already? How disappointing."

I whirled around and Clive Richter, one of the council members, was standing there, a smug look on his seedy face. I didn't particularly like any of the council members, although I'd had little personal interaction with any of them, but Clive seemed to be the most unlikable of them all. He sat up in front at Temple week after week, trying to hide his yawns and checking something in his pocket repeatedly, while looking disdainfully at the workers. I didn't know if anyone else noticed, but I did. Clearly Clive Richter had a very high opinion of himself and a pretty low opinion of the rest of us.

"It was an emergency."

Clive laughed mockingly. "You can return to your own…lodgings and take care of your emergencies there."

"In the future, I will," I said tightly, and went to move around him.

Clive grabbed my arm and I stopped suddenly, moving my head slowly to look at his hand holding tightly to my forearm. I looked down at him, about six inches shorter than me, and narrowed my eyes. This man, who probably in any other arena on the face of the earth would never dare to touch me, thought he could overpower me here.

I grabbed his arm and whirled him around, bending it

behind his back the way Xander and I play fought when we were kids—only I wasn't playing this time. He choked out a sound of pain and I leaned in to speak right against his ear. "Don't. Touch. Me." I leaned in even closer. "Ever. Again."

Clive let out a small pained laugh, so I bent his arm up just a little more and he cried out, "Okay, okay, let me go."

I pushed him roughly away from me, and when he turned around, his face was red with rage. "You'll be sorry for trying to make me look like a fool," he gritted out.

"Probably," I said. "But even if I'm punished, it was worth it. And you were a fool long before I came along anyway." I pushed him aside as I passed him and returned to "my" room, where I waited for Hector to summon me like the dog he apparently thought me to be.

———

The rain started falling a few minutes after I'd returned to the laundry room, large drops that spattered against the windowpane next to my bed. I put my hands in my pockets and looked out the window, wondering how I'd protect Eden from the rain once we left this place.

My thoughts were interrupted suddenly when the sound of a wailing alarm started up on the loudspeaker outside of the main lodge.

It was a flood drill.

My body tensed and I opened the door and moved into the hall. People were already leaving the main lodge; all the council members and their families were heading quickly to the front door.

Hector stood in the large main room, smiling serenely and reassuring people as they passed by him. "Don't be concerned. The gods are protecting us. This is only a drill

204

so we're prepared when the floods come. Rest assured, be calm."

I looked for Eden but didn't see her anywhere. Maybe she'd already left the lodge. I moved toward the front door when Hector's voice boomed out, "Calder Raynes."

I clenched my jaw and turned around slowly.

"I require your services here, Water Bearer," Hector said.

I walked back to where he stood, people passing me as the last of them filed out the door, a little girl crying in her mother's arms.

"Yes, Father? What can I do for you?"

"You can wait here until you're sure everyone's gotten out safely," he said. "I need to go and reassure my bride-to-be. She must be frightened. She doesn't like small spaces."

I kept my expression blank and remained quiet. As if he knew one thing about Eden. He knew nothing. To him, she was only what he wanted her to be: a possession.

But I stood still and watched him as he walked away. He shut the door behind him, and I moved very quickly to the window and looked out to see him opening an umbrella and heading around the main lodge to the door that led to the large cellar belowground.

I moved quickly toward the council members' wing of the house and called out, "Anyone here? Flood drill." I paused and there was only silence and so I opened the first door I came to and peeked inside, calling out one more time, "Flood drill." Silence met me again and so I entered the room, glancing quickly behind me.

Immediately, I saw a dresser holding a wallet and walked to it quickly. Inside the wallet was money: three twenties, two fives, and seven ones. I hesitated momentarily, but then pulled out two of the twenties, one five and three of the ones.

My heart beat harshly against my ribs and adrenaline rushed through me.

I heard footsteps right outside the door and spun around. Duke, the larger of the two mutts came trotting into the room, whining at my hand for pets. I exhaled. "Hey, boy." I scratched his head for a minute, attempting to slow my heart rate.

I stuffed the money in my pocket and returned the wallet to the dresser top and left the room, closing the door behind me. I did a similar search of several of the other rooms, coming away with three more twenties, three tens, and twelve more ones.

I had been bold in my stealing, but we needed to leave this place as quickly as possible. I was willing to risk someone questioning their missing money if it meant Eden, Xander, and I could leave that much sooner. No one could prove it was me.

As I was passing through the kitchen, I saw a plastic bag on the counter holding some crackers. I emptied the crackers into the garbage and put the money into the bag.

I started to head toward the front door when I noticed that Hector's office door was slightly cracked open. I hesitated for just seconds and then turned and entered the large room. I went immediately to Hector's desk and opened the drawers one by one, looking for cash. I didn't find any and I touched nothing. Everything in his drawers was lined up, just as everything on top of his desk was, and I didn't want to disturb anything. He was strange when it came to the order of his things, constantly adjusting items over and over.

I went to the large filing cabinet by the window and tried to open the drawers. They were locked though, all except the one on the very bottom. I hesitated, stilling for a moment and listening, thinking I may have heard something. After a silent minute, I pulled the drawer open and saw only files. I tilted my head to read the tabs and saw that each council member's name, all six of them, were spelled out. I frowned and started rifling through the paperwork. At the front of each file was a newspaper clipping. I brought the first one out, for council member Rodney Sarber. I scanned the article briefly and saw it was about how Rodney had run a large ministry in Kansas City, where he apparently had been embezzling money from his own church. The article told of the scandal that had followed and showed a tearful picture of Sarber being led away in handcuffs. I put the article back and rifled through the other folders, intending on reading the other articles, when I heard the same noise outside Hector's office again. I closed the drawer quietly and tiptoed to the door, where I opened it and strode out as if I had every reason to be in there. The man himself, Rodney Sarber, was standing outside Hector's office. He looked surprised when he saw me. "What are you doing here?" he asked suspiciously.

"Hector asked me to check the lodge to make sure everyone was out," I said calmly.

"In his office?"

I shrugged. "Just being thorough."

His eyes narrowed but then he nodded. "Go on, then, I'll be behind you."

I'm sure you won't be, you damn coward.

I headed out the front door and put the baggie of money under a rock on the side of the house where Xander and I had once sat waiting to see Eden for the first time so many years ago.

The heavy concrete door to the cellar squeaked open when I pulled it, and I walked down the five steps to where everyone was waiting, bodies pressed against bodies in the space that didn't quite fit two hundred people. Workers were segregated in one section, while the council members and their families gathered near Hector, who was standing on a small platform at the back of the space. Next to him was a storage room that held food items being preserved for the winter.

This space was built so we would all be together when the floods came, none of us being washed away. We would all hold hands as the water finally broke through the ceiling and began filling up the belowground rooms. We shouldn't be afraid—paradise waited. We would be led to Elysium by Hector and Eden, where we would all look down on the earth as it began again, rulers of the new humans.

And I couldn't do anything now except hope it was all a great big lie. And yet the very thought brought not only hope but grief and anger too. I had believed once, hadn't I? And now the lie felt cruel and intentional, meant to harm me and rob me of a life.

As I stood there in the throng of bodies, I felt like I was spinning. The only sounds were of rain outside, restless children, and a few crying babies. I looked around for Eden and finally spotted her next to Hailey, to the right of Hector.

I was taller than most of the people around me, so when I craned my neck, Eden spotted me and smiled, glancing quickly in Hector's direction. I followed her glance and saw Hector was looking at her and then looked over at me when Eden did. We both quickly looked away, and when I glanced back at Hector several minutes later, his stony face was still focused in my direction.

I stood taller, responding in an instinctual way to what felt like a male threat, even from across a very, very crowded room. The hairs on my neck bristled and I worked to keep my breathing steady. So many bodies were between Eden and me. I'd have no way to get to her if I needed to.

I looked around for my own family but couldn't see them in the crowd. This couldn't be good for Maya's health. I hoped, at the very least, she wasn't scared. I had always been next to her during these drills in the past, squeezing her hand three times after she squeezed mine.

Outside, the rain seemed to increase in intensity, as if great sheets of water were falling from the sky. The noises around me got quieter, all the people looking upward as if the ceiling over us would give any view of what was going on outside.

"The gods are simply testing our patience, our faith in them," Hector called out over the noise of the pounding rain. "Don't fear. This is what it will be like when the great floods come! All of us together, rejoicing because we are about to be led to the most glorious place imaginable. We *know* this is a drill because my blessed one hasn't yet become mine. Without that, we cannot be led to Elysium. Without that, we are not complete. Without that, we are not yet balanced."

Hector dropped his head and weaved slightly, a council member to the side of him reaching out to keep him steady. Hector pointed to a corner of the ceiling. "There. There is where the water will start trickling in." He closed his eyes again. "It will become a mighty gush very, very quickly, and the water will begin to fill this space." He raised his arms. "But we will not fear because we will feel the presence of the gods among us!" Then he dropped his arms and went silent, seeming to come back to himself as he simply stood waiting and looking around with a small satisfied smile on his face.

After what seemed like hours and hours but was probably

more like thirty minutes, the sound of the falling rain grew faint and it felt like we all let out a collective sigh of relief.

"You may open the door now," Hector called, and a man standing next to the staircase went up and pushed the heavy door open.

The people behind me pushed forward, and I walked out quickly and moved to the side. Everyone was eager to get out into the fresh air and the open space.

Everyone began walking toward the temple, for Hector always gave a sermon after a flood drill, and I followed behind them, knowing I'd be close to Eden soon, even if I did have to sit on the floor.

I went inside the temple and took my new place, kneeling at the side of the council members' chairs.

A few minutes later, Hector walked in with Eden on his arm. I tensed to see him touching her, repeating in my head *not long now, not long now* again and again until I could relax, picturing that money sitting under the rock in front of the main lodge.

Hector guided Eden to her chair, and then he walked to the podium, where he waited until everyone had entered the temple.

"My people," he began. "I know a flood drill isn't the most pleasant experience, but it always reminds me that someday very, very soon, we are all going to be standing in that space belowground, knowing the *real* flood is above us and the world is being scrubbed clean. It fills me with humility to think about the fact we, all of us here"—he waved his hand around—"have been chosen by the gods. We are *blessed*. And so these drills fill me with happiness, with pride, and with love for all of you."

Hector looked down. I couldn't see the expression on

his face well from where I was sitting, but I imagined that it looked thoughtful, intense.

"The gods have chosen me as your father, your protector, and your leader. Nothing fills me with more gratitude and honor than that." He paused again. "And yet, like any good father, I sometimes must correct the actions of my children, my family. In any obedient group, discipline must exist or there is no trust, no faith in the rules of how we must live. Yesterday, I told you about the gods creating the gentle river and the turbulent sea. Today, I must act on behalf of the gods and help one of our own find his way back to peaceful waters. Unfortunately, one of my children has lost his way, veered off the course the gods would have him take. Calder Raynes." Hector turned toward me and I looked back at him, unblinking. I looked out into the audience and my mother's hand was over her mouth and Maya's head was buried in my father's chest.

Hector continued to hold eye contact with me as he spoke to the congregation. "Despite the fact his baptism was just yesterday, Calder Raynes has committed the sin of selfishness and has disrespected a council member by using physical violence against him."

Hector turned to the crowd. "Is physical violence acceptable from one of the blessed people of the gods?"

"No, Father," the people said.

"No, no, it's not. Do we all feel safe here when there is an undisciplined person living among us?"

"No, Father."

"Does sin and disobedience harm us all?"

"Yes, Father."

"Yes. Yes, it does. And so it pains me, *it breaks my very heart*, but Calder must kneel on the punishment board for the rest of my sermon and then he must serve one day in the people's jail underground for his transgressions. This pains me as much as it will pain you, son, my once-trusted water bearer."

My vision clouded and I felt like I might lunge at Hector.

"Or perhaps," Hector went on, "you are so selfish that you'd have someone else bear your punishment for you? Perhaps"—he waved his arm out to the crowd—"perhaps your mother?"

I forced my expression to remain passive. "I take my punishment happily, Father," I said, my voice especially raspy, even to my own ears.

I sat there incredulous as Clive Richter stood to get the board, shooting me a triumphant glare as he walked past me, and then placed it on the floor to the right of Hector, where I was meant to kneel with my back to the people, in humiliation and shame. I felt sad my parents and Maya had to witness this and might believe the charges brought against me. But I couldn't feel shame about what I had done to Clive. I'd said I'd take my punishment happily, and I would.

CHAPTER FIFTEEN
Eden

Fear and horror gripped me as Calder stood slowly, his jaw tense and his eyes unreadable. He walked to the board and began to kneel on it. He paused in his movement, his eyes narrowing at something on the board and a confused look passing over his features. But I couldn't tell what he was seeing from where I was. His eyes moved to Clive Richter's and he stared at him as he kneeled, a very brief flash of pain moving across his face before it again went blank.

What is happening? I didn't understand.

I leaned forward, wanting so badly to go to him, but his eyes shot to mine, warning me to stay still. I clasped my hands in my lap and looked away miserably. His message was clear: if I said anything, I would only make it worse for him and for myself. I was helpless. I wanted to scream.

When I looked back at him again, my eyes widened in shock when I saw blood pooling on the metal beneath Calder's knees and shins. This form of punishment had been used before in the temple, but bleeding had never occurred.

Something was wrong. Something had been done to the mat to make it cause injury. And yet, Calder endured it, his back straight and his body unmoving, but I saw the sweat trickle down the side of his cheek. It was taking him great effort to kneel there, suffering, without it showing on his face. I didn't know if he held a look of cool indifference for me, for himself, or for the people around him, but clearly, it was costing him dearly. *Oh, Calder.*

For the next hour, I sat silently, tortured *inside*, while Calder kneeled in front of me, blood pooling until it ran off the metal and onto the tile floor of the stage as if in slow motion, the blood falling drip by drip echoing through the room during moments of silence. Hector preached on, quoting mostly from his own Holy Book about selfishness and Satan and those who commit sin. I heard only a few words here and there as I said my own prayers to the gods to be merciful, to send strength to Calder, to make the time pass more quickly for him.

Once we're out of here…once we're safe, I said to Calder in my mind, *I'm going to look at the scars that will surely be on your knees and your legs, remembering the bravery you showed while the wounds were forming, and I'm not going to feel sadness. I'm going to feel only one thing. Pride.*

When I came back to myself, Hector was saying the final prayer, the crowd speaking it along with him. I looked around at the people and saw many of them were looking uncomfortably toward Calder as the blood rolled slowly across the floor. I glared at the men—some of them much bigger and stronger than Hector. *This is wrong, and not one of you is doing anything*, I thought. *Not one of you cowards.*

I found Calder's family in the group and saw his father and mother looking solemnly ahead while Maya's face was turned into her father's chest.

I found Xander in the group and saw blatant hatred on his face as he stared at Hector. I caught his eye. His expression gentled very slightly, and he nodded his head once as if to say, *We have a plan. Hold tight.*

Hector finally turned to Calder. "You may rise, Water Bearer." He looked down at the blood. "The gods believed you needed an extra-harsh punishment for your crimes. And who are we to argue with them?" He looked around at the crowd, apparently no one believing they were anyone to argue with them.

"But wounds cease bleeding eventually and then they heal. If you have learned from your actions, then the physical pain was worthwhile. Was it worthwhile, Water Bearer?"

"Yes, Father," Calder said in a strong, unwavering voice.

Hector paused. "Very well. You may rise and face your family. Please offer them an apology."

Calder remained unmoving for a moment, finally leaning forward and putting his palms on the floor before lifting one knee and then the other, each one sticking briefly before he pulled his broken flesh loose. I saw agony cross his features before he again schooled his expression and stood slowly, unbending each leg. My eyes, locked on his face until then, moved down to his knees and I brought my hands up to my mouth, so as not to cry out. The flesh was broken and mangled as if each metal bump on the mat had been filed down until each one was a piece of raw, jagged metal. Small rivulets of blood ran from each wound. Calder stood to his full height and turned to face everyone.

"I offer you my apologies for my selfish behavior and I'm sorry you had to endure what happened here today. I'll be considering my actions as I sit in jail."

"Now turn and offer the council an apology as well," Hector instructed.

Calder turned slowly. I didn't look at his legs again. I looked only at his face even though he wasn't looking back at me. His eyes were on Clive Richter as he said, "I offer you my apologies and regret my need to prove that some people in this world are made stronger than others. My actions were purely selfish."

Clive narrowed his eyes but remained silent. Hector waved his arm indicating the council should begin the exit of the temple. We each stood up and filed out. I kept my head raised high, not making eye contact with anyone as we exited the building.

I glanced back once as I climbed up into the carriage that brought Hector and me to and from Temple each week and saw Calder walking up the aisle, his lower legs a blur of red, looking straight ahead as I had done.

———

I spent the rest of the day in my room, sitting grief-stricken on my bed. What was Calder feeling right now? Were they mending his legs, or was he sitting alone, bloody and uncared for? I didn't know how I could bear the not knowing, but guilt filled me at the thought alone. Calder was the one who was suffering.

An hour or so before dinner, there was a soft knock on my door, and when I answered, Hailey was there. "Are you okay?" she asked, taking my hand in hers as we sat down on my bed.

I couldn't help it. Tears came to my eyes and I shook my head no.

"I see the way you look at him, Eden. Everyone does."

216

My face crumpled and I blurted out, "I love him, Hailey. I'm in love with him." I hadn't thought about saying it, but Hailey's comforting face made a spear of neediness lance down my spine. I was desperate for someone to talk to.

Hailey's face paled. "Oh, Eden. How could you? How could you let this happen?"

"I couldn't help it. There was nothing I could do to stop it."

"You could have stayed away from him."

"I didn't want to. I want nothing else but to be with him."

Hailey sat up taller, pursing her lips for a second. "Then you've been selfish. You've put us all in a terrible position. You've risked our future—*our destiny*—by following your own self-centered heart."

I felt a thud in my spirit and a heaviness pressed against my chest.

"If I only achieve a spot in paradise by ignoring the desires of my own heart, then I reject paradise," I choked through my tears.

"And what about the rest of us?"

I stood up. "What *about* the rest of you? You all depend on *my* misery for your deliverance? You wish for me to sacrifice my deepest heart's desire so you can rule with the gods eternally? Isn't that selfish as well?"

Hailey stood up. "You will rule with the gods eternally too, Eden."

"I don't want to rule with the gods if it means I have to do it without Calder. I'd rather burn in hell," I hissed.

The fight seemed to go out of Hailey as her shoulders slumped and she looked away from me, out my window. "This is in part my fault. I gave you too much freedom and look what happened."

Tears pricked my eyes again. "You're the only one who

was ever kind to me here…the only one who has ever…who has ever shown me any love." I reached for Hailey's hand, but she pulled it away. "Please, Hailey, you've been like a mother to me when I needed one so badly. Please don't hate me. Please try to understand. Please help me," I whispered the last sentence.

"And who will help the rest of us?"

I pulled in a breath. "What if Hector's wrong about the flood? What if…what if it doesn't come to pass?"

She shook her head. "It will. Hector, he…knows things. His marriage to you and the foretelling of the flood is the one thing that has never changed. He is very sure, and so am I."

I looked down at the floor, tears still rolling down my cheeks. "I'm sorry." I didn't know what else to say. I raised my eyes. "Please, please don't tell Hector what I've said."

"I would never tell Hector. He'd punish us both. And rightly so."

I grimaced in shame.

"I'll tell everyone you're not feeling well and won't be at dinner tonight. I think it's best that way," she said.

"Okay," I croaked, knowing she was saying she didn't want to look at me anymore that day.

Hailey turned and left my room. I sunk back down on my bed and put my face in my hands and sobbed. I'd been so happy Hailey and her boys would remain in our wing of the main lodge, even when Mother Miriam returned. But now Hailey was disgusted with me too. I felt overwhelmed by loneliness and despair.

A little while later, I looked out my window to see Xander walking away from the main lodge, glancing back over his shoulder.

I snuck downstairs, listening toward the large dining room,

where I heard the sounds of everyone eating dinner. I opened the front door quietly and moved stealthily down the front steps to the plantings below and then reached inside the bush, removing a folded-up piece of paper. I stuffed it in my skirt pocket and rushed back to my room, where I unfolded it.

Eden,

I think you'll agree that after what happened today, we need to leave here as soon as possible. Two months from today at the very latest. When you hear the call of a night-hawk three times in a row, pause, and then twice, you'll know it's time to meet Calder and me at the spring. Make sure no one follows you.

In the meantime, if you see any money lying around, and if it's not too risky, take it. We'll need all we can get, every cent.

Xander

Two months? I took in a deep, shaky breath. Two months seemed like an unbearable time to wait but I had no other choice but to try to be patient. I would try my best not to look at Calder with the love I felt in my heart. And I'd pray the next two months went by without incident.

I didn't put this letter with the ones Calder had given me, the ones I couldn't seem to part with. Instead, I lit a candle on my dresser and held the paper by the edge as it burned. When it was just a small burning corner, I let it fall into the large glass container the candle was in. I blew it out, went back to the window, and stood there simply staring out, thinking of Calder and trying to picture us far, far away.

CHAPTER SIXTEEN
Calder

The jail room at the far end of the cellar area was damp and musty. I'd never been in here before, but I'd heard it was a cold, miserable little space that made repenting quickly an easy choice. There was a rusty drain in the corner to piss in and the stench of mildew filled the air. The only seating was a narrow concrete bench where I currently sat with my throbbing legs stretched out in front of me. I grimaced as I adjusted them, thankful I didn't have the added element of holding the pain inside now. Someone had shaved or altered the bumps on that piece of metal and my bet was on Clive Richter. But if he thought I was going to give him the pleasure of witnessing my pain, he was wrong. Wounds in my skin would heal, no matter how bloody they looked now. And the memory of the pain would keep me strong and filled with the motivation to leave Acadia.

The sound of the key in the lock of the thick metal door drew my attention, and a moment later, a small old woman with frizzy white hair was let in and then the door was closed and locked again.

"Mother Willa," I said, starting to stand.

She made a sound of impatience, waving her hand to indicate I should stay seated. I sunk back down, grateful.

She opened a large crochet bag she had slung over her shoulder and started taking out small fabric pouches and a little bowl that looked like it had once been a rock of some sort. As she mixed various items together with a small amount of water in her bowl, a strong herbal smell rose around me. She began smashing it and mixing it together until it was a dark green paste. Then she came closer and set it down as she examined my legs, making tsk-tsking sounds while she used her hands gently to turn them this way and that.

"The gods had nothing to do with this," she said, almost as if to herself. "Here, take this. It will help with the pain." She handed me a small packet of powder and a wooden jug she had uncorked. "Drink it all."

I tipped the packet of powder into my mouth and drank, emptying the jug. My body immediately felt warm and the throbbing in my legs began to abate. I sighed and leaned my head back on the wall. I felt something cool being applied to my legs but didn't watch as she tended to me.

After a minute, Mother Willa asked, "What in this world did you do to displease Hector?"

"I...think I threatened him, challenged him," I said, my eyes still closed. My head was starting to swim, but in a good way.

She was quiet for a good long while. "You must leave, then. Things will only get worse for you."

I opened my heavy eyes and studied her. Crystal-clear blue eyes met mine and I stared into them for a few seconds.

Her skin was leathery and wrinkled, her hair was brittle and pure white, and she only had a few teeth, but I swore in her eyes, she was as young as a girl.

"I'm going to make things better," I said.

She shook her head, applying more cool paste to my wounds. "You've permanently upset the balance. Things cannot be made better. No. You should leave now."

"There are people I love here."

She removed strips of white linen from her bag. "Even more reason for you to leave. As soon as you are released from here, begin walking, and do not stop until you're far away."

The air around me seemed to shimmer as I shook my head slowly. "I can't do that. There are people here I have to take care of."

Mother Willa sighed loudly. "You have made your sacrifice in this life, Calder Raynes"—she applied a fabric strip to my knee and tied it around the back—"whether you know it or not."

"I don't understand," I said. My tongue felt thick and I worked to form the words.

Those crystal eyes met mine. "You were very young. You must not remember coming here."

"Coming here? No. Me and Maya, we were born here."

"Aye. Maya, yes. Not you, Calder. You were not born here. But you belong to Hector all the same. And now you've crossed him, threatened him, and he won't abide by that. And so if you want to protect the people you love, you leave here, do you hear me?"

"Why? What? I don't..."

Mother Willa patted my foot softly. "A gift to them— that's what you were. Such a perfect boy, so very, very beautiful, to balance the imperfection they were given in your sister."

It felt like fog was moving through my head, and I couldn't wade through it to grasp my own thoughts, or separate the ones that mattered from the ones that didn't. Surely this ancient woman was crazy or suffering from some sort of dementia.

"You're really old," I somehow managed, my words slurring.

Mother Willa cackled as she continued wrapping strips of white material around my legs.

"Someday you will be too."

Did Mother Willa not believe in the prophecy of the great flood? If not—if she believed Hector was wrong or being dishonest—then why was she here? "Will I grow old?" I asked.

"I think so," she said, looking slightly confused before her expression cleared. "If certain things… Yes."

I had no idea what she was talking about, but I didn't care. Nothing seemed to matter except for the warmth flowing through my veins and the absence of pain. "Do you like it here, Mother Willa?"

She took a minute to answer. "I suppose I do. There is room for me here. And"—she inclined her head toward my legs—"I earn my keep. Here, I'm useful."

I nodded. I'd never been doctored by Mother Willa, but I'd heard women who gave birth here sang her praises, and many wounds would have festered without her herbs and, of course, like Hector always said, the healing will of the gods. Only…that part seemed questionable now.

"But you, Calder, there is no need for a boy like you to hide away in a place like this."

"Hide away? Is that what people here do?" My words seemed to run together.

"Aye. And sometimes we all need refuge. This world is painful. Some people seek to belong." She shook her head. "But not when there's too great of a price tag attached."

I frowned. "What is the price of taking refuge here, Mother?"

She stopped what she was doing and looked at me, her pale eyes glistening. "Death," she said so simply the word almost didn't compute. "So much death."

The room pulsed around me. All I wanted to do was sleep. "And if we leave here?" I asked.

"Life," she said.

The words floated around in my mind, coming together and then drifting apart again. I couldn't connect them, couldn't apply meaning. Instead, I closed my eyes and rested.

What seemed like a few minutes later, she patted my foot. "All done. This will keep the infection away. Keep them on, even if they itch—at least as long as you're in here—then remove the bandages, clean them, and reapply. If they get wet, apply new dry ones."

My eyes were so heavy, but I opened them anyway and made eye contact with her. "Thank you, Mother Willa," I slurred. "Thank you so much."

She nodded, looking at me sadly. And then she muttered as if to herself, "I tried so hard to help him understand his gift, not twist it." Pain moved across her features, making her, impossibly, look even more ancient. I blinked sleepily as she packed her things away in her bag. I wanted to question her further, but I was so tired. I let my eyes close again and this time, darkness took me, images seeming to swoop forward from the darkness of my own mind: large spitting snakes;

Eden, arching her back in pleasure, her lips parted as she moaned out my name; and flowing water that turned from a trickle to a flood, dragging me under, into blackness so deep I knew I'd never surface again.

———————

I slept in that small box for most of the day. Mother Miriam, Hector's sour-faced mistress, delivered my meals. She set my tray on the floor, took the empty one, and then quickly left. I didn't attempt to engage her in conversation. There was no point, and she made it clear she wouldn't be receptive to niceties, anyway.

The next day, when my head was clear of the herbs Mother Willa had given me, Mother Miriam also delivered a copy of the Holy Book and set that on the floor along with my meal. I placed it on the bench, but I never cracked it open.

When the door was opened by one of the council members' sons the next afternoon, I emerged into the sunlight, squinting and drawing back from the bright glare around me.

"Hector says you should go straight to the fields once you're washed up."

I took a minute to adjust my eyes and then simply walked away from the boy without replying.

I sat by the side of the river, removing the bandages Mother Willa had applied, tending to my still-raw wounds. I washed the grime from my hair and body and then reapplied the bandages I had left drying on the river's edge in the sun.

By the time I started for the fields, the sun was high in the sky and it beat down on me. It felt good. Being clean and in the sunshine made me feel human again.

As I passed by one of the cabins, a hand reached out

and grabbed me and pulled me back behind it. I stumbled, swearing softly, and then looked up into Xander's intense expression. "You scared the living hell out of me," I said.

"Sorry. We only have a few minutes. I don't want anyone to see us talking."

"Why not? We're friends. It wouldn't be strange to see us talking."

Xander paused. "You're probably right. I just think it's better if we don't call attention to that fact. It'll make it more likely that people aren't watching me. They're already watching you and there's no going back from that."

"I think it's better if we act totally normal. More attention will be drawn to you if we don't."

Xander looked impatient. "Okay, fine."

"Okay, so let's walk. No hiding behind cabins."

Xander glanced down at my legs and then we both started walking toward the fields.

"How are you?"

"I'm fine. Sore but fine."

"Kneeling in the fields isn't going to be easy."

"I'll live. What's our next move?"

Xander looked around. "Kristi was able to come up with five hundred dollars in cash to loan us. She doesn't have a lot of money, she just works at the ranger station part-time, so that's the best she could do."

"That's incredible. Okay. So we have over six hundred dollars then. How far will that get us?"

"Not far. Kristi offered up the extra room in her apartment to us, but she's moving soon, going off to a four-year college, and so she'll be gone if we don't leave within a couple months or so. She said she might have some suggestions about places we can stay if it takes longer."

I nodded. "So you think it will take a couple months for us to be ready to leave?"

"Yes, but no longer than that. Things are only going to get worse for you, and for Eden. Plus, wedding preparations have already started with the workers. Eden's eighteen in what, three months?"

I let out a harsh exhale. "A little less."

Xander was quiet for a minute. "Okay, so you take what you can without getting caught. Jewelry, money, whatever we might be able to sell. The longer we have to find a job, the better, because we're going to have to use our cash to eat until then." He looked at me pointedly. "And no going near Eden. We can't risk it."

I sighed, but nodded. "We need to tell Eden too."

"I did. I'm hoping she might have a way to get into Hector's room and see what she can find in there of value."

I clenched my jaw. "I don't want her anywhere near Hector's room."

"It's for our survival, Calder."

"No. I'd prefer to risk finding a way into his room than to send Eden."

"Fine. We'll figure out the details. Like I said, I've already talked to Eden. I told her to be cautious. She'll be ready to meet us at the spring as soon as I give the signal."

I raised a questioning brow. "What's the signal?"

He raised his hands to his mouth and did a nighthawk call very softly.

I chuckled, despite the seriousness of the situation. "That's not bad." *Not exactly good either, but convincing enough.*

Xander winked. "I know. It's virtually indistinguishable. A man's got to practice something to keep his mind occupied when he's walking alone for hours a day."

"You're a man of many talents. So how will we be able to tell if it's you or an actual nighthawk?"

"I'll do it three times in a row, pause, and then twice," Xander explained.

"Got it." I looked behind me and around. "I better go."

"Yeah."

I paused. "Xander, do you think you can help me with something? I need to see Eden one last time before I don't see her for months."

"No, Calder. You need to stay far away from Eden. Don't even look in her direction—"

"I know. I will. Just one time. Please. It will get us both through the next few months. I promise."

Xander looked down, clearly not happy with my request. "Fine. We'll do one practice run of her sneaking out of her room and meeting us by the spring."

"Thank you. Only I want to meet her there alone."

"Yeah, I kinda figured I wasn't invited."

I smiled. "Thank you," I repeated.

"Thank me when we're walking out of here."

"I will. We need to meet again. I have some other things I want to talk to you about. But I need to get to the fields now before I'm missed and Hector forces me to sleep on jagged metal tonight."

Xander gave a small chuff. "We'll sit by each other like usual at breakfast in the morning and come up with a meeting place."

I nodded. I was glad Hector wouldn't allow me to eat up at the main lodge. It worked out better for us. I turned and started to walk toward the fields. Xander softly made the nighthawk sound behind me and I laughed softly, shaking my head.

228

Xander had been my friend for so long, I couldn't imagine life without him. Our plan had to work; we had to get out of here. The pain in my legs was nothing compared to that of my heart when I considered being separated from Eden for more than a few months. Our plan *had* to work—*it had to.*

CHAPTER SEVENTEEN
Eden

I sat on my bed, Hector's Holy Book in my hands, not reading but playing a game where I asked a question about the future and then opened it to a random place and used my finger to blindly point to a word, wherein I opened my eyes and used the word to discern the answer.

It was a game I'd played with one question or another since I was young. It was immature, I knew, but I was *bored*.

"Will Calder and I live happily ever after?" I whispered.

I opened the book, closed my eyes and used my finger to settle on a place on the page, and then opened my eyes. The word sitting directly above my finger was *perchance*.

"Perchance?" I grumbled aloud. "Really?" I huffed out a breath. "Best choice out of three," I murmured, beginning to open the book to a random spot once again.

A knock at my door startled me and I sat back against my pillow and brought the book up as if I'd been studying it. "Come in," I called.

Mother Miriam opened the door holding something

white and gauzy in her hands. She set it down on the end of my bed. "Your bridal veil," she said, the same disdain in her voice that had been present all my life.

"Oh," I said, my heart sinking. "Well, thank you."

Mother Miriam nodded. "The girl who brought it, that simple one, wanted me to tell you the lace on the bottom might seem heavy, but it's only because extra stones were used in the adornment. She repeated herself six or seven times. I suppose she's worried you'll complain," she said, rolling her eyes and shaking her head as if she'd endured some torturous event in having to have a conversation with her at all. I gave an internal eye-roll. I'd give anything to talk to Maya for just a few moments, to know the girl whom Calder loved so fiercely.

"Thank you," I said, moving down the bed and toying with the delicate material of the veil.

Mother Miriam regarded me for a second and then turned to leave.

"Why do you hate me so much?" I asked matter-of-factly, still staring down at my veil.

Mother Miriam turned around to face me again, her expression neutral. "I beg your pardon?"

I looked down at my fingers on the white gauze and then back up at her, holding eye contact. "It's just...I've never done a thing to you. I tried so hard to make you proud by being the best piano player I could be. I tried to be polite and obedient. I...tried to make you love me. And you never showed me a moment of tenderness, not one. Why? What did I do to you to make you look at me with such hatred?"

Mother Miriam was silent for a second as though she was deciding whether she'd even answer me. Finally, her eyes seemed to dim. "You took him away from me," she said simply. "I've hated you since the day you arrived."

My lungs constricted, pain piercing my heart. I wished I could have shrugged off being hurt by Mother Miriam long ago. "I was just a little girl," I said.

Her gaze moved to my breasts and then away. "You're not any longer, though, are you?" Then she turned and walked out of my room, shutting the door quietly behind her.

I sat there for a minute, staring at the place where she'd just stood, wondering at the unfairness of life and of love. And wondering, if the gods were real, why didn't they intervene in situations like this, where I loved Calder and Miriam loved Hector? Maybe if they interfered just a little bit, we could all have the love we wanted.

But the gods weren't interested in our piddling problems I supposed, not when they had bigger issues to handle, like floods and famines and how exactly to end the world.

My eyes went back to the veil sitting at the end of my bed and I touched it again, picturing Maya's fingers sewing the fabric to the lace, attaching each and every gem with the utmost care, piecing together the veil that would ultimately take me away from her brother.

I rubbed a finger over one of the larger pearls. Maya hadn't called them gems. She'd called them stones. Six or seven times, Miriam had said. *Extra stones were used.*

I stared at the veil for another few seconds and then I picked it up and began moving my fingers along the hem, feeling over the lace and the gemstones until I came upon a place where there weren't any gems sewn to the outside but a hard lump that indicated something was sewn between the lace. My heart picked up speed. It felt flat and hard and about the size of a coin. I brought my teeth to the lace and ripped it right open. What did I care? It was beautiful, but I'd never wear the thing.

I stuck my finger in the small tear and ripped it open wider. My fingers touched something hard and so I turned the piece of hem upside down and a small river rock fell out onto my lap, almost perfectly round and as smooth as any one of the pearls Maya had used on my veil. I sucked in a breath.

He sifts through all the pebbles until he finds the smoothest one he can and presents it to her as a token of his love.

I brought the pebble to my chest, holding it there for several minutes as my heart burst with happiness. Then I placed it under my pillow, laying it in my "nest." "Yes," I whispered, "I accept you. A thousand times yes." And then I grinned to myself as I set the pillow back over my offering of love.

Was there anything else hidden in that veil? I picked it back up and dug my fingers into the spot where I'd removed the pebble. After a second, I felt two very small pieces of paper and grasped them between my fingers, removing them both. The first one was small. I unfolded it quickly, my breath hitching again.

On the inside was a drawing of our rock at the spring and the number twelve written above it, inside a full moon. I frowned, glancing over at the calendar on my wall. *Tonight was a full moon.* Calder wanted me to meet him tonight—midnight—at our spring? My heart sped up again, practically tripping over itself.

The second piece of paper was even smaller and said, "Open carefully," on the outside in tiny letters. I did and when I unfolded the final corner, I looked down at a small pile of white powder. Written underneath were three *Z*'s. Sleeping powder? For Hector?

I sat there for a minute longer, looking at the items, my mind going over what I'd been given and why. I knew we weren't ready to leave just yet, so the meeting at the spring had to be solely because he wanted to see me. And I wanted to see him—desperately. And to do it safely, I needed to get this powder into Hector's evening tea. My fingers shook at the thought of the risk. I'd do whatever it took though. I'd do anything to see Calder.

"Thank you, Maya," I whispered. "Thank you for being so very brave." I only wished I could tell her in person.

Later that night, after I'd carefully put the white powder in Hector's tea and served it to him as he read in front of the fire, and he'd woozily walked up the stairs to bed, I climbed carefully out my window. I had thought about exiting through the front door, but several of the council members were home and their eyes followed me as I walked through the main lodge. I retired to my room directly after Hector. Leaving my window open a tiny crack, I shimmied along the roof on my behind, careful not to make a single sound, and then when I got to the far side of the house, I counted to three and made a quick leap to the only tree tall enough to reach. I bit my tongue, forcing myself not to cry out when a sharp branch struck my side and the one I'd grasped onto swayed precariously under my weight. I gave myself a second to settle and reached for another branch, and another, until it was safe to jump to the ground.

Just as I landed, car headlights turned into Acadia, and I let out a tiny gasp of breath and made myself as small as possible behind the large trunk of the tree, squeezing my eyes shut in fear. If they got out of the car and looked carefully enough, I'd be easy to spot.

I heard heavy footsteps walking to the left of me and I stayed frozen until the front door opened and closed. I released a slow breath and then sprinted quickly across the open area to the grove of trees that led to the path down to the spring.

My body was filled with energy and excitement when I finally pushed the brush aside and ducked into our oasis, breathing heavily, almost giddy.

And there he was, bathed in moonlight and the glow of dozens of candles placed all around. I froze and stared unabashedly, his beauty so overwhelming it made my knees weak. And he'd done all this…for me. I sucked in a shaky breath, suddenly feeling the weight of this moment. It might be the last one we had before we left here.

I brought my eyes to his and we both moved at once, rushing toward each other until he picked me up and swung me around. I tipped my head back and laughed at the clear night sky as Calder buried his face in my neck, his smile growing bigger against my skin.

After a minute he set me on my feet and then he brought his hand to my cheek as I leaned into it. "Are you okay?" I whispered. "I was so worried. Your legs…" I couldn't help it. Tears welled in my eyes at the memory of watching him endure such horrendous pain.

Calder used his thumb to brush away the one tear that escaped. "My legs are fine, Eden. I promise you." He gave me a sweet smile. "It's my heart that hurts from missing you."

"I miss you too. So much. I thought I would die watching you suffer."

Calder leaned forward and took my face in his hands. "Shh, it's over now."

I nodded, but the floodgates had opened and now tears were running down my cheeks.

"I didn't worry about you because I know how strong you are," he told me.

I shook my head. "Look at me. I'm not that strong."

Calder smiled. "Yes, you are. You're stronger than anyone I've ever met in the whole wide world."

I laughed, a strangled sound in the midst of my tears. "You've never left Acadia."

"It doesn't matter. I stand by my statement." He grinned, but his eyes moved over my features before he leaned in and kissed me gently, sweeping his tongue over my lips. "Mmm, not just strong, but sweet."

I closed my eyes, my tears stopping, and a smile tilting the corners of my lips. "You're trying to distract me."

He smiled. "Is it working?"

I gave a small laugh and nodded right before he leaned in again and kissed me. We explored each other's mouths for long minutes, both sighing in pleasure. When we came up for air, Calder smiled, brushing a piece of hair off my cheek. "The sleeping powder—"

"I put it in Hector's tea. It was easy. He was falling asleep in his chair twenty minutes later. Mother Miriam walked him up to bed."

Calder gave a nod. "I asked Mother Willa for a little more of the powder she gave me for pain."

I couldn't help the sadness that swept through me again. "The pain—"

Calder put a finger to my lips, smiling gently. "Let's not waste any of our time talking about that. We have so little. We can't risk this again. I just had to see you one last time before we're apart again for a little while. Let's not waste one second, Eden."

"Okay," I whispered. "Not a second." I looked around at

all the flickering candles. "It's so beautiful," I said. "Thank you. I love candlelight."

Calder smiled. "I can't give you much right now, Morning Glory. But candlelight, that's one thing I can provide in spades."

I smiled back but it quickly dwindled. "Will anyone be looking for you?"

"No. Not for now, I don't think. I'm sleeping in the sick tent and Xander switched places with me for tonight. In the dark, no one will be able to tell, even if they do look in on me."

I chewed at the inside of my cheek. We were risking so much for this one night.

"How'd you get out of the house?" he asked.

"I climbed out my window and walked along the roof until I got to the big tree on the side of the lodge."

Calder leaned back, his brows dipping. "Eden, that was dangerous. I thought with the sleeping powder, you could sneak out the front door."

I shook my head. "The council members are all watching me. I feel it. Hector's instructed them... I don't know, but I couldn't risk that. It was safer to go out my window."

Calder looked worried but then sighed and leaned in to kiss me. After mere moments, I was lost to everything except all things Calder. I felt drugged from the taste of him. His smell—clean water and that certain something that was just him—spoke to a deep and secret part of me. It brought me alive in some essential way I didn't even understand. It made my blood run faster and joy spread through my limbs. It made my stomach ache and my heart soar. It made me feel heavy and light, and like laughing and crying at the same time.

I blossomed under his touch like a flower drinking in the

warm sunshine, my nipples tightening, my thighs clenching, and my core beginning to throb.

I felt him harden, and I moaned into his mouth, bringing my hands up into the silky hair at the nape of his neck. He moaned too, that beautiful, throaty sound vibrating on my tongue. Moisture settled between my legs, my pulse beating in that inner place that called out to be filled. I broke away from Calder's mouth and he gazed at me with heavy-lidded eyes.

"Make love to me, Calder. Right here, under this moon, in the place that's only ours."

Calder's expression was tender as he leaned in and kissed me softly again. "Did you accept my pebble?"

"Yes. It's tucked away in my nest. Does that mean we're married?" I asked on a laugh.

Calder grinned. "Yup."

"I don't imagine the state of Arizona recognizes the laws of penguins."

"I don't care about the state of Arizona. It will be the law I'll live by for the rest of my life."

Oh, Calder. My love. "And your vows? What are your vows?"

He took hold of my hands. Overhead, the moon cast its golden glow on everything around us, and the warm air caressed my face. In front of me stood the most beautiful man I'd ever seen, the man I'd loved as long as I could remember, the one who loved me back. All around me, the night glowed with miracles, both great and small.

Calder's gaze moved slowly over my face, a gentle smile on his lips. "Eden, I vow this: My heart is yours. My life is yours. My body is yours. My art, my dreams. You own each and every part of me."

My heart hitched. "And I vow this: Calder, my heart is yours, as is my life, my body, my dreams. You own each and every part of me, in this lifetime and any other."

Calder pulled me to him, wrapping his arms around my waist and lifting me up to his height. I laughed and kissed him again and again, planting small kisses all over his face as he laughed too.

"I love you, Morning Glory."

"I love you too, Butterscotch."

"I brought something," I said as Calder set me on the ground.

"Show me."

I walked over to the canvas bag I had dropped by the rock entrance and brought it back to the small grassy area and then pulled out the large white blanket that was kept in my wedding trunk. It had been sewn especially for my wedding night: a beautiful combination of wool, cotton, and linen, with silvery threads woven throughout. It sparkled in the candlelight. I spread it out on the grass as Calder joined me.

I unbuttoned my shirt slowly and let it fall off of my shoulders. Calder watched silently, his lips parting slightly when our eyes met. He removed his own shirt, tossing it aside and moving closer until we both stood just inches apart.

The water splashed softly, the foliage whispered in the warm breeze, and to me, this moment seemed holy, warm, real, and right.

We removed the rest of our clothes very slowly until we both stood naked before each other, his eyes caressing my skin, my nipples pebbling as his gaze moved over each part of me.

I too allowed my eyes to move over him unabashedly. I loved him, and I felt no shame. I admired his muscular arms and shoulders, his flat, ridged stomach, and the indents that formed a V on the inside of each hipbone. Something about those lines made my own body clench in reaction to the sight of them. My eyes continued their journey, traveling slowly downward, over that sparse trail of dark hair that led straight to his manhood, standing stiff and rigid, straining toward me.

I remembered Hailey's instruction and went slowly down on my knees before him. Calder sucked in a breath and said my name, his voice raspy and unsure.

I noted the bandages still wrapped around his lower legs but didn't remark on them. I knew he wouldn't want me to. *Let's not waste one second.*

I laid my cheek against his stomach and then turned my face to his skin, inhaling his scent and then leaving a slow trail of kisses before I kneeled lower. Calder's breathing became heavy and he wove his fingers through my hair. "Eden…"

I took his shaft in my hand and kissed the tip of it, darting my tongue out to taste him. He groaned and swelled even more in my hand and I exalted in the knowledge that I owned him completely in that very moment, feeling powerful and beautiful and loved.

"I love the way you feel," I murmured, sliding my hand up and down him once as the skin slipped beneath my fingers. "So different from me." Then I took the tip of him in my mouth and sucked gently and Calder gasped out an unintelligible word, his fingers tightening on my scalp. He pulled away from me and I made a sound of loss as he kneeled down—just a little stiffly, I noted—and took my mouth in a deep, breathless kiss. When he finally pulled back, he looked drugged, his eyes dilated so that his normally deep brown eyes were almost black.

Calder inclined his head toward the blanket and I scooted over until I was able to lie back down on it. He gazed down at me for only a beat before he moved over me and we continued kissing, his skin burning into mine. Between my legs, I was wet and needy and aching. Was this normal? Was it *normal* that Calder filled me with so much heady desperation? I had no way to know—no comparison, no one I could ask other than Hailey, who hadn't even been comfortable *talking* about it. But it felt too good not to let myself enjoy it. It felt too *necessary* not to lose myself in the sensations Calder brought. Would the gods have created our bodies to experience so much pleasure if they didn't mean for us to? I didn't think so. I couldn't imagine the gods were that cruel, not when we were expressing our love for each other this way. And I did—I loved him with every part of my heart.

"Calder," I groaned. "I need you."

"I need you too, Morning Glory," he said, sounding strained. "But I don't want this to end either." He leaned down and kissed the place between my breasts. "I want this to last forever."

I arched my back as his warm mouth closed over my nipple, sucking it gently. I felt the pulse of the pleasure between my legs as he licked the hardened peak and ran his tongue around it and then moved to the other one, where the delicious torture continued. I panted his name and wrapped my legs around his hips, pressing myself upward into the heat of his hardness. He brought his mouth off my breast and groaned softly.

Calder rolled to the side so that his weight was on the blanket and brought one hand down and parted my thighs. I sighed dreamily, opening for him, and when his finger dipped inside me, a spark of pleasure shot through my core. "Oh!" I gasped, arching off the blanket. Calder put his mouth back to my breast and explored me with his fingers, finally circling the spot that made me cry out his name and move my head from side to side as delicious bliss pulsed through me.

He circled his finger there until the feeling was so intense it took over, plunging me into an abyss of bright pleasure. As my body clenched and shivered, I gazed up at the stars, their glow burning into my eyes and the feeling of bliss burning into my flesh. It lit the moment from within, from without, in a way that made me feel changed forever, as if somehow that one blinding second of intense light had singed my very cells.

The thought itself seemed dramatic and fantastical, but it also felt true and real.

Calder leaned in and kissed my lips softly, moving over me once again and I tilted my hips upward, offering myself to him. The look that roamed over his face was wonder and I felt him shiver slightly as though he was straining to hold back his passion. But I didn't want him to. My heart squeezed with love. Tonight, I'd give him my body, but he already owned my heart and soul. I wanted to belong to this beautiful man in every way possible. And I wanted him to belong to me. "Are you sure?" he asked.

"Yes. Very sure." I wanted it as a reminder of what my sacrifice was for—why it would all be worth it in the end. In the *end*, Calder and I could do what we were doing anytime we wanted, without fear, without shame, without having to plan and conspire and sneak out windows and down trails in the dead of night. Although for now, I wasn't complaining. For now, I'd take him any way I could. *He is mine for tonight.*

Our gazes held for several intense moments. "I love you, Eden," Calder said, before taking himself in his hand and guiding his hard shaft to my wet opening. His eyes held mine as he pushed slowly inside me. His lips parted, his lids dropped for just a moment, and I closed my eyes too, as he pushed farther. I felt overly filled, too tight to accommodate his size, and I grimaced, willing my body to relax.

Calder halted and my eyes flew open. "No, please don't stop," I said.

"I'm hurting you," he said breathlessly.

"Just this time. The next time won't hurt at all. Or the time after that...or—"

Calder gave a choked laugh. "Morning Glory," he murmured as he kissed me softly. Then in one stroke, he plunged all the way into me, and I broke from his mouth, crying out at the stab of burning, tearing pain. "Are you okay?" he asked.

"Yes. Yes. I'm fine," I said, as the burn abated.

Calder paused, watching me, before he began moving inside me very slowly, groaning into my neck. "I'm so sorry. You feel so good," he panted out. "So good."

I stared up at the night sky as Calder stroked in and out of me. The stinging sensation remained, but only slightly. For a few minutes, I still felt too full, too stretched, but that began to lessen enough that I was able to focus on Calder above me. I ran my hands over his smooth back, down to his firm backside, the muscles contracting as he worked his body into mine. I marveled at the fact that he was all around me, *inside* me, and it seemed both strange and wonderful.

I knew the blissful thing that washed over me when he touched me with his fingers wasn't going to happen again, but I gloried in the feeling of his flexing muscles and the look of pleasure in his expression. He began moving faster and with less finesse. I saw the war in his face between being gentle with me and moving as his body was telling him to. I was intoxicated with the knowledge I was doing that to him; he had lost all control because of me. I encouraged it, grabbing his backside and pushing him into me at the pace I could tell he was barely holding back from. His eyes flared and then closed, and I wrapped my legs around his hips, bringing my hands up to his arms to feel those flexing muscles as he held his weight.

"I love this. I love you, the feel of you, the smell of you, just you," Calder panted.

I smiled. I loved how words started pouring out of him sometimes when we were physically intimate. It was another way he lost control, and I loved it. I pressed up into him and sighed out blissfully.

Calder leaned forward, brought his mouth to mine, and moved his tongue in my mouth to the same rhythm our bodies moved together. I felt a small spark as his chest rubbed against my nipples, and relaxed completely into him, moaning into his mouth. Calder groaned back and then his thrusts grew jerky as he let out an exhalation of breath with each one. And then suddenly, he pulled out of me and I cried out softly at the unexpected loss of him.

I felt something hot and wet on my stomach and Calder groaned into the side of my neck, repeating my name again and again.

I ran my hands leisurely up and down his back as we lay there, our limbs tangled together, our hearts beating as one, his heart rate slowing as his breath ghosted against my skin. It had been everything I'd dreamed and more. A spike of sympathy ran through me for Hailey, for any woman who didn't experience what I'd just experienced with Calder. And I knew it would only get better. The discomfort would go cease, and soon it would only be pleasure.

He shifted his weight to the blanket next to me and gazed down at my face. "You're so beautiful," he murmured, kissing both eyelids, and then my nose, and finally my lips as I smiled and sighed in pure happiness.

"Are you okay?" he asked.

"Better than okay. Perfect." I smiled. "The rest of them can have every square inch of Elysium all to themselves. I'll take this."

Calder smiled but it seemed slightly unsure.

"Really," I said, bringing my hand up to his hair and running my fingers through it. "You didn't hurt me."

"Well, you destroyed me," Calder said on a sigh. "I'll never be the same." He rolled to the side and we both lay there, staring up at the sky, the warm breeze blowing across our skin, candlelight flickering and the wetness on my stomach growing cool.

I reached my hand down and touched the sticky substance, rubbing it between my fingertips.

"I don't want you to get pregnant," Calder said. "At least not here, not now."

"Oh," I whispered, piecing together the way babies were made.

Calder turned his head toward the sky and I rolled toward him, putting my elbow on the blanket and supporting my head on my hand. "I want to know all the science of it… eventually. Another time."

Calder looked at me, laughing softly. "Have I mentioned recently that I love you?" he asked.

"Not recently enough. Say it again."

"I love you…I love you…I love you."

I grinned and kissed him. "I love you too."

I lay my body over his, burying my face in his neck and wrapping my arms around his neck. We lay like that for several minutes until he brought his hands down to my backside and squeezed gently. I giggled and squirmed on him and he groaned softly. "Let's wash off," I said, rolling off him and kneeling up. I looked down at the blanket where I had been laying and heat rose in my face. There were smears of blood marring the perfect white fabric. I saw that Calder was looking at the blood too, but not with embarrassment, on the contrary with something that looked like pride. He held out his hand and I took it silently and we walked hand in hand to the spring, where we both waded in.

When the water was up to my chest, I stopped and turned toward Calder. We stood there in the moonlight, the water sparkling around us. I brought some up over my breasts, my nipples puckering at the cool wetness. Calder's eyes lingered on me and then I dipped down in the water, dunking my head and coming back up. He laughed as I stood, sputtering water and grinning. Calder kneeled down on the sandy bottom and pulled me to him, where he held me against him so I was at his height. We kissed and floated there for several minutes, nuzzling each other's mouths, Calder nipping at my lower lip playfully until I laughed and threw my head back. He laughed too, and swirled us around, the water like cool silk sliding against my bare skin.

After a moment, Calder considered me thoughtfully.

"What?" I asked.

"I'm memorizing every detail of your face," he said quietly. "The next time I get to look at you close up like this, we're going to be away from here."

I took a deep breath. "How long do you think?"

"Two months, maybe less."

"It will pass so slowly," I said, feeling the weight of what would be our separation press down on me.

"It will be worth it," he said. "A little more sacrifice, and we'll finally be free to be together, free to live the life we want to live."

I nodded, clasping my hands around his neck. "More sacrifice," I said. "I don't want to sacrifice anymore. I've had enough sacrifice for three lifetimes. I'm ready to *live*."

"I know, Morning Glory. Me too. Just a little longer."

Calder set me down and we washed each other slowly, me glorying in his smooth skin and the way he watched my hands as they ran over the different parts of him. "You're the most beautiful man in the whole wide world," I said.

Calder smile. "Just wait until we get out in the big community. You'll see how unfortunate-looking I really am. There's not a lot of competition here."

I laughed as we began to wade out of the water. We made it back to the grassy area and began pulling our clothes on. *The big community.* We'd always called it the "big community" in Acadia, but suddenly it *felt* big. Huge. Overwhelming. The place where so much would be different. I chewed at my lip as I gazed out to the spring. *My safe place. My comfort. The place I won't have access to anymore.*

"What?" Calder asked, using his fingers on my chin to turn my gaze toward him.

"Well, what about clothes and stuff? People don't wear what we wear here."

He dropped his hand. "I know. I see what people arrive here wearing. We'll figure all that stuff out. It's why we need a little time."

247

I nodded, searching his face. "Are you afraid?"

"Sometimes. But mostly I'm filled with excitement for the future for the first time in my life. We've always lived with this great flood looming over us, and I don't know, it's hard to imagine a day when I don't use that as the compass for the way I spend each and every day. But I *want* that. I want to know what that feels like. I want to know what it's like to live without constantly thinking about dying."

"Even if dying's supposed to be glorious."

"Yes. And maybe it is. But"—he ran a hand through his hair, looking up at the sky—"there are glorious things right here on earth too, and I think they're meant to be enjoyed. We weren't created not to notice them…our hearts weren't formed not to take joy in the things we've been given right here."

We both sat down on the blanket, and when Calder lay back, I snuggled into him, his body warming me. I was so sleepy. "So you believe the great flood…it isn't true?" I yawned. I still didn't know exactly what I thought.

"I don't know," Calder said very quietly. "I used to believe in Hector so strongly. But he isn't the man, the leader, I always saw him as. He's not a man I want to follow any longer. And so if the floods do come, I'll take my chances with the rest of the people Hector considers sinners. I'm certainly among them in his mind anyway."

I nodded, growing sleepier, so warm and happy with Calder's arms around me. I'd take my chances wherever he was too.

"All I know for sure," I heard him whisper, "is that you belong to me and I'm going to protect you. I'm going to make a life for us. *Somehow.*"

And I believed him.

The next thing I knew, Calder was shaking me gently. "Wake up, Eden, we have to get back."

I blinked and looked around, sitting up as Calder moved away from me. I oriented myself, suddenly realizing I'd be saying goodbye to him for quite some time. I stood as my breath hitched. I felt tears forming, and my chest ached. I hadn't known this pain before. "I'm going to miss you so much," I whispered.

Calder had picked up the blanket but stopped folding it at my words. He set it down on the ground and moved toward me, wrapping me in his arms. He hugged me to him tightly, his chin resting on the top of my head. "I love you so much, Morning Glory. Every single day we're apart, I'm going to be planning our life. It will get me through, and you remember that too, when it gets hard. When wedding plans are going on around you, when you see Hector treating me like a dog, you remember I am planning our life and doing everything I can to make that happen. And I swear to you, we will leave here."

I looked up into his eyes. "Okay."

"My brave Eden. I won't worry about you because you are so strong. I'll know you're fine."

I nodded, resolve filling me. "I will be fine. I'll be strong and I will wait for that call from Xander telling me to meet you right here."

After I'd put the blanket back in the bag, I almost swung it over my shoulder but thought better of it and set it down behind me, between the rocks where the sketchpad was still kept. There was no reason to carry it with me back up the tree and across the roof. I turned back to Calder. "I'll see you here soon, very soon," I said.

"Yes," he said, "very soon." He took my face in his hands

and kissed my lips softly and then rubbed his nose along mine tenderly. I kissed him one last time and turned to leave. I ducked through the opening in the rocks and hiked up the trail, knowing Calder would be behind me in a few minutes. I wondered if he'd leave the unlit candles where they were or take them back with him. I pictured somebody stumbling upon our little spring years and years from now, when we were long gone, and wondering what had gone on there, what it all meant. I couldn't help smiling to myself. Only he and I knew the story. It was only ours.

I climbed the tree easily and then tiptoed across the roof back to my window that I had left open just a crack. I pushed it up slowly, pausing when it creaked softly. When I didn't hear another sound, I opened it all the way and climbed through. Two minutes later, I was changed and in my bed.

The next morning, the only clues that the beautiful night at the spring with Calder hadn't been a dream were the delicious smell of him still on my skin and the glorious ache between my thighs.

CHAPTER EIGHTEEN
Calder

The morning after I made love to Eden at our spring, I sat down next to Xander in the community dining hall.

"Kicked out of the dogs' quarters or just here for a meal?" Xander said, spooning scrambled eggs into his mouth.

I laughed a humorless laugh. "I don't know just yet. Hector hasn't said a word to me."

Xander eyed me and then looked back down at his empty plate. I knew him; he was trying to decide whether to go back for thirds.

"You look tired," I said, biting into a piece of buttered bread.

"Yeah, I can't imagine why. Maybe because I tossed and turned all night in the sick tent, waiting to get caught for posing as you."

I chewed, feeling remorseful. I hadn't realized Xander would be so nervous he wouldn't sleep at all. I had been selfish. "I'm sorry, and thank you. I owe you," I told my best friend.

Xander smirked. "Yeah, you owe me for about a hundred lifetimes. I've been keeping tally. You'll still be paying your debt to me in Elysium."

I grinned. "Happily."

Xander drained the rest of his orange juice. "Was it worth the risk?"

I pictured Eden's pale skin glowing in the moonlight, her eyes filled with love and passion and trust.

"I'd risk my life to relive last night," I said truthfully.

Xander studied me, a slow smile taking over his face. "Okay, then." His eyes made a slow survey of the mostly empty room and then came back to me. "I hope you didn't get her pregnant."

I felt a flush of heat move up my neck. "I know better," I said.

Xander gave me a slow nod but didn't exactly look convinced.

"So," I finally said, smiling around my food, "let's get these plans underway so I *can* relive last night."

I'd expected him to laugh, and when he didn't, I frowned, watching him. He seemed suddenly troubled. "What's—"

"Gods, Calder," Xander said tensely, "this isn't only about you and Eden. I have my own dreams too, you know. Life isn't all about you."

I set my cup down. "I know that," I said. "Hey, Xander, I'm sorry. I've been selfish. This is about you too. I'd want to get out of here whether Eden existed or not. And I *know* you have your own dreams. I'd want you with me regardless of the circumstances. I'm sorry if I gave you any other impression."

Xander rubbed the back of his neck. "I know. Damn this place." He shook his head. "I know. I'm just tired."

"Listen, Xander, we'd be doing this together anyway. Unfortunately, we're on a time limit because Eden's birthday is looming, so we have to do it sooner than I'd like. I'm sorry for that, I really am."

Xander let out a breath. "No, I'm sorry. It's just stressful."

"I know. Thank you."

"Don't thank me. We're in this together. Whatever I have—"

"You have half." I finished.

Xander nodded, glancing around again as several families walked in the front door and over to the food line. "So with that in mind, we have six hundred seventy-six dollars and that's including the money Kristi's lending us."

I did the math. "Where'd the extra twenty-six come from?"

Xander tapped his fork on his plate. "I had it under the floorboard from years ago. I found it in a wallet in the ranger station. I don't know who it belonged—"

"Okay," I interrupted, knowing Xander felt guilty for stealing from the people who turned out to be his friends. "So realistically, what's the bare minimum we need before we can safely leave? I don't want to stay here a second longer than we have to."

"Agreed. Let's try to get two thousand. Hell, let's try to get every cent we can. But that's the minimum. With that, we have at least a month. We just need *one* of us to score a job. Even if it's Eden."

"No, not Eden. I want to navigate things before I send her out anywhere by herself."

Xander took a sip of his coffee. "You can't keep her locked up somewhere in the outside world like she's been locked up in here. She deserves her freedom too."

"That's not what I mean. I just…I need to protect her."

"We might all need protection, brother, in ways we can't even comprehend yet. How about we all take turns when it comes to that?"

I nodded, considering the wisdom of his words. "Deal."

"Okay, so take money whenever, however you can."

I nodded. "Clothes?"

"I have some for you and me."

"How?"

"I was supposed to burn the clothes from some people who've joined us over the years. I took them and put them under the floorboards."

"For the love of the gods." I laughed. "You have a major problem."

Xander glared at me.

"You're like a squirrel," I said.

"Yeah, damn lucky for you."

I chuckled. It felt so good to laugh a little. It gave me some hope and made me feel like my old self for a few minutes. Plus, I was on such a high from my night with Eden. Life seemed full of promise, despite my aching legs. I'd taken my punishment like a man and hopefully Hector was done with me. Maybe I was overconfident because of what we'd just gotten away with, but I felt it in my bones that this was going to work. I'd sit on a jagged metal mat again if I had to, but by gods, this was going to work.

"What about clothes for Eden?"

"Kristi's going to bring in something of hers for Eden to borrow."

I chewed a bite of toast and swallowed. "We couldn't do any of this without Kristi. Talk about still owing someone in Elysium—"

"Kristi doesn't believe in Elysium."

I smirked. "Good for us. Seriously, though, will you tell her how much we appreciate this?"

"I do. All the time. You can tell her yourself soon enough."

I couldn't wait because that would mean our plan worked and we'd be free of Acadia. "So the only thing we really need is cash."

"Yes. I'll work out the details with Kristi once we're close to having what we'll need."

We both ate in silence for a minute. "Hey, Xander. When I was in the cell and Mother Willa came in to tend to me, she said some weird stuff."

Xander rolled his eyes. "She's crazy and senile, Calder. I wouldn't waste too much time trying to interpret her ramblings." He glanced up as the door opened. "Your dad's on his way over here."

I looked back to see my dad walking quickly toward the table where I was sitting with Xander.

"Calder, Maya's had some sort of seizure. She's in the sick tent."

My heart dropped and I stood up quickly, leaving my dishes on the table and following him out the front of the hall. Xander was close behind me.

When we entered the small room, Maya was lying on one of the cots under a heavy blanket. I moved to her side and knelt down on the floor, taking her clammy hand in mine and moving her bangs out of her eyes. "Maya, I'm here. How are you?" I asked gently.

Her eyes moved to me, but they moved slowly and alarm filled me to see how sick she was. I looked back at my dad and mom, standing at the end of the bed, Mom wringing a handkerchief in her hands. "How long has she been like this?" I asked.

"She seemed to be doing well this morning, just the same cough," my dad said. "She had a seizure…and then—"

"Mom, go get Mother Willa," I interrupted.

"Mother Willa? I don't think Maya's in pain."

"Just go get her!" I raised my voice, then closed my eyes momentarily at the look of pain that crossed my mom's features. "Please. Maybe she can do something… anything."

My mom nodded, but it was Dad who left the room to go get Mother Willa.

Fifteen minutes later, Mother Willa entered the small room where we all waited; I was still holding Maya's hand. The old woman moved to the bedside and stood there, simply looking down at Maya with sadness on her face. "This child was never long for this world," she finally said.

"What's that supposed to mean?" I demanded. "We don't need your predictions; we need your help. What can you do for her?"

Mother Willa met my eyes. "There's nothing I can do for her, boy. Her heart is weak. It always has been. You're lucky you've had her for as long as you have."

I groaned. I felt stunned and helpless. How had this come on so suddenly? Was I not paying enough attention? Was I too caught up in my own world, focused on my own needs and desires, every waking thought on Eden?

Life isn't all about you. Xander's words from less than an hour before came back to me, causing me to flinch. Had I missed something that would have told me Maya needed more care than she was getting because I was so wrapped up in my own plans?

"Move aside," Mother Willa said. "I can at least make the child more comfortable."

"She's not a child. Are you in pain, Maya?" I asked.

Maya's eyes met mine and she shook her head. "I just feel sleepy," she said, blinking her eyes in an effort to keep them open.

Mother Willa put her hand on her own chest and looked up as she inhaled a breath. Then she put her hand on Maya's chest. "Not enough air," she finally said. "Because of the heart. She will simply fall asleep."

I relaxed a little. "She just needs to sleep and she'll be better?"

Mother Willa shook her head, regret in her expression. That regret enraged me and made me feel even more desperate. I pulled her arm gently and she followed me a little way from Maya's bed as my parents took my place at Maya's bedside.

"Tell me what's going on with Maya if you know."

"It's like I said. Her heart is weak. It's failing. Soon it won't be able to provide her with enough oxygen and she'll fall asleep. She won't wake up."

"No." I shook my head, shaking off the very idea. "No. You're not right. How would you know that anyway? Just from looking at her?"

"Aye. I see it. When things are imminent, they grow very clear." She put her hand on my arm. "I'm sorry. I see your love for her too. It's like a brightly colored butterfly."

I studied her ancient face, those ageless eyes, not knowing what to think, and then pulled loose from her hold and returned to Maya to sit on the other side of her bed.

I clasped her hand in mine and sat with her as Mom and Dad prayed. As I listened to the words from Hector's

Holy Book, the room seemed to sway and blur all around me. When I blinked my eyes, I realized it was because I was crying. I sat up straight and looked out the window. I wasn't going to cry. Maya was still here, her warm hand holding my own and a small serene smile on her face.

As I stared at her, she opened her eyes and looked right at me and then just over my shoulder. She smiled just a little bit bigger. "Oh, Calder, it's so beautiful, and so simple," she whispered.

I furrowed my brow, not understanding what she meant. She met my eyes again and her hand squeezed mine, so gently, three times. *I. Love. You.* I squeezed back and her smile grew bigger. "I know," she whispered. And then she closed her eyes, a small puff of air escaping her mouth, her hand slipping from my own.

"Maya?" I choked, putting both hands on her shoulders and shaking her just a little. She remained unmoving, her eyes closed, the small smile still on her lips. My mom began to cry and my dad bowed his head. I looked up and saw Mother Willa standing quietly in the corner, her eyes downcast as her lips moved silently in some kind of prayer.

My dad picked up Maya's wrist and put his finger to her pulse, and we all watched as pain traveled over his face. After a minute, he laid her arm down gently. "She's gone," he said.

I stood up quickly, the chair beneath me scraping against the floor. I felt hot, short of breath, like all the light in the room was suddenly too bright, piercing. I needed to get out of there, away from Maya's still body and the seemingly tangible feeling of loss all around me.

I stumbled toward the door as Mother Willa reached out her arm and clutched mine. "This is not your fault," she said.

I looked at her, reeling, the strange sensation that my

eyes might bug right out of my head at any second. "Whose fault is it, then?" I asked too loudly.

"There is no blame here."

"Brother…" Xander said, stepping forward from beside the doorway, where he'd been standing, offering support with his presence.

I looked away from him, pulled free of Mother Willa, and stalked out the door, my feet leading the way, until I found myself down at my and Eden's spring. I stood there looking around dazedly at the place that had only ever brought me happiness and joy. In that moment, I *needed* to be there. Grief clawed at me. How would I go on without Maya? I loved her so deeply. I had never been apart from her for one day my whole life. I fell down on my knees on the grass and put my head in my hands and sobbed, letting the tears fall for my big sister.

Maya's body was laid to rest in Acadia's burial ground, a quarter mile to the west of the river. The ground was hard and rocky, and it took my dad and me half a day to dig Maya's grave as Mom and several other women anointed her body with oils and dressed her for burial.

Hector led the funeral procession through desert wildflowers to her grave. The rest of our family came to pray for Maya's safe journey to the afterlife. Eden stood to Hector's side, a look of utter sorrow on her face. I glanced at her once, but my longing for her was too much, and I couldn't look back again. I needed her so desperately that even looking at her was too painful of a reminder of what I couldn't have when I needed it the most: Eden's loving arms around me, her warmth, her comfort. I saw she was trying to catch my eye, and I was sure she was confused by my lack of attention, but I had to remain stoic or I would crack.

I was even more desperate to leave Acadia now. There was nothing for me here. My mom and dad wouldn't understand, but I had to live my own life. And they had each other. They had the life they'd chosen. They had Elysium.

As Maya's funeral procession made its way back to the main dining hall where all the workers, Maya's family, would gather over food and drink, I saw Hector lead Eden away, back to the main lodge. The two council members who were there followed behind them. I saw Eden glance back several times out of my peripheral vision, but I didn't look her way. I couldn't.

As I sat in the corner of the dining hall, watching the gathering around me, I talked to my sister in my mind. *Maya, I don't know how this all works, but if you're able, help us…help us get out of here safely.*

If Maya heard me, she gave no indication. I felt utterly alone despite being surrounded by people I considered family.

CHAPTER NINETEEN
Eden

I felt like my heart had shattered into a million jagged pieces. I couldn't go to Calder, I couldn't offer comfort, I couldn't hold him or take away any of his sadness. And I grieved for the girl I'd never know, the girl who had such a large piece of Calder's heart. I saw the stark misery written on his face and yet he wouldn't meet my searching gaze. I didn't want to be selfish; this wasn't about me. But I didn't understand why he wouldn't even glance my way. I was hurt and confused, and I felt completely helpless.

I thought about writing a note and leaving it in the bushes in front of the main lodge for Xander, but I knew he wouldn't come looking for it and it would sit there, possibly creating the risk of being found by someone else. And so I wandered through the days—existing as best as I could— praying for the hours to pass by more quickly, to bring me closer to the moment when I would hear that birdcall outside my window.

Every morning, I had a moment of peace before the

hole inside would gape wide and I would remember, even though Calder was close, he was so very far away.

Hailey hadn't spoken to me since our conversation about me being in love with Calder. I had lost her too and that knowledge sat heavy on my heart. Despite what she believed, I loved her. Not quite like a mother but like an older sister or an aunt, and her rejection stung.

Three weeks after Maya's burial, Hector called me down to his office.

"Come in," he called when I knocked quietly. I entered the room and Hector motioned me to a chair in front of his desk. I sat down and crossed my legs at the ankles, my hands resting in my lap. I couldn't help but notice that Hector looked more unkempt than I'd ever seen him before. Hector had always been meticulous in his grooming. But today his hair was uncombed, his shirt slightly untucked, and there was a small piece of food at the corner of his mouth.

It was so unusual, it alarmed me.

Hector leaned back in his chair, regarding me with a small smile. "I hear your bridal gown is coming along nicely."

I lowered my gaze. "Yes, my veil is complete. It's lovely. Of course, it means all the more because it was handmade by Maya Raynes."

Hector was quiet for a moment. "Yes, Maya Raynes." He looked out the window thoughtfully. "Even the gods make mistakes sometimes. It's up to us to create balance. It pleases them. It makes us *worthy*."

"Mistakes?"

Hector raised his brows. "Surely you noticed the mistake Maya Raynes was?"

A tidal wave of sadness and anger rose in my chest and I clamped my lips shut as if it might come pouring from my lips. "I didn't see Maya as a mistake," I said after a moment. "She was a beautiful, talented girl."

"You're very generous with your praise, Eden, a lovely trait. It never ceases to amaze me how very pure you are."

You know nothing of me. You're blind to who I am.

I looked down at my hands, wanting nothing more than to leave Hector's office. "What can I do for you, Father?"

"First, stop calling me Father. Call me Hector now, as I've already asked you."

I cleared my throat. "Yes, Hector."

"Thank you. Now speaking of Maya Raynes, I have some good news. Her brother, Calder Raynes, will be married in the temple a little over a month from now. I'd schedule it sooner, but the workers need some time to prepare a proper wedding."

My heart dropped into my feet. "What?" I croaked out.

Hector looked out the large window to his left. "You're going to be my wife, Eden, in this life and the one after. As the leader of Acadia, I won't seek your counsel. But you are allowed to know my reasons, and especially on this matter, I think it prudent that you do."

I sat silent, still trying to wrap my head around what Hector had just told me. Was this some kind of trick? My throat felt like it was closing up. "Married to whom, Fa—Hector?"

"To Hannah Jacobson. She was born here, just like Calder. She's only seventeen, but her father has consented to her marriage."

I conjured a vision of Hannah…the small, dark-haired girl with the pretty smile who had caused me a moment of intense jealousy the year before. I sat up straighter. "And why are you telling me about this?" I asked. Hector had never called me to his office to inform me about the unions of the workers before now.

Hector steepled his fingers and regarded me for a minute. "When I built Acadia, it was my vision that this be a place of peace and harmony for those who chose to make their home. The luckiest among us are the ones who don't have to adjust to life here. It's all they've ever known. However, what I neglected to consider is that young men, especially, need continued purpose. I tried to provide that to Calder Raynes by appointing him my personal water bearer, but that didn't work and I excused him from that position. I don't often make mistakes, but I've watched him grow increasingly dissatisfied with Acadia. I've watched him stray from our righteous path. And if Calder, a boy…" He paused. "No, a man now, whom many other boys look up to, begins to stray, what affect will that have? It will cause them to consider straying as well. The balance here, *the harmony*, will cease to exist. Clearly, our family can't have that if we're to stay intact, strong, and free of sin. Do you agree, Eden?"

I stared at him as I clasped my hands in my lap, attempting to control the trembling. "I just don't understand what marriage has to do with this, Hector."

"Marriage and family focus a man and give him purpose. The responsibility provides goals beyond his own. The gods have spoken to me and they have made it clear it's what Calder Raynes needs." He paused, a storm passing over his face. "Him especially. He has sin and evil in him, Eden. You have no idea." He paused, his expression settling into neutrality again. "It's my job to care for my family, and although Calder has disappointed me, it's my duty to help him back onto the righteous path. I believe a wife will assist in that endeavor. I suggested it to him, and he agreed."

I froze. "He agreed?" I whispered.

"Yes, he did, quite enthusiastically so."

"But…his sister just died," I said, feeling bile rise up in my throat. *Please don't let me be sick right here*. This couldn't be right. This was all some kind of mistake. Calder was taking me and leaving here. He wasn't marrying someone else. Calder loved me. Didn't he? Doubt crept in. Had Maya's death altered Calder's commitment to leave here with me? Dread settled in my stomach.

Hector nodded, tapping the pads of his fingers together. "Yes, all the more reason to give him the purpose he obviously craves…to help him value his family more, rather than focusing on his own selfish motives." Hector glanced out the window again. "His sister's death may have been just the thing to help Calder realize how far he'd veered off course." Hector pushed his chair back and stood. "In any case, we should meet more often about Acadian business, my love. It will bring us closer, especially as the flood draws near." He smiled but I couldn't manage one. Instead, I stared at the small piece of food to the side of his mouth, unblinking.

"Well, then," he said, clearly excusing me.

I stood up on shaky legs. "Have a good day, Hector," I said, turning and leaving his office.

I could barely walk. I could barely *breathe*. I needed to talk with Calder, to know what he was thinking. *Does he still love me? Want me?* Was he somehow blaming himself for Maya's death? *Oh, Calder. I need you.*

———

I watched Calder pledge his engagement vows to Hannah Jacobson two days later as all of Acadia stood in the temple. I felt like I was hovering just outside my body, a lump in my throat so big I could barely swallow. Once again, Calder wouldn't look at me, although my heart leapt with hope when I saw the morning glory pinned to his shirt. Had he done that for me? I had no way of knowing and no chance to speak to him. Was he going along with this because he was being forced to in some way? Why hadn't he sent me a message of some sort? Didn't he know this was killing me inside? He had to.

Calder's face was blank. I couldn't read it. But Hannah looked serene and happy, a wreath of flowers in her hair. I watched her as she glanced repeatedly at Calder, a shy look of admiration on her face. Of course. Who wouldn't admire Calder, or even just the way he looked?

My heart throbbed with jealousy when I watched them together. They really were a lovely couple, both with their dark glossy hair; she was small and petite, and he was tall and strong. I held a scream back, but only barely.

After Hector performed the commitment ceremony, Calder leaned forward and kissed Hannah chastely on her cheek. I looked away, misery clouding my vision.

We all filed out of the temple, the rest of the people chatting and laughing, ready for the celebratory feast. Hector took my arm and started leading me back to the main lodge. I turned my head and craned my neck, attempting to look at Calder one last time, but there were so many people in my way, on every side, I couldn't see him. *He is mine, all of him, every part*, I reminded myself. We vowed it to each other beside our spring, under the light of a full moon. I suddenly couldn't stand all the people, the close confines of the temple. Fierce anger billowed inside, and I broke free of Hector's arm. I walked ahead for a few steps before Hector caught up to me, grabbing my arm.

As I spun around, that's when I caught Calder's eye, standing still, watching me between two groups of people who were chatting. For just a brief flash, I saw the wild look in his eyes as he took in Hector's hand on my arm. But he didn't move. And then Hannah came to stand beside him and his eyes broke from mine as he smiled down at her.

I looked away in misery. Perhaps it was unreasonable that I was experiencing such anguish and craven that I suddenly felt such doubt. But all my life I'd been expected to sacrifice and *give* to others and it felt like the only thing in the world that mattered to me might suddenly be in jeopardy. I wanted to *fight* for it—for him—but there was no way for me to do that.

I took in a shaky breath. "I don't feel well," I said to Hector. "I need to lie down."

A knowing look came into Hector's eyes as he stared at me. "Yes, of course you do. Go rest. Rebalance yourself. I'll see you at breakfast tomorrow morning."

I turned and walked away, back to the main lodge. I couldn't help but note, in all the years I'd been in Acadia, it was the first time I'd been allowed to walk anywhere publicly by myself. I supposed it was not only because Hector sensed I needed time alone but because there was nowhere else I could go.

I'll kill Hector in his sleep tonight, I thought wildly as I ran up the small slope to the main lodge. Every minute of pain in my life was because of him. But when I got inside and closed the door behind me and stood breathing hard against the wall, the idea seemed desperate and stupid. And I didn't think I had the heart to kill anyone, even Hector.

In my room, I lay down on my bed and curled into the heartbreak. If Calder married, how would things work out for us? Even if we were able to leave, Calder would be married to someone else. Didn't he have a duty to take care of her? Could he just abandon her here when we left?

If I were married to Hector though, it wouldn't stop me from leaving. Calder was doing what he had to do and I had to gather my courage and trust him, despite the unexpected circumstances. *Be strong, Morning Glory.*

I skipped dinner and went to bed early, so emotionally exhausted I could barely stand. Surprisingly, sleep claimed me easily and I sunk gratefully into her dark nothingness.

The next thing I knew, the gentle patter of rain was hitting my window. I rolled over and tried to drift back to sleep, but the hard pinging of a drop hitting a particular surface kept me from falling back into my dream. I groaned and put the pillow over my head, but the pinging every few seconds continued.

For a minute, I let the memories of watching Calder pledge his commitment to someone else assault me, feeling the hole in my chest open again. Now I'd never fall back to sleep. I'd lie here all night imagining Calder and Hannah sharing the same bed…eventually.

Ping!

I stayed in bed for a few minutes, listening. The pinging stopped, so I threw back my blankets and put my feet on the floor, rubbing my eyes and standing to look out the window. I startled and clamped my hands over my mouth when I saw a form right outside, looking in at me. As my eyes widened, I saw it was Calder. *For the love of the gods!*

I hurriedly opened my window and grabbed onto his shirt, pulling him inside. He climbed over my desk and stepped to the floor, a puddle already pooling beneath him.

"What are you doing?" I hissed, closing the window.

"I had to see you."

I stood back. "We promised not to risk this."

"I know, but, Eden, after today, I had to see you. You know I had no choice about the engagement."

My shoulders sagged. "What did he do to you?"

Calder ran his hand through his hair, droplets spraying out around him.

"He told me to leave here or marry Hannah."

"Then why didn't you leave?" I whispered. "Maybe that would be the better thing to do. You could have gone ahead and waited for me and Xander—"

"With a hundred and something dollars? I've never even met the girl who's going to help us." He stepped closer and cupped my face in his hands. "I can't leave you here, Eden. I did what I had to do to stay near you. And maybe this way, Hector's attention will be off us even more. I made it sound like I thought it was a good idea."

"You didn't even look at me," I said, tears filling my eyes. "Not once did you even look my way. If you had, I would have understood. You could have told me with your eyes—"

"I couldn't. Hector was watching me like a hawk. And if I had looked at you, my feelings would have been all over my face. And I knew." He took my chin in his fingers and tilted my face up to his. "I knew you were being strong, Morning Glory. I knew you trusted I wouldn't be going through with any of this if it wasn't for us."

"It just made me wonder…it made me wonder if *you* wonder what it would be like…" I shook my head, the words all jumbled in my head, more feeling than rational thought.

"Then ask me, Morning Glory. All you ever have to do is ask me."

I stared up into the dark beauty of his eyes, the suppressed emotions and doubts clarifying under his loving gaze. "Do you wonder what it would be like to be with another woman?" I asked. It would be natural, wouldn't it? He was a young man who'd only kissed—only made love to—me. Did he wonder what it would be like to experience intimacy with someone else?

"No," he said. "I've never wanted anyone except you. Not for one second, not ever."

I released a breath, love and relief causing my breath to come easier. Calder was stronger than I gave him credit for. I almost felt sympathy for Hannah. She wouldn't be able to help but love him, even if only a little. I didn't wish her pain, but I couldn't bear for her to be with Calder in any way physically. "I just… there has to be something we can do…if you get married—"

Calder shook his head. "The only person I'll ever marry is you."

"How will you avoid it? Can we leave sooner?"

"If we have to. It doesn't make me feel very secure in our plan. But yeah, if we have to."

"I'll be ready anytime."

"I know," Calder said, taking my hand and leading me to my bed. Outside, the rain came down harder.

"Does Hector ever check on you?"

"He checked on me once, but I don't think he will anymore. Hector put a lock on the outside of my door a few days ago. I'm not sure why."

Calder studied me for a second. "Bars will go up on your window once he contemplates whether you're brave enough to scale the roof."

I let out a very quiet laugh. "Or that *you're* stupid enough to scale the roof."

Calder grinned. "I think he simply believes we've caught

each other's eye, nothing more. He doesn't know about our spring."

I nodded but didn't mention how I'd confided in Hailey. That hadn't been wise. I had just hoped for a brief moment she might help us. But she hadn't.

Calder looked at me seriously. "Just the fact that I've looked at you has made him crazy though, Eden. This"—he moved his eyes around my room, indicating where he was—"is truly stupid. I just couldn't stand you not knowing what I was thinking. It was killing me that you might be in pain."

"You could have sent a note somehow…someway."

"Yes, I could have. It would have been safer." His gaze roamed over my face as if in the last month, he had forgotten what I looked like.

"Yes," I agreed. *I should make him leave.* But he was right in front of me, his hair slicked all the way back from his gorgeous face, droplets still shimmering on his skin, and the delicious smell of him invading the air around me, making me want to close my eyes and inhale deeply.

And I understood the frantic feeling of *needing* to offer comfort to the one you loved, against all reason, all rational thought.

I put one hand up to his cheek, and he closed his eyes and turned into it. "I'm so, so sorry about Maya," I whispered, tears pricking my eyes. "I wanted so desperately to come to you."

Grief crossed Calder's features and he allowed it to remain there. Something about that made me fierce with protectiveness. He loved and trusted me enough to bare his pain to me. I leaned forward and wrapped my arms around him, and he turned his face into my neck and just breathed as I rubbed his back and turned to kiss his cheek again and again.

271

When I leaned back, Calder said, "It was so sudden. I didn't have time to prepare. It still doesn't seem real. I wondered if the gods were punishing me for what we did."

"By causing Maya's death?" I shook my head. "Are the gods that cruel?"

Calder sighed. "I don't believe so but I have no proof."

"When we leave here, I'll find you proof. I'll study every piece of information available until I find you proof that the gods are good and merciful."

Calder gave me a sad smile. "My Morning Glory."

He leaned forward and placed his forehead against mine, and for several long minutes, we simply breathed together, finding solace in each other's nearness. Calder's fingers found the edge of my nightgown and he rubbed the fabric between his thumb and index finger. "So this is what you sleep in," he said.

I nodded my head slowly, suddenly feeling self-conscious. "I'll wear something nicer when we sleep together," I said, feeling like a child in the modest, unattractive piece of night-wear. I knew women in the outside world showed skin sometimes. I very vaguely remembered wrapping my own arms around my mother's bare legs, her skirt just touching her knees, as she smiled down at me. It seemed like a dream now. Maybe it was.

"No," Calder said. "I love it. You're like a present I get to unwrap." One side of his lips quirked up teasingly.

"What do *you* wear to sleep in?" I asked. Did I get to unwrap a present too? The thought brought a smile to my face.

"Far more than I'll be wearing when I sleep with you," he said, grinning and leaning forward to kiss my neck. I leaned my head back, moaning softly.

"Calder..." I started, glancing back at my door. "We

272

promised we'd be careful until we can leave… The sacrifice will all be—"

"I know," Calder whispered against my skin. "I'll leave in a second. Just another taste of you and I'll go."

"Mmm," I murmured as his lips feathered against my neck, sending a bolt of arousal straight between my legs. "The rain's stopping. You need to go," I said, running my fingers through his hair and pushing him slightly.

Calder brought his head up and I stared in his lust-filled eyes, his lips barely parted. With everything in me, I wanted to kiss those lips until I was dizzy and breathless. But Hector was right down the hall, and if we were caught, it would ruin everything.

Calder stood and pulled me into his arms where he held me tightly against him. "I hate saying goodbye to you."

I nuzzled my face into his chest and then tipped my head back to meet his eyes. "Just promise me once we get out of here, we'll never say goodbye again."

"I promise."

He kissed me softly on my lips and then I walked him to the window. It was just drizzling softly now. "Don't slip," I said worriedly, eyeing the slick roof outside.

"I won't." He kissed me one last time, quickly, and then climbed through the window. I closed it behind me, watching him until he moved around the corner of the roof and disappeared into the rain.

I mopped up the water on my floor with a blanket at the end of my bed and then got back under my covers, feeling relieved yet still unsettled. I closed my eyes and said a prayer to the God of Mercy.

CHAPTER TWENTY
Calder

The speakers went up the morning after I sneaked into Eden's room. Twelve of them in all, placed so wherever you were on Acadia, you could hear one of Hector's sermons being broadcasted.

I saw a few workers shooting each other confused looks as the sermons played on and on, only quieting once the sun set. Then it was like a sigh of relief just to be able to hear your own thoughts again. Everyone seemed to want to stay in the quiet of their own head after that, and the usual chatter and laughter around the evening bonfires workers built mostly ceased. If we did talk, it was in quiet whispers. The mood shifted and no one seemed to know exactly what to make of it. My parents, however, seemed to be quietly accepting.

At Temple, as I sat next to Hannah, Hector didn't explain the meaning of his broadcasted sermons. Instead, he repeated some of the same ones he had already given, growing quiet here and there as he stared off into space as if listening to someone, before he found his place again and continued on.

I saw him watching me, though, his eyes meeting mine and lingering there, appearing as though he suddenly didn't know who I was and was trying to recall. He didn't look at anyone else like that. I grabbed Hannah's hand and held it in mine and Hector's eyes moved down to our laced fingers and finally moved away. I couldn't help but to exhale. I didn't know what was going on with Hector, but something wasn't right. His hair was a mess, it looked like he'd slept in his clothes, and there were bags under his eyes. We needed to leave as quickly as possible.

Hannah squeezed my hand in hers and a pang of guilt twitched inside. Not just because I was touching a woman who wasn't Eden, but also because Hannah was a nice girl, and she seemed happy with our engagement. It would hurt her when I simply disappeared. But it couldn't be helped. Hector had forced my hand and used Hannah as a pawn.

At the front of the temple, Eden looked away. *Be strong, Morning Glory.*

A week after the speakers went up, Hector declared we'd all be participating in special prayer sessions three times a day at the temple. Truthfully, the prayer sessions were a quiet blessing. The heavy walls kept the broadcasted sermons out, and we all were able to sit quietly for an hour at a time.

I didn't talk to the gods anymore. Instead, I talked to Maya in my head, telling her about everything that'd gone on since she died. I told her all about Eden and the things I'd never gotten to say to her when she was alive: she and Xander had always been my best friends, I was so proud of her, and I missed her every single day.

Xander and I also used the prayer sessions to quickly update each other on the progress of our money situation. Xander had been able to sneak into the council members' cars and take thirty-seven dollars total in change and dollar bills. He thought he'd left just enough to not make it look too suspicious. He'd even scored a gold chain in one car and a gold keychain in another. Apparently, the price of gold in the city was pretty high, or so Kristi had told him, and it was common for people to sell it.

He kept it all under his floorboard at home, all ready to grab, along with the clothes he'd saved.

The problem with being in Temple so much during the day was the crops were being neglected and under the intense heat of the Arizona sun, the neglect began to take its toll. Only a few weeks later, our beans and vegetables were wilting, and the fruit from the fruit trees ripened and fell to the ground, where the birds pecked at them.

If this went on much longer, we'd all starve to death. Hector had to know that.

One quiet morning in Temple, Hector walked to his podium and stood looking at us quietly for several minutes before he finally spoke. "There is a thief among us."

My heart dropped and I glanced very quickly at Xander, who continued to stare straight ahead at Hector, unblinking.

Hector's eyes moved over the congregation. "There was a gold necklace stolen from one of the council members' cars. Who knows something of this?"

Holy hell.

No one said a word. You could have heard a pin drop on the other side of the room.

"No one?" Hector questioned. He leaned forward on the podium and waited, looking around again, his eyes landing on me and staying there for several beats before he looked away. "Eden, will you step forward, please?"

Eden's confused gaze rose to Hector but she stood and joined him where he stood.

"If no one has the courage to stand and confess to their crime, an innocent will suffer the punishment. My own true love will suffer the punishment. For you see"—he stood back—"*I love you so much, I am willing to sacrifice my own for your sins,*" he shouted. Eden startled and stepped back. "*I will mar my beloved's perfect skin for you,*" his voice boomed.

Shocked fury caused my body to tense, my spine snapping straight. I saw Hannah in my peripheral vision looking over at me, but I didn't look back.

I started to step forward myself when Xander's voice rang out. "It was me, Father. I stole the necklace."

Hector's head swiveled over to Xander and his eyes narrowed on him. The crowd shifted nervously, glancing between Xander and Hector.

I opened my mouth to say something, but then closed it again. If I said something, I'd likely make this worse for all three of us. Every muscle in my body was primed for fight, and my brain started working out the path I'd take to Eden and how quickly I could get there.

Hector leaned forward casually on the podium. "Xander Garen," he said, pushing his now overly long hair out of his eyes. "Where is this necklace?"

Xander hesitated. "I'll go retrieve it for you, Father."

"No, I'll send someone to retrieve it. Tell me where it is."

Oh no. All the items he'd stolen—our precious stash were in the same location under that damn floorboard. I closed my eyes briefly. Out of the corner of my eye, I could see Xander open his mouth and then close it again. He was stuck.

"The truth is, Father, I couldn't explain it exactly. I'd need to accompany the person."

Hector stared at Xander and I held my breath. "Very well," he finally said. Maybe if Xander went along, he'd have time to push the other items out of the way. Something. *Anything.* If not, we'd be back to square one. I felt like I might vomit.

"Clive," Hector barked, "escort the boy to retrieve your stolen property."

I dared to quick glance at Eden, and her face was blanched of all color, her expression shocked.

Clive walked to Xander slowly, took him by the arm, and they exited the temple as my heart sped. My mind raced too, trying to figure out what I could do. Hector's hand was still on Eden. If I ran after Xander, making a spectacle of my disobedience, I'd be leaving Eden alone with Hector. Would he harm her in order to punish me? Something had come unhinged in his mind. I didn't even want to consider what it might be.

Hector stood with Eden at his podium, finishing his sermon, although what I focused on sounded disjointed and Hector stumbled over his own words several times. Eden stared down at the floor, the color barely returning to her face.

What seemed like a lifetime later but in reality was probably only twenty minutes or so, Hector began the final prayer. When we all filtered out, I noticed people glancing at others with questioning expressions on their faces. Everyone recognized that something confusing was happening in Acadia. And everyone was uneasy.

Suddenly, the sight of Xander, kneeling on the ground with his hands tied around a post came into view. Clive

Richter stood behind him, a long cord in his hands. I didn't even have time to consider what I was doing before I started running toward them.

"Grab him!" I heard Hector yell and somewhere in the back of my mind, I thought Eden screamed.

Strong arms grabbed me from the side and pulled me back, and as I turned to fight the person holding me, someone else grabbed me from the other side. Council members Garrett Shipley and Ken Wahl held me as the first whipcrack sounded. Adrenaline coursed through my system and I elbowed Ken in the face and then used my free arm to punch Garrett, sending blood spraying as he yelped and brought his hands up to his broken nose. As they both let go of me, I shot forward again.

"Stop, Calder," Xander yelled. I skidded in my tracks, breathing hard. Xander's head was hung and his jaw was tight, but he widened his eyes and shook his head, instructing me to stay back. I didn't know what to do. Everything in me was screaming to fight for my friend, but he was asking me not to. I brought my hands up into my hair and raked my fingers across my scalp, wanting to roar with anger and helplessness.

Garrett and Ken came up behind me and grabbed my arms again. This time, I didn't resist them.

Clive brought the whip back and let it fly again, and I watched as it hit Xander's naked back, opening his skin in a long raw red line. Xander jerked but remained quiet. *Oh, Xander. My brother, my friend.* I locked my jaw and balled my fists.

Clive brought the whip back again, the expression on his face filled with some sort of disgusting glee, and let it fly, creating a third welt on Xander's flesh.

Two more times the whip flew, and two more times Xander jerked but didn't utter a sound.

"That's enough, Clive," Hector called. Clive looked over at him, seeming to come back to himself, his chest rising and falling in heavy pants. "I think justice has been served for the thievery. Did you retrieve your property? Do you feel vindicated?"

Clive seemed to consider the question, his head turning toward Xander, who was hunched over, his back a mess of blood and open wounds. "Yes," he said, dropping the whip on the ground and turning to walk back toward the main lodge.

Hector nodded over at Garrett and Ken. "Let him go. I think this served as a lesson to him too. You can accompany your friend to the sick tent." I heard women crying around me, but I didn't turn to look at anyone in the crowd.

My arms were released and I rushed forward to Xander, kneeling down in the dirt beside him. "Hey, brother," I said gently, "let's get you off here."

Xander grimaced as I began to untie the rope binding his wrists. "Fuck me, it hurts, Calder," Xander grunted. He must have been in excruciating pain because I had never once heard him use the obscenity some of the people who came from the big society let slip once in a while.

I let out a breath, forcing my hands not to shake as I worked the knot as gently as I could, so I moved Xander as little as possible. "Why didn't you let me pull him off you?" I asked, not able to keep the bitterness from my voice.

"He would have just whipped you too. And then probably locked you up."

"I would have taken it."

"I know," Xander said as the rope came free and he fell

forward, using his palms to brace himself on the ground. "Whatever I have—"

"That's right." *Even injury. I'd have taken half the lashes for you. Hell, I'd have taken them all.* I pulled Xander to his feet and took his arm and put it around my shoulders, so he could lean on me as we walked.

"He got our money. Every cent of it," Xander said, his voice breathless and pained. "The only thing I was able to push out of the way as I reached in was the bag of clothes. I told him there was a nest of snakes that lived under our house and that I couldn't remember which floorboard it was under. That's the only reason he didn't reach in himself. Coward. And hypocrite, he stuffed the rest of the cash in his pocket. I doubt if he's even going to mention it to Hector."

My heart fell at the news that our money was gone. But talking about it was the last thing Xander needed. "*Is* there a nest of snakes that live under your house?" I asked, trying to distract him as we made our way to the sick tent.

"No. A few mice, but thank the gods they were moving around when Clive was there or else he'd have gotten our clothes too."

I couldn't help it—I laughed, a hollow sound. "What are we gonna do with the clothes without the money?"

"We're gonna walk out of here, that's what."

I considered that as we moved toward the sick tent. I thought we might have to, considering how close the date of my wedding to Hannah was and now that our thievery had been discovered, but it was far from the way we'd originally planned it. Dread settled in my gut. We'd be leaving with absolutely nothing except the clothes on our backs—clothes that would blend in, in normal society, true. So I guessed there was that. Still I felt like I might be sick. It wasn't nearly enough.

We got to the sick tent and I helped Xander to one of the clean cots and he lay down on his stomach. There was a small cabinet I knew from being there with Maya over the years that had bandaging supplies. I hoped Mother Willa would arrive soon with the pain medicine she'd given me for my legs, but for now, I'd have to do what I could for Xander.

As I washed his wounds with a cloth and clean water, I talked to distract him. Even so, each time I brought the water to his back, he grimaced and ground his face into the pillow.

"Remember that time you gave me chicken pox?" I asked.

"You gave *me* chicken pox," Xander said, turning his head. I wrung the cloth out, the water turning red.

"And the worst part about it," he continued, "is I only had about six of them and you were *covered*, and I'm the one who got a scar." He tapped his finger on the small round divot next to his eyebrow.

I laughed softly, bringing the cloth to his back again as he winced.

"As soon as you're ready to leave the sick tent," I said, "you can do that stupid birdcall and we'll meet Eden at the spring. We'll have to wing it." Fear prickled my skin at the thought of not being able to guarantee I could keep Eden safe and fed.

"Stupid?" Xander's eyes began to close. "That birdcall is perfection. Other nighthawks can't even tell I'm not one of their own."

I chuckled, patting Xander's back dry with a clean cloth. "I'm sure they can't."

"Will you go get those clothes, Calder? My parents will be out on the perimeter right now. I think we should keep them in here with us, so we don't have to go back there." A

282

sad note came into his voice when he mentioned his parents. I frowned. We were men, but we'd never been away from them a day in our lives. And this would break their hearts. But with what was happening in Acadia, I had to believe it would do everyone good if we left. Of course, Eden was another story altogether. We'd be leaving with their "blessed one."

My thoughts were interrupted when Mother Willa bustled through the door. She ambled to the cot where Xander lay, now drowsing. I stood and gave her a nod. She obviously didn't require any instruction.

"Xander, I'm gonna make a trip to the outhouse. I'll be back."

Xander made a soft half grunt, half snore.

As I passed her, Mother Willa grabbed my arm. Her eyes looked misty, unfocused, and something about them had unease filling the space between my ribs.

"Go to the far left corner," she said.

"What?"

"The far left corner," she repeated with intensity. "It's the only place where you'll live."

"Live? I... What?"

She let go of me and went to Xander, who was still snoring.

I left the tent and instead of going to the outhouse, I made a quick detour to Xander's cabin, knocking on the door once. When no one answered, I snuck inside, closing the door behind me. I didn't have to try to guess which floorboard it was. The one Xander used as his storage facility was still out of place. I kneeled down next to it and reached my hand inside. Something skittered by my wrist and I jerked my hand back, grunting in surprised disgust. "Mice. Just mice," I murmured, reaching back inside.

When my arm was under the hole all the way to my shoulder, my fingers touched fabric and I gripped it and pulled it out. It was a canvas bag, secured at the top with a rope, and obviously full of what would be our getaway clothes. I didn't bother to return the floorboard to its place. Instead I ducked out of the cabin, the bag over my shoulder and walked purposefully back toward the sick tent. When I was almost there, someone grabbed my arm and I dropped the bag and spun around, ready to fight whomever it was off of me.

It was Hannah. She stood in front of me wringing her hands. It looked as if she'd been crying. "Hannah," I breathed.

"Calder, that was awful." She let out a small cry. "Why did Xander do that? Is he okay?"

I picked up the bag and considered how to answer. "He'll be okay. I need to get back in to check on him. You go on home, all right?"

She blinked at me with worry. "I'm scared, Calder," she whispered. "Something's happening here, and I'm confused. My mom and dad say it's just because the great flood is drawing nearer and more is being asked of us, but...it scares me."

I paused, not knowing what to tell her. I cared for Hannah. I'd grown up with her. We'd played together as kids. I didn't love her, however, not like that. "Hannah, listen, if anything...happens to me, there are, well, you have choices. You don't have to live here all your life if you don't want to."

Her eyes widened and she took a small step toward me. "I want to. I want to marry you, Calder. I want to go to Elysium with you."

I released a breath. "I have to get inside. Just...just remember what I said, okay?"

"Okay." But the troubled look remained on her face. I pulled her toward me and kissed the top of her head.

When I got inside the tent, Mother Willa was already gone, but Xander's back was bandaged and he was snoring quietly.

I stuffed the bag under my own cot and lay down next to Xander to rest. I clasped my hands behind my head, dying inside because I couldn't go to Eden right now. I had to believe she was locked safely up in her room, away from Hector. In a couple days, we'd call to her and make our escape. Images swam through my head of Eden climbing out her window, Hector's hand reaching out to grab her, then Eden scaling the roof, falling, the sound of breaking bones barely muffled beneath her screams. I startled awake and looked around wildly. I'd fallen asleep without meaning to. "Just a dream," I whispered, falling back onto the cot.

But then I heard the sound that must have woken me the first time—a faraway nighthawk cry—only this one was strange and imperfect, and in the voice of a female. *Eden.*

Xander raised his head and looked around dazedly, still lying on his stomach where he'd fallen asleep. He fell back onto the cot, out cold. I remembered what it felt like after Mother Willa had given me the pain powder. I didn't even know my own name, regaining consciousness in fits and starts, unable to move or think clearly.

I jumped off my own cot and picked Xander up as gently as I could, trying not to touch his wounded back. He mumbled some slurred words I couldn't understand and went limp. I hoisted him over my shoulder and bent to pick up the bag of clothes I'd hidden under the bed.

Eden was giving the call that said we needed to leave. Fear surged through my body. Eden would never risk that unless there was something horribly, horribly wrong.

CHAPTER TWENTY-ONE
Eden

The spring was bathed in golden moonlight when I broke through the brush and stood drawing in gulps of air, my entire body shaking. *Please let Calder and Xander have heard my call.*

I dropped the canvas bag I had thankfully been able to grab as I escaped and wrapped my arms around myself, rubbing my hands up and down my goosefleshed skin as I tried to get my raging emotions under control. *It's safe here.* When I heard the footsteps coming through the brush on the other side of the rock wall, I cried out in relief, knowing it could only be Calder and Xander. No one else would be coming toward me to this secret place with such direction and purpose.

Calder burst through the brush, panting heavily, Xander hanging limply over his shoulder. Alarm made me stumble. "Is he okay?"

"He's fine, just out cold."

I exhaled as I rushed toward him. He lay Xander down gently in the grass and took me in his arms as I sobbed out his name.

"Shh, Eden, it's okay. I'm here. Tell me what happened.

What happened, Morning Glory? What did he do to you?" He ran his hand down the back of my hair, whispering the soothing words into my ear.

The sobs I'd barely been holding back rose up in my chest, the hysteria now finding a safe place to land in Calder's strong arms. "I… He…" I drew in a big breath, gathering myself. It wouldn't help any of us if I went stark raving mad. "He found your letters, Calder." I leaned back, looking up at his worried face with shame and regret. "I'm so sorry. I"—I shook my head—"shouldn't have kept them. But I wanted to take them with me when we left. They were mine. They were part of *us* and I wanted them." A tear spilled from my eye.

Calder used his thumb to wipe the wetness from my cheek. "We're all okay. We're here. Together now. What did he do to you? Tell me."

I shook my head again, trying to move the memory away. "He…went crazy." My breath hitched as I pictured Hector's beet-red face, the bulging vein at his temple, his crazed eyes. "After what happened with Xander, I was so upset." I glanced at Xander, snoring quietly on the ground. "I'm so sorry, Xander," I said quietly, knowing he couldn't hear me but needing to say the words anyway. "You paid the price for all of us."

"He's okay, Eden. Really, he is. His wounds will heal."

The ones on his skin, yes. But what about the ones inside from enduring that cruelty? But Xander had been so brave. He hadn't uttered a single noise even as the whip made contact, splitting his skin. I straightened my spine, focusing back on Calder. "I helped Hailey put the boys to bed and then I went back up to my room, and he was there, sitting on my bed, reading your letters." The dread of that moment gripped me, just as it had when I'd walked into my bedroom.

"Did he touch you? Did he hurt you?" Calder asked, his jaw tense.

"No. He just kept saying, 'He burns for you? He burns for you? I'll show you how he burns for you.'" I choked back a sob, shuddering with the memory. "He wanted to kill you," I whispered. "And maybe me too."

"What did you do? How did you get out?" Calder asked, running his hands over me as if to prove to himself I was whole.

"He locked me in his office. I dragged the filing cabinet in front of the door and then broke a window with the fireplace poker. They were all banging on the door as I climbed outside. A council member, Ken Wahl, I think, I don't know, came around the outside, but I was already hiding and he didn't see me."

Calder shook his head slowly, a small disbelieving smile on his lips. "Morning Glory," he muttered.

"I didn't have a choice," I said. "It was that or…who knows what. Something bad." I chewed at my lip. "I'm just sorry we have to leave before we're really ready."

"No, you did the right thing." Calder brought his hands to my cheeks, his gaze meeting mine. "You were so brave." He leaned forward and kissed my forehead. "And we'd have had to leave soon anyway," he went on. "My marriage to Hannah is supposed to take place next week. And after what happened today, Xander and I had already decided to leave earlier."

We stared at each other for a few seconds; I drew strength from the face I loved so very, very much. I felt calmer already. We were together. We were safe—for now.

"Our only issue now is we don't have a cent to our name," Calder said.

"Oh," I said, stepping back. "No, that's not true." I walked to the canvas bag I'd hidden in the bushes behind the main lodge. Thankfully, I'd been able to sneak around and retrieve it quickly after I'd jumped out of Hector's office window. From there I'd snuck to the grove of trees a hundred feet or so from the sick tent, done my best nighthawk call three times, and then made my way quickly to the trail that led to the spring.

I knelt down on the grass and dumped out the contents of my bag, all the loose cash I'd stolen all over the main lodge and all the jewelry I'd swiped from the council members and their wives. I had become especially brazen as Calder's marriage to Hannah drew near. I should have been whipped today as well.

I reached inside the bag and scooped out all the loose change I had and then looked up at Calder, whose mouth was hanging open. Xander rolled toward the loud sound of the change clinking onto the ground, his eyes half-open. "Well, holy hell," Xander slurred.

"For the love of the gods, she's worse than you," Calder said, looking over at Xander.

"Where'd you find her?" Xander asked woozily. "I think I'm in love."

Calder laughed, his dark eyes filled with warmth. "Oh, I just happened to find her by this pretty spring one time…"

I smiled and Xander attempted a grin but promptly passed out again, his head falling back on the grassy ground. "Isn't this what you wanted me to do?" I asked, waving my hand over the stolen money.

"Hell no," Calder said. "It was far too dangerous." He let out a breath, one side of his lip quirking up. "But since it's done, I'm damn glad you did."

He knelt down on the grass next to me and started taking inventory of what we had. After a few minutes, he said, "Three hundred eighty-three dollars." He set the paper money in a neat stack and then handed it to me so I could return it to the bag.

"I have no idea how much this other stuff could be worth," Calder said, holding up a gold ring with a red stone in it, a ruby maybe. "But it's gotta be worth something, especially if this is real gold." He paused. "You did really well, Eden," he said. And when I glanced up, I could tell by the look in his eyes that he was thankful and relieved. I smiled proudly.

"So now the only thing we have to do is get changed and get out of here," Calder said. "Eden, you're gonna have to help me change Xander."

I nodded but frowned. "If he can't dress himself, how's he going to walk?"

"He's not," Calder said. "I'm going to carry him."

Calder grabbed the bag he'd dropped by the entrance to the spring and perused the clothing items for a few minutes, holding each piece up and then deciding who should get what.

Calder and I dressed Xander in jeans and a blue button-up shirt, trying our best not to hurt his back. But he was pretty out of it and didn't seem to be in any pain. I turned my head when I was at risk of seeing something too personal and let Calder take over.

As Calder was dressing, I packed everything up in the bag and then turned around. *Oh, wow.* Calder was wearing blue jeans with a light gray T-shirt that was just a little bit too fitted over his lean muscles but in a way that made my mouth go dry. And he was wearing a cap with some kind of orange logo that looked like an S and an F entwined together. "How do I look?" he asked.

"You'll do." I smiled. "But what am I supposed to wear?"

"We were going to wait for Kristi to give you something," he said. "So you'll have to wear what you're wearing for now. Hopefully with us dressed this way, you'll blend."

I nodded. There was no other choice. "So what's our plan?"

"We get far away from here, and we find a hotel until Xander can call Kristi. I think we're about twenty miles from the city. Maybe fifteen. Do you think you can make it?"

"Yes." I'd do whatever I had to do to get far, far away from Hector and his crazed eyes. I'd walk barefoot if I had to. I glanced down at our feet. We all still had on the same simple sandals we always wore. There was one woman who made them on Acadia, and her craftsmanship was about to be put to the test.

"But, Calder, you can't possibly walk twenty miles carrying Xander," I said.

"I don't have a choice because I'm sure as hell not leaving him here."

My heart swelled with love for my brave, strong boy, who loved his friend so much he was willing to carry him on his back to safety rather than leave him behind.

"I think it's a good idea to stick to the desert area as much as possible, since Hector most likely sent someone, or many someones, after you," Calder said.

A chill went down my spine and I considered what was in store for us as Calder picked Xander up gently, his strong thighs flexing through his jeans as he stood and situated Xander over his shoulder.

I wished so desperately I could just snap my fingers and

we'd be in a room somewhere deep in the city, safe and locked behind a door. But of course, life didn't work that way. You had to survive every minute of the hard part in order to get to the good. Perhaps that made it all the sweeter though. If you could just skip over the bad parts in life, the good parts would start to feel bland and emotionless. In that moment though, with fear and trepidation moving through my body, *bland* sounded just fine.

"Ready, Eden?" Calder asked, and by the look on his face, I wondered if his question went deeper than whether I was ready to hike out of here. Was I ready for a new life? A different life? One filled with questions and hardships? Perhaps a long and terrifying journey to get there?

"Yes," I answered simply. *As long as you're beside me, I'm ready for anything.*

Calder adjusted Xander. "Drink as much water as possible," he instructed. "We don't have a container to carry it in and it might be hours before we have access to more. I gave Xander a little water before I heard your call, so he should be okay, especially since he won't be the one exerting himself."

I leaned over the side of the spring and put my mouth under the trickling waterfall, and then Calder did the same.

It was time to leave.

We exited through a very small opening between two large towering rocks on the far side of our spring. Before we left, I made a point of moving the brush in front of the opening where we entered, so it was covered completely and didn't look out of place. I didn't want anyone to find this place…not just because they'd know where we escaped from but also because, to me, this place was sacred. I didn't want anyone else tromping through it, at least not before we had a *new* sacred ground, our own little piece of Elysium on earth.

As we hiked upward and climbed over and between rocks, we grew quiet, listening for the sounds of other people. The only sound I heard was Calder's huffing breaths as he carried Xander on his back straight uphill. I didn't want to think too much about who Hector would have sent after me, or that feeling of dread would descend once more as I pictured his warped expression, eyes darting everywhere as though voices were chattering around his head. Instead, I daydreamed about what Calder's and my little slice of peace would look like once we got to where we were going. I had such a small frame of reference, so I mostly used the feelings I remembered from being with my own family before they died and even the things I loved about the main lodge.

I'd want a bedroom with a huge window, like the one at the back of the lodge that looked out on a beautiful view. Not the desert, for we'd be far away, but maybe a body of water, or trees or a forest of some sort. I'd have a big kitchen and I'd cook dinner for Calder every night. I hadn't been taught how to cook, but I'd watched Hailey in the kitchen, taking note in my mind about how she made bread that rose perfectly and melted in your mouth. I knew all the basics, not because anyone had taught me but because I'd paid attention.

And there would be babies. I wanted ten babies and I wanted each of them to look like Calder. I wanted to make them, and raise them, and I wanted to teach them all the things I'd learn before they came.

Calder glanced back at me and did a double take at my expression. Did I look dreamy-eyed? I couldn't help the blush that heated my cheeks. Here I was, planning out *his* whole life for him in detail as we climbed away from danger. Surely, that wasn't the appropriate focus right now. But I couldn't *help* dreaming. I had been denied dreaming for so long, too afraid of letting the details come into focus, too afraid they'd be ripped from my grasp. But now, with each step, each foothold, my dreams came just that much closer to coming true. The world felt *almost* wide-open to me right now. I wanted to raise my arms and laugh up at the sky. I wanted to seize my own dreams and hold them close. *This is what hope feels like.*

When we reached higher ground, we stood together catching our breath for a few minutes.

"Do you need to rest for a while?" I asked.

"No," he said and started walking again.

I looked around, getting my bearings. We were about a half mile away from the main lodge now. I could see it in the distance, the lights glowing from within. It appeared as though every light in the place was on. I shivered and leaned toward Calder as I gazed at that room on the second floor where I'd been held captive—or at least that's what it'd felt like. Calder put his arm not supporting Xander around me and pulled me into him, looking off in the same direction, lost in his own thoughts. Over his other shoulder, Xander snored.

"That way." Calder pointed to my right. "It'll eventually bring us to the main road, but it looks like there's plenty of rock cover in case we see or hear a car coming." Calder gave me a quick squeeze and we started off again, walking as fast as we could.

"If we keep up this speed," Calder murmured, "we can make it to the city before daylight. That's the goal."

We walked for hours, our path the one that provided the most cover, even if it meant walking in a sort of zigzag pattern now and again. Cover was more important than time, although time was important too. We saw cars go by on the road twice but had plenty of warning ahead of time because of the black desert night, and the noise of the engines. Each time we ducked safely behind rocks as the cars drove by slowly.

"I need water," I finally said hours later, parched and unable to keep silent about my need to quench my thirst.

Calder stopped walking. "I do too. I think I see lights from houses about half a mile away." He pointed and I squinted my eyes to see what he meant.

I, too, saw a few very distant lights but couldn't tell what they were.

We started walking again. We didn't talk. The cloud cover was low, so the light from the stars was muted and dull, casting just enough light to see where we were going and what immediately surrounded us.

About ten minutes later, we were able to see that, indeed, Calder had been right. We came upon a few small houses, far apart and set back off the road. I followed Calder as he walked quietly around the side of the nearest house. There was a hose there connected to a faucet on the brick. I breathed out a sigh of relief, practically able to taste the wetness in my dry mouth and feel it on my chapped lips. Calder glanced around, looking edgy.

I was too thirsty to be nervous. I squatted down by the house and turned the faucet. It came on with a squeak and the hose filled as the water traveled through it, bursting out the end that I held up to my lips. I drank thirstily for a few seconds—the water sweet and delicious—and then handed it to Calder, who laid Xander down gently, and straightened his own back, stretching before taking the hose and drinking thirstily.

Once we'd had as much as we needed, Calder turned off the water and stood staring down at Xander again before he picked him back up, putting him over his shoulder. Calder had to be in pain; there was no way he wasn't. As we began to walk to the front of the house again, something big and dark suddenly lunged at us and I screamed, stumbling backward against Calder.

"What the hell?" he yelled, stumbling backward too.

A large dog started barking and lunged at us again. I screamed one more time, until I realized the dog was chained up and was only lunging toward us as far as he could go.

The front door of the house burst open and the porch light came on, illuminating a man holding a shotgun. "Who's there?" he called. "Show yourself!"

"Run," Calder said, so low I almost didn't hear it. He yanked my hand, and I lurched after him. A shotgun blast sounded behind us and I let out a small scream again and kept running, holding on to Calder's hand for dear life.

I heard Xander slur loudly, "Wha?" as we ran. When we made it to a grove of trees far enough away to know we weren't being followed, we stopped and I put my hands on my thighs, attempting to catch my breath. Calder lay Xander down on the ground and Xander sat up slowly, rubbing a hand over his face and looking around in utter confusion.

"What the hell?" he asked under his breath.

"Are you okay, Eden?" Calder asked, gasping for breath.

"I'm fine. My feet are torn up, but other than that…yes, I'm fine." I sucked in lungfuls of air, trying to get hold of my rapidly beating heart and burning lungs.

"Yeah, mine are pretty bad too," Calder said. We both looked down at our feet. Our sandals were barely hanging on, the straps that crisscrossed over the tops of our feet in serious danger of snapping and the soles coming loose, so each time we stepped, they slapped against the ground.

Calder looked behind me and pointed and I turned and squinted through a break in the trees. The city looked close. Hope soared, and I faced Calder, a grin spreading over my face. "How far do you think?" I asked in a rush of words.

Calder scratched his chin and looked over at Xander, who was slowly standing up. "Three hours maybe?"

Xander kept looking in the direction of the city and then back at Calder. "You carried me all this way?" he asked.

"You'd have done it for me too," Calder answered.

Xander's shoulders hunched just a bit, his expression filled with some emotion I couldn't define in the low light. "Yeah," he said, the word sounding slightly strangled. "Yeah." He looked back out to the city, seeming to compose himself.

"How's your back?" Calder asked.

Xander moved a little as if testing it. "It feels like a million bucks," Xander said. "Too bad we can't sell it for cash because damn do we need it."

Calder chuckled, and then without speaking, we all turned and began to walk again. I had been exhausted, almost falling down with tiredness before we'd come upon the houses. But now I felt energized. We were so close.

We briefly told Xander what had happened with Hector and why I'd called them. He glanced over at me and put his hand on my shoulder briefly. "You did the right thing, Eden."

After that, we walked silently again, Calder leading the way and Xander in the rear, the only sound our flapping sandals. When I glanced back at Xander, he still looked slightly out of it, like he was trying to clear the fog in his head. But his legs were working just fine and I was thankful Calder didn't have to bear his weight any longer.

Again we stuck to the areas next to the road that provided the most cover. Luckily, even though the large rocks were few and far between now, the vegetation had increased, so we moved between groves of trees and behind brush where we could.

When we had been walking for a couple hours, we saw bright lights moving closer to us in the distance, and all stopped and moved behind some large flowering bushes. The red and blue lights on top of a fast-moving car shot by us, and as we watched it move away, the lights turned off, but it continued to drive in the opposite direction. I released the breath I'd been holding.

"Police," Xander said.

I nodded. "It was going toward Acadia. Do you think Hector called the police?"

"Maybe," Calder said, standing up and taking my hand.

About three miles from the edge of the city, Calder's sandal gave out. He made an angry, frustrated sound and threw the broken straps into some brush. He dropped the useless sole onto the ground and turned around, putting both hands on the back of his neck, as he looked up at the sky.

"Here," I said, ripping off the hem of my skirt.

"What the hell are you doing?" Calder asked. He moved around me quickly to block my suddenly bare legs from Xander.

"I'm making you a shoe," I said. "My legs aren't going to get torn up on the road for being bare, but your foot is."

Xander chuckled. "She's right, Calder. Sit down. I'll use it to attach the sole to your foot so you can walk. We're so close."

Calder sat down on the road and let Xander tie my skirt

hem around the sole and over his foot and around his ankle. When he stood up and tried it out, he shrugged. "This one feels better than the other one now."

I smiled. "Well, good. I've got enough skirt to go around if we need more."

"Oh no you don't," Calder said, but a corner of his lips quirked up. He took my hand and we started walking again. Holding hands hadn't been something we could do before that moment. It made the sense of freedom that much sweeter.

The dirt road turned onto a highway, and we walked along it for a while, keeping as far away from the actual road as we could so we were mostly out of sight from drivers passing by. Very large trucks roared past us with different names written on the sides in bold, bright lettering, their engine noise swelling and then receding.

We made it to the edge of the city just as the morning sun crested the horizon as if in welcome. We'd walked all night long, but we had enough energy to grin at each other and grasp hands tightly as our feet stepped onto the first sidewalk I'd walked on since I was a small child. I figured Xander and Calder had never seen a sidewalk, but I was too tired to ask at the moment.

After another half hour or so, Calder pointed. "There," he said. I followed his finger to a sign that read, "Holiday Inn," and the word "Hotel" beneath that. I wanted to weep with relief and happiness. Our destination. We'd made it.

Calder pulled me into a large doorway and Xander followed, groaning softly as if in pain and leaning back against the wall. "Listen," Calder said softly. "I think Xander should go in and try to buy us a room. He knows the most about money and talking to people. Plus, he's in their clothes and his shoes look better than ours since he didn't walk for as long in them." Calder addressed Xander: "Eden and I will walk inside in twenty minutes or so and you wait somewhere where we can see you. We'll follow you from there."

Xander gave a nod. In this light, I could see that his face was pale. "Sounds like as good a plan as any."

Calder studied him for a minute. "Let me see your back."

Xander looked like he was considering protesting but then turned around. Small dots of blood stained the back of his shirt, making the dark material darker in spots. I sucked in a breath. "It's really not that bad," Xander said. "I think I just need to change the dressings."

Calder lifted up Xander's shirt and checked under an edge of the cotton bandage. I couldn't see what he was seeing from where I was, but Calder frowned and put the shirt back down. "Okay, we'll get you cleaned up when we get inside." He pushed Xander gently toward the hotel and handed him the canvas bag so it looked like he was a traveler. "Make me proud," Calder said.

Xander laughed. "Don't I always?" He turned around and walked backward for a second. "Twenty minutes," he said. We nodded and he turned and walked quickly to the front door as we watched.

I sighed and leaned back against the doorway like Xander had just done.

"How are you doing, Morning Glory?" Calder asked softly, taking me in his arms.

I burrowed into his chest, inhaling his comforting scent. "Fine. I'm fine." I turned my head to the side so that my cheek was resting against his shirt. "Do you think he's looking for us?"

Calder was silent for a few seconds. "I don't know. But it doesn't matter. He won't find us. This is a big, big city, and by tomorrow, we'll just be any ordinary people, in ordinary clothes, doing ordinary things."

I nodded, but inside, I wondered if I'd ever feel ordinary.

I closed my eyes and rested against him. After what seemed like mere seconds, Calder nudged me. "I think it's been about twenty minutes. Let's go."

I took a deep breath as Calder stepped back and took my hand. "Stay just a little behind me and don't make eye contact with anyone. But don't look nervous either," he instructed as we started walking.

A minute later, we were pulling open the doors of the Holiday Inn, me holding Calder's hand and walking slightly behind him. The lobby was mostly deserted, except for an older man using a vacuum on the carpet. He was humming softly as he worked and he didn't even look back at us. There was a sign that said "Check In" with an arrow pointing around the corner. I released a breath. We wouldn't even have to walk past anyone.

Suddenly, Xander appeared from a hallway. "Hey, guys," he said, "going up?" He winked and walked toward a sign that said "Elevators."

Calder squeezed my hand and my heart leapt with hopeful excitement as we followed Xander. Xander frowned in confusion at the doors on both sides of the hallway as he looked between them and the card in his hand. I leaned forward and pressed the up arrow. Sometimes I knew something and I couldn't remember how or why—I figured it had to be something I'd learned in the past, but the specific memory or memories of actually doing it were gone.

A second later, the doors in front of us dinged open and

we all peered inside, Xander stepping in first, Calder and I following behind. When we were all inside, Xander looked at the card in his hand again and said, "Ten," under his breath before pressing that number on the wall.

The doors closed and the elevator lurched. Calder let out a small gasp and put one palm on each wall, bracing himself. I laughed softly and Xander grinned over his shoulder, and then the elevator was rising swiftly. When it stopped and the doors opened, Calder grabbed me and jumped off, stumbling away from the open doors as quickly as possible. "That can't be natural," he said.

Xander snickered. "You can take the stairs tomorrow." He pointed at a sign that said, "Stairway."

"I will." He looked back at the sign. "At least everything's labeled in the outside world."

We followed more signs to get to the door with the number on the card Xander carried and then took a few minutes to figure out that we opened the door *using* the card.

When we spilled into the dim room and shut the door behind us, we stood still there for a minute, gaping around. Were we really here? Had we made it? Joy, swift and complete, filled my body and I let out a small incredulous laugh and launched myself into Calder's arms, laughing and crying at the same time. He picked me up and laughed into my neck, squeezing me tight. "We did it, we did it," I repeated.

"Well, thanks for nothing. I'm the one who got us in here with my easy charm and winning smile," Xander complained as he walked to the bed by the far wall and put down the bag we'd all taken turns carrying once Xander could walk.

Calder set me down and we both walked over to Xander. I pulled his shirt so we could all hug, although Calder and

I were both careful not to touch his back as he laughed and patted our shoulders. "We did it, partners," he said. "Holy hell, we did it."

"Was it hard?" Calder asked. "Getting this room, I mean?"

"Nah," Xander said. "It was easy actually. The kid at the front desk looked like he was falling asleep, probably about to get off shift. I paid in cash and signed a form and that was that."

"How much did it cost?" I asked.

"Two hundred forty dollars," Xander said. "I rented it for two nights. I know that's a lot. But now we have time to get in touch with Kristi, get some clothes for you"—he nodded at me—"and try to pawn the gold."

I nodded, stifling a yawn.

"First though," Calder said, "we're going to get cleaned up and get some sleep. Xander, go shower and then I'll rebandage your back."

"Okay, the guy at the front desk said there was an ice machine on every floor. Maybe if I put some ice on it for a little while, it will help with some of the pain now that those magical herbs are wearing off." Xander grimaced slightly as he rolled his shoulders forward and then headed toward the bathroom.

After he shut the door, I turned to Calder. "Have you guys ever used pain relief? Like Tylenol?"

Calder looked at me blankly. "I've heard of it," he said. "That's one of the things people who lived outside before Acadia talk about missing, but no, I've never used it."

"We need to get some for Xander."

Calder sighed and ran a hand through his hair. "That'll have to wait until tomorrow. I think we all need rest more than Xander needs pain relief. Especially since he's done without it all his life."

"Okay, go get ice and come right back."

"Do you think it costs money?"

I frowned. "I don't know. Take some money just in case."

Calder nodded, grabbed the bag on Xander's bed, and took out some change and put it in his jeans pocket. He pulled me toward him, kissed my lips, and then turned and walked out the door.

I sank down onto the other bed and lay back, sighing at the feel of the soft mattress beneath my back. I started drifting off and forced myself to sit up. If I fell asleep, I'd never wake up. And I wanted to shower and tend to my practically black, dirt-crusted, blistered feet before I got in this clean bed. I was going to sleep in a bed with Calder for the very first time. A thrill shot down my spine despite my exhausted state. Yes, we were in a hotel, and yes, Xander would be sleeping right next to us, but still, I was going to be under blankets with Calder. I felt giddy.

Deciding I should have gone with him to get the ice because it would serve to keep me awake, I left the hotel room and stepped out into the hallway, peering in both directions. The floor was quiet, not a person in sight. I turned a corner and saw a sign for ice and couldn't help smiling. Everything *was* labeled in the outside world, thankfully. I followed the sign, and when I rounded the corner, I saw Calder standing in front of a big Coke machine. He turned and startled when he saw me and then, for some reason, looked embarrassed. "I got some food for us," he said, glancing at the machine just a little ways down the hall.

I tilted my head, looking between him and the Coke machine. "Soda," I said. "Do you want to try one?"

Calder put his hands in his pockets. "I've had Coca-Cola before," he said. "Ranger station."

"Ah." I studied him, swearing I saw longing in his gaze. "Well, let's get one."

"No, no, we shouldn't waste our money on this."

"Calder, it's only a dollar. Let's splurge. Just this once. We deserve a reward, especially you."

He looked so torn. "I don't really need it," he said, drawing out the word *need*.

I reached in his front pocket and grabbed a handful of change and then went up on my tiptoes and kissed him quickly. "It's okay to want things once in a while. We'll buy one and share it. By the way, I haven't had a chance to tell you how much I like you in jeans." I shot him a grin and then stepped to the machine and deposited four quarters. The soda can dropped noisily and I bent down and retrieved it, handing it to Calder. He took it and studied it like it was a delicate piece of expensive jewelry. "I'm going to make a wild guess that you liked those Cokes you tried."

He chuckled softly, turning the can one way and then the other "Yes, I liked it. Coke? Not Coca-Cola?"

"Yeah, it's like the shortened name. It's what most people call it."

He nodded, frowning at the can. "I feel like there are so many things to learn, so many things to catch up on. I feel like I just moved to another planet."

"In a way, you kinda did." I was quiet for a second, thinking. "I know how you feel. I know I experienced more up at the main lodge, but I still have a lot to figure out too." I held out my hand. "We'll figure it out together, okay?"

Calder smiled. "Yeah." He grasped my hand, brought it up to his lips, kissed it, and then feathered his lips over it softly. Even in my exhausted state, butterflies fluttered between my ribs. "We better get back with that ice," he said.

We turned the corner into the small alcove with another sign for ice. There were a few small containers sitting next to it and Calder picked one up and started filling it. I looked behind us and saw the small machine on the wall holding Tylenol, Advil, feminine protection products, and, I moved closer, reading the last product: Trojan Condoms. I didn't know what those were and so I squinted at the small package. "Ultra-thin contraception," I read.

Calder came up behind me. "Oh, lucky. Tylenol."

I counted out the coins and dropped them into the machine and retrieved the two small square packages of pain relief, putting them into my skirt pocket.

I noticed a supply closet. "Let's see if there's something in there to use for bandages for Xander."

Calder opened the door and we looked over the shelves of toilet paper and towels.

"A first aid kit," I said excitedly, bending down and retrieving it from the lowest shelf. "Perfect. There will be bandages in here."

"Good," Calder said. "Let's go."

We made our way back to the hotel room and knocked softly and, a few seconds later, Xander swung it open, standing in only a towel wrapped around his waist. "*Hot* water comes right out of the faucet!" he exclaimed.

"Here," I said on a smile, handing Xander one package of Tylenol. "Take this and Calder will get you bandaged up. I'm going to go take advantage of some of that hot water."

I headed off to the bathroom as Xander moved toward the bed. I cringed when I saw how bad his back still looked and pictured him tied to that pole as his flesh was ripped open with a whip. *We're far away from there*, I thought. *We're safe.*

In the bathroom, I stripped out of my clothes, balled them up, and put them in the trash. There was a robe on the back of the door. I'd have to use that until Calder and Xander could get out and buy me something to wear. My clothes were filthy tatters. I dropped my sandals in the garbage too, and cringed down at my feet. I washed my underwear and bra in the sink with soap and hot water and then hung them to dry.

I turned the shower to as hot as I could stand it and then stepped under the spray, sighing as the warmth cascaded over me. I washed my hair twice and conditioned it, and then sat down on the floor of the tub and used a washcloth and a bar of soap to clean my feet. Once they were clean, the red blisters were easier to see, but they still looked a hundred times better.

As I sat there on the floor of the tub, a wave of emotion suddenly overtook me. I pictured Hailey and the four little boys I had grown to love. I'd never see them again. I'd never go back to our magical spring. I'd never hear the distant singing of the workers as they sat around glowing fires at dusk. As happy as I was to be out of Acadia, as happy as I was to be free, a feeling I could only call grief swept through me when I realized everything I knew and was familiar with was no longer a part of my life. I hadn't expected that. I had thought I'd only feel joy at escaping Acadia; I hadn't antici-pated feeling sorrow and loss, but I did.

When the shower curtain was suddenly pulled aside, I squealed and startled, scooting backward and hitting my tailbone on the side of the tub.

"Whoa, sorry, sorry," Calder said, stepping into the shower with me. I stood shakily as I wiped my tears away. "Hey, Morning Glory," he said softly, pulling me into his chest. "What's wrong?"

I shook my head, a new batch of tears rolling down my cheeks. "I don't even know," I breathed. "I just realized I'd never see Hailey again...never see our spring... We fell in love there."

Calder looked into my eyes, his expression soft. "We'll fall in love a thousand times again," he said, "in all kinds of new places."

I managed a small smile and sniffled.

"Okay?" he asked, brushing his lips over mine.

I nodded. "Okay," I whispered back.

Calder's gaze moved over my face. "I'm going to take care of you, Morning Glory."

"I know," I whispered. And that was the thing I loved most about Calder. He didn't just protect me in physical ways; he protected all of me: my heart, my feelings, and my moods. I loved him so much. "I'm going to take care of you too."

"I know."

He kissed me gently, and when our heads moved under the spray, he broke free and laughed, and put his hand out to feel the water. "It is, it's hot!" he said. He stuck his head under it and then pulled it away, a smile lighting his face. I suddenly realized this was his very first shower.

I turned us around so he was the one directly under the showerhead and he sputtered and grinned. I laughed. His joy was contagious.

"Xander?" I whispered, inclining my head toward the room outside where Xander was, feeling strange he would know we were in the shower together.

"He fell asleep again before I was even done bandaging him. I think the Tylenol started working and the relief put him right out."

I nodded, picking up the bottle of shampoo and pouring

308

some in my hand. I reached up to rub it in his hair and he bent forward so I had better access.

I lathered his hair and ran the pads of my fingers over his scalp, working the shampoo through. He moaned softly, closing his eyes. I smiled, running my fingers behind his ears and around the back of his neck. "That smells like…" His forehead wrinkled as he sniffed. "What is that?"

I glanced over my shoulder at the bottle. "Mango splash."

His forehead creases deepened and I couldn't help laughing softly. "Mango? What is that?" he asked.

"It looks like a fruit," I said, glancing at the picture on the bottle once more. I'd used shampoos and other products that smelled like apples and honey and vanilla and different things before, but I didn't think I'd ever encountered a mango. They certainly didn't grow at Acadia, and if I'd had one as a small child, I couldn't remember now. "Do you not like the smell?"

He sniffed the air again. "No, I do. It smells sweet." But he appeared dubious.

I smiled as I continued to wash his hair. There would be a million things to question as we walked through the world. But I suddenly felt better, the feeling of loss subsiding as I experienced "mango splash" with Calder. We'd navigate new places, new roads, new feelings, and strange new bottled fruits together. "Lean back," I instructed, tilting his head under the water.

Once the shampoo was rinsed from his hair, I took the bar of soap and nudged him gently so he turned around. I lathered my hands and ran them over the beautiful muscles of his smooth back, massaging his shoulders with the slippery soap. He hung his head and braced one hand on the tiles in front of him and sighed. He was wet and sleek and big. I ran my hands down his muscled backside and cleaned the backs of his legs. When I got to his feet, he turned around and I reached for the washcloth and did the same thing for him I had done for myself, washing the hours and hours of road grime off him, taking care not to hurt the wounded parts of his feet.

I worked my way back up the front of his legs, kissing the healed but scarred skin from the wounds he'd suffered so bravely. I slowly massaged his muscular thighs. It was difficult not to notice that between them, he was hard and rigid, and when I leaned my head back and looked up into his face, his eyes were half-lidded with lust. I swallowed, standing slowly.

"Sorry," he whispered. "I can't help that. Your hands feel so good."

"There's nothing to be sorry for," I said. I loved the way he reacted to my touch. I wouldn't want it any other way.

I lathered my hands once more and slid them over his chest, his muscles tensing as he tracked my movement with his gaze. I slid my hands down his arms and then brought each hand up, cleaning between his fingers slowly. His chest rose and fell as his breathing increased, and with his obvious excitement, my heartbeat accelerated as well.

I met his gaze as I brought one of his fingers to my lips and feathered them over it before opening and sucking it gently into my mouth. He drew in a sudden breath and pushed his finger in slowly. I sucked at it again, licking around it and closing my eyes.

Calder moaned deep in his chest.

Suddenly, he removed his finger from my mouth with a pop and took my face in his hands, bringing his mouth to mine. I met his tongue with mine, swirling and tasting, bringing my arms up and around his neck, pressing our naked flesh together and moaning softly at the feel of my nipples rubbing against his chest. Around us the steam swirled and the water rained against the tile, blocking out all other sounds except for our mingled breath and very soft moans.

Calder kissed down my neck as he pressed that hot, hard part of him into the side of my hip, moving it in slow circles. I leaned my head back and sighed. The tingly feeling grew between my legs, the blood there pumping in a slow, steady rhythm. "I want you inside me," I whispered. This was our reward for what we'd just endured. We deserved this, needed it.

Calder's mouth came back to mine as he walked me a couple steps back until I was pressed against the wall of the shower. I put one leg up on the small corner edge of the tub and Calder bent his legs and guided himself to my opening. We laughed softly when it took him several tries to get things lined up properly. But finally, he pushed into me and we both sighed in bliss. Calder moved slowly and deliberately. I took my arms from around him and used my palms behind me to keep steady and to stop my skin from slapping against the tile.

"I love you so much," Calder panted against my neck, thrusting steadily into me. For me, this time felt much better than the first time and I relaxed into him, moaning softly as I gripped him deep inside me.

"I love you too."

"Things are going to be just fine, Eden. I'm going to make sure of it."

"I know. I know."

Calder used his thumb to circle slowly on the sensitive bundle of nerves just above where he'd entered me and I pressed forward, seeking more. My nipples pebbled and I leaned my head back against the tile, finding newness and joy in the varied sensations and emotions that all came together to create such intense pleasure. I'd never forget this moment. It felt like a celebration that we were alive, that we were free. It felt necessary to declare with our actions that this wasn't a sin. It was beautiful because we did it in love.

When I felt his warm, wet mouth cover one nipple, I gasped, hot pleasure shooting from my breast to between my legs, right where Calder's thumb circled faster and faster. "That's...oh, please, don't stop, it's so good," I panted. I felt rather than heard Calder's own moan as he switched nipples and drew it deep into his mouth, sucking gently.

I had no idea where he ended and I began, only that we moved together, seeming to have melted into one unit. The heat of the shower—of him—had gotten to my head, surely. I was half out of my mind with emotion, exhaustion, *love*, and awe-inducing pleasure.

That overwhelming tingly feeling increased, and more intense, hot pinpoints of light grew and burst, white pleasure shimmering around me as I clenched and shuddered, and then cried out softly in his arms. Wave after wave of glorious pleasure overcame me. Calder's thrusts grew short and shallow, and I watched him as his eyes closed and his lips parted, and he appeared almost pained. Nothing in this world could possibly be more beautiful. My own body clenched again as an aftershock swept through me at the sight of his pleasure.

Right then, if he had asked me to walk another twenty miles, I would have.

Suddenly, he grunted, a sound somewhere between bliss and pain. He pulled out of me quickly, pressing into my stomach and falling forward as he moaned against my neck.

For long moments we just breathed that way, the calming sound of the cooling shower still beating down around us. I wrapped my arms around him and held him, relishing the feeling of not being scared that we were going to be caught and punished for what we'd just done.

"I'll never ever forget my first shower," Calder whispered.

I laughed softly. "As far as showers go, that was a pretty good one for me too."

Calder grinned. We cleaned ourselves quickly and then turned the water off, stepped out, and dried each other tenderly.

Calder used the towel to blot my hair dry until it was just slightly damp. I put on the robe on the back of the door and Calder tied a towel around his waist.

We didn't have toothbrushes but used a small bottle of mouthwash provided by the hotel. Calder watched me as I swished it in my mouth and then spit it down the drain and then followed my lead. We'd have to get a few necessities tomorrow.

We turned off the light and stepped into the room, where the air-conditioning was on high, creating a steady hum blocking out any noise. Xander was lying on his stomach on the bed near the window, snoring softly.

It was morning, but the heavy drapes were pulled tight and blocked out almost all light.

Calder and I climbed under the blankets and turned toward each other in the dim room. "I love you, Morning Glory," he whispered.

"I love you too, Butterscotch," I said back, my heavy eyelids closing of their own will. Calder's warmth surrounded me. I was finally sleeping in a bed with him. I fell asleep with joy in my heart.

When I woke late that afternoon, disoriented and heavy with sleep, the smell of mangoes surrounding me, I reached for Calder, but he wasn't there.

I sat up, bringing the blankets with me, as my robe had fallen open while sleeping. I immediately spotted the note on the nightstand next to me.

Morning Glory,

We went to get some clothes and shoes and other necessities. We'll bring back some food too.

I love you. C.

P.S. Sleeping on an actual mattress for the first time came in second to sleeping next to you.

I grinned and set the note back down, noticing he'd left a bag of peanuts and the still unopened Coke on the table for me. *Sweet Calder.* I stretched and got out of bed. After using the bathroom, I ate the bag of peanuts and drank a bottle of water the hotel provided, recalling Calder's longing gaze at the can of soda and saving it for him.

I flopped back on the bed, staring up at the ceiling, feeling happy, feeling safe, and finally, finally feeling *free.*

CHAPTER TWENTY-TWO
Calder

I had woken to the feel of warm skin against my face, the scent of Eden and sweet fruit meeting my nose. *A dream*, I thought, *a beautiful dream*. But it hadn't been. It had been real. The peace I felt had been as unfamiliar as the new scents and different surroundings and I had wanted to stay wrapped in her warmth all day, her soft breath lulling me into tranquil dreams. But I had to take care of her. There were things she needed.

So now Xander and I were walking the aisles of a store called Target that the hotel clerk had directed us to when we told her what we needed. "Our stuff was stolen," Xander had explained. "We need everything." And then he'd shaken his head and shrugged his shoulders, as if to say, *What can you do? The state of the world is such a bummer.*

"Good thing you're not just an accomplished thief but an accomplished liar too." I ribbed him as we walked out the door of the hotel.

"Don't forget nighthawk call expert." His lips turned

down. "I'm still pretty disappointed I never got to use that."

I laughed. I was still wearing a bandage wrapped completely around the foot that had no shoe. Hopefully, if people noticed, they'd just think I had an injury, not that I was using it to replace my lack of footwear.

We walked across the large parking lot of the store and both took a startled step back when the double doors in front of us opened before we even touched them. "What the…?" Xander asked under his breath as we both peered at the doorway in confusion. We ducked through tentatively and entered the massive, brightly lit store.

As we wandered the aisles, I looked over at Xander, his mouth open and his eyes filled with awe. I was sure I had the same expression on my face. There was *so much* of…*everything*. And it was all so…colorful. One part of the store had clothes and shoes, and another part had soaps and grooming products, and one huge section even had food, all packaged up with bright pictures on the boxes.

"Have you ever seen stuff like this?" I asked Xander. Everything came in a box or a bottle or had a paper tag hanging from it.

"Yeah, some at the ranger station but never this much." He looked around in wonder.

"Let's find what we need and get back," I said. "We probably look like we're aliens from another galaxy the way we're looking around."

"Yeah, that or on some sort of drugs."

I laughed. It was either do that or cry. I'd known I'd feel out of place in the outside world, but I hadn't imagined feeling like a different species.

We each picked out a pair of shoes and made sure they fit

on our feet. When I put my foot inside the padded sneaker and walked a few steps on it, I sighed with happiness. "Wow, this is nice," I said, bouncing slightly.

Xander laughed. "You look like an idiot."

"Look who's talking," I said, taking the shoe off. "You're trying on slippers."

Xander looked down at the brown leather bootie on his foot. "These aren't slippers."

"Yes, they are. It says so right on the tag."

Xander turned over the tag at his ankle and read it. He took the bootie off and hung it back up on the rack. "I knew that."

I shot him an eye roll, which he ignored.

"Listen, we only have about a hundred fifteen dollars, so let's spend as little as possible," he said.

I nodded, checking the price tags on the shoes I'd just tried on. "Hopefully we can replenish some cash with the jewelry."

"But that's not a sure thing yet."

I nodded. "We probably have enough in change to eat until we can get ahold of Kristi."

"Yes, I'm gonna try her later. She leaves the ranger station at eight o'clock. I guess she'll be home at about nine…hopefully."

"Do you even know how to use a phone?"

"I'll figure it out. Anyway, Eden will know how."

"Oh, right, she will. Speaking of Eden, what size shoe do you think she wears?"

"Small."

"I don't think shoes come in small."

"I don't know then. Just take half your size. That's probably hers."

I picked out a pair of sandals that didn't have a back strap. I thought they'd be forgiving of size, even if I was a little off.

We were okay on clothes for now, but Eden needed something. We wandered through the girl's clothes, confused.

"Can I help you with anything?"

I turned around and a girl with a red shirt on was standing behind me. I looked down; her Target name tag said, "Ashleigh." She blinked at me. I was sure I looked pretty bad. I hadn't shaved in two days now and I was wearing a bandage on my foot. "Hi, Ashleigh, uh, yes, I need something for my girlfriend and I've never picked out girl clothes before."

Her face fell slightly, and confused, I glanced at Xander, wondering if I'd said something wrong.

"Of course," she said. "Well, is this for an occasion or just something casual?"

"Something casual."

"Well, a sundress always works. What about one of these?" She held up a dress with bright blue and green flowers that looked like it would barely cover Eden's breasts.

"Uh, something more…covered?" I asked.

Ashleigh sighed. "She could put a sweater over it." She held up a very, very short sweater with short sleeves. I looked between the dress and the "sweater," unsure if Eden would like either one.

"Is that what girls wear?"

Ashleigh stared at me. "Well…yeah."

"Looks good. We'll take it," Xander said.

Ashleigh glanced at him. "What size is she?"

"Small."

She nodded and dug through the racks, pulling out another one of the same dress and same sweater.

"Thanks for your help," I said as I took the clothes.

"No problem. Thanks for shopping at Target." She gave us a fleeting smile and walked away.

We headed back to the aisles where we'd seen soap and picked up toothbrushes, toothpaste, and a brush for Eden. The hotel had all the other stuff we needed, and we didn't want to waste any money unnecessarily.

Our last stop was the food department. We looked around, confused about what everything was. I wanted to pick things up and read about them, but we didn't have time right now and, although it was supposedly the food department, half the stuff didn't resemble food at all. Finally, we settled on a loaf of bread, some cheese, and a bag of apples.

We returned to the front of the store where we had seen people paying for their items and followed along behind a mom with two kids sitting in her cart. We watched as she put everything on the counter and then the counter moved her things right to the clerk's hand.

"Whoa!" Xander said, his eyes widening as he watched the woman's items move forward.

I looked up at the clerk, who had her eyes narrowed suspiciously on us as she ran each item over a machine that beeped loudly.

When it was our turn, we did as the woman ahead of us had done and watched as the clerk bagged our items, our heads moving back and forth as each item was pulled forward.

"One hundred fourteen and thirty-six cents," the clerk said, her eyes still watchful. We were obviously doing something wrong again.

"I added it all up in my head, and I thought it only came to a hundred five or so," Xander said out of the corner of his mouth.

"Tax," the clerk said, overhearing him.

"Oh," Xander said back. "Right. Tax. Yeah, I forgot about the tax."

"We've never been in a Target before," I explained.

Xander sighed and shook his head.

The clerk stared at us. "Are you boys Amish or something?"

"Yup," Xander said, handing over our money. We'd just spent practically every cent of it.

The clerk nodded knowingly. "I thought so. I watch those shows." She took our money and put it in the drawer and scooped out some change.

"Oh, uh, that's good," Xander said, clearly confused.

"How accurate are they?" the clerk asked.

Xander stared blankly at her, and at his ridiculous expression, I laughed. I couldn't help it. But I quickly sucked it back, feigning a cough.

"You'll do fine," she said, giving us a smile and handing Xander the change. "Good-looking boys like you, you just ask for help if you need it, m'kay?" She winked at us.

"Thanks," Xander said, staring back at her for a minute. "Oh hey, we're looking for a place to pawn jewelry. Can you tell us where to go?"

The clerk tapped her fingers on the counter. "Well, I can't say exactly, but if you walk about a quarter mile in that direction"—she pointed her finger out the doors in front of us—"you'll run into a neighborhood that most likely has a dozen of those."

"Right. Okay, thanks."

Outside Target, we sat on a bench and unpackaged our shoes and put them on. They felt incredible. I could practically hear my blisters sighing in happiness.

We walked in the direction the clerk had pointed us, and about ten minutes later, the buildings started looking more run-down and groups of people stood on street corners, some laughing and others just seeming to mill around. There were also a few reclining in doorways or even on curbs. Xander and I didn't talk. We were so busy looking around, taking everything in, trying to understand how the big society that we were now a part of worked. I thought I had understood a lot of it from the people who talked about the lives they'd lived before Acadia, but being among it was a completely different experience.

"Look," Xander said, pointing his finger across the street. I turned my head to see a giant sign that said, "Pawn Shop," and had blinking lights surrounding it.

"Well, that's not easy to miss. Come on."

We crossed the street, entered the shop, and went to the counter, and a moment later, a man came from the back. "Can I help you?"

Xander took the piece of jewelry he'd brought out of his pocket and put it on the counter. "I want to sell this."

The man picked up the heavy chain and looked it over, squinting and rolling the small stick in his mouth. My heart raced. What if this didn't work? We'd have basically no cash left.

"You got ID?"

"No, all our stuff got stolen," Xander said.

The man gave him a glance. "You need an ID to pawn something in my shop."

Xander made a sound in the back of his throat, opened his mouth and then closed it as he looked down at the chain in the man's hand, obviously at a loss of what to say or do.

"But I'll buy it from you, no ID required," the man said.

I wasn't too stupid to see we were about to be cheated. "How much?" I asked.

"Five hundred dollars."

Which meant it was probably worth four times that. "We'll take it," Xander said.

I sighed. What other choice did we have? Plus, we had some more jewelry. Maybe Kristi would help us out next time and we'd get a fairer price.

The guy nodded and went to the back. When he returned, he counted out five one-hundred-dollar bills and put them down on the counter. "Nice doing business with you boys," he said, turning his head slightly and belching.

I grimaced and pulled Xander's arm as he picked up the cash. As we walked to the door, I couldn't shake the feeling that someone was going to reach out and pull us back, so when the heavy door closed behind us, I released a breath of relief. "Let's get back," I said, suddenly not liking the feel of this particular neighborhood. My gaze hung on a woman sitting on a bench rocking back and forth and muttering to herself. Was this one of the places where Hector came to find those who needed saving and then led them to Acadia?

Xander glanced around nervously, seeming to feel as uneasy as me. We walked in the direction of the hotel at a quickened pace.

Being in the city with cars racing by us, sudden noises I wasn't acquainted with, shouts of people I didn't know, eyes of strangers on me caused a brief longing for Acadia and all I was familiar with. It was confusing since I'd wanted so badly to experience the outside world and now here I was doing that. But inside, I longed for the familiar, for the things and surroundings that made me feel confident and in control, for the way of life I understood and the people who greeted me as I passed by.

Eden—I needed Eden, my comfort, my purpose, the other half of my heart. I picked up my pace even more and Xander jogged to catch up with me, not asking any questions, obviously understanding why I was in such a hurry.

Xander used the key to open the hotel room door and I practically pushed him aside to get through. "Eden?"

All the curtains were open, showing the night sky. The beds were made and everything looked like it'd been straightened. But where was Eden? I dropped the bags I was carrying on the bed, my worry increasing. "Eden?" I called again.

"In here," she said, coming from the bathroom.

I released a breath and rushed toward her and picked her up in my arms as she laughed and I squeezed her tight.

"Success?" she asked.

"Success," I confirmed, burying my nose in her fragrant neck. "We got money and clothes and food."

"Big success. Let me see. Oh, and I'm starving. Feed me."

I chuckled as I set her down, taking a few steps to the bed and opening and handing her the bag with the clothes inside. "I hope they're okay," I said.

"Anything other than a bathrobe will be fine," she said on a small laugh.

As I got the food out, Eden went back in the bathroom. When she came out a few minutes later wearing the sundress and sweater, I stopped what I was doing and simply stared. Her slim but shapely legs were fully on view, and the fitted sundress hugged her curves. I raised my eyes to look at her face and she was biting her lip, waiting for me to speak. "You look beautiful," I said. It was so strange to see her in what I knew were "regular" clothes in the outside world, when I'd only ever seen her in long dresses or skirts with blouses that buttoned to her neck. For a brief moment, she felt like a different person to me and that longing for familiarity came back again. I pushed it aside though. She *wasn't* a different person. She was still her despite new clothes and despite that she'd cast off the role of savior and princess.

Eden smiled and then did a small twirl that made me smile back. "Thank you."

I looked over at Xander and he was staring at Eden too. "Whoa," he said. But then he looked at me and the smile vanished. "It's really...bright, that's all."

We sat down and ate bread, broken-off pieces of cheese, and apples. We told Eden about our "adventures" in the aisles of Target and the pawnshop.

As Eden and Xander laughed and chatted about something, I chewed my apple and watched them, my lips tipping. Whatever happened from here on out, whatever struggles we had, I'd never forget this moment. For some reason, it felt important to take a mental picture that very second. Hope shimmered around us, the knowledge that— hopefully—the hardest part was over and now we could focus on one step at a time as we searched for our place in this new big world.

"I'm gonna try Kristi now," Xander said. "Eden, will you walk me through this phone thing?"

Eden and Xander went over to the phone on the bedside table while I cleaned up the food.

I glanced up when I heard Xander say, "Kristi?"

Eden came over and wrapped her arms around me from behind and nuzzled her face into my back. I turned around and gathered her in my arms, kissing the top of her head as I listened to Xander give Kristi a brief breakdown on what had happened since yesterday. Had it only been yesterday? It seemed incomprehensible that life had changed so much in twenty-four hours.

"Yeah," Xander said, "okay…right. Half an hour? Okay, yeah."

I looked at him questioningly over Eden's head.

Xander hung up the phone and stood there for a second, looking at the wall. Finally, he turned toward us. "Kristi's going to pick us up in half an hour. She said the police were all over the ranger station today asking about Eden."

Cold dread pooled at the base of my spine. Of course I'd already known that Hector wouldn't be searching for us, not only because we were of legal age, but he was likely glad to be rid of us. But he would definitely be searching for his chosen one, Acadia's ticket to Elysium.

"Kristi doesn't think we're safe here at a hotel, especially one of the first ones at the entrance to the city," Xander said.

I nodded, and Eden took a step back. "Right. Okay," I said, starting to gather up our stuff. "Is it safe to go to Kristi's house?"

"Probably safer than here. She suggested we get out of town as quickly as possible."

"Out of town?" Eden asked, stuffing things into the canvas bag.

"Yeah. We can ask her about it when she picks us up."

"Can we get our money back for the room since we won't be staying tonight?" Eden asked.

Xander shook his head. "We have a thousand dollars now with Kristi's money. I don't think it's worth drawing attention to ourselves right now."

We were packed up in ten minutes and watched the clock for the next twenty. I paced while Xander and Eden sat on the bed, watching me. It wasn't only Hector searching for Eden; he'd called the police. I didn't know why I had doubted he'd alert the authorities. True, Eden was a minor for now, but she wouldn't be for long. And Hector had always seemed so adamant about keeping our community separate from the big community, operating by its own laws—the laws of the gods as spoken to *him*.

When thirty minutes had passed, we left the hotel room and descended the stairs out onto the street. A minute after that, a red car pulled up to the curb and a pretty woman with dark-blond hair pulled up into a ponytail stepped out. She immediately went to Xander and gave him a hug.

"Kristi, this is Calder and Eden," Xander said, opening the back door so we could get in.

"Hi, Calder. I've heard so much about you," she said as she gave me a handshake. Then she turned to Eden with a warm smile and shook her hand too.

Once Kristi had instructed us on how to attach our seatbelts, she pulled back into traffic and I sat back, watching nervously out the window as the buildings flew by. I tightened my grip on Eden's hand and she squeezed it back.

"So," Kristi said from the front seat, "you guys really did it. You made a break for it."

Xander chuckled softly, but I heard the nervous edge to it. "Yeah, we were kind of forced to."

Kristi looked over at him. "You did the right thing, Xander."

"Gods, I hope so," Xander muttered.

"God, singular," Kristi said. "You'll call attention to yourself if you refer to plural gods."

"Right." He looked back over his shoulder at Eden and me. "I forgot to mention to you guys, in the big society, people pray to a singular god."

326

"Yes…I think I remember that," Eden said. She leaned forward slightly. "Which one is it?"

I smiled over at her. I knew which one she was hoping for.

"Uh, just, you know, the creator of the universe," Kristi said, looking in her mirror at us and shrugging. "But there's also Jesus, Buddha, and Muhammad…Allah. Different people, different religions and cultures pray to different gods, or prophets, or whatever. But only one…generally."

Eden sat back, a dissatisfied look on her face. I squeezed her hand again. Gods, I loved her. *God*, I loved her.

"Xander mentioned that you thought we should leave town," I said after a moment.

Kristi nodded. "If it were me, I would. The police came to the ranger station today, said you were an underage runaway, Eden, and they were looking for you. Obviously I didn't say anything about ever having seen any of you." She glanced at Xander. "But I'd get far away from here if I were you." She paused. "If you decide not to, I know some people who I'm sure would help you get a start here. But I encourage you to get far away."

"Where should we go?" Xander asked.

"Well, that's up to you guys. You don't know anyone at all?"

"No one except you," Xander said.

"Which, by the way," I said, "we can't thank you enough, Kristi. I don't know where we'd be if Xander hadn't met you, and without your help."

Kristi met my eyes in the mirror. "Hey, if I were in your position, I'd hope someone would help me too."

I nodded, but I didn't completely understanding her meaning.

"Speaking of help, we have some more jewelry we were hoping you could help us sell," Xander said.

"That's no problem," Kristi said. "I've sold gold before. It's easy. And there are plenty of reputable places."

"I don't think the place we went to yesterday was very reputable," Xander said.

Kristi shot Xander a confused frown. "You'll have to tell me about it." She pulled into a parking lot, turned off the car, and got out, and we followed with our meager possessions.

We walked behind Kristi down a path and up a stairway and watched as she took out a key and opened a door that had "8C" on it in chipped gold paint.

Kristi shut the door behind us and we all looked around at the large open apartment, with a giant window on one wall overlooking a courtyard. In addition to the comfortable-looking pieces of furniture, there were boxes piled up against one wall.

"I know it's small," Kristi said as though she was embarrassed. "And the boxes take up even more room. You guys know I'm moving in a couple weeks, so..."

I met Xander's eyes and we both started laughing.

"What?" Kristi asked.

I knew it was rude, but I couldn't get a hold of my laughter, and Xander apparently couldn't either as we both doubled over, clutching our stomachs. It was almost as if the stress of the last few days had crumbled our self-control.

"Don't mind them," I heard Eden say. "It's just they both grew up in a whole cabin about an eighth of this size." I was still laughing, but I had to admit I was proud of her fraction usage in ordinary conversation. *I taught her that.*

"Sorry, sorry," I said, containing myself. "Kristi, to us, this is a palace, I swear. You have no idea. It's beautiful and we're grateful you're taking us in."

Kristi grinned. "Okay, then, you're going to be really

excited about this. Calder and Eden, you have a whole room to yourselves right through there. Xander, you get the couch."

"Story of my life," Xander said, throwing our stuff down on the piece of furniture. I chuckled and pushed him slightly, which he took good-naturedly.

"So, guys, I know it's still early," Kristi said, "but I'm going to turn in because I have class really early and tomorrow is my last day of work at the ranger station." She yawned. "But help yourselves to anything in my kitchen and we'll talk more tomorrow about your plan. The thing you're all going to need is IDs. But we'll discuss that. Also, Xander, leave the rest of the jewelry on the coffee table there. I'll grab it in the morning and stop at a jewelry store on my way home from work."

I nodded. "Hey, thanks again, Kristi, for everything." I reached out to shake her hand, not knowing exactly what to do. She smiled and shook my hand and then we all said good night.

I took Eden by the hand and pulled her into the room that Kristi had pointed us to. There was nothing except a mattress sitting on a metal frame, made up with sheets and a blanket folded up at the end of the bed.

I took Eden's face in my hands and kissed her long and deep. I couldn't believe we were in a room together and could simply enjoy each other so freely.

"Your bed is my bed now," she whispered.

"Forever. From this day forward, we'll never sleep apart again."

There was peacefulness in Eden's smile and my heart rejoiced to see it. All the fear, all the worry and hardship had been worth it. As I watched her, she covered her mouth to hide a yawn. "Sorry, I have no idea why I'm still so tired."

"Because you went through a really scary experience and then walked twenty miles practically barefoot." I led her to the bed. "Let's get a really good night's sleep and then we'll get up early and figure things out."

Eden nodded. "Do you really think we should leave here right away?"

I considered it for a second. "Yeah, I think so." I didn't want to constantly look over my shoulder. I wanted to focus all my attention on getting a job and all the other things that would be necessary to live a good life, and that would be difficult if we stayed so close to Acadia.

"Your parents…" Eden said.

My chest tightened. "Someday…maybe we'll go back… For now, I have a life to build for us. That's my focus, my *only* focus."

Eden nodded, but her frown remained.

I leaned forward and kissed her lips gently again. "You go use the bathroom first."

Eden took her turn in the bathroom, using the products we'd bought, and then I took mine, using toothpaste for the very first time in my life. It was overly sweet and tasted odd to me, but after I'd brushed, I loved the slightly minty taste in my mouth.

When I got back to the room, Eden was already under the covers, half asleep. I stripped off my clothes and joined her, taking her in my arms, feeling her warmth envelop me. Our hands started roaming, but we must have been overly tired because the next thing I knew, the first dim light of dawn was streaming through the edges of the shades on the windows and I heard the faint sound of birds chirping outside the glass.

A little later in the morning, after getting some quick instructions from Kristi as she was on her way out the door, Xander and I left the apartment to see what we could do about getting copies of our birth certificates for ID purposes and to find out about bus tickets. I left Eden curled up in bed, her long hair spread over the pillow, her breathing smooth and even. We'd agreed the night before that she'd stay in the safety of Kristi's apartment while Xander and I went out. It made me breathe easier. Plus, the only one being looked for was Eden.

We stepped back through the apartment door at three thirty. "Eden?" I called as Xander shut the door behind us.

"Hi," she said quietly. I hadn't even seen her curled up in a chair on the opposite side of the couch, books scattered all around her.

A grin spread across my face despite the fact that I didn't have much good news to give to her. I'd missed her, and I'd *allowed* myself to miss her. I'd never willingly done that before; it'd never been safe to do that, but now...now everything was different in ways I was going to have to navigate moment by moment.

Eden started standing, her face flushed and her eyes bright. She looked...feverish. "Are you okay?"

She nodded and set down the book she had in her hands and walked over to me, grabbed my hand, and started pulling me toward our room. "Hi, Xander," she said as we moved past him.

I glanced back at Xander, confused, and Xander shrugged before picking up a small black controller and pressing a button. "Television," he called behind me. "I watched some last night. You've gotta check this out."

"Okay, we'll be out in a few minutes," I said, closing the door behind us. Eden turned toward me, lifting the bottom of my shirt. "Whoa, hi." I laughed, letting her pull my T-shirt up and over my head.

She stood back, her gaze moving heatedly over my bare skin. "You have a beautiful body, Calder. It's...so manly and"—she ran her hands up my chest—"sexy." She leaned in and kissed one nipple before dragging her tongue around it.

Gods. God. I groaned, hardening. That was one thing about jeans—they didn't allow much...expansion. Also, where had this come from? "Uh, Eden, this isn't unwelcome, but what exactly have you been doing for the last several hours?"

She looked up at me. "I've been reading." She sighed dreamily as she stood straight. "Beautiful love stories about people destined to be together."

"People? What people?"

Eden ran her hands down my arms and then started unbuttoning my pants. All thoughts fled my brain. Who cared what she had been doing? If this was the result, I wanted her to do more of it.

She dragged my pants down my hips, and let them fall to the floor. I kicked them aside, and her eyes went to my straining erection, and they seemed to grow even glassier as she reached out and stroked me once. I sucked in a breath.

"Lord Darkhaven and Lady Flowervale."

I had started leaning forward to kiss her and paused. "Dark what and Lady who?"

"The people you asked about. Their names are Lawrence and Elinor." She sighed, another dreamy look washing over her face. I was completely lost. She stroked me again and I groaned.

332

I took her face in my hands and kissed her lips. They immediately opened and our tongues met, the fresh taste of her bursting across my tongue, filling my mouth. She whimpered and my entire body, my heart, my mind—they were focused on one thing and one thing only: Eden. She kissed me like she hadn't seen me for decades. She kissed me like I had just come home from war, unexpectedly alive and unharmed. *Whatever I have to do to keep this girl kissing me like this every day of my life, that's what I'll do*, my lust-fogged brain somehow pieced together.

I walked her backward to the bed, and we both went down on it, my mouth coming off hers as she laughed. I grinned too, and then began kissing the smooth, fragrant skin of her neck.

"I love *love*," she declared. "I love *you*. I love being yours."

"I love you too," I said, between kisses. "I love being yours."

Eden pushed me, and I rolled over onto my back and she climbed on top of me, nestling my erection right against her core. My thoughts began to dim once more.

She leaned down and kissed my neck and then began stroking my erection. "That feels so good," I breathed. "Don't stop."

She stroked me for another minute and then leaned back a little and used her other hand to cup and fondle my balls. I sucked in a breath and my eyes flew opened. *God.*

Eden's eyes met mine and widened as a pink tinge rose in her cheeks. "Do you like that?" she asked.

My mouth opened but no sound came out, though I finally managed to nod, doing whatever I needed to do so she didn't stop.

Eden's eyes were focused on me, and the dreamy smile

only made me harder. Wherever this had come from, I had to make sure to provide more of it.

"Tell me about this book you read today," I said, my voice raspy. I was thinking that as soon as I had a job and was bringing in some money, I'd ration my food to buy her more of these books.

Eden stood up and quickly removed her clothes as I watched. I started to sit up so I could touch her, but she pushed me back down gently. "Lawrence, brave and noble lord, dark-haired and strong, just like you," she said, as she climbed on top of me and took me in her hand again.

I fell back on the bed, my erection throbbing in her hand. "Eden…" I groaned.

"I know," she said, "I want you too. I've wanted you all day. I've been feverish with it, ever since Lord Darkhaven took Lady Elinor's maidenhead on the kitchen table of the servant's cottage."

"Maidenhead?"

Eden nodded. "Lady Elinor was hiding as a servant from the evil Duke of Wallington." She guided me to her opening.

My vision grew blurry as I watched the tip of my penis enter her slowly.

She stopped moving and I groaned, a sound of desperation and need.

Eden closed her eyes and lowered herself, the wet warmth of her squeezing me so tightly, I thought I could easily pass out from the pleasure. "Mmm," she murmured, and started moving slowly, her eyes still closed and her head tilted back.

"But he found her anyway, and he captured her!" she said.

I jerked at her tone of outrage, trying to remember what we'd been talking about, who "he" was, and why she might be suddenly irate but my thoughts were all blurry, my brain cells not firing properly, and the one thing I knew for sure was that she wasn't angry with me.

Eden's nipples tightened and she moaned, and the sight of her, along with the feel of her wet friction, was almost torturous. I gripped her hips but resisted guiding her. I wanted to see what she was going to do. I wanted to see her move in the way that pleasured her the most.

She bounced on me a little faster and each time she came down, she let out a tiny gasp of pleasure. She reached her own hands up and touched her nipples and I had to close my eyes for a second not to climax right then and there. "Eden," I groaned, "I can't... You're—"

"What feels good to you?" she asked on a breath, her eyes fluttering closed and her full lips parting. God, she was exquisite.

"It all feels good to me, Eden. At this point, anything you do feels good. Move the way you like."

"Just a second... Oh, you feel good too," she breathed. "Lady Elinor was right. This is very good."

Thank you, Lady Elinor, I thought blearily. My vision blurred even further and I felt my own climax swirling through my abdomen. I held it back, gritting my teeth and straining my stomach muscles.

Then, thank the heavens, Eden began moving in earnest and panting my name. She fell forward on top of me, gasping one final time as she moaned and pressed into me.

I flipped her over in one swift movement so she was on her back, and I thrust into her hard and deep, my toes curling as the bliss spiked through my body. My own pleasure hit me, hard and intense, stars bursting before my eyes as I jerked and swelled inside her and pulled out just in time for my seed to spill on her stomach. I groaned into her neck, rolling my hips lazily, milking the last little bit of my climax. I couldn't wait for the day it would be safe to come inside of her. But for now, I couldn't risk that.

We lay there together, my head right under Eden's chin. "But valiant Lord Darkhaven rode his trusted steed over mountains and into valleys, through the blackest of nights to rescue Lady Flowervale. And even though there was a twist, and they discovered that Lord Darkhaven wasn't actually a lord at all, but a penniless pauper without a title or a castle or even a shilling to his name"—Eden ran a hand through my hair as my head cleared and my breathing slowed—"Lady Elinor chose him anyway because he was her one true love."

I lifted my head and looked up at her. My eyes widened as tears came to her eyes, one escaping down her cheek.

"'Lawrence,'" she whispered, bringing her other hand to her chest, "'whether a lord or a pauper, a prince or a gutter-snipe, I worship you and no other. Until no breath remains in my body and my bones have turned to dust, you, my love, you and no other.'" She exhaled shakily and then beamed at me as more tears flowed from her eyes.

Um… Was she *crying* over two characters from a book? I was utterly at a loss for what to say to the beautiful girl under me who I loved fiercely and yet was completely baffling me. Maybe there was a good reason Hector had banned fictional books so long ago.

"I know it's just a story," Eden explained, as though she'd seen my confusion, "but it made me believe that even seemingly hopeless situations can work out in the end. Even when everything looks to be a mess—and you're not sure how or why or where to turn—that with love, everything will be okay, that *we'll* be okay."

336

I couldn't help smiling even though I was still slightly dazed. "Morning Glory," I murmured, my lips lingering on her forehead for a moment. "Where do you find your strength?"

"From you," she whispered.

We rolled to the side, so that we were facing each other on the bed, and I ran my hand down her long hair, working out the tangles we'd created.

"Tell me about today," she said softly.

I sighed. "No luck today. There doesn't seem to be any record of our births. Kristi thought there might be, since we were registered in school, but evidently, after our births at Acadia, no birth certificates were obtained. We're not sure how it all works—we're trying to figure it out. But until we do, we're not going to be able to work anywhere that requires identification, so no restaurants or stores. Xander and I have some ideas though, so I don't want you to worry, all right?"

"I'm not worried. I know things are going to be okay."

"Right, Lord Dark…"

"Haven," she continued. "Yes, Lord Darkhaven. I pictured him to look just like you, only his hair curled up over his collar, in a rakish fashion."

Rakish. I laughed softly. "I don't know what a 'rakish fashion' is exactly, but if growing my hair gets me more of what we just did, then…"

"I think it just might." She put her head back down on my chest and I felt her smiling against my skin. A wave of sudden protectiveness crashed over me and I gathered her more tightly in my arms. Sometimes the depth of my love for her stunned and scared me. It made me aware of my own vulnerability and all the ways I might disappoint her.

I breathed deeply, drawing strength from her trust in me. There were parallels between us and the fictional couple she'd just wept over. Eden had forsaken her role as a princess to follow a pauper out of the desert and into a life of uncertainty. The mere idea of letting her down made me feel like I was bleeding inside. *My beautiful girl, I will protect your sweet and hopeful heart. I vow to shield you from any ugliness in this world and always be your shelter in the storm.*

Eden ran her finger lazily over my skin and I sighed, relaxing under her touch, allowing the doubts and pressures to float away, at least for now.

"What should we do for dinner?" Eden asked after a few quiet moments.

"Are you hungry?"

She nodded. "I worked up an appetite."

I smiled. "Then let's get you some food. Kristi should be home soon too. Hopefully she was able to sell our gold." I paused. "I feel like a pirate every time I say that."

Eden laughed. "I think Kristi had a book with a pirate in it out there. That'll be next on my reading list."

I grinned. "I support that plan."

We remained lying there, enjoying the feel of being in each other's arms, the quiet around us, the knowledge no one was going to try to separate us, and that we would sleep tonight and every night from here forward, just like this.

An hour later, we all sat on the couch as Xander flipped through television stations, showing us how it worked. It was loud and bright and too much seemed to be going on at once for me to focus. "Turn it off," I said, grimacing and turning away. It had given me a headache and I'd only been watching for ten minutes.

"You don't like it?" he asked, incredulous, pressing buttons on the controller again.

"No."

The door opened and Kristi came in, smiling happily at us. "Hey, guys," she said, closing the door behind her. "Good news: I have cash for you. Over a thousand."

"Holy hell. You're kidding!" Xander exclaimed, clicking the television off and standing up.

"Nope. Here you go." Kristi opened her purse and handed a stack of cash to Xander.

"Well, let's celebrate," Xander said. "Dinner is on us." His smile dropped. "Wait, how much is dinner?"

Kristi laughed. "We'll go somewhere very affordable."

"Okay, and hey, we don't need your money now."

"Well, you're getting it anyway," Kristi said. "A deal's a deal and you can use all you can get. I just wish I could give you more. Let me freshen up and we'll get going."

Xander, Eden, and I grinned at each other. Things were falling into place. "What do you think, Lady Flowervale?"

Eden laughed. "I think we're gonna be just fine, Lord Darkhaven."

"Ready?" Kristi asked, coming out of her room.

"Yup," I said, taking Eden's hand in mine.

We descended the stairs, chatting and laughing. When we turned the corner to the parking lot, a police car rolled slowly to a stop. A police officer with a black mustache and wearing sunglasses stepped out of the passenger side to our right, his hand on the gun at his belt. I squeezed Eden's hand more tightly, adrenaline spiking through my system. "It's okay," I said quietly, "just follow my lead. Maybe they'll help us."

I glanced behind me, searching for an escape route just in case. There was nothing except a solid concrete wall.

That's when the officer driving the car stepped out and turned toward us.

It was Clive Richter.

CHAPTER TWENTY-THREE
Eden

"We've been looking for you, Eden," Clive said with a strange smile that didn't come anywhere near his cold eyes.

"Clive?" Calder asked, sounding incredulous. He stepped slightly in front of me, shielding my body. "She's fine," he told Clive. "She doesn't want to live with Hector." The other officer was leaning against the car, watching Clive who was clearly his superior.

"Well, unfortunately, *son*, Hector's her guardian and she doesn't have a choice." He squinted at me, resting his hand on the gun at his waist. "You do, though. You're free to do as you please. You're eighteen. Hector doesn't want you back anyway."

Clive Richter is a police officer! I tried to wrap my mind around what was happening as my eyes darted between Clive and Calder.

"No way I'm leaving her," Calder said, squeezing my hand tighter as I peered around him. My brain reeled. My body swayed. I felt vomit rise up my throat. How had we been laughing and joking just minutes ago, and now my whole world was crashing down? Clive looked pleased somehow at Calder's declaration that he wouldn't leave me. *Why?* Was it what he had wanted him to say?

"Do you know the man you're bringing her back to is a cult leader?" Kristi said, her voice rising as she stepped forward. "He runs a wackadoodle cult out in the desert where he brainwashes people to think he speaks to gods about a great flood."

Wackadoodle? Brainwashes? A cult leader? Kristi's description of Acadia wound through my brain, the words not quite making sense.

The other police officer lowered his sunglasses and looked at her. "You call it a cult; he calls it his religion," he said. "And regardless, he's still her guardian. He has legal rights."

Kristi shook her head, looking confused. "What? That…" But she didn't seem to know how to continue. He must be right.

"You're lucky we don't arrest you for harboring a runaway," he said. "And we *really* don't want to shoot you, but we will if we have to." He laughed and touched his gun again. I had no clue what was funny.

"Get in, both of you," Clive said, his face turning stony as he pointed to the police car. "Don't make me have to cuff you."

"Calder…"

Calder looked back at Xander and I caught a widening of his eyes and a small nod from Xander. What they'd communicated, I didn't know. Then Calder made a sudden movement, throwing himself in front of me and facing the officer. Calder pushed me backward to Xander who took my hand and started to run. I screamed, looking backward as the officer dived at Calder.

And then suddenly, I was being slammed to the ground, the breath leaving my lungs as I hit pavement. I desperately tried to pull in air as someone yanked me up. Clive stood in front of me, breathing hard. He snapped cuffs on my wrists, a wild, excited look in his eyes. "Little fighter. I like that," he said with a high-pitched laugh. Then he dragged me backward to the police car as Xander swore behind me, Kristi rushing to his side.

I swallowed, a drumbeat of terror pounding inside me as I was pulled along.

Calder was being shoved inside the police car and I was pushed in behind him. Calder's expression was panicked as he tried to reach out and touch me with his cuffed hands. "Are you okay? Eden, are you okay?" He made a sound of desperation in the back of his throat as his eyes flew over me.

"I'm okay, Calder. I'm okay." I reassured him, even though my heart thundered in my chest and fear pumped through my veins.

Xander ran to the door of the car, but Clive held him back. "He doesn't want you," Clive said.

He. Hector.

Calder leaned around me and called out to Xander. "I'll meet you…"

Xander walked away backward, his face a mask of shock and anger but he nodded at Calder. "I know where, I know when," he told him.

I didn't know what they'd arranged, but Calder nodded and slumped down in the seat. "It's going to be okay. I promise you, we'll just leave the second we can. We have somewhere to go now; we have money."

I nodded, incapable of forming words, refusing to cry.

Clive and the other officer got in the front seat and pulled away from the curb. I glanced through the back window to see Kristi and Xander standing there, twin expressions of shock on their faces as they watched us drive away. It had all happened in less than five minutes. *How? How did they find us so quickly?*

I was numb, shocked, stunned. Clive looked over his shoulder and laughed mockingly. "Hoowee. Hector's gonna be happy to have you back, princess. I gotta say, he's lost it a little, but this should put things right again."

He turned back to the road and I saw his eyes in the rearview mirror, looking at Calder. "You made a bad call getting into this car with her," he said, his eyes shiny with cruel amusement. "In this case, chivalry was a poor call." And then he laughed mockingly.

Calder and I remained silent, scooting as close to each other as possible. My hands had grown cold and clammy and I couldn't stop shaking.

I looked out the window as we drove down the highway and then eventually turned onto the dirt road leading to Acadia. *Did we really walk all this way? Did Calder carry Xander on his back all the way down this very road?* Tears pricked my eyes and I blinked to keep them back. We'd be making this walk again soon, my mind insisted. We'd be escaping again the second we could. And then we'd *stay* gone. We'd be smarter, safer. And I'd be eighteen in two weeks and then there'd be nothing Hector could do anyway. I straightened my spine and held my head up. Two weeks. It was all we had to bear.

I met Calder's gaze and he gave me a barely perceptible nod. "That's my strong and brave Morning Glory," he said very, very quietly.

We pulled into Acadia, the gravel crunching beneath

the tires of the police cruiser. I blinked around. It looked deserted. No one was in the fields, no one was tending the animals, and no one walked the paths. What was going on?

Clive came around and opened the door for us, and I stepped out, the sound of Hector's voice surrounding me. I turned in a slow circle and saw it was only the loudspeakers, turned up to full volume, blasting through Acadia.

Clive pushed Calder roughly, and he let go of my hand and stepped back, catching himself. Calder's lips thinned and a muscle jumped in his jaw as he eyed the gun at Clive's belt. Clive stood taller, cold amusement glinting in his eyes. "Try it, *Water Bearer*. Make my day."

"Hey, come on, Clive," the other officer said. "We delivered them. Let's get back to work."

Clive kept his eyes on Calder and spat on the ground next to him. That's when I saw Hector coming out of the house, Hailey next to him, running to keep up.

Hector's hair was long, the way he used to wear it when I was a little girl. But it wasn't pulled back now. It was wild and stringy, and it made it more obvious how much hair he'd lost on the top of his head. He had lost a lot of weight too and his cheeks were gaunt and hollow. And the look in his eyes…the look in his eyes as he got closer…it was just like the night I'd run…only…worse. Had that only been a couple of days ago? Hector looked like he'd aged years since then.

Hailey looked like she'd been crying, and when they both came to a standstill in front of us, she lowered her gaze and clasped her hands in front of her. The loud recorded sermon continued to fill the silence.

In my peripheral vision, I saw Clive Richter and the other officer get in their police cruiser, and a moment later, the car drove off.

Hector took a deep breath and smiled. "I'm so pleased to have you back, my love."

Hailey's eyes darted to him, to me, and then back down. Three worker men I didn't know came out of the main lodge and stood behind Hector, their eyes downcast as well.

"Hector, please," I implored. "Let me go. Let us go. If you ever loved me, *please*, just...let me go."

The pleasant look on Hector's face didn't alter. "Let you go? Let you go?" He put his finger to his lips and stood there looking up at the sky for a full minute. Then his expression filled with frigid anger. "*So that Satan's spawn here can possess you?*" He screamed, spittle flying form his mouth. He jerked his head toward Calder. "*So that the rest of us can rot in hell for eternity?*"

I startled as he shouted the words, and Calder made a move to come toward me, but the three worker men suddenly leaped forward and grabbed his arms. He looked back at them in shock and confusion. "What the hell are you doing? You know me. You *know* me!"

"We thought we did," the tallest man said. Oh gods in Elysium, I was in a nightmare. *Please make this stop!*

"Take him to the cellar," Hector said, smoothing his hair back and standing up straighter as though gathering himself from his outburst.

Calder reared back and punched one of the men in his face, and the man reeled as the other two scuffled with Calder to get a good hold on his arms. I brought my hands to my mouth, not able to hold back my sobs any longer.

Suddenly Hector moved behind me, and I was pulled roughly against his chest. "I'll slit her open," Hector hissed.

Everything stopped. I froze. Calder froze. The men holding him gripped his arms tightly and ceased moving too. Hailey let out a sharp cry.

346

Hector pressed the knife he was holding to my throat, and I flinched as the point of the blade pierced my skin.

"There's power in her blood," Hector said. I cried out in disgust as he brought his face forward and licked the drop rolling down my throat.

"If she refuses the foretelling, there are alternate ways to bring her with us to Elysium…even just a small living part of her." Again, he licked another droplet of blood on my throat and I clenched my eyes shut, my stomach roiling.

"You're out of your damn mind," Calder grated, his voice cracking.

Hector raised his head to stare at Calder. I felt his hot breath at my ear and smelled the stale stench of it. He pressed the knife to my skin again and I whimpered. *Oh God of Mercy, please don't let him kill me.*

"All right," Calder said, bringing his arms up to show his surrender. "You win. I'll do whatever you want me to do. Just please, please don't hurt her." Calder's eyes were wide with fear as he watched Hector.

Hector withdrew the knife slowly and I heard him suck in a deep breath of what seemed like satisfaction. "Take him to the cellar. Lock him up," he told the worker men holding him.

Calder's eyes bored into mine as he gave a singular nod. I acknowledged his nod with a small one of my own. *It will be okay*, he was telling me. *It will be okay.*

Somehow.

He went willingly with the three men, one of them now bleeding profusely from his face.

Hector let out a breath and smiled pleasantly. "Shall we go inside? Perhaps you'll play for me, my love?" Hector took my arm and I tried desperately to catch Hailey's eye, but she looked away, trailing behind me and Hector.

Later, after I'd played the piano for hours and was bent over the keys in exhaustion, Hector finally excused me, and I shuffled to my room. As I began to climb the stairs, Hector grabbed my arm. I gasped and turned to him. "The foretelling will come to pass, my love. Don't have delusions that it will not. And if you attempt to stop it, I'll kill him. Do you understand?" Then he let go of me and I used the last of my strength to bolt up the stairs.

I closed my door behind me and, moments later, heard it lock on the other side. On the window, heavy metal bars had been installed. I clamped my hand over my mouth, holding back my horror. I was a prisoner in every sense of the word. I collapsed on my bed and sobbed. Where there had been light and hope only hours before, now there was only darkness and despair.

———————

Over the next two weeks, I was rarely allowed to leave my room. Mother Miriam brought food to me, although there wasn't much. The fields weren't being tended; food was ripening and falling to the ground, uncollected. The animals were sick and hungry now too. I could hear the goats bleating miserably outside whenever there was a pause in Hector's broadcast. I thought I would go insane. I had to tamp my emotions down as best as I could and live with the one thought that kept hope alive: we would get out of here... *somehow*, someway. We would, at the very first opportunity.

I didn't know how Calder was and it filled me with stark terror. Were they feeding him? Was he okay? I vowed to be his strong Morning Glory. I vowed not to crumble.

On the afternoon of my eighteenth birthday, Hailey entered my room quietly and laid a white dress at the end of my bed. Her eyes were filled with sorrow as she looked at me sitting at my desk, staring out the barred window.

I ran to her and threw myself at her feet, hugging her legs and sobbing. Her hands stroked my hair. When I looked up at her, there were tears in her eyes. "Please help us," I begged.

"There's nothing I can do. My boys—I have four boys... He...he'll..." She put her face in her hands and cried softly for a minute.

He'd threatened their sons to keep her in line. I pulled in a breath. "Calder. Do you know how he is?" I asked when she'd dropped her hands.

"He's alive," she said. "He's being fed and given water. I have no way of knowing more than that."

Tears coursed down my cheeks. "If I marry Hector today, we'll just leave tomorrow," I whispered.

Hailey shook her head. "He won't let you. He'll never let you leave before the foretelling comes to pass."

"The foretelling isn't coming to pass!" I yelled. Hailey startled and my shoulders dropped. "I'm sorry, Hailey, but... you know that, right?"

She didn't answer me either way, just kept staring at the floor. I watched her, my hope dwindling. I wasn't going to be able to convince her to help us. Still...I had to try one last time. "Hailey, if I marry Hector today...and the time comes when I can get Calder out, will you at the very least distract Hector?"

Her gaze moved slowly to me and she stared seemingly unseeing for several breathless moments, but then she nodded. I released a breath of relief, hope sparking once more. I'd come up with a plan. I'd get Calder out and we'd run, and this time, we wouldn't get caught.

"Get dressed. I'll be back to do your hair. Hector means to marry you in an hour," Hailey said.

I swayed in shock. "In an *hour*?" I began trembling all over. I felt as if I was going to be sick. *An hour?*

"Yes, everyone is waiting at the temple. Councilman Daniels has the legal authority to perform the ceremony," she said. *No, no. This can't be happening.* I distrusted Councilman Daniels almost as much as Clive Richter. I wondered if he was a policeman too. Maybe they all were. I didn't understand any of it.

Do you know the man you're bringing her back to is a cult leader?

Be strong, Morning Glory.

I let out a deep breath and straightened my spine. Maybe there was more opportunity in me acquiescing. At least I'd be out of my locked room. "I'll be ready," I told Hailey.

She turned to leave my room but when I called her name, she stopped and turned back toward me. "Will you gather a few of the blue flowers that grow on a small bush on the west side of the field? I've always wanted to wear them in my hair on my wedding day."

Hailey appeared momentarily confused but nodded and then closed the door behind her.

I dropped to my knees. *Oh dear God of Mercy, please help me*, I prayed. *I need you. We need you. Please.*

An hour later, I rode to the temple in the carriage alongside Hector. He wore a suit of white, and I wore the long, flowing wedding gown someone had sewn for me. Morning glories adorned my hair. Pain gripped my heart.

We said our vows in the temple in front of the Acadian people, Hector's eyes shining with some form of fever I couldn't begin to explain. He looked like a madman. I tried

350

not to make eye contact as I murmured the words I did not mean. *The gods know my heart*, I thought. What did so-called vows mean if they were uttered as lies? I would never love this man. I would never be faithful to him. I belonged to Calder and only him.

I looked out to the audience and spotted Calder's parents. Their heads were bowed and they were praying reverently. They still believed.

He runs a wackadoodle cult out in the desert where he brainwashes people to think he speaks to gods about a great flood.

My head swam. The room felt overly hot. Maybe I'd caught Hector's fever. Maybe this place drove everyone mad.

When the ceremony was over, Hector turned to the people and raised his arms, his voice ringing out strong and sure. "My beloveds. This is a glorious day. Eden is now my lawful wife in the eyes of the state and as witnessed by the gods. And we are all one step closer to fulfilling our true destiny." He beamed out at them, his eyes unfocused but his smile wide. They all stared back at him, some looking happy, others looking stunned, troubled, and hungry. Several children were crying.

"A feast has been set up for you in the main dining hall. Please, eat. Rejoice. This is a day made for joy and celebration!"

Hector peered out at the crowd. "My beloveds, the flood draws near. The fruits of our sacrifice draw near. Cling to me; cling to your mother, Eden; cling to Acadia. Know we are holy now. Satan tempts you in all kinds of ways as our hardship grows, as the end draws near. But do not be tempted. Do not be forsaken. We are so close to paradise, my beloveds. Go now and celebrate."

He took my hand and led me up the aisle and back

outside to the carriage, where he took the reins and started back to the main lodge.

"Won't we be celebrating?" I asked in a voice that sounded dead, even to me.

"Yes, we'll be celebrating in my bedroom," he answered.

I stared straight ahead, trying to control my racing, aching heart, knowing what I had to do. I glanced to the right, where the door to the cellar was behind the main lodge. *Oh, Calder, my love. I'm doing this for us. I have no choice. I only pray it works.* I clasped my hands in my lap to disguise my trembling.

Hector took my hand and led me through the main lodge and up the stairs to his bedroom. I'd been in here before, when I'd stolen money and a couple pieces of jewelry. My heart clenched in pain when I thought of that moment at the spring when I'd shown Calder and Xander. There had been so much hope then. I had to push that aside so I didn't start screaming.

Hector approached me from behind and I felt his warm breath on the back of my neck as he lowered the zipper of my dress slowly. I pulled away from him, and when I turned, his expression was settling into displeasure. "Please, let me undress for you," I said, looking up at him through my lashes as though I was a shy bride.

His gaze dipped to my lips and his hand moved to the growing bulge in his pants, petting himself. Bile rose up my throat, but I swallowed it back down and attempted a pleasant smile.

Be strong, Morning Glory.

I slid off my shoes and brought my dress down my shoulders, letting it fall in a puddle at my feet. I wore nothing underneath. I stood before Hector naked, the very small swell of my pregnancy completely on show.

I ran my hand over it with shaking hands. It had only become obvious in the past couple of weeks, and more so because I'd lost weight due to the lack of food at Acadia. In my room alone, while Calder sat in the cellar not more than three hundred feet from me, I'd discovered a tiny beautiful secret. I was carrying his child. I knew I wouldn't be able to hide it from Hector when I stood before him naked. I had no choice but to beg for our lives.

"Let us go," I whispered. "It's not only my blood that runs through my veins now. It's his blood too. His child grows within me. And the baby is strong, just like its father."

Hector stood frozen, mouth gaping, eyes filled with deep confusion. "He's tainted you." He said it almost matter-of-factly.

Hope surged inside me. I was no good to him now. Was he going to give me up? I nodded, imploring him with my eyes. "Yes, Hector. I wanted to be tainted. Let us go. You don't want me. Please. Just let us go. Let us make a life together. I'm going to have his child. We're in love. That's all. It's that simple. Please." I fell down on my knees in front of him. "Please just let us go," I begged. "Have mercy, Father."

"Get out."

The calmness with which the words were said startled me more than a sudden yell would have.

"Leave my presence while you carry his spawn. I should have known how strong Satan was, how hard he'd try to stop the foretelling." He began swaying, lifting his head and squinting as if hearing voices in the air around him. "Yes. Again, I've underestimated his strength, his deviousness," he croaked, looking almost lost.

I stood quickly, gathered my dress, and pulled it on, not bothering with my shoes. Hector took me harshly by the arm and led me out of his room and down the hall to mine, where he practically threw me inside and slammed the door behind me. The latch sounded and I sat down on my bed and ran my hand over my tiny rounded bump. "It's okay," I said, attempting to soothe myself as much as the baby nestled inside me. "It's okay. You're safe. We're going to be okay."

I removed the gold band from my finger, laid it on my bedside table, and put my arms around myself, trying to get control of the shaking. I allowed myself to feel the relief that I hadn't had to endure lovemaking with Hector, but now I was even more scared for Calder.

The next morning, I woke up and blinked at the bright sunlight streaming through my window. I'd forgotten to close the shade before I fell asleep. I lay there for a few minutes, my hand going immediately to the small swell of my stomach, and for just a second, I felt like everything was going to be okay. I had no reason why I felt this. Everything was awful—a terrible, terrible mess. A nightmare. Yet for those brief few moments between dreams and complete wakefulness, a calm peace settled in my heart. Everything was going to be okay...*somehow*. But then the details of reality came flooding in, filling the void, and the hairs stood up on the back of my neck. Nothing was going to be okay.

I heard a key in my lock and sat up quickly, pulling the blanket up over my now fuller breasts.

Hailey walked in with my breakfast tray. She was looking down and I immediately saw that she had a large red mark on her cheek. "Hailey—" I started, throwing the covers back and getting out of bed.

"Don't, Eden, please," she said, her voice sounding

hoarse. "There's not much food. Sorry. Our steadiness is tested now. My boys are hungry too. So hungry…" She set the tray on my bedside table and left, closing the door quietly behind her. My heart squeezed.

She was their mother. Why didn't she take them and run? How could she watch them be hungry and do nothing? Not me. I'd fight the gods themselves rather than let my baby starve. I picked up the breakfast tray and set it on my lap and then sipped at my tea as I considered what could be done.

Hector had rejected me as his wife. That had to be good. I couldn't play the role in his foretelling now. It was over. Still, a chill went down my spine despite the warmth of the liquid making its way into my body. Hector wasn't going to give me up. I knew he wasn't. Otherwise, he'd have thrown me out last night rather than lock me in this room. I had only bought us some time. And if my instincts were right, not much time. I finished my tea, ate the few morsels of food on the tray, and then swung my legs out of bed. I knocked on my own door, and a few minutes later, Mother Miriam came and answered it and I used the bathroom as she waited outside.

I searched the drawers in the bathroom and found that everything that could be used as a potential weapon had been removed. No fingernail clippers. No bleach. Nothing. I leaned against the counter, feeling defeated. The problem was not so much me escaping. I could probably manage to do that. But how would I get Calder out too? And if I didn't, what would Hector do to him as punishment for both our actions? I felt hopeless.

As I opened the door to the bathroom, a sharp pain lanced through my abdomen and I doubled over, crying out at the sudden intensity of the cramp.

"What is it?" Mother Miriam asked, coming to my side.

"I don't know," I said breathlessly, still clutching my stomach. Another stabbing pain assaulted me, and I grabbed the wall, doubling over once more. "I'm pregnant," I cried. "Something's wrong!"

Mother Miriam drew back, shock registering on her face. "No," she said simply.

"Ahhhh!" I cried out as agony ripped through my stomach, and I bent over and vomited on the hardwood floor of the hallway.

"Take her to the sick tent," I heard behind me in Hector's deep, cold voice.

Mother Miriam wrapped her arm around me and held me upright as we walked…limped down the hallway to the stairs. Sweat had broken out on my face and everything swayed around me. "What did you do?" I asked weakly as we passed Hector. "What did you put in my tea? What did you do to me?" I cried out more loudly.

"It had to be eliminated," he said behind me. "What has been foretold cannot be unwritten or undone, not even by Satan himself."

"Ahhhh!" I screamed in horror and agony, the pain ripping through my body and through my very soul.

Mother Miriam gripped me more tightly and practically carried me out the door of the main lodge.

I vomited again right outside the door. "He's killing my baby," I sobbed. "Oh, God of Mercy, help me, help me, help me." I fell to my knees in my own sickness, shaking and sweating and half-crazed with terror.

"Shh, child," Mother Miriam said behind me, picking me up again and dragging me down the stairs. "I'm here."

"You hate me," I sobbed. "You did this. You did this too!" I beat weakly on her arm wrapped around my waist, but I had no energy left to do anything but bear the pain and sickness.

"I would never do this," she said. "I've lost too."

"Ahhhh!" I screamed again, doubling over in the courtyard and vomiting again. The world blinked on and off, everything swimming around me as I tried to pull myself upright. Something warm and wet was running down my leg.

I heard my name somewhere from far away and even in my delirious state, I knew it was Calder. "Calder," I screamed. "Calder!" My voice broke on his name as I called out a second time and then doubled over in a blood-curdling scream again, a river of liquid sliding down my leg. I tried to lurch toward where he was calling to me, but Mother Miriam pulled me back. "I have to get you to the sick tent," she said. "If you want to live, I have to get you there."

I went limp in her arms as another pain tore through me, too weak even to scream this time.

The world dimmed and faded around me and then came into focus again as I saw men running past me toward where I had been trying to go to Calder.

The next thing I knew, I was in the sick tent, lying on a cot, the pain still ripping through my body as I sweated and cried and screamed out the agony.

I lost time as everything went in and out of focus around me, the morning sunlight slanting in through the window one second, and then the early evening twilight sky greeting me the next. All that day, I cried and writhed and endured the pain as Mother Miriam came and went, attending to my body in ways I couldn't even focus on.

"The worst of it is over now," Mother Miriam said quietly from the end of the cot where she was cleaning my thighs and between my legs.

"Is it…is it…? Did I?" I sobbed.

She was quiet for a minute. "Yes, Eden, I'm sorry. Your baby is gone."

Gone? Where? Where is my baby now? The small being I only just began to love so fiercely. What do I do with that love now?

I fell back on the cot and wailed, tears of grief and loss and horror. "I did this," I choked out. "I told him about the baby. This is my fault. This is all my fault."

"No, this is not your fault. And you will see your baby again in Elysium."

I wailed harder. "I'll kill Hector when I get there," I spat out. "I'll hunt him down and kill him! I don't care if he'll already be dead!" I choked on my own sobs.

"There is no hate in Elysium, Eden."

I rolled into a ball and cried in misery.

"Calder tried to get to you when he heard your screams."

I looked at her through wet, swollen eyes.

"He fought like a warrior to get to you, child," she said softly, rubbing a cool washcloth on my forehead. "But in the end…there were just too many of them."

"Too many?" I squeaked out. "Is he…?"

"He's alive."

But I understood that he might not be for long. "Did they send Mother Willa to attend to him?"

"Mother Willa died last night," she said simply.

I struggled as I tried to get out of bed.

Mother Miriam pushed me gently back down. "There is nothing you can do, Eden. They won't let you near him."

"Why are you letting this happen?" I cried.

Mother Miriam pursed her lips. "In Elysium, all our dreams will come true. In Elysium, we will be gods and goddesses. In Elysium, I will see my own children again too."

"Then go to Elysium by yourself. Don't make us go with you," I yelled, another sharp cramp suddenly making me grab my stomach and wince.

"You'll have afterpains. It's normal. You need to rest."

She got up and left the sick tent, saying something to someone outside the door. A deep male voice answered back. They'd put a guard outside.

I turned over on the cot and sobbed. So much pain. Physical. Emotional. This was agony. I didn't know if I could endure it. *Calder, I'm trying to be your strong Morning Glory, but I don't think I can do this without you.*

After a few minutes, the room grew measurably darker and I brought my head up and blinked, turning to the window. Outside, I had a perfect view of the moon. A shadow was moving across it. My heart lurched and I grasped the bedsheets. Confusion and disbelief descended, joining the cloud of despair hovering over me. My mouth fell open and I stared. *No, no, it can't be.*

But it was. It was an eclipse.

CHAPTER TWENTY-FOUR
Calder

I bellowed in rage and helplessness and then sunk to the floor, gasping for breath. The hem of my shirt—the one I'd donned before our escape with so much hope—now served to mop the blood running from my lip to my chin.

But I couldn't just sit, and so I paced the cage they'd put me in—the same one I'd been pacing in for two weeks now—as I tried to fathom a way to get out of this underground prison. The door was made of heavy steel, food brought only occasionally, with no regular pattern. I rationed the water they'd placed in the corner in one of the large jugs I used to carry down to the spring. *The spring. No, don't think of that. Not now.*

They'd come when I'd started hollering and yelling like a banshee after I'd heard Eden scream. And I'd gotten through the first three, but then ten more workers—I didn't even recognize all of them in my crazed state—had come running down the stairs and overtaken me. They'd fought me like I was the devil himself. *Why?* They'd once been my friends. My family.

I'd failed Eden. I'd told her I'd keep her safe, protected, and she'd trusted me. I fell onto the small bench and put my head in my hands. What had she been forced to endure? Yesterday had been her birthday and no one had come in at all. I'd thought I would go out of my mind.

I'd been reduced to begging at the door for someone to help me, but still no one came.

A small scraping sound outside my cell caught my attention and I leaped up in time to see a small piece of paper being slid under my door. "Hey," I yelled. "Please! Let me out! Whoever's out there! Please!" Footsteps moved away, and moments later, I heard the outer door slam.

I grabbed the note and tore it open.

She is Hector's wife now in name only. Today, your baby was taken from her. She bore the pain with strength. She lives.

The words hit me like a body blow and I gasped as cold horror dripped down my spine. *Your baby was taken from her...* My baby? Taken? My brain reeled, trying to grasp the meaning of the words in front of me. I stumbled backward as I gripped my hair on the top of my head and attempted to calm my racing heart. Eden was carrying my baby? Had she conceived the first time we'd been together at our spring? That would have been about three months before. She *had* seemed just slightly...fuller, rounder in the last month. I just didn't think...I didn't think... My chest tightened and for a moment I didn't realize the strange choking sound filling my cell was coming from me. *Oh Gods. Oh no.* I'd tried to be so careful. No! I fell to my knees and wailed, lifting my head to stare at the ceiling as I shouted my grief and pain and unrelenting guilt. What had she experienced because of me? My beautiful Morning Glory.

I only registered the sound of keys in the lock as the

door was opening. I jumped up and then rushed forward as it opened but came to a halt when I saw Clive Richter standing there with a gun on me. Options raced through my brain. Could I survive a gunshot? Could I rush him before he got a shot off? I had no idea how guns worked. I had no idea what to do when faced with one. Adrenaline surged through me, but I'd be no good to Eden if I were dead.

I backed up slightly, raising my hands to let him know I wouldn't fight—not yet anyway. He sneered at me. "Turn around and put your hands behind your back."

I turned slowly, doing as he said. My mind was spinning a million miles a minute. I just needed to get out of here, make it to a place where I could help Eden. I could fight as long as it was fair. I could even fight as long as it wasn't fair, assuming the men I was facing down weren't fighting with the same passion as I would.

But, of course, the men here were fighting to be gods. They'd fight to the death for that possibility.

Clive led me out of the small cell. When we climbed the stairs and the door was flung open, I expected the sun to blind me, but the world was dark. *I thought it was day.* I'd been given breakfast hours before. I glanced up and immediately saw why the world was dim despite what I assumed was the early hour. My blood pumped furiously through my veins and I fisted my hands in the cuffs, testing their resistance. The sun was moving in front of the moon. It was an eclipse. Holy gods, it was an eclipse.

I didn't know what to think, what to feel, *what to do.*

The two council members, Garrett Shipley and Ken Wahl, who had held me back during Xander's whipping, joined us, walking beside Clive and me. Garrett's nose had a small splint on it and both eyes were a greenish yellow where his bruises were fading. They both glanced at me nervously. They *should* be nervous. If I had the chance, I'd kill them with my bare hands. I'd *relish* it.

They looked up at the sky as it dimmed further. "Hector says he was off on the foretelling. The gods didn't say two months, six days. They said two *days*, six *hours*. One of those unfortunate misunderstandings." And then they started laughing like hyenas about a joke I wasn't sure I understood.

As we walked past the end of my irrigation system, I glanced backward, toward the river and squinted. Someone, probably one of the workers, had fixed the areas that Hector had kicked over.

The sight of that irrigation system suddenly filled me with boiling hot rage. And grief. Such blinding grief. The twisting emotions coursed through my body, making me feel crazed, animalistic. I let out a yell as I kicked out with my leg and brought a section of it down. That system was the symbol of all my stupid, ridiculous, naive hopes and dreams. That system had been built when there was still a fire in my heart for what life might offer me. I wanted to fall on my knees and weep for that naive kid who knew nothing, realized nothing, and was blind to the way things really were. I wanted to knock him senseless, beat him, kill him, and render him unrecognizable. I hated everything about him and I wanted desperately to be him again. I missed him with my whole damn heart.

When I came back to myself, I had destroyed a long section of it and Clive, Garrett, and Ken were standing back, laughing at the show I'd just given them. I stood there, breathing hard, every part of my body hurting, from my face to my feet to my wounded heart.

"Come on," Clive said. "Hector's going to let you go."

I stopped. "He's letting me leave?" I asked, my heart lurching in my chest. "Why?"

"I don't give a fuck why."

"Why am I handcuffed then?"

"Because you're acting like the fucking animal you are, that's why."

"I won't. I won't, I promise," I begged. "Just free me and I'll go get Eden and we'll leave."

Clive smirked. "You don't get Eden, you fool. Eden belongs to Hector. You get nothing except your freedom. And you're damn lucky for that."

Okay, okay. If I was set free, I could come back for Eden. I could come up with a plan. I could get help...*something*. If I was free, there was hope. "Let me go, then. I'll walk out of here. You'll never see me again."

Clive laughed. "Oh but Hector wants to say goodbye to you first."

We came to one of the large wooden poles that held a speaker at the top. Clive instructed Garrett to unlock my cuffs and put them back on once my back was against the pole and my arms were wrapped around it behind my back. A hot burst of panic surged through me. *Oh no.* I wasn't going to be restrained to a pole. *No.* Something awful was happening. *What is he going to do to me?* I brought my head forward and slammed it into Garrett's face, his nose crunching again and blood spurting out as he screamed a high-pitched, shrill sound of agony. I brought my knee up and caught him square in the groin. He made another sound that resembled a squealing pig and doubled over.

I heard a gunshot ring out somewhere, but I had no idea where.

And suddenly it seemed like thirty more men were on

me, and just like earlier that day when I'd tried to get to Eden, there were just too many of them. I fought off as many as I could, but finally, one held my arm and twisted it, and I yelled as he freed it quickly and then brought it around the pole. Someone else was punching my face again and again as I slid down to the dirt and my other arm was brought behind me. I heard the click of the handcuffs again and it hit me in the gut harder than any of the punches that had connected with my body so far. I roared in fear and agony, my body broken, my spirit destroyed. Blood was dripping into one eye, the other already swollen shut. It felt like my arm might be broken, sharp, stabbing pain radiated up to my shoulder. I slumped on the ground, my legs spread out in front of me, my head hanging. Beaten. Broken. *I'm so sorry, Eden. I'm so, so sorry.*

"Did you think you were stronger than me, Satan?" Hector's voice came to me from very close by. "Did you think you could worm your way into my community with your beauty? You tricked me once, long ago, but not again. Never again!"

I felt something hitting my foot but didn't raise my head. Hector circled me and then stopped in front of where I was sprawled. I squinted up at him. He was a massive black shadow against the dim sky.

"I tried to help you," Hector said. "I tried so hard to wash you clean, but I underestimated your power. I underestimated your evil ways, your ability to charm my blessed one right out from under me. And I invited you here. That was my greatest mistake. I *brought* you to Acadia. I let you in—Satan's spawn himself. But good will always prevail. Good will always win. And evil will always lose." He brought his face mere inches from mine. "You burn for her, don't you, Satan?

Hmm? You burn for *my* property, for the property of the gods? You burn for her? Oh, you *will* burn for her. You will. And your evil will finally be destroyed." He laughed, a shrill, crazed bark. And then my gaze lowered to the ground in front of me and realized what he was doing. He was building a fire. He was going to burn me.

My feet scrabbled in the dirt as I struggled to pull myself up the pole, standing now and breathing harshly, terror slamming into me as Hector added to the piles of sticks he'd laid around the pole, just out of the reach of my feet.

"Father, no. Please, no," I begged. "Please, I'll walk out of here. I won't come back," I lied. "You'll never see me again. Please don't do this. It's murder, Father. It's a sin. You taught me that. You taught me that taking a life is a sin against the gods."

He barked out another high-pitched laugh, appearing like a demon himself.

"What the fuck, Hector?" Ken Wahl yelled, standing a little ways back. "You're gonna burn him to death?" He raised his hands, backing away. "I won't be part of this. This is not what I signed up for." But he didn't leave.

"Help me, please," I called, looking at him through my one good eye, my voice so hoarse with fear I could hardly get my words out.

Clive was directly behind Ken and he looked confused— but also excited as his gaze darted back and forth between me and Hector.

"Clive…please," I appealed, but then let my words die. If he was going to help me at any point, he already would have.

"Anyone," I called to the people who were standing in a huddle in the main lodge's courtyard just a hundred feet away. "Help me. He's gone mad. If we all band together, we—" And that's when I saw her being led toward me by

Mother Miriam. Her face was pale, expression blank, her skirt covered in blood. The blood from our baby. *Eden. No.* I lurched toward her, but the cuffs caught me, and pain arced down my arm. I yelled and kicked at the pole with all my strength, hoping to get it out of the ground. But I knew it was to no avail. I'd watched the holes being dug for these poles, the cement being poured in. I roared in hopelessness.

I looked up to see Eden trying to run to me but being held back by Mother Miriam, who wore a grim look on her plain face. Eden looked too weak to put up much of a fight. She fell against Mother Miriam and sobbed. *Eden, Eden, oh, Eden, my love, my Morning Glory.*

"Light the fire, Abe," Hector instructed. My head swiveled. Horror and heartbreak rose up my throat as my dad walked slowly toward me, a box of matches in his hand. Tears were running down his face and his hands were shaking.

"Dad. Oh no, Dad," I said, the last word breaking, the final piece of my heart shattering. My dad wouldn't look at me, his hands shaking as silent sobs wracked his body. He was praying under his breath. "Mom," I yelled. "Mom!"

A loud wail rose from the crowd, and I saw my mom fall to her knees, but she didn't move to help me.

"The greatest sacrifices hurt most deeply, Abe," Hector said to my father. "Your rewards will be great. You will be a god among gods. All the suffering you've endured in this life will be worth it."

All the people had joined hands and were reciting Hector's admonition of Satan, some calm, eyes closed, some crying.

I heard Eden wail again and focused my blurry eye on her. "Eden," I called out, attempting to make my voice as strong as possible. "Eden!"

"Calder," she sobbed. "No!" She tried to fight her way

toward me, but two of the men who had fought me held her back. She struggled uselessly. She looked too weak, and they were too strong. She threw her head back at the sky and let out a blood-curdling scream.

My gaze darted to my dad, whose shaking was so severe, he dropped the first match, unlit, on the ground and bent to retrieve it.

"Eden. Stop. Just listen. Please." The tears came then, streaking down my cheeks. "When they light the fire, look away. Don't watch this. Please, don't watch."

She shook her head violently back and forth. "No! I won't leave you! Not even with my eyes. I won't leave you alone. I'm with you. I'm here!"

The second match lit and my dad cried out as he dropped it on the pile of kindling next to my feet. A small fire caught and I returned my eyes to Eden. "Please, Morning Glory. Please, I can't bear it if I know you're left with this image. I'll inhale the smoke. I won't feel the flames. But I have to know you've looked away. Please."

The fire grew, leaping to another pile of sticks. I felt the heat of it on my lower body.

Eden threw her head back and screamed at the sky again, her chest rising and falling in heavy sobs as she struggled to get loose. The men gripped her more tightly, each one holding an arm, turned away from her just enough that she couldn't kick at anything vital. It wouldn't matter anyway. She didn't have the key to the handcuffs that kept me bound.

Eden dropped her head, her face a mask of defeat and agony as her gaze met mine. She nodded, her shoulders shaking in violent sobs, despair evident in every part of her: her expression, her posture, her futile cries. And I could do nothing.

"I don't know what's going to happen after this, Eden, but

whatever it is, be brave, Morning Glory. And know there's a spring somewhere in Elysium. And I'll be waiting for you, Eden. I'll be lying on a rock right by the water. Picture me there, under the sunshine. And when it's time, come find me. I'll be waiting. I hope I'll be waiting a long time, Eden, but know I'll be there. I'll be waiting, Morning Glory."

Eden threw her head back once more and I understood that she was screaming at the gods, begging them for help. It sounded as though she had no voice left to scream with though. Seeing her anguish ripped me apart, the grief of witnessing her pain rising above my desperate fear. I felt helpless as I watched her torment and suffering. This was my fault. All my fault.

As the flames leapt, she sobbed silently and turned her head away as I'd asked her to do. *Oh, Morning Glory, be brave. Be brave and I will too.* The smoke began to rise and I prepared to inhale huge gulps of it. I prepared to die. Fear and horror and rage and, yes, *love*—every single part of who I was in that singular moment—coalesced and began swirling inside of me like a hurricane, speeding faster, gaining power.

Where are you God of Mercy? I tilted my head toward the heavens, clenched my eyes shut, and opened my mouth in a silent scream. And as I did so…it began to rain.

Not a light rain that started slowly, drop by drop, but a sudden, drenching downpour that fell in heavy sheets. The fire was extinguished.

Hector stepped forward, letting out a disgusted grunt of anger that was barely heard over the falling rain. He grabbed the box of matches violently from my father, who had turned away, his shoulders shaking in sobs. Hector attempted to light another match. But after several tries, he threw the box down and screamed, "*Run to the cellar! Everyone! The great flood is upon us! Run to the cellar and bring my blessed one!*"

Hector turned to Clive. "Unlock him and throw him back in the cell."

"Aw, Jesus Christ," Clive yelled. "This is it. This is the last thing I do here."

I looked around dazedly, the storm making everything blurry and unclear. But I saw Eden being dragged toward the cellar in the midst of the others. *Eden. Eden.* My heart pounded and I squinted through the water rolling into my eyes as Clive unlocked my handcuffs and pushed me roughly away from the pole. I stumbled, my right leg buckling from under me. I fell down on my knees in the kindling that had been spread around me and saw the hole in my thigh, blood trickling out slowly and being washed away by the rain. I was shot? "Get up," Clive commanded coldly.

"I can't," I said, my broken arm hanging lank by my side.

"Somebody drag him to the cellar," Clive called. "I'm out of here." Then he turned and walked into the driving rain, disappearing after about three steps.

"Eden," I said weakly, using my one good arm to drag myself through the mud.

I felt someone grab me and screamed as red-hot agony went shooting through my broken arm, my numb legs following helplessly behind me.

My broken body bumped roughly down the stairs, my head hitting the edge of a riser as others practically trampled over me and clattered behind. Screams from the community members drowned out my own sounds of misery. I was thrown back into the same cell, where I crumpled onto the floor. The world began fading and I fought to stay conscious. "Eden," I choked out weakly, reaching toward the locked door. "Eden." Then all went dark.

CHAPTER TWENTY-FIVE
Eden

The rain beat down on the roof as I was dragged, kicking and screaming, into the dim, already crowded cellar. The fighting took the last of my energy, but I had to get to Calder. He'd looked half dead when they'd freed him from the pole.

Hector held me firmly by my waist and his strength was too much for me to fight against. He had lost weight and looked gaunt and sickly, but his power seemed to be that of a hundred men. Or perhaps it was just that I was utterly weakened, and woozy with terror and grief. *They were going to burn him to death. But the rain. The rain. Oh, thank you for the rain.*

When Hector brought his hand up to maneuver me to the corner of the cellar, I leaned sideways and bit it. Hard. He roared, the metallic taste of his blood filling my mouth. I spat it in his face.

He bared his own teeth and then pushed me harshly toward two worker men standing next to us. "Put her in the food storage closet," he said disgustedly. "She'll still be here for our journey to Elysium. Satan's cells are still draining from you. He'll be gone by the time the gods come for us." And then Hector held up the small silver key to the main cellar door, his eyes crazed as he swallowed it.

I sobbed and pushed at one of the men, but he didn't budge. They walked me easily the short distance to the room where food was usually stored and pushed me inside, slamming the door behind me. I heard something heavy being pushed in front of it. I banged and banged on it, but the door was thick, whatever had been put in front of the door provided more of a sound barrier, and the rain was still pounding on the roof. I was so weak from sickness and blood loss. And no one would save me anyway.

There was barely enough light coming in from under the door to see the room. It was mostly in dim shadow. I could see the empty shelves, no food on them now. The ceiling was slightly higher in here as it sat under a part of the main lodge, whereas the other parts of the cellar had only ground on top. There were no windows, no way out. I slid down to the floor and rolled in a ball and cried. Hopeless. Calder might already be dead or dying. There was nothing left. Nothing left to hope for.

Perhaps I slept, or maybe I faded in and out of conscious-ness again. I lost time as the rain continued to pound all around me, or so it seemed. I was still drenched and I was shivering. Dreams drifted through my mind, misty, half-formed. I saw Calder swimming in the water at our spring, a gentle smile on his beloved face. Suddenly the water was fire, engulfing him, and he yelled and was pulled under, into the flames, to the depths of some place I couldn't fathom. He was lost to me as I screamed and tried to reach for him, my own arms blistering and turning black as I plunged them into the fire. I startled awake, the scream hanging on my lips. There was a puddle of water beneath me and I heard the cries of people outside the door.

I bolted up and fell against the wall as all the blood rushed to my head. I took deep breaths and put my ear to the wall. It sounded like water was rushing in from somewhere and when I looked down at my feet, the puddle was growing bigger, water flowing in from under the door. I swayed as my blood ran cold, my heart slamming in an erratic beat.

The foretelling is coming true.

As the water rushed in faster to where I stood, people's cries increased in volume on the other side of the wall. I heard Hector preaching loudly and someone else, a male voice, yelled to give them the key. There was scuffling, more screaming, and then Hector's voice rose again. I only caught portions, only a few of the words through the wall. "No fear...the gods...destiny..."

I would die with the rest of them. The room was quickly filling with water and there was no escape. I stood there, breathing in, breathing out, swaying on my feet as I came to terms with my reality. An unexpected feeling of acceptance came over me—a strange peace I could only imagine was the realization there was no way out of this situation. I leaned back against the wall and tried to shut out the sounds of the screams, the deep yells of the men, the terrified cries of the children. *The wails of the innocents.*

Somewhere out there, Calder was among them.

"One times one is one," I said. "One times two is two..." By the time I'd gotten to nine times nine, the water was up to my shoulders. I closed my eyes and thought about the many things Calder had taught me down at our spring, the least of which was academics. I did division in my head as the water rose to my chin. I climbed to the highest shelf in the room, which brought my head about two feet from the ceiling. This was where it would end. I wondered what Elysium would look like. Would I immediately wake up there? Or would there be a journey? What was Calder doing now? Had the water swallowed him yet? Was he already waiting for me by that spring? "I'm coming, my love," I whispered. "I'll be there soon."

When the water got to my chin once again, the light from under the door went out, and the screams turned to sobs and whispers and...sputtering death. I sobbed quietly until my own heartbeat thudding in my chest lulled me into some sort of hollow calm. It was utterly dark and silent now except for the sound of the rain, still beating down. Was the whole world underwater? Were the penguins floating? Watching as the skies darkened and the planet became one vast, unending ocean? The water rose over my nose and I closed my eyes.

Can I teach you an even better way not to expend energy in the water?

My eyes came open. I swore I had heard his voice whisper in my ear.

I let the water take my body with it as it rose higher in the room. *Take a big breath and then let yourself float so that the back of your head is just above the water. Just let the water support you. Then, when I touch your arms, let them float toward the surface with your elbows bent. Have you got it so far?*

Yes, yes, I remember.

I floated to the top of the water and did what I had been taught to do once upon a time, under the sunshine, in the water of a spring where I had fallen in love with the most beautiful boy in the world. And where he had loved me back.

You never know when a small piece of knowledge is going to come in handy or maybe…maybe even change your life.

I floated there, just like that, until I realized the water had stopped rising. I felt above me to find there was about three inches of air at the top of that taller ceiling, three inches that kept me alive. The rest of the cellar would have been completely underwater about a half an hour before, when the screams had stopped. They were all dead. All except me—the only one they'd wanted to take with them.

Be strong, Morning Glory. I'll wait for you, but I hope I'm waiting for a long time.

Fierce longing assaulted me. It would be so easy to let myself sink to the floor and suck in a big lungful of water. But what if the sin of taking my own life meant I ended up somewhere else? What if *that* was the thing that separated me from Calder forever? He wouldn't be alone. Our baby would be with him. He'd learn of her existence there. He'd know her right away. He'd teach her how to swim in the spring. He'd teach her to be brave. He'd teach her what love felt like. *Just like he once taught me.*

I'd heard it said that when you die, your life flashes in front of your eyes, every moment of it. But for me, there was only Calder. *There is only him.* Because he was my life. I saw his laughter as I turned toward him at our spring. I saw us lying together under the stars. I saw Calder's fierce expression as he took my face in his hands and put his lips to mine. I saw pleasure wash over his features as he made love to me. I saw his sudden grin, like sunshine, as the warm shower water rained down on him. Every blissful moment with him floated through my mind in vivid detail. I closed my eyes and I lived in each memory, letting them comfort me and bring me peace.

And I floated. All through that cold, dark, pitch-black night, the now softly falling rain was the only sound around me. I floated and I *lived*. And at some point, the water level began to lower and the top of the shelf hit my foot. I stood on it, half-awake, half in a place deep within my mind where I had gone as I floated, in shock, in disbelief, in unspeakable grief.

The water receded slowly and by the time I was standing back on the floor, it seemed like hours had gone by. I felt along the wall, and when I came to the door, I pushed against it and wedged it open just a fraction. Whatever had been put in front of it must have floated up in the water and come back down a little bit away from where it'd been. With the small crack in the door, I was able to wedge my body into it and push enough to squeeze through. The water on the other side was still up to my thighs. I stood there, panting from the exertion of pushing at the door, trying to focus my eyes in the very, very dim silvery glow filtering under the door that led outside.

Morning had broken.

My eyes adjusted fully to the low light and I blinked around and then brought my hand to my mouth, horror causing my knees to buckle before I barely caught myself. Bodies floated everywhere. Men, women, and children. Hailey's little boy, Myles, floated by and I turned my head and sobbed silently, covering my face.

And that's when I heard it, a splintering followed by the deep groan of wood giving way. A portion of the ceiling crashed down on the other side of the room, right by the door, the light of a new morning sky streaming in like the arrival of a thousand angels. I didn't have time to scream. I only reacted, wading among the bodies, pushing them aside as I moved through the water, toward that heavenly light. Another loud wood groan and then another portion of the ceiling fell in, slamming down next to me, crushing the bodies that had been floating there. I looked to my right and Hector's face rose up from the water, bloated, tinged purple, but his expression serene, peaceful. Rage ripped through me. "You did this," I whispered hatefully, not knowing if I had actually spoken aloud. "You did all of this."

His expression remained tranquil, his body bobbing gently in the dirty water. There was nothing I could do to punish him, nothing I could do to exact revenge. I sobbed into my hands and moved past him, away. I made it to the place where the ceiling had just crashed in and climbed up the pieces of broken wood and fallen concrete until I could grab on to a still-intact piece of the roof and pull myself up. I fell on the ground, panting and sobbing. When I heard another loud creak, I lurched away and dragged myself as far from the cellar roof as possible.

A minute later, the entire roof collapsed in one loud, violent crash that brought the entire weight of the ceiling and the ground above it down on the bodies below. Beneath the wreckage was still a low lake of water. I fell to my knees and bawled. If I had had any hope Calder was alive, I knew there was no hope now. Deep inside of me, I felt my soul curl up and quietly die. My body was thoroughly spent and my heart broken into a million tiny shards of utter desolation. I lay looking at the ground numbly, clutching a handful of mud and watching as I squeezed it through my fingers again and again and again. All emotion seemed to drain from my body, leaving only hollowness and a heavy black grief just under the surface.

Finally, I sat up slowly, looking around in detached interest. A flock of birds flew across the sky and I could hear the animals in our fields making their animal sounds. Far up above, a plane flew by as I shielded my eyes and squinted into the bright sky. The whole world hadn't been washed away. Only Hector's people, all except one. *All except me.*

I stood on shaky legs and walked numbly to the main lodge, lifting one foot and then the other. Once inside, I stripped my blood-and-dirt-stained clothes off as if in a trance and dropped them in the garbage. I changed into a clean skirt and shirt and washed the grime off my face and arms in the sink. I refused to look in the mirror. I felt dead, and I couldn't take looking at another dead face right then.

I went back to my room and gathered the pressed morning glories wrapped in a plastic bag and put them in my pocket. I found the small pebble in my desk drawer and put that in my pocket too. If Hector had found these at some point, he didn't know what they meant.

Hector's room was next. I rooted through his drawers, feeling nothing. The last time I'd done this, I'd been shaky with nervousness, fearful of getting caught and punished.

There was some money, but I didn't count it, just stuffed it in my pocket. In another drawer there was the locket portion of a necklace. I hadn't seen this the first time I'd gone through these drawers. I picked it up and studied it, something about the piece making my dead heart pick up a rhythm. I *recognized* this. I had worn it once upon a time. I turned it over and saw that on the back was the name of a jeweler and the city, Cincinnati, Ohio. I opened it, but there were no pictures inside.

I stuck the locket in my pocket too, and I walked downstairs. I did a brief search of the council members' rooms but found nothing of any value. Maybe they discovered my thievery after I'd escaped and removed or hidden their money and jewelry. I left the main lodge. I didn't look back.

Later, I remembered some of the walking, but not all. I'd made the same trip before, only that time with two brave boys. This time I was alone. When cars passed on the road, I used rocks for cover as we'd done before. I collapsed behind one as morning became afternoon and I slept. When I woke, it was evening.

At some point I stopped at the same house we'd stopped at before for water, and I drank from the hose and stole clothes from their clothesline, a pair of women's jeans, a long-sleeved white T-shirt, and a lightweight jacket. Again, the dog barked and pulled on his rope, but I ignored him. No one came to the door with a shotgun this time. I wondered if I was disappointed. My body was alive, but my soul was too distraught to care.

Somewhere inside a voice whispered, *You survived, and now you have to live.* I didn't know whose it was, certainly not my own.

It was morning again by the time I made it to the city. I wandered the streets for a long time, trying blankly to spot something familiar. Somewhere, Xander was here, but I didn't know where, and I didn't know how to find out. Kristi would have moved by now and Calder had told Xander to meet him somewhere, but I didn't know where. Kristi had said she knew people who might help us. I had to believe Xander was safe somewhere. I *had* to.

A police car drove by on the street and I started breathing raggedly, pulling myself into a doorway and pressing my body against the wall until it had passed. Clive was still out here.

I wandered for a little while more until I saw a sign for the bus station. I looked bleakly at it and went inside, where I asked how much it would cost for a ticket to Cincinnati. I couldn't think of one other thing to do, not that I could think very clearly at all. I had just enough money, so I bought a ticket and sat in a plastic bus station chair, staring at the wall. Finally, I reached in my pocket and pulled out the locket, the only thing I had of any value, the only thing that might bring me safety. I studied it again, turning it over and over, wondering if it could lead me to someone who would care about me. The thought made sorrow rise suddenly in my chest and I sucked back a sob.

The bus headed to Ohio boarded half an hour later. I sat in a seat by a window and closed my eyes. And again, I slept. It was the only thing that didn't hurt.

EPILOGUE
Calder

I was in Elysium. The light was silvery white and the air was warm and I had a spring to find. Only there wasn't supposed to be so much pain in Elysium. If I was in paradise, why was every part of my body crying out in agony? And why did it smell like rancid death? I swallowed down the vomit trying to make its way up my throat.

"I've gotta grab your arm," I heard Xander say. And I screamed. "I'm sorry, brother. So damn sorry." Why was he crying? There weren't supposed to be any tears in Elysium either.

"I have to find the spring," I said. Only it came out, "Hash tofin the spr." My face didn't seem to want to move.

"Shh," I heard Xander say. "Don't talk. I've got you. You knew I'd come back for you, right?" He choked back what sounded like a sob. "I'm so sorry I was too late."

"Hash tofin the spr," I repeated, trying to make him understand.

Loud things were crashing around me and I felt more warmth on my skin, the light suddenly brighter.

"This is going to hurt. I'm so sorry, brother," Xander choked out once more, but I didn't understand why.

Then agonizing pain flooded my body as I screamed again, feeling myself being lifted upward. The world blinked out.

To Be Continued in
Finding Eden
Available Now

Want more Calder and Eden? Read on for an excerpt from

Finding Eden

AVAILABLE NOW FROM

PIATKUS

PROLOGUE
Eden

"I promise you I will do everything just as you ask. But come closer. Let us give in to grief, however briefly, in each other's arms."

—Homer, *The Iliad*

I woke under heavy blankets, my eyes popping open so I could take in the room around me. I didn't move, just listened and looked, trying to understand where I was. It was then I heard footsteps moving toward me and the older man, the jeweler, came into view. It all came back…breaking the vase, paying for it with the locket, the homeless shelter, fainting. I blinked up at him, my fight-or-flight instinct kicking in as my eyes darted around the room, seeking an exit.

"It's okay. You fainted. My driver helped me put you in my car. You're at my town house."

I sat up, pulling the covers up against my chest. I still had all my clothes on, but someone had removed my shoes.

I opened my mouth to say something, I wasn't sure

exactly what, when the door opened again and a woman walked in with a tray in her hands.

Food. My stomach lurched and my mouth immediately started to water at the smell wafting off whatever was coming toward me.

The woman set the tray over my lap, and my gaze roamed it greedily—some kind of soup and several rolls with neat little pats of butter melting on top. My body took over and I grabbed for the spoon with shaky hands and started shoveling it into my mouth. I'd get out of here after I ate. I had to eat. In that moment, the hunger ruled me and it was too much to resist. I didn't care where I was or why or with whom. The food was the only thing that mattered. When I glanced up at the jeweler and the woman in a housekeeping uniform who stood just to his side, I saw that both of them were watching me with sad, curious eyes.

The woman took a step toward me. "Slow down, little one. You haven't eaten for a while. You'll make yourself sick if you eat it too fast. Force yourself to slow down." Then she put one hand on my back and moved it in slow circles while I slowed the movement of the spoon from the soup to my mouth. For several minutes, the only sound in the room was my unladylike slurping and then my chewing sounds as I picked up each roll and ate them in three bites apiece. The woman's gentle circles on my back never stopped, calming me, reminding me to eat as slowly as I could. A few times it felt like the food would come back up, but it didn't, and when I was finished, I picked up the napkin and wiped my hands and my face and then set it down, embarrassed to look at them. My dignity trickled back in now that my hunger had been satisfied.

"Well then, that's better," the woman said, and I raised my gaze to her sympathetic face. It felt like so long since someone had been kind to me. Tears filled my eyes, but I looked away before they could spill down my face. She took her hand off my back, picked the tray up, leaned into the man and said something softly, and then left the room.

I swung my legs over the side of the bed, but the man put his hand on my shoulder and said, "Please, you're welcome to stay here tonight. There's a bathroom over there." He inclined his head to the left, and I glanced at the closed door he was indicating. "And this room isn't used by anyone anymore. Please stay. It's the least I can do after…today."

I licked my parched lips, trying to decide what to do. I desperately wanted to stay here in this warm place, where I could sleep in an actual bed, but I didn't understand why this man had taken me in.

"I broke your property today," I finally said.

He pursed his lips. "Yes, and you paid for it. And it could have been handled differently. I'm sorry I didn't step in."

I wasn't sure what to say to that and so I remained silent.

"Please. Let me put you up for the night. We can make other…arrangements tomorrow. Yes?"

I fidgeted with my hands in my lap. It was either say yes or go back out into the cold street. But I didn't know what his "arrangements" might be and that worried me. Still… I nodded tentatively, deciding I'd stay at least a little longer, and when I looked up at him, he seemed pleased.

"Good. Take a shower. Get some sleep. I'll see you in the morning." And with that, he turned on his heel and walked quickly out of the room.

Once he had left, I scurried over to the door and turned the lock and then stood there taking in the details of the room for the first time. It was beautiful. There was a sort of floral fabric on the walls, and I walked over to one and ran my hand over the smooth, slightly textured surface. I tried to muster up some gratitude for the lovely surroundings, but there was only numb observance. I turned toward the bed, my gaze moving over the luxurious silk and rich velvet bedding in various shades of cream and lilac. Inviting. I walked back over to it, the call to sleep too great to resist now that my belly was full. I'd shower in the morning.

I climbed back in between the crisp sheets, still fully clothed. Sleep took me under her dark wing, sweeping me away into blessed oblivion.

I dreamed of morning glories, *I dreamed of him, my love*, wispy images that twisted and turned and washed away under a wave of water so massive I was crushed beneath it. There was no breath in my lungs left to call his name, to whisper the words I needed him to know in the end—that I loved him, that I'd always love him, that he was my strength and my weakness, my endless joy and my greatest sorrow.

I woke up crying, breathless but silent.

In the bathroom, I stripped my clothes somberly and stood in front of the mirror for a moment, running my hand over my flat belly and sucking back a sob before moving quickly to the shower stall. The gentle drumming of warm water was soothing and I tilted my head back, wetting my hair. But that wave came again, rising, crushing, and I hung my head forward and let go of that which I had held so tightly inside for the past week. I sunk down to the marble floor, pulled myself back against the wall tiles, and finally allowed myself to sob as the sound of the running water masked my cries.

After I'd showered and dressed and relieved a small portion of the burden of my grief, at least for the moment, I stepped out into the quiet hallway.

The distant sound of dishes clattering drew me and I peeked into a large kitchen where the jeweler was seated in front of a plate of food, an open magazine on the table next to it.

"Good morning," he said as he stood. "You look refreshed. Did you sleep well?"

"Yes, thank you." I eyed the food sitting on the table—a plate of bacon and eggs, and a dish of fruit.

The jeweler waved me over to him. "Please, sit. Eat. We can discuss the arrangements I mentioned last night."

I nodded and took a seat at the table as he dished up food and set it before me. I took a few bites as I gathered my resolve. I wanted to stay here. The man was nice, or so it seemed. But I was pretty sure what his "arrangements" would include, and I didn't think it was possible for me—I couldn't fathom it. Not after what I'd been through. I would return to the street—I might die there, but death didn't scare me, not anymore.

I'll be waiting for you, by a spring. Come find me. I'll be there.

I cleared my throat. "I can't accept the arrangement you propose," I said, lowering my gaze.

Through my lashes, I saw his coffee cup halt midway to his mouth. "I haven't proposed anything yet."

Heat moved up my neck. "I understand what you want," I said softly.

The jeweler watched me for a minute and then set his coffee cup down, causing it to clatter against the saucer. His expression was…angry? Sad? I couldn't be sure. "That's not what I want."

I stared at him in confusion. "You said you had an arrangement we could discuss."

He took a deep breath. "First of all, I don't think we've met properly. My name is Felix Grant. Please call me Felix.

Acknowledgments

It takes many people to complete a book, and I am so blessed to have the very best on my team. Special, special thanks from the bottom of my heart to my storyline editors: Angela Smith, who not only talked story arrangement with me to the point of exhaustion but provided wine and emotional support often and tirelessly, and Larissa Kahle, who spends what little free time she has helping me to ramp up the emotions of my story and perfect the character development. Thank you to my developmental and line editor, Marion Archer. She is new to my process, but I'll never write a book without her again—*never*. Her expertise and enthusiasm—not to mention the little notes she wrote in the margin of my manuscript that made me laugh and swoon—not only taught me things but made my story richer and full of more depth. And to Karen Lawson, whose bionic eyes perfected my manuscript even further.

I am also lucky enough to have an incredible group of beta readers who provided invaluable feedback on Calder and Eden's story and cheerleaded for me when I needed it most: Cat Bracht, Elena Eckmeyer, Michelle Finkle, Natasha Gentile, Karin Hoffpauir Klein, Nikki Larazo, and Kim Parr. And to my author beta, A.L. Jackson, who read the first draft of my manuscript when it was just three hundred pages of my ramblings and before I'd even spell-checked it. Her feedback and assurances gave me the courage to continue on.

Thank you as well to my wonderful sprinting partner, Jessica Prince. Many of these words would not have been written if not for her diligent 9 a.m. texts that generally included one word: *sprint?*

Big thanks to my amazing formatter, Elle Chardou, for saving my sanity and my carpal tunnel.

An updated dose of gratitude to Bloom Books for reintroducing this story, and assisting me in adding some finesse.

Love and gratitude to my husband for his patience through this process—and for being understanding when every date night for three months included plot talk. You make it all fun—and you make it all possible.

Steamy, addictive and emotional . . .

Available now from

PIATKUS